OUT OF TIME

A Casey Jones Mystery

BY KATY MUNGER

DEDICATION

For Cabana Boy—who taught me
that life is a daring adventure.

BOOKS BY KATY MUNGER

LEGWORK
OUT OF TIME
MONEY TO BURN
BAD TO THE BONE
BETTER OFF DEAD
BAD MOON ON THE RISE

ANGEL OF DARKNESS
ANGEL AMONG US

WRITING AS GALLAGHER GRAY

PARTNERS IN CRIME
A CAST OF KILLERS
DEATH OF A DREAM MAKER
A MOTIVE FOR MURDER

WRITING AS CHAZ MCGEE

DESOLATE ANGEL
ANGEL INTERRUPTED

Visit http://www.katymunger.com for more
information on the author and her books.

CHAPTER ONE

I was hungry enough to eat the wrong end of a skunk. Fortunately, I wouldn't have to. My case was about to crack wide open, courtesy of a dumpy brunette wearing ill-advised spandex who was teetering toward the bar on wobbly four-inch stilettos.

"One Bahama Mamma and a margarita," she told the muscle-bound bartender, fingering her fake-gold necklace. Her voice was so squeaky, I narrowed my eyes in speculation. Could it really be the mayor of Munchkinland in drag? Or, more likely, could I really have just downed my third drink of the evening? *What was I thinking?*

I pushed my Tanqueray on the rocks to one side and took a deep breath. I needed to slow down. Bar surveillance could take all night, and you couldn't fake the drinking without making the bartender suspicious. Especially this one. He smelled a spotter in the air and had already thrown me a few curious looks. If I kept up this pace, I'd pass out before I discovered the scam. Except—thanks to the munchkin—I was just about to nail his trim little butt.

"I meant to say a frozen margarita," she squeaked across the counter, stopping the bartender in mid-pour long enough for me to realize he was standing in the wrong spot for tequila. And that the label on the bottle did not match the house brand. I watched more closely as he corrected the order, drawing a frozen margarita from a machine along one wall and tossing the rejected drink down the drain without comment. The Bahama Mamma looked legit, if you consider Bahama Mammas legit, but when he rang up both drinks, the munchkin did it to him again. "How much was that Bahama Mamma?" she asked, anxiously counting the dollar bills in her pudgy hands. He stopped ringing up, and I

1

saw that the total on the register was zero, but the guest tape had been credited with nine dollars. That greedy iron-pumping bastard sure had ambition. He was doubling up on his scams. Looked like I would finally be able to explain to his boss why, after his place had been named the hottest bar in town, his profits had scarcely inched up.

"Nine dollars," the bartender grumbled, shoving the drinks across the bar. His eyes slid sideways toward me and I knew he had me made. Realization had finally penetrated his steroid-soaked brain. I didn't care. My job was done. By tomorrow, his career would be history.

"I'll get that," I told him sweetly, sliding a ten across the bar. After all, the munchkin had just helped me solve a three-day case. The least I could do was buy her a drink. "Keep the change," I told him. He shrugged, unimpressed.

"Gee, thanks," the munchkin piped up, but when she got a better look at me, she turned nervous. "What did you do that for?"

"Relax," I told her, throwing her a wink. "I'm not after your body, cupcake. I just admire your fashion sense. It's so distinctive."

She brightened at this and scurried over to her table, casting a final suspicious glance my way. Hey, when you're a woman as big and as bold as I am, you get a lot of those looks from other ladies who're afraid I'm out to drag them for a walk on the wild side. It's unfashionable of me, I admit, but I'd be a big disappointment in that department. Though others are perfectly welcome to go where no man has gone before, I'm strictly a younger-man woman myself. Just give me a negligee that rips off easily and a twenty-five-year-old boy that doesn't rip off at all. I've got the soundtrack to *The Graduate* cued up and ready to go.

I left the bar with a nice rosy glow, courtesy of too much gin and a smug sense of law and order. Casey Jones, watchdog of civilization, scourge of bar cheaters everywhere, defender of the oath, keeper of the cheap drink. Casey Jones, 160 pounds of pure brain and muscle. Casey Jones, too damn tipsy to drive.

It was true. My reach had exceeded my grasp. I was forced, by the prospect of Chapel Hill's unmarked drunk-driving task force, to take a nap in the backseat of my 1965 Valiant before I could proceed. This was no small order. The backseat was my auxiliary office. In addition to current case files, it held assorted sweat suits, a large plastic cooler crammed with Diet Pepsis, three empty bags of Lay's potato chips, a single can of Slim Fast (who was I kidding?) and four bundles of magazines I kept meaning to recycle, but where the hell did Durham, North Carolina, recycle its magazines anyway? I pondered the mystery as I fell into a deep snooze, waking an hour later, when the couple in the car next to mine mounted a show that made Tonya Harding and her ex's honeymoon night look like the amateur hour that it was. An eyeful of their action sobered me up fast. The guy's BVD-clad butt was pressed against the side window, which said a lot for his flexibility, but not much for his foreplay. Besides, I think guys look pretty silly in briefs, even when they don't have toy cars or superheroes printed on them. I decided it was time to go, pronto. If I stayed in the parking lot of this singles bar for another instant, who knew what madness might overtake me. These days, I'm too old to wake up the morning after with regrets—or worse. When in doubt, I put the fire out. It keeps a woman healthy, wealthy and wise.

I rolled down the windows and headed to Raleigh, where my grossly obese boss, Bobby D., was anxiously awaiting my progress report on the bartender scam. This new client— like my boss—was a big one. He owned a lot of bars in the Triangle, and keeping his staff honest could turn into a steady gig. Best of all, it was yet another task that Bobby D. could foist off on me. I didn't mind. It's a dirty job sitting at bars drinking all night, but someone's got to do it. And that someone is me. Because the only work Bobby D. actually does for himself involves either the telephone or a soon-to-be-grieving divorcee who is vulnerable to Bobby's practiced words of love. That man is a genius. He makes Barry White look like a piker. He also makes Barry White look underfed. At 360 pounds of pure fat, Bobby is a favorite of the ancient staff that mans the Big Man Department at Hudson Belk's.

The fresh air sobered me up. I arrived in downtown Raleigh on top of the world. After all, it was only nine o'clock on a balmy Saturday night in March. Spring was in the air. My hormones were racing. The night was young, even if I wasn't. And I had a non-date with Bill Butler at eleven o'clock, when he got off his shift at the Raleigh Police Department.

Bobby D. put a big dent in my mood. For starters, I thought he was dying.

"Bobby," I called out. "How's it hanging?"

He didn't answer. He was too busy asphyxiating. His face was bright red and he was pointing a half-eaten chicken drumstick toward my office.

"What?" I asked, eyeing him suspiciously. As usual, he was parked in a long-suffering chair that tilted back from a desk heaped high with junk-food wrappers so ancient I was surprised he hadn't tried to foist them off as antiques at the fair-ground weekend flea market. The trash can at his feet held a six-pack of Bud Lite. Fat lot of good it did him when he was known to down a case a day. A cardboard bucket of chicken leaked grease onto the desk. It ran in slow rivulets over the edge, and dripped on his polyester slacks. His face was shiny with chicken fat.

"Can you breathe?" I asked, readying myself for the Heimlich maneuver. I'd have to jump up and down on his chest just to penetrate his fat.

"Of course I can breathe," he said indignantly. "I look like a corpse to you?"

"Then why are you waving a chicken part at me and turning red?" I asked.

"You've got company," he said grimly. "And it don't smell good." He turned his back on me. After all, he had better things to do—like polishing off a twelve-piece family dinner for four before it got cold.

Okay, I told myself. It was a little unusual for a new client to come knocking on a weekend night, but, after all, I was a professional. I hadn't gotten into this business to punch a clock, I'd gotten into it to punch the bad guys.

I turned the hall corner toward my office—and froze. At least ten pairs of eyes trapped me in the dreaded country-lady glare. That glare is a North Carolina classic, designed to scrutinize every detail of your being. With a single look, the assembled women were toting up my hair, my attitude, my age, my weight and my worth in the world now and far into the future. It's as powerful as any laser Obi-Wan Kenobi could wag around.

"I'm Casey Jones," I said, squeezing myself as far away from them as I could get. I counted quickly. Eleven women, of various ages, sat on the edges of my desk and on the windowsill, leaned against the walls and spilled out the door into the hall. How the hell had they all fit in there? The older ones shared the same no-nonsense short-cropped haircut and sun-worn faces that displayed just enough makeup to make it clear they were women. The younger ones had lots of big hair, makeup that was heavy on the pink and they wore embroidered country-western blouses above skin-tight blue jeans. By god, I'd never be able to breathe in those things. Among them, they probably had enough yeast infections to shut down the local Taste-Tee Bread bakery.

"Can I help you?" I asked when no one said anything.

"I'm Carol Ann Honeycutt," the oldest woman finally said. She looked like human beef jerky and twice as tough. "Most people call me Nanny."

I found it hard to believe that anyone could call that old goat a nanny, but I kept it to myself. I pegged her age at seventy or so.

"We thought it best to wait for you here," she said, nodding toward Bobby D. as if he were a grizzly about to run amok. "I didn't want that man out there to hear."

Okay, I thought, they were some sort of country lesbian group. Or maybe that women's choir I kept hearing about. What the hell did they want with me?

"And these are?" I asked, gesturing toward the crowd.

"My family," she said impatiently. "Do I have to introduce every one of them?"

"Of course not. I just like to know who I'm doing business with is all," I assured her. "You are here on business, right?" Could they be a particularly belligerent branch of the Seventh-Day Adventists?

"Of course we're here on business." She peered at me suspiciously. "You are Casey Jones, aren't you?" she said. "The lady detective who got that girl off over there in Zebulon, the one they said burned down that store when it was really the owner?"

"That's me," I admitted. "In the flesh." I heard a sniff or two, letting me know that they thought I had a little too much flesh for my own good. Ah, let them think it was fat. Lots of people made the same mistake. It wasn't fat; it was muscle. But when it comes to fighting, surprise is my best weapon.

"Then I suppose you're nobody's fool," Nanny Honeycutt conceded. A few heads nodded in agreement. Gee, I was winning over the crowd. "We want to hire you."

"To do what?" I asked.

"To save my granddaughter's life."

There was a silence. I waited for more. None came.

"Is that all?" I joked.

"It's not a joking matter, young lady," she snapped. "My granddaughter is Gail Honeycutt Taylor. Only she's dropped the Taylor part for obvious reasons. Does that name mean anything to you or are you too smart to read the newspapers like most of the damn fools running the world these days?"

She had a point, but I wisely ignored it as a sense of dread permeated the working parts of my brain. "Yes, I know who your granddaughter is."

"Well, she didn't do it," the old woman told me. "Gail didn't shoot her husband any more than I could do a striptease."

I considered the possibility. She wasn't that damn old.

"Take my word for it," the old gal snapped, interrupting my thoughts. "If her husband hadn't of been a police officer, she never would have been convicted. Those people were out for blood, and she was in the wrong place at the wrong time."

"Wasn't she found just a few feet from the body?" I asked, recalling the case. "With the gun in her hand?"

"See what I mean?" the old woman retorted. "Wrong place. Wrong time."

"I thought she had an appeals lawyer," I said, thinking back to the case. I measure my life in ex-boyfriend eras. The Roy Taylor killing occurred back when I was dating a Guilford County deputy sheriff who had a thing for handcuffs and ladies' underwear. On him, not me. That would have made it about eight years ago.

If I remembered correctly, Gail Honeycutt Taylor had shot her husband, a Durham police officer, one night during a drunken brawl and it hadn't taken the jury very long to give her the death penalty. The case had snaked its way through the appeals process and gotten Gail nowhere. She was currently one of four women on death row in North Carolina. And she'd been there for a while. I suspected she was next up to bat.

"She's got her a lawyer," the woman admitted angrily. "And that's why we're in this mess. If we hadn't of listened to that snooty Northern girl, we wouldn't be standing here with only a month to go before they kill Gail."

"A month!" I shouted, taking a step backward. "Oh, no. No way. How can you come in here and ask me to help you when she's only got a month left? How can I possibly say no without feeling guilty?"

"We're counting on that," the old woman said, folding her arms. "People have a conscience for a reason, you know."

I groaned. She sounded like the nuns in the Catholic school that kicked me out after a week when I was seven years old. I felt a headache beginning at the back of my eyes. Too much gin, too early in the evening, ignited into a headache by incipient guilt.

"I know it's last minute," a softer voice interjected. "Nanny Honeycutt doesn't mean to be rude, but we're desperate." A woman in her early forties stepped forward. She wore a sweater decorated with two giant red hearts. Even the QVC network would have turned down that beauty. "We would have come to you sooner, but the lawyer told us that everything was under control, that the case would be reversed on a technicality."

"But it wasn't?" I guessed. Their lawyer should have known better.

The woman shook her head. "After the state Supreme Court turned down her automatic appeal, we got Gail a new lawyer. She filed an appeal with the federal Court of Appeals in Richmond. They turned her down, too. Now she's filed a second appeal with them, but I haven't got much hope."

"None of us have," Nanny Honeycutt interrupted. "We think her only chance is a stay by the governor. I read up on it. He can do whatever he wants. They say his power is 'absolute.' If we can come up with enough evidence to show that maybe someone else might have done it, then he might put the date on hold while we convince the police to find out more. It's our only chance."

In that case, Gail Honeycutt didn't have much of a chance at all, whether I helped her or not. The current governor of North Carolina had recently been elected for the third time, in part thanks to an anticrime platform. A few years ago, he'd even convened a special session of the legislature—at the cost of hundreds of thousands of public dollars—just to come up with new ways to punish criminals. He had really gotten the creative juices of our local politicians going. One state senator had gone on record as saying that N.C. ought to bring back public hangings in the courthouse yard, then suggested we invite all the citizens of our fine state to witness these executions. He didn't specify whether refreshments were to be served or not. But few people had contradicted him.

"We need you to find enough evidence to convince the governor," the younger of the two women said. "We don't know where else to turn. Please, the whole family knows she's innocent. You've got to help her." She tried to say more, but broke down in tears. A dozen arms reached out to pat her, and little clucks of sympathy ran through the crowd. She had to be Gail's mother.

I gritted my teeth against her tears. I hate it when anyone over the age of two years old cries. If you're old enough to be toilet trained, by god, you're old enough to keep a stiff upper lip. Especially if the crying makes someone like me feel guilty. "Haven't you got any men in your family?" I asked. "What do they think?"

Nanny Honeycutt snorted. "They're too busy watching football or plowing their fields to take a stand. Don't look for the smarts in the Honeycutt family on the male side, honey. What you see here in this room is what you get."

"It's a touchy situation," another younger woman explained. "Most men in the family think that Gail isn't worth the trouble."

"Not worth the trouble?" I asked. That was a hell of a way to put it.

The woman shrugged. "She's had a knack for getting in trouble her whole life. They think this is just the end of a long road for her."

"How can you be so sure she's innocent?" I asked.

"Honeycutt women are not stupid," the old lady said proudly. "Gail is not stupid enough to shoot her husband in her own home and then lay there with the gun in her hand. She couldn't even hold a gun properly. I know. I tried to teach her myself. You can't tell me she could fire off six shots and hit him with four of them. No way on god's green earth."

I sighed. Intelligence has nothing to do with committing a crime, only with getting caught for it. What the hell could I do to help at this late date anyway? I'd have to go back and dig up a crime that was eight years old, then convince the governor to give her a break, and who knew if I'd find anything that would help? On the other hand, a nagging inner voice reminded me, you once spent eighteen months in a Florida prison paying for something you didn't do because no one believed in you. Great, I thought, even my own conscience was turning against me. "Is there any new evidence?" I asked. "Or should I call up Johnnie Cochran and ask him to help me invent some?"

"Her sister thinks there is and she's a prosecuting attorney."

"Gail's sister is a prosecuting attorney?" I asked, surprised.

"Yes," Nanny Honeycutt said briskly, annoyed I hadn't learned her family tree by osmosis. "Here in Wake County. Brenda's the one who suggested hiring you in the first place."

I was silent as I paused to think it over.

"We don't have anyone else," the old woman reminded me grudgingly. I noticed for the first time that her fists were clenched and her mouth had grown tight along the edges, sending wrinkles fanning out across a grim face. "Please, I'm asking you from my heart. She is my granddaughter and I love her no matter what people say she did."

Oh god, that did it. I had been raised by my grandfather and I knew how heartfelt those words could be. If I turned my back on this proud old woman, I'd feel lower than a centipede's instep. And I'd never be able to look my grandpa in the face again.

"Okay," I said. "Let me look into it. I'll let you know in a day or two."

"You better make it a day and not two," the old lady warned. "We've only got a month now. One month."

"I know, I know." I involuntarily looked up at the clock. "You really know how to put pressure on a person."

A few minutes after the women left, a huge shadow loomed in my doorway. I spun around, my mouth hanging open in disbelief. Bobby D. had actually moved from his chair and walked a good fifteen feet to my office. Hallelujah, he has risen.

My astonishment showed. "Got a new filling on the right side," he observed.

I nodded. "Heard there was a cute new dentist in Chapel Hill. They were right, but he's no fun. Doesn't believe in laughing gas."

"What did those women want? Are they all gone now?" Bobby asked, running a hammy finger around his collar to loosen it. "They sure know how to make a man nervous."

"They want me to look into the Roy Taylor murder," I said. "They say the wife didn't do it. She's kin."

"Gail Honeycutt?" Bobby D. shook his head. "That's a real shit storm, Casey. Don't do it. She killed a cop and we need the cops on our side. Capiche?"

"I haven't said yes for sure," I told him. "I'm going to visit her in prison and talk to her first."

"It's your funeral," he warned.

Yeah, my funeral and his fee.

He ambled back to his desk, satisfied that the country ladies were gone. He eased into his chair with a grunt. I had no doubt he'd stay right there for the next five hours, at least, gathering his strength to haul his big butt up again. "I been thinking about getting me a computer like yours," he confessed suddenly. "So I can go into them chat rooms I keep hearing about and get me some computer dates."

Oh, lordy. It was time to save the women of America a lot of unpleasant surprises. "Bobby, you're a master technician when it comes to love, but you might lose something in the translation. Besides, you can't even type. Stick to working your magic in the flesh. Trust me."

He brightened. "That's true. Why mess with perfection?"

"Why indeed." I kept my face as solemn as possible.

"So what's the word on the bar gig?" Bobby asked, dollar signs dancing in front of his eyes.

"Got him. It's the head bartender, I regret to say. Double dipping. Experienced at it, too, if my eyes are telling me the truth."

Bobby sighed. "Client ain't gonna be happy. Good bartenders are hard to find."

"Yeah, well, this one was bleeding him dry." I sketched in the details of the scam while Bobby took down a few notes on the ancient notepad he kept near his telephone.

"I'd better phone him tonight," Bobby decided. "Before the perp moves out the bottles and clears the tape." His smile reappeared. "This could get us a lot more work."

"Get me a lot more work," I corrected him. "It could get you a lot more money."

"Synergy!" he said happily.

"What?" I stared at him warily.

"You and me, baby—we're synergistic!"

"Don't go corporate on me, Bobby. Whatever you do, don't go corporate."

I fled to the privacy of my office and put the next half hour to good use re-applying my makeup, changing dresses twice and inspecting a dozen minute flaws in my compact mirror. Damn. I still didn't look like Cindy Crawford. Maybe I should ask for a refund on my new eye shadow. Good thing I didn't have a real date with Bill Butler. I'd have spontaneously combusted from tension and missed the whole thing.

I looked pretty good when I was done, if I do say so myself. I was unlikely to scare anyone under the age of sixty-five. I had exchanged my cat-eye glasses for contact lenses, swapped my high-tops for sluttish high heels, refreshed my eyeliner, toned down my semi-punk look in honor of my police officer dining companion and fluffed up my blond-going-black hairdo. I admit I have a rather in-your-face fashion sense that favors thrift-shop clothes and unorthodox color combinations. But I'm a big girl and it's hard to hide it, so I don't bother. I wear tight dresses when I'm in the mood and, if someone has a problem with that, they're welcome to Indian-wrestle the point.

I was in the mood for a tight dress that night. Bobby whistled when I sashayed past.

"Wee doggies, baby," he said, shaking his toupeed head in admiration. "I can see the wrinkles on your wrinkles in that dress. What is it? Spray-painted on?"

"You really know how to flatter a girl," I told him, letting the door slam shut behind me.

Bill was waiting at the bar of a massive downtown nightspot. Two enterprising young men had gutted a tobacco warehouse and converted it into a huge restaurant that included a nifty bar area that certainly did not look as if it were situated in Raleigh, North Carolina. Handmade stools from funky pieces of wood. Blue halogen lighting. Copper-topped bar. Very New York City, only a whole lot cleaner and a whole lot cheaper.

"Christ, Casey—you got a license to wear that thing?" Bill asked, checking me out from neckline to hemline.

I was pleased. Best to get his attention early on. "This old body?" I said. "I've been wearing it for the past thirty-six years."

"Then it's time you let someone else try it on for size," he suggested.

"One size fits all," I said. "And, believe me, it has."

I slid onto a stool next to him and noticed his appalled expression. "I'm kidding, Bill," I assured him. He didn't look too convinced.

"Pretty quiet," I said, glancing around.

"Basketball play-offs," he explained. "Everyone's home glued to their tubes. What is it with this state? I don't get the big deal about basketball."

"It's simple," I explained. "We can't root tobacco farmers or hog farmers to victory. Basketball is the thing we do next best."

"Speak for yourself," he said, signaling the bartender to bring us a round. He didn't bother to ask me what I was drinking, he just ordered the same brand of beer he was having.

That's Bill Butler for you.

"Aren't you afraid we'll run into someone we know?" I asked, searching the few occupied tables for familiar faces. No one I recognized, either from in person or from glossy eight-by-tens. Just a couple tables of wealthy-looking senior citizens squinting at the trendy hand-printed menu. North Raleighites out for a funky night on the town at the funky new restaurant. I hoped their pacemakers could take it.

"Starting trouble early, aren't you?" Bill asked. "Can't even be nice to me for five minutes?"

"I can't take the pressure," I admitted. And it was true. It was one thing to hop gaily from bed to bed with a string of younger boyfriends, all of them all too willing to let me love 'em and leave 'em. It was another to get involved with a man who wanted to steer the ship once in a while, and Bill Butler definitely qualified for captain. He was a detective with the Raleigh Police Department and considered a newcomer to the area, having arrived from Long Island a mere four years ago. He was currently working with the Sex Crimes Unit, which had done nothing for his potential libido in my book. In fact, he'd seemed to be downright uninterested lately, which hurt me deeply. I had recently rejected him and, instead of retreating, by all laws of men and women, he should have been leading the charge in the battle of the sexes by now. What fun is war if the other side doesn't even notice we're fighting?

"Casey," he explained, clinking his beer bottle with mine in salute. "You have to learn to play the game. You can't just say things like you're under pressure when you're dating. It doesn't work that way—"

"We're not dating," I interrupted firmly. "I told you. No dates. I don't date. Either you're in it with me or you're not. I'm not going to spend my evenings shopping for another human being."

"Okay, okay." He backed off quickly. "I forgot, this is a non-date. Is there any chance we could have a little non-sex at the end of it?"

"Watch it, Buster," I warned him. "I've had a long day."

"I'd do all the work," he offered.

"Damn straight you would," I replied. An involuntary sigh escaped from me. It really had been a long day, and the thought of surrendering to Bill's long fingers had its appeal.

"So, how did it go?" he asked. "You sound tired. I thought you were on a bar job. How hard could that be?"

It took me a moment to answer because I made the mistake of glancing at him and it was always hard to think when you had Bill Butler in your line of vision. He hadn't been raised around here and it showed. This was not a body bred on biscuits and bacon grease. He was tall and lean, with a full head of hair that was rapidly turning a well-earned gray. His hands were big and it was impossible to watch them spread gracefully over the copper bar without thinking of them spread elsewhere. A long black mustache that pushed the limits of departmental regulations crept down either side of his mouth. He had a great mouth on him, when he could keep it shut. It was thin and almost always curled into a smile no matter how tough he tried to look. But his eyes were his most deadly weapons. They were deep brown and he had those long lashes that it's really unfair to waste on straight guys. His eyes always looked as if he were about to strip some girl of her virginal white in a Mexican bordello somewhere. There was no doubt about it—the man made my pitter go pat and my patter go pit.

"Why are you staring at me?" he demanded. "Are you trying to be alluring or something?"

I shoved him so hard he almost fell off his stool.

"Sorry," I said. "I had a weird day is all." I told him about the office full of country ladies, all related to Gail Honeycutt Taylor. He did not exactly react as I had hoped. He shifted into indignant overdrive and committed one of my personal seven deadly sins: he tried to tell me what to do.

"Jesus, Casey—let it lie," he ordered me. "That case is over and done with. She popped him. He was a fellow officer, for god's sakes. Don't tell me you're going to try and help her? Stay away from it."

I stared at him incredulously, both because he knew about the case—which had been well before his time—and because he'd done it again. "Don't tell me what to do," I warned him in a voice that usually worked with twenty-six year olds, but had damn little effect on the forty-four year old before me.

He shook his head angrily. "Casey, that mess was bad enough when it first happened They were still talking about it when I joined the force down here, and they're still talking about it today. I've heard the rumors; the family's been saying Roy was a dirty cop and I'm not going to buy it."

That interested me. "Really?" I asked. "I hadn't heard those rumors."

"You always get them when a cop goes down like that," Bill explained. "It doesn't mean they're true."

"It doesn't mean they're not true, either," I said.

"See, that's my point." He inched away from me. "That's why civilians shouldn't go poking around in police business. The first thing that comes to your mind is that he was dirty and now your whole investigation is going to revolve around that rumor, whether it's true or not."

I was indignant. I slammed my beer bottle down on the bar and a couple of the old coots looked my way. I considered flashing diem, but didn't want to be responsible for performing CPR on them if I did. "I think I'm experienced and intelligent enough to be able to separate fact from fiction," I said. "I believe I have just about as much experience as you, in fact."

"Doing what? Following around cheating spouses and lousy bartenders?"

"What brought this on?" I asked. "A little touchy on the subject of cheating spouses, aren't we?"

Wrong point to bring up. It was why he had moved south in the first place. His anger edged up a notch. "Casey, I can tell that you're in over your head with this one. It's a bad case, is all I'm saying. A good officer was killed. His wife did the killing. She was a drunk. The evidence was there. She deserves her punishment. Let it lie."

"You mean let her die," I countered angrily. "And I can't let that happen if there's a chance she didn't do it. It seems to me that she hasn't had a whole hell of a lot of competent help in proving her innocence."

"I suppose you're one of those bleeding-heart liberals who opposes the death penalty," he said, rolling his eyes.

Now I was madder than a bull on the wrong side of the fence. Politics had nothing to do with it. I knew what it felt like to walk around with anger burning in my heart, searching for someone to blame, aching for someone to punish. I understood why people wanted the death penalty, and I didn't appreciate being labeled by some paranoid cop who thought it was us versus them—and who was a little confused about which side I was on.

"You haven't got a clue as to who or what I am," I snapped back. "Or what this case is about."

"Neither do you. Just stay away from it," he ordered me abruptly. It was enough to seal his doom. No one tells me what to do twice in one night. Not ever. Not now. Not in the future. And certainly not Bill Butler.

"I knew this date was a bad idea," I said.

"Non-date," he corrected me. Another big mistake. I shot him my version of the country-lady glare and marched out the door.

The effect was spoiled a bit when I caught one of my idiotic heels on the entrance-hall rug. I heard him snicker, but at least I had the satisfaction of knowing that he had watched me go.

CHAPTER TWO

I hate waking up alone on Sunday mornings. Having sex while everyone else is stuck at church is my idea of a good time. Besides, forget reading *True Confessions* and eating bonbons. It is my god given right as a bawdy woman to lounge among plush pillows while a strapping young man feeds me bits of fresh apple fritters from Harris Teeter.

So what was I doing on a spring Sunday slouching around in my torn chenille bathrobe and pink bunny slippers searching for a clean coffee cup? I refused to admit that, perhaps, my pride had gotten me in this predicament. Instead, I blamed it on the weather.

We'd had no winter that year, a Carolina phenomenon that happens more and more these crazy-current, ozone-impaired days. The skies had stayed a steady gray for several months straight, with only occasional cold blasts and blue skies, courtesy of the Great Lakes. It was like being forced to watch reruns of the same unfunny television show day after day. And now, like millions of my fellow Carolinians, I was desperate for warm winds and those silly daffodils that pop up in every traffic median around here. I pulled a chair up to the window that overlooked my little patch of backyard and surveyed the pathetic stubs of green dotting my tiny lawn. I sighed. Daffodils were a long way away. How depressing. So was being alone.

Oh, what the hell, I told myself. Get a grip, girl. Life could be a lot worse. For example, I could have been up early slinging hash and cleaning house for some fat-ass husband who was parked on the couch frantically flipping through the channels for a sports event so that he could avoid talking to me. When I thought about it that way, living alone didn't seem so bad after all.

I roused myself with a weight-lifting session performed to *Aretha Franklin's Greatest Hits* and then enjoyed a long shower while I pondered the mystery of Bill Butler. I couldn't decide if he was turning out to be a lot of trouble because I really cared for him and it irked me—or if he was simply a plain-old garden-variety pain in the ass. What I needed, I decided, was a sign from the gods; what I got was a blast of cold water when my meager hot water supply ran out. Shivering, I dressed in my favorite sweat suit and selected a pair of red high-tops for comfort. Hey, I was going to spend the day behind a computer and at the women's prison. I didn't exactly need blue velvet and pearls.

Since it was Sunday, I devoted a good five minutes to feathering my nest. In other words, I looked at the vacuum cleaner and considered cleaning the kitchen counter. The rest of the mess I could live with since the chaos was confined to two rooms. I may be the only person in all of Durham County who prefers apartment living. I have several big rooms in a converted tobacco warehouse—there are a lot of those around here—just a stone's throw from the railroad tracks that run through downtown Durham. I love the sound of the train whistle and the wheels clacking down the track in the afternoon and deep into the night. The train always seems to be heading south. I imagine it pushing slowly through the flat fields of South Carolina, skirting the edges of the coastal swamp and sandy shores of Georgia, plowing ahead down into Florida to pass by my grandfather's fields in the heart of the Panhandle, that no-man's-land of hopeless soil and unforgiving skies. One day, I'll be on that train, but sometimes it seems like going home is a lifetime away.

Once I had whipped my domestic department back into shape, it was time to get to work. I hacked my way through the lobby; the owner had recently gone nuts with the potted plants, hanging them willy-nilly from every rafter she could reach in an attempt to fool yuppie Duke students into thinking they were living in a SoHo loft. I didn't see lights on in any other apartments, and regret reared its ugly head once more. I imagined all the other residents luxuriating behind closed doors, snuggling with assorted significant others, stretching lazily and eyeing one another for another go-around while they chatted about that poor lonely old maid who lived on the first floor.

Geeze, I needed to get a grip. At this rate, I'd commit suicide before I reached I-40. I was loved, I reminded myself. Deeply. By my landlady. She kept my rent cheap because I lived at ground level and seemed impervious to the usual fears of women living under such circumstances. I did not stay awake at night wondering if some hulking rapist might climb in my window and overpower me. Not only was I pretty tough to overpower, but I'd also been through worse and it took a lot more than that to scare me now. Besides, she knew that I was packing an Astra Constable .380 semiautomatic pocket pistol, a Spanish knockoff of the Walther PPK. I kept it locked in a drawer in my office much of the time, but just remembering that I had it made me feel so much better that I abandoned my pathetic whimpering and drove to Biscuitville, where I broke the bank ordering a boatload of their miniature country-ham biscuits. Hey, those suckers are small. It takes two dozen to last a girl the thirty miles to Raleigh.

I arrived at the office with my monthly sodium intake taken care of and a powerful thirst for a cold beverage. Fortunately, Bobby D. was still beached at home and I was able to snag a Bud from his wastebasket without fear of drawing back a bloody stump. The can was still cold from the night before. Yes, I know, it's disgusting to drink beer on a Sunday morning, but the water cooler was out of action. Trust me.

Even as I turned on my beloved Mac, I knew that I would probably take the Gail Honeycutt case. The fact that Bill Butler opposed it made it a near certainty. Otherwise, I would not be going through my new case ritual: connect to the World Wide Web, access NandoNet—a locally based database with former ties to the *News & Observer*, Raleigh's only major newspaper—then hack my way into the bowels of the N&O's archives via an outdated access route they failed to block when they sold the network. Finally, I would pull up every article and photo I could find on the case.

There was plenty on Gail Honeycutt Taylor. I'd lived in Raleigh for twelve years and should have remembered the scandal better. But my early years had been a blur of alcohol and odd jobs, which gradually gave way to semi-sobriety and doing office chores for Bobby D. Finally, I started taking on a few cases of my own, mostly following soon-to-be ex-husbands or ex-wives or locating missing persons. It wasn't for another few years that my cases got much more interesting than that. In short, I hadn't given the newspapers much of a look when the Taylor case broke eight years back.

It had been a doozy. The murder of Roy Taylor had gotten bigger headlines than the time our lieutenant governor was caught frolicking nude in the downtown Hilton fountain with a well-known transvestite. And no wonder: the Taylor murder had it all—a decorated policeman shot to death in his home, a wife gone bad who was found passed out a few feet from the body with the murder weapon in her hand, a child sleeping through it all in a nearby bedroom and an anonymous call alerting the cops to the event.

I kept reading: Roy Taylor had been shot with his own service revolver, a Smith & Wesson 4506-1 model, standard issue of the Durham Police Department. Six bullets had been discharged. Two had lodged in the pasteboard walls, high above the doorway where Roy Taylor was found sprawled. Four bullets had lodged in the victim. Some serious shooting had gone down. Three of the slugs hit his chest—one drilled him right through the center of his heart, for god's sake—and the fourth bullet took off a chunk of his head. It was damn fine shooting, though I doubted Roy Taylor would have agreed.

Lord, I hoped the kid hadn't stumbled in and found him. I kept reading for more mention of the child. She had been nearly four at the time of the killing; that made her eleven or twelve today. She had not testified in court, and I hoped she had slept through the entire mess.

To my surprise, Gail had not been defended by a public lawyer. Nanny Honeycutt had forked out some big-time dough for the services of a well-known feminist lawyer who specialized in representing battered wives. I'd run into her on a few major divorce cases some years back. She looked—and acted—like F. Lee Bailey in drag and had the personality of Margaret Thatcher on steroids. But she'd been effective as a lawyer. Gail had been one of her few losses. It would have helped to talk to her, but a few years ago she choked to death on a piece of ham in a local restaurant while arguing with her husband over their impending divorce settlement. Move over Mama Cass. It was sort of a Greek tragedy, if your idea of Greek is a cross between Animal House and animus. At any rate, I wouldn't be able to ask her a whole lot of questions about Gail's case.

The judge was another surprise. Peyton Reynolds Tillman came from not one, but two, old North Carolina families, bringing a better pedigree to the bench than the last winner of the Westminster Dog Show. But unlike his forebears—one of whom held the Confederate flag at Gettysburg—Peyton Tillman was a firm opponent of the death penalty. What the hell had motivated him to approve the jury's sentence of death?

In North Carolina, where juries are inevitably working class and not exactly hesitant about sending convicted felons to their maker, the law required the presiding judge to sign off on every death penalty recommendation. Judges were also given a lot of leeway in how they could instruct the jury, and often swayed them one way or another during the sentencing phase. Signing off on Gail's death had been a first for Judge Tillman, as was the wording of his jury instructions. Before then, he had barely stayed within the confines of the law in urging juries to consider life imprisonment over death. In Gail's case, he had been objective—which meant that, while he had not technically sprung the trapdoor, he had certainly helped to tie the noose.

I wondered if his subsequent tumble from grace had anything to do with fallout from the Taylor case. The story of Judge Tillman was not one of North Carolina's finest: about five years ago, he took to drinking, which was certainly not unusual around these parts, but not advisable either, especially as a public vice for an unmarried judge in a god-fearing, church-going state. Two drunken-driving arrests had put a dent in his credibility, as had the tender young ages of the coeds found with him in each instance. During the Republican sweep that balanced Clinton's first election, Judge Tillman had been defeated by a fundamentalist candidate running on a family-values platform. The voting public did not seem to find it unusual that his opponent was acting as a spokesperson for family values even though she'd been divorced twice and her stepchildren had gotten a restraining order against her. They were more concerned that Judge Tillman was tooling around town tipsy with twenty-year-old babes—and not seeming to care that he was caught. If only he'd been polluting the rivers with hog waste or accepting illegal tobacco-company campaign contributions, he might have been forgiven by the voters. But his transgressions smacked of someone who was enjoying his sins, and that was a big no-no in these parts.

I also suspected that his attitude had done him in. He never spoke publicly about his arrests, never apologized to his mama for sullying her name and never appeared on "NC People Today" to weep his repentance for everyone's entertainment. His silence might have translated into arrogance for N.C.'s no-nonsense folk, though I thought it might simply have been outdated dignity in a tabloid-mentality world. I also wondered if his motives for remaining silent hadn't included embarrassment, shyness or something much deeper— like regret at sending a woman to her death.

After he was defeated, the public learned that Judge Tillman had a whole lot more to him than a law degree and liberal leanings. An enterprising reporter who, in my humble opinion, missed the boat by about six months, uncovered his war record: Peyton Tillman had served two tours of duty with the Marines in Vietnam, and saw the heaviest action possible for a young man in the late '60s—and that had been heavy action indeed. Why hadn't he capitalized on his war record, I wondered. It could have saved him the election.

I wanted to get my hands on Tillman to ask him about the Taylor case, but the chances of that were slim. I made a note to find out about his current whereabouts and kept plowing forward through the newspaper accounts.

Gail's case had gone through the usual appeals process without any apparent success. Judge Tillman's skill in the courtroom had left little grounds for appeal on a technicality, and the evidence against Gail had been strong. She did not take the stand in her own defense, and the mitigating circumstances presented during the penalty phase of her trial had been duly dismissed as a bunch of hog swaller by a jury of her peers. Analysis of her blood had measured an alcohol level of .15 of one percent, nearly twice the legal limit, but certainly not high enough to support her contention that she had blacked out the night of the murder.

Blood analysis had also revealed traces of antidepressants, barbiturates and various other prescription drugs, but nothing in significant quantity. There were no witnesses to support her lawyer's contention that she was a battered wife. There was no medical evidence either, and much had been made of the fact that she weighed at least as much as her husband—though what that had to do with the price of tea in China Grove, I could not fathom. Weight has nothing to do with meanness. I've seen a ninety-pound woman on crystal meth knock a 280-pound biker on his ass.

I read the summaries of testimony with interest. Numerous people took the stand to testify that the Taylors had been experiencing marital problems, and at least five people had sworn that they witnessed a public screamfest by the couple the night Roy Taylor died. This display had taken place in a police bar called the Lone Wolf that was located on the outskirts of Durham. Presumably, the Taylors stumbled out of the Lone Wolf to weave their way home for a final battle.

They had also instigated divorce proceedings against one another, and, according to some witnesses, Gail was worried she might lose her right to ownership in the couple's fishing cabin up at Lake Gaston.

Roy Taylor seemed like a pretty good guy. A string of commanding officers testified that he had been the perfect cop. No one mentioned any possible dirty dealings. I was at a loss as to how and why Bill Butler kept hearing all those rumors. There was a leak somewhere, but it hadn't been to the media and it hadn't been during the trial.

In short, what the newspaper articles told me was that Gail Honeycutt had never had a prayer. North Carolina's Correctional Center For Women was filled to the rafters with self-made widows who soon learned that shooting your husband was not as easy an offense to wiggle out of as shooting your wife was in most of the world. Especially when your husband was a well-respected police officer and you were widely acknowledged as a drunk, pill-popping slut.

The final public chapter in the case was a sad one. Gail's daughter had become the object of a bitter custody dispute between maternal relatives and Roy Taylor's parents. The whole wedlock mess had been brought out and speculation as to the identity of the child's real father had been cruel, protracted and, ultimately, useless. In the end, the judge awarded custody of little Brittany Honeycutt Taylor to an unnamed relative of Gail's on the grounds that blood was thicker than money. I've never understood why being genetically connected to someone should in the least affect suitability as a parent one way or the other, but the courts seem mighty keen on the concept.

The series of articles about the custody dispute had all been written by the same N&O reporter. They were remarkably restrained, given the sensational nature of the material. I wrote down the reporter's name and reminded myself I could always call her if I hit a brick wall. She might know something that never made it into print, something she'd be willing to share.

I printed out the most important articles and started a case file—yet another sign that I was rapidly being sucked into the vortex of the Gail Honeycutt case. I jotted some questions in the margins and made a few notes about possible counter theories. When I was done, I had a thick manila folder of information that I tucked into my knapsack for safekeeping. I come from a

superstitious lot. Where I go, my current case files go with me—
even if I was off to as depressing a place as the women's prison.

If I thought the morning had been rough on my psyche, I
knew the afternoon would be worse. There isn't a place on earth
I'd rather avoid more than a women's prison. I had bad
memories of my own eighteen months spent behind bars. It had
been a long time ago, when I was dumb enough to believe that
the man I loved was a good man. Fortunately, that was also when
I was young and strong enough to survive the rude awakening
when it came. It had been many years since I'd willingly entered
such a place, but I could remember the suffocating loneliness as
if it had been yesterday. Not to mention the bad B-movie reality
of the experience.

No matter. That was then. And this was now. I shouldered
my knapsack and moved on.

The women's prison was on the south side of Raleigh, nestled
among the town's largest black neighborhood. The churches
were just letting out from eleven o'clock services, and the streets
were clogged with families dressed in their Sunday best which, in
Raleigh on a nearly spring Sunday, could be pretty damn spiffy
indeed. Tiny boys in white suits. Little girls in pastel dresses with
big bows tied in back. Mothers in cobalt-blue and ruby-red
dresses, their hair carefully tucked up under stylish hats. Fathers
in somber gray and black suits, scrubbed and dignified in their
praying clothes. Like me, everyone was just waiting for spring.
They stared up at a heavy sky, wondering where all the sunshine
had gone. I basked in this last glimpse of normalcy before I
turned down the road that led to the prison.

The parking lot was only a quarter full, mostly, I suspected,
with the cars of guards. The parade of children here to see their
mothers under the supervision of weary grandmothers had not
yet started. They were all still driving in from their coastal,
country and mountain homes, wondering what the hell they
would say to each other this time. I knew the rap.

As I followed the long brick sidewalk over a muddy lawn to
the first guardhouse, my heart pounded and a muscle in my right
thigh started to twitch. Bad memories can be a powerful force. I

showed my I.D. to the guard manning the front post and was waved through to checkpoint two. It took a while to negotiate the various gates and administrative watchdogs, nearly all of whom were women. At least I think the guards were women. While a few looked like they could go either way—standing up or sitting down—odds were good they were female. They aren't stupid in the penal system here. They know better than to stick a bunch of male guards in a women's prison, and they have full confidence that the countrybred females of North Carolina can keep just about anyone in line, thank you very much. They're right.

The prisoners were on their noon break, filing into a low brick building that held the cafeteria or lingering on the lawn to look up at the sky, just like their free brethren. They moved about in small groups, smoking cigarettes and whispering to one another, every now and then shouting an insult to another group. Most of the women were young, and all of them looked royally pissed off.

A tiny black female guard acted as my tour guide. She didn't waste much time on small talk. "This is one unhappy lady you're about to see," she said, unlocking the door to a smaller brick building set apart from the other brick structures. They're big on brick in prison.

"Yeah?" I asked. "She on medication?"

"That girl is so high she needs an air-traffic controller," the guard replied, unlocking a small room and leaving me to wait at a wooden table.

They were pretty informal at the prison, if you were a mere murderer, drug dealer or abuser of small children. But death-row inmates were housed in separate quarters from the general population, in a building they shared with regular inmates who had violated prison rules. They lived an isolated life, with only one hour of solitary recreation allowed per day and a single outside visitor every twenty-four hours, clergy and lawyers excepted. As prisoners reached the end of the line, this rule was often relaxed to give families time to say good-bye—or at least the surviving family members. There weren't a lot of husbands visiting wives on death row. Gail's cohorts included a woman who had stomped her elderly husband to death with cowboy boots and several who had used their spouses as targets in their own private turkey shoots.

Two guards brought Gail to me without comment, unlocking her handcuffs and parking her on the other side of the table. They left us alone and looked away discreetly as they waited on the other side of the room's glass windows.

"Hello, Gail," I said, doing my best to erase any forced attempts at cheerfulness from my voice. It wasn't hard. I felt like I could hardly breathe. Either my living bra was turning on me or I was on the verge of a panic attack.

Gail looked at me for a moment before abruptly asking, "What's the matter with you? You don't look too good." Her southern accent was thick and much rougher than that of her relatives. Tough girl in prison talk.

"Prisons do that to me," I said.

"Oh, yeah? You should try being in one." She leaned back and crossed her arms, waiting for me to apologize. She was in for a surprise.

"I have been in one," I told her. "For eighteen very long months." I am not above pandering my past if it furthers my future.

She stared at me, expressionless. "Got a cigarette?" she asked.

I shook my head.

"Never mind. That stuff'll kill you." She made a rusty coughing sound that was supposed to be a laugh. "I cracked a joke, did you notice?" Her words came out in disjointed intervals and her pupils were small. The lady was bombed on prescription drugs. Medical management, they called it. I called it zombie time. It was no way to spend the last thirty days of your life.

"Do you know who I am?" I asked.

"Yeah." Her sullen attitude returned. "Nanny Honeycutt said you were coming. I don't know why the hell she doesn't let me die in peace."

28

"Maybe she loves you?" I suggested sarcastically. "It's just a wild guess, of course." Her passiveness was getting on my nerves. I could imagine she drove her lawyers up the wall.

"I can't help you," she said, looping a long string of black hair behind one ear. She had been a pretty, though overweight, woman in her pre-prison photographs, with a catlike face and big eyes. Now she was puffy, and her country tan had faded to a sickly pallor. Her shirt strained at the buttons and a roll of soft fat spilled over the waistline of her blue jeans. Her hair was still glossy and thick, however. It was brushed into the familiar prison shag that's a cross between feminine and butch, and has never looked good on anyone other than David Cassidy. I wondered at this small vanity. It gave me a little hope.

"I haven't decided whether to take your case yet," I announced, hoping to shake her up.

"Really? I haven't decided whether I should let them kill me by drugs or the gas chamber. Maybe we should both flip a coin?"

So much for that strategy. "Look, I met with your family and promised Nanny Honeycutt I'd talk to you and let her know if I could do anything," I said. "I know you don't care if you're going to die, but your family sure does."

"Some of my family cares," she corrected me. "I bet my daddy wasn't at that meeting, was he?"

"No men were," I admitted.

She shrugged. "Big surprise. How about my sister Brenda?"

"She wasn't there either," I answered. "But I'm supposed to meet with her as soon as possible."

Gail began rapidly drumming her fingers on the tabletop as if I bored her. I gritted my teeth, reminded myself of what it had been like and tried again.

"Listen, Gail. I know you don't think you can help me and I know that you don't really care what happens to you. I've been behind bars, like I told you. A place like this has a way of sucking the hope out of you. But you've been in here too long to be able to see things clearly anymore. You might be able to help me and not even know it. Why don't you just tell me what you remember about the night Roy died and let me decide what's important and what's not?"

She shrugged again. "I don't know what the hell I did or did not do that night. I blacked out. I knew something like this would happen one day. But I couldn't seem to stop drinking. All Roy and me ever did was drink together. That was what we had in common. I drank four, maybe five, drinks that night. I was okay for a while, but then everything kind of went dark."

"When did it go black?" I asked. "Before or after the bar?" I was curious as to why she would black out after five drinks. She was a big woman and sounded like she'd been a functioning alcoholic. Five drinks shouldn't have put her away like that. Hell, I was two-thirds her size and I could go a whole fifteen rounds before the lights went out.

She thought for a moment. "After the bar, I think. On the way home in the truck. Roy and me had been fighting. I can't remember over what. We left and we were still fighting. That was about all I remember until I woke up in the backseat of a police car on my way to jail." She glanced around the tiny room. "It's not so bad inside," she added. "People are nice to me in here. Especially now that I'm going to die."

How heartwarming. I wondered which one of these nice people would be the one to kill her. "Did you tell your lawyer about blacking out?" I asked.

"You mean my first lawyer?" she asked. "I told her. She didn't want to hear. She just wanted me to say that Roy beat me and that was why I shot him."

"Did he?" I asked.

"Hell, no." She held up one arm and flexed it. I had to admit she was built pretty good for a woman. I estimated it would take me thirty seconds to whip her ass instead of the usual ten.

"You think any man would try to beat on me?" she continued. "I'd have kicked his tail faster than he could sneeze. Besides, me and Roy, we got along fine. We just didn't love each other."

"Why'd you get married in the first place?" I asked. "It's customary to love your husband."

"On what planet?" She laughed bitterly. "We got married because Roy wanted to. He loved my kid is what he loved."

"Your kid?" I asked, my voice rising involuntarily.

"Not that way," she complained. "You got a dirty mind. He loved Brittany like she was his own little girl. He couldn't have kids of his own and he felt sorry for us. Me, I married him because, what the hell, it was better than living with my parents."

"Does Brittany come to see you often?" I asked.

Her mouth clamped down in a tight line. "She doesn't come to see me at all. Children got no business seeing their mothers like this. The sooner my daughter forgets about me, the better. I am going to die, you know. There's nothing anyone can do." She sounded both resigned and relieved at the prospect.

"God almighty, Gail. Don't you care about that?" I asked. "It's not a game. You are going to die if no one does anything about it."

She let her hands drop to her sides. "Don't you get it? I give up. I'm tired of all of this. I'm tired of my family acting like I'm a big disappointment. I'm tired of always being the one who screws things up. I'm tired of thinking things are going to be better and then finding out they're the same old bullshit. Shit, I'm just plain tired."

"Maybe you need to cut back on the tranquilizers?" I suggested.

"They took away my booze," she said. "The least they can do is leave me my pills."

"Were you on pills the night Roy died?"

"Of course I was on pills," she said impatiently. "I been on pills since I was fifteen. But I wasn't taking black market like people are always saying. I didn't do those kinds of pills. People who say I did are liars."

I sighed. "Nothing else you can tell me?" I asked.

She shook her head. "I can't tell you what I don't remember."

I slid one of my cards across the table. "Will you call me if you think of anything?" I asked. "That's my office number and that's home."

She shrugged again. I was starting to seriously dislike that shrug. "You live in Durham," she said. "I might have to call collect."

"So call collect." I stood to go and shook her hand goodbye. It was soft and puffy behind the old calluses, a work-worn hand without any work left to do. "Good luck," I told her. "Whatever happens."

"Whatever," she repeated and treated me to a final shrug.

"Told you," the tiny guard said as she led me out through the labyrinth of walkways and buildings. "Only one person can get through to her and that's a girl who just might have worse luck than Gail. She's over there." She nodded toward a skinny woman hunched over on a bench, smoking a cigarette.

The woman felt us watching and glanced away like she'd been caught doing something bad. She had a sharp face, like someone who has been hungry for a long time, and she sure as hell didn't need to be pulling tobacco smoke into her lungs. She was coughing up a storm as we passed by.

"Her girlfriend?" I asked.

The guard shrugged. "Hey, I'm like the military," she said. "I don't ask and I don't tell."

As we turned a corner near the front gate, I palmed a business card in my left hand and slipped my knapsack behind a bush. I don't normally leave my personal possessions lying around in a compound of convicted thieves, but I had a plan in mind.

"Thanks," I told the guard, shaking her hand.

"Good luck," she replied and walked away briskly.

"Any luck?" the front-gate guard asked. He was reading an out-of-date issue of *Sports Illustrated* and looking monumentally bored.

I shook my head. "Not much." I paused to give my escort time to disappear. "Oh, damn," I complained. "I left my knapsack in the visiting room."

"I'll call," he said, picking up the phone.

"Don't bother." I put my hand on his to stop him. "I know the way. It'll only take me two minutes."

"Suit yourself." He turned back to his magazine as I quickly walked up the sidewalk toward the skinny girl sitting on the bench smoking a cigarette. She jumped when I dropped my business card in her lap and I caught a glimpse of a furtive, frightened face. "Call me," I said. "It's about Gail Honeycutt."

Before she could reply, I was heading back to the front gate. The last thing I needed was to have my visiting privileges cut off. I grabbed my knapsack from behind the bush, waved a cheery good-bye to the guard and fled to the familiar safety of my car. It felt good to leave the brick walls behind.

What an uplifting Sunday it had been so far, I thought as I sped my way back home to Durham, hoping to beat the rain and the extra gloominess it would bring. I couldn't make up my mind about the case, but I couldn't think about it anymore today. Those brick prison walls were sticking with me and I needed to find a way to escape.

I returned to my apartment to find two phone messages. The first was from Bill Butler and it was to the point: "If you're expecting me to call and apologize, don't. I'm not going to." All this was uttered quite cheerfully before he hung up with a click. Jerk. He had no right to be cheerful. He was supposed to be at home suffering, swearing off women forever and, hopefully, gouging his eyes out in agony. Maybe women ought to pass out instructions when they get into relationships. It would cut down on a lot of confusion.

The next message was from Nanny Honeycutt wanting to know how my visit with Gail had gone. I steeled myself and called her back.

She answered the phone like she'd been sitting on it, waiting for it to hatch. "Did you talk to her?" she asked when she heard it was me. This was a lady who didn't waste a lot of time on small talk.

"Yeah, and it got me nowhere. But I'm going to take the case." I said it fast before I could change my mind. I had no idea why I had agreed. It was just that I couldn't walk away.

There was a silence. "God bless you," she finally said.

I was embarrassed and covered it. "How about that appointment with Gail's sister?" I asked.

"Brenda is expecting you anytime tomorrow," she said, and I realized she knew I'd take the case all along.

"There's one more thing," I warned her. "I need some answers."

"About what?" she asked calmly.

"About a lot of things. Like, what is this I hear about your family starting a rumor that Roy Taylor was a dirty cop? Where's that information come from?"

There was another silence.

"Well?" I asked, remembering what Bill Butler had said the night before.

Her tone was indignant. "There's not a person in my family that would say such a thing. And if I heard them, they'd have to answer to me. Roy Taylor was a fine man and an honest policeman. No one would dare insinuate otherwise. My family does not lie."

"They did about Roy beating Gail."

The silence that followed this observation was downright poisonous. "Young lady," she snapped, "I let myself be talked into shading the truth because I was desperate. It blew up in our faces. No more. It's nothing but the truth from here on out. Take it from me, Roy Taylor was not a dishonest man."

Well, how do you like that? Those Honeycutts had no concept that the truth was a moving target. They'd have made lousy politicians.

"Okay," I said carefully. "Thanks for setting me straight."

She hung up without wishing me a nice day.

It would have been a waste of words. Day had given way to night and it was barely four o'clock. Outside, it was dark, and rain clouds rumbled, ready to split open and pour. I'd done my work for the weekend and now I needed a way to fight off the residual doom in my heart. That meant an SOS to Jack.

In the realm of younger men, Jack reigned supreme, both as a lover and as a friend. He was handsome and fickle, with a talent for serious bodywork and a knack for making me laugh. He did not have a committed bone in his body and women who expected him to stay around longer than an evening were uniformly disappointed once morning came. But he was upfront about his failings and so god awful cute that I loved him just the way he was.

We had known each other for almost five years, and, if you didn't ask much of him, he delivered more than you would expect. He looked like a well-fed pirate, with dark Irish coloring, blue-black hair that curled around his nape, flashing eyes and the rosiest complexion I'd ever seen outside of a Bertie County peach. Jack was also disgustingly healthy, given that he was a bartender who kept horrendous hours and was not averse to a drink or ten himself. I knew Sundays were his days for lying comatose and recouping for the week of womanizing ahead. I was sure he'd be at home and willing to entertain the thought of a pizza.

He was. We argued awhile over whether or not to add black olives to the sausage and onions, but finally compromised by getting one large pizza with olives and one without. He promised to pick up all the extras that such a feast demanded and arrived at my doorstep within the hour, just in time for a double-feature horror-film festival on TNT. The thunder and lightning outside added to the atmosphere. We stuffed our faces and belched in companionable silence, our feet parked on the furniture and pizzas balanced on our bellies.

When the movies were over and the pizzas mere spots of grease on cardboard, we moved the party into the bathroom and reenacted a series of famous naval battles in my tub, sending bubbles and water splashing over the tile walls. Jack's best quality is that he is resolutely immature. Well, maybe that's his second best quality. His very best quality showed itself later on in the bedroom, where we romped for hours and thoroughly erased any signs of doom and gloom from our souls. He had me purring like a fine-tuned Porsche by the time we were done. By midnight, we fell as sound asleep as a pair of puppies after a wrestling match, belly to belly, snoot to snoot.

CHAPTER THREE

I arrived at the office late the next morning, ready to tackle, if not the world, at least the Gail Honeycutt case. I still wanted to talk to Gail's sister as a starting point, and Nanny Honeycutt had set up the appointment for me. And if I was heading over to the district attorney's office anyway, I might as well aim high. Bobby D. could help. I found him parked behind his desk in all his obese majesty. I tossed him a box of Krispy Kreme doughnuts as a bribe. "Monday morning sacrifice to the gods," I said.

"I am a god," he agreed, though the closest he got to being one was his Buddha-like belly. God or not, he was no fool. "What do you want?" he asked, peeking inside and counting his treasures. Never mind that the flat box with green and white polka dots lying empty at his feet told me that he had already scarfed down a dozen that morning.

"Know anyone down at the D.A.'s office?" I asked. "I want to talk to the head man for a minute or two." If I wanted to hear what the other side said about Gail's case, there was no better place to start than at the top.

Bobby D. groaned. "You're going to take that damn Taylor case, aren't you?"

"Look, old Nanny Honeycutt, who runs the family, shelled out plenty to hire an expensive lawyer to defend Gail. She didn't get her money's worth. She wants to try again. I want to help."

Bobby looked thoughtful. "If she could afford to pay double our usual rates, that would make the embarrassment worth it."

"Embarrassment?" I repeated incredulously. "Bobby, you are physically, emotionally and constitutionally incapable of feeling embarrassment. Can you get me in to see the D.A. or not?"

"Of course I can get you in, babe. Give me a minute or two."

I sought refuge in my cubby while I waited. Bobby D. may be on the fast track to a heart attack, but he is a master at maintaining connections throughout the North Carolina judicial network. Like I said, he specializes in divorced middle-aged women starved for romance, and there's one of those in every office in the state. Including the Wake County District Attorney's Office.

"If you can get your gorgeous butt over there by eleven, my source can squeeze you in for fifteen minutes," Bobby hollered down the hall.

"I'm on my way," I yelled back, hightailing my gorgeous butt out the door.

The walk through downtown Raleigh gave me hope. Crocuses were starting to break through the well-trimmed grass on the Capitol lawn, and the bright copper dome of the building actually sparkled in the stray beams of sunshine. If only the clouds would move up north where they belonged, spring would burst out like a ripe peach, saving us all from permanent depression.

The Wake County courthouse offices were quiet on a Monday at mid-morning. Strategy meetings hummed behind closed doors. Secretaries yawned as they steeled themselves for another mind-numbing week ahead. And those hardy few who were actually working were already arguing their cases in courtrooms located on the upper floors. I found the office for Ham Mitchell pretty easily: the man must have been a megalomaniac, since signs pointed the way at three-foot intervals. Either that or he had Alzheimer's.

Ham Mitchell had been Wake Country District Attorney for going on ten years now. His real name was Hampton but, take it from me, Ham suited him to a tee. Not only did he look like a big old pig wearing a stubby brown wig, he also hogged the cameras like a pro. He was always in front of a reporter, issuing statements on cases that were out of his jurisdiction and none of his damn business to begin with. He was also shameless about his ambitions: as soon as the state attorney general had the decency to die, Ham was planning to slide into the post quicker than a piglet slicked in grease.

In the meantime, he was practicing his intimidation skills. "Who the hell are you and what the hell do you want?" he demanded after I introduced myself. Well, gracious me, what ever happened to old-fashioned southern hospitality?

"Donna!" he bellowed out his door, but Donna had wisely beat a hasty retreat to the little girl's room.

"Relax," I said, sliding into one of those huge leather contraptions that pass for chairs in the offices of people who think they're important. I inched my dress up over my knees and crossed my legs to appease his temper. Trust me, I know what I'm doing. "I just need ten minutes of your time to talk about Gail Honeycutt Taylor."

That cheered him up. I do believe the old boy was fond of her memory. It had been one of his most publicized cases as district attorney. He had bellowed, stomped and cajoled his way to victory, taking great pride in sending yet another North Carolina woman to death row. His win put the state at the top of the charts when it came to female felons waiting to die. It probably made him proud. He was the kind of guy who shoved old ladies off the front-row pew at church each Sunday so he could get a good seat and show everyone how pious he was.

"Well, young lady," he said, lacing his stubby fingers together. I forgave him the "lady" because he'd tacked on the "young." He licked his lips. "What can I do for you in ten minutes?"

You have no idea what raced through my mind at that offer. But I thought ten minutes was probably eight more than he typically needed, so I held my tongue.

"You prosecuted that case," I reminded him. "I'm looking into it on behalf of her family. She's only got a month left before her execution. They want to be sure they've done everything they can do for her, so I've been asked to verify the evidence against her one more time. I was wondering if you could give me your impressions about the strength of her case, if you thought her defense had any merit? If there was anything I should look into?

I am sure you would want to be positive before you sent a woman to her death."

"It's a shame when anyone has to die," he said sadly. "But we must maintain the boundaries of civilization, young lady. An eye for an eye." He oozed so much sincerity, I felt like wiping my shoes on the carpet.

I didn't get into it with him. This state is full of sincere church-going people. Letting a bible-spouting hypocrite like Ham Mitchell get under your skin makes them defensive, and I admire them too much for that. So I let it pass. "It doesn't make sense," I said instead. "Gail and her husband always got along well until that night. Why would she suddenly kill him?"

"Got along?" he countered. "The man slapped her around, beat her, kicked her when she was down. You call that getting along? She just snapped is all. Picked up a gun and evened the score."

"You believed her defense?" I asked, as close to speechless as I ever get. "Yet you went for the death penalty? If you believed her, wouldn't that constitute mitigating circumstances? Wouldn't life with a chance for parole have been a more appropriate punishment?"

He rolled his huge shoulders. "If every woman who was slapped around took justice into her own hands, there'd only be a handful of men left in this state."

"What century are you from?" I asked incredulously. I just couldn't help it.

"Pardon?" he asked, blinking his tiny eyes.

"You seriously believe that?" I said. "That must go over big at Junior League rallies."

"See here, young lady," he said. "Abuse is a serious matter and I don't take it lightly. But it's no excuse for taking another person's life. Why even Gail's own sister felt she deserved the death penalty."

"I would doubt that," I said emphatically.

"Then you would be wrong." He rose, irritated, and his bulk seemed to fill the room. He was also starting to sweat. Was it my imagination or did he smell like barbecued pork? At any rate, I'd had enough. I'd get nothing out of him, that was for sure. My skeptical look said it all.

"Why don't you go ask her for yourself?" he suggested. "She's right down the hall. I have work to do. Donna!" he hollered again. This time, a well-dressed brunette in her late forties scurried into the room, notebook in hand.

"Sir?" she chirped, a professional smile curling her lips.

"Take this young lady down the hall to see Brenda Polk, would you? I have to attend to more pressing matters. I am sure Brenda would be happy to help her. I can't understand whose idea it was to let her in to see me in the first place."

"Why, it was your idea, sir," she lied politely. "You thought it would be good for your standing with female voters if you appeared fair. Remember?"

"Oh." He paused, momentarily confused, then picked up enough steam to sputter a dismissal. "I've changed my mind. Get her out of here."

We filed out dutifully, with me feeling like the poodle who's just peed on the new white rug. Well, I thought with determination, we'd just have to wait and see whose nose was rubbed in what.

"God," I said when we were safely down the hall. "Is he always like that? I wanted to pop him with a pin to see if he'd deflate."

"When he's unrehearsed he is," his secretary admitted. "Usually he has the office press secretary telling him what to say. You caught him off guard and he couldn't read you, so he didn't know what you wanted to hear."

"How can you work for him?" I asked. "Scraping dishes down at the K&W would be more fulfilling." Her friendship with Bobby D. aside, she seemed like a sensible lady.

"I have a front-row seat," she explained. "Ham's getting old and he's out of touch. Blabbing his mouth more and more at the wrong time. Worse, he's starting to garble his bible verses. One day soon, he's going to go down big time. I want to be around to see it. I've earned it. I can't wait for the big show."

We reached a small office at the end of a long hall. The door was shut. "I hope you get to see that show soon," I told Donna and we slapped each other a high five good-bye. Sisterhood, ain't it grand?

"Come in. It's unlocked," a raspy voice called out when I knocked on the frosted-glass window. Brenda Polk's voice was much more cultivated and controlled than her sister's.

She was a raw-boned woman with a determined face. She was on the short side, with a well-developed rib cage and skinny legs. I pegged her for a long-distance runner, both literally and figuratively.

"I'm Casey Jones," I told her. "Your family met with me a few days ago."

"Sit down," she said. "I know who you are. Nanny called. There are some things we need to discuss." She shoved an ashtray my way and lifted a bottle of Pepsi. "Want one?"

I shook my head. "No thanks, I'm trying to quit."

"Cute. I'm not." She took a swig, then flicked a slim cigarette from a nearby pack while she studied me. I doubted crossing my legs would help warm her up, so I kept still and waited. She lit the cigarette without ever once giving it a glance, telling me she was at least a two-pack-a-day smoker. I reconsidered the long-distance running theory.

"When Nanny Honeycutt gets her mind set on something," she finally said, "there's no stopping her." She blew out a plume of smoke and watched it rise up to the ceiling. "I made the mistake of telling her about some crackpot caller who claimed to have new evidence that would help Gail. Now Nanny won't let it drop. I should never have told her. It's nothing, just a troubled individual with a guilty conscience. But now her hopes are up. I'm sorry I ever opened my mouth."

She stared intently at me again and I wondered if my bra strap was showing. For a Southern woman, that was an impeachable offense.

"Can I ask you something?" she said.

"Sure." I'm a sucker for that question.

"You bleach your hair, right? I mean it's obvious. It's almost white."

"Sure." I nodded.

"But you have at least two inches of black showing at the roots. Right?"

"Right."

"Why?" She seemed genuinely interested in my answer.

I thought about it. "I bleach my hair because I can. It's my head and I'll do what I want to with it."

"Okay," she said. "I'll buy that."

"I let my roots grow out so that people know I have better things to do than sit around and obsess about it. Also, I'm too busy to care."

She nodded thoughtfully. "I like it. It's sort of a subtle screw you. I wonder what John would do if..." Her voice trailed off and she stroked her hairspray-stiffened helmet of short brown hair absently. "Naw. I don't think so. But it looks good on you."

"Thanks." We stared at each other for a moment. "Ham Mitchell says you think your sister deserves the death penalty," I said, getting right to the point.

"Ham's a complete asshole. And that's his best quality."

"So you don't want to see your sister die?" I asked.

"What kind of person do you think I am?" She locked her eyes on mine and I stirred uncomfortably. They were nearly black and hyper-alert. I doubted many people had the guts to get in her way. I had to fight the urge to duck every time she looked at me. "I did everything I could to help my sister," she said slowly. "I always have. But it looks like we're nearing the end of the line."

"It looks that way," I agreed. "Were you involved in the case?"

"Hell, no." She looked at me incredulously. "You think they'd let me near it? Besides, I didn't work here at the time. Ham hired me a few years later. I go by my married name. He didn't even know that I was related to Gail until I'd worked here for six months. Then he walked around feeling proud of himself for the next five years. He felt that hiring me showed compassion and justice on his part."

"Why would you want to work in the office of a district attorney that sent your sister to her death?"

"Lurid fascination?" she suggested, raising her eyebrows and picking a fleck of tobacco off of her well-glossed bottom lip. "This is what I do," she explained. "I'm a prosecutor. There aren't a whole lot of places where I could work and get decent cases in North Carolina. Better still, I'm a capital-crimes specialist—one of a handful in the country. And I've had the opportunity to learn from one of the best capital specialists in the business. When my boss retires, I'll probably get to take over and then I can run the show. I don't want to work for the Feds. Too much interference. And I want to stay near the rest of the family."

A sister on death row and she decides to specialize in trying death-row cases? A shrink would have a field day with that one.

"Did you help Gail at all in her defense?" I asked out of curiosity. The two sisters seemed so different—in a *Whatever Happened to Baby Jane?* sort of way, unfortunately.

She nodded. "Sure. I'm the one who told Nanny to hire Kaitland Cameron. She was Gail's defense lawyer. Big mistake. She'd just hit it big and had taken on too many cases at one time. She wasn't prepared. Just threw up her usual dog and pony show and hoped it would fly. It didn't. My sister paid the price. People weren't in the mood to let a woman off, whether she was battered or not. They still aren't. I suppose you remember the Sherwood case?"

I nodded. Betty Sherwood was a convicted killer who gave new meaning to the word "nightmare."

"I remember," I said. "She claimed she accidentally shot her husband through the head in the middle of the night with a gun she kept conveniently stored under her pillow. It was rather inconvenient for her husband, of course."

"Right," Brenda Polk said. "And she got away with it, in that she was sentenced to life in prison instead of death. Even after it came out that her first husband had died under suspicious circumstances. It made the public madder than a swarm of killer bees. Lots of people felt she got off easy. That happened right before Gail's case. I think Gail paid the price."

"Why didn't you get Nanny Honeycutt to fire Kaitland Cameron once you knew her legal strategy wouldn't work?"

"I tried, but I got nowhere. By then, Kaitland had convinced Nanny and the rest of the family that the battered-wife defense was Gail's only chance to get off."

"And Roy wasn't battering her?"

"Hell, no." She rolled her eyes and took another swig of Pepsi. "I'm addicted to this stuff. The caffeine. Coffee wrecks my stomach." She looked at a big stack of manila folders on one side of her desk and sighed. "You wouldn't believe my case load. No, Roy wasn't beating Gail. That's one thing she wouldn't stand for. She worked alongside of my daddy in the fields every day after school. She liked that stuff. Not me. I was too busy twirling batons and being homecoming queen and studying to be a lawyer. I was really obnoxious, I admit it. But Gail was a physical person, she liked all the lifting and hard work. She was strong and she didn't like being bullied that way. My daddy tried to hit her once when she was fifteen and had stayed all night with this loser who worked at the convenience store down the road. She clocked our daddy before his hand hit her face. He went down like a dead man. Didn't try to hit her again, though."

"Whoa," I said. "That sounds a little violent."

She stared at me and her level gaze made me feel at least three inches smaller. "You and I both know there's a difference between standing up for yourself and pushing people around. Gail protected herself physically, abused herself emotionally and never hurt anyone else if she could help it."

"Then how did she end up in this mess?" I asked.

"Gail's always done the wrong thing since she could walk. She was born under an unlucky star. When she was five, she accidentally strangled my kitten when she hugged it too hard. When she was nine, she drove my father's car into a river and hit an old fisherman in his boat. When she was thirteen, she accidentally burned down the barn trying to smoke cigarettes.

And when she was eighteen, she got herself knocked up and wouldn't tell anyone who the father was. Never has. That's the story of Gail's life. She was born to lose."

"That's some story," I pointed out. "A lot of people would say it's the classic portrait of a serial killer, for chrissakes. Torturing animals, setting fires, inappropriate sexual behavior, running down old men in rowboats." I wasn't being serious. I'd been too much of a fuckup myself. But she took me at my word.

"Oh come on, since when is getting knocked up at eighteen unusual behavior?" Gail's sister demanded. "And if it sounds bad, it's just like I told you. She was born under an unlucky star. It's only been worse for her because I was such a goody two-shoes. I got straight A's and a scholarship to UNC. I married a rich farm boy from Virginia, then talked him into living down here. I went to law school. I got a job as a special prosecutor with the state. Blah, blah, blah. Sometimes I make myself sick, so I imagine Gail feels the same way. My father holds it against her for not measuring up. I hate it—and believe me, I'd love to let my father down— but I can't sabotage my own life just to make Gail feel better."

I sided with Gail. Overachievers like Brenda could be a right royal pain in the ass for the rest of us mere mortals. "What makes you think Gail is innocent?" I asked. "Can you give me anything besides the lousy-shot theory?"

"No motive," Brenda said promptly. "That's the one thing that really bothers me about this whole mess. I can't figure out why Gail needed to shoot Roy. They were already getting a divorce and it was amicable."

I looked at her skeptically. There is no such thing as an amicable divorce and I see living proof of it almost every day. I make a lot of money following future exes around. Show me an amicable divorce and I'll show you a spouse who's being blackmailed into cooperating.

"It's true." Brenda insisted. "Look, Gail liked Roy. He married her with a bastard kid and all. And stuck by her when she got accused of stealing from the hospital."

"That would have been at age twenty-two, right before the killing," I guessed. "She seems to hit a snag every four years or so."

"She didn't steal anything," Brenda said. "And I'm the suspicious sort. She was set up. Believe me, Gail is a natural patsy. I know. I've watched my cousins take advantage of Gail's bad luck her entire life. She's taken the rap for everything from stealing pies to snitching car keys to dynamiting our Uncle Billy's pond and killing all the fish. She never did a tenth of what she was accused of. My cousins just smelled a sucker when they saw one."

"And so did someone else the night Roy Taylor was killed?" I suggested.

"I think it's possible," Brenda said hesitantly. "But I can't be sure." Leftover tendrils of cigarette smoke curled from her mouth and vanished in wisps. "I think there's also a chance she killed him," she finally said. "Gail had been drinking more and more, and there was all this talk about pills. Who knows how they change a person."

"But Gail denies popping pills, and Nanny Honeycutt says she hated guns," I said. "How could she drill him right through the heart?"

"That would be Gail's luck for you," she offered. "Nothing she does ever works out, except the one thing she shouldn't be doing. Like shooting Roy in the chest. But, yes, you're right. She wasn't a deadeye shot like the rest of my family. Never even picked up a gun to the best of my knowledge. Not even when Daddy wanted her to go out hunting with him and, believe me, Gail would have done anything for that man's approval." Brenda shook her head. "Gail never understood about the Honeycutt men. They don't show anything on the outside, and I'm not so sure they ever feel anything on the inside. Expecting one to love you and show it is a losing proposition. I never bothered. I just did the best I could to get the hell out on my own as soon as possible."

"Why didn't the jury think the bullet holes drilled perfectly through her husband's heart was unlikely?" I asked.

"The jury didn't believe she was a bad shot," Brenda explained. "That's the trouble when you throw up a defense that's a lie from the start. They smelled a lie and thought it was all a lie."

"What about the fact that Roy was working with an antidrug unit when he was killed?" I asked. "Did anyone look into that? If he'd been putting drug kingpins behind bars, that's a pretty large pool of potential suspects right there."

She nodded her head. "Her legal team spent a month and over $20,000 of Nanny's money having that angle looked into. There wasn't a whisper of threats against him by dealers. He didn't put that many behind bars, anyway. Roy died before most of his arrests came to trial. So the drug connection was a dead end."

"What about the rumors that he was dirty?" I asked.

"We looked into his financial records and followed leads up and down the Eastern seaboard. If Roy was dirty, he sure as hell wasn't getting rich from it. He had zippo assets except for their home. He didn't even own their fishing cabin. His stepfather did. I think Roy was clean."

"Why didn't Gail's daughter testify during the trial?" I asked. "She was there that night."

"Brittany couldn't add anything that would have helped, and Gail didn't want to put her through it. I agreed, but for a different reason. It would have made Gail look bad if Brittany had been put on the stand. What kind of a person would shoot a kid's father practically in front of her? Her lawyer wanted to avoid that issue."

I groped for another lead. "What about the two bullets in the wall above the door frame?" I asked. "The trajectory is odd. Does that mean anything to you?"

"Well, Ham contended during his closing argument that Gail had lied about blacking out, shot Roy through the heart then discharged her gun wildly into the air. In victory, to hear him tell it."

I stared at her incredulously. "What? Like Pecos Pete getting a snoot full of tequila and shooting off his pistol for fun?"

She shrugged. "You and I both know that Ham's an idiot. The jury would probably agree. But I don't think they found the extra shots important."

"What about her appeals? Who's handling them?"

Brenda's sigh was a long one. "Ever heard of Northern Lights?"

"You're kidding?" I said. The Northern Lights Foundation was a nonprofit organization devoted to overturning death-penalty convictions everywhere. But, it seemed, mostly in the South. You would have thought they'd have better sense than to send a bunch of Yankee lawyers marching into the South to bring enlightenment to the masses under the name "Northern Lights." But they didn't.

"Gail has a good appeals lawyer," Brenda explained, "but she doesn't know southern judges. During the first federal appeal, she argued that Gail had been so medicated during the trial, she had been unable to assist in her own defense. I thought we had a pretty good chance, but it was turned down. A second appeal was filed with the Fourth Circuit. We expect to hear from them sometime next week. I don't think we have a chance."

"Why?" I asked.

"We filed on the grounds that Gail's original defense lawyer was not allowed to present all of the mitigating circumstances during the sentencing phase," Brenda explained. "Gail's lawyer wants to try this angle because, of all the death-penalty appeals successfully filed over the past five years, twenty-six percent have been overturned on those grounds. It's an easy way for the judges to assuage their consciences without looking too liberal."

"What mitigating circumstances weren't presented?" I asked. "It seems to me that they aired every scrap of your family's dirty laundry."

"She's claiming severe alcohol and pill abuse impaired Gail's ability to distinguish right from wrong," she said.

"It isn't going to work," I warned her. Gail abused alcohol, but she wasn't going to get any sympathy on that point. Here in the South, we tell ourselves that if people want to be damn-fool drunks and destroy themselves, that's their business. But in return, we hold them responsible for what they do while they're drunk. Plus, you can't persuade a bunch of southern judges through rhetoric alone. Once a jury of peers has said someone deserves to die, you have to show new evidence that at least points to the possibility of someone else having done it. More important, every one of the Richmond judges had graduated from a law school in Virginia, North Carolina or Georgia. Like a lot of southerners, they came from families that had been ripped off by outsiders who made pretty speeches too many times over the past two hundred years. We're a skeptical lot, even if we do seem mighty polite on the surface. Only new evidence would impress those judges.

"Is there any point in looking into the case?" I asked. "It seems like you've done about all you can do and I have no new leads."

Brenda hesitated. "Yes," she finally said. "There's a big point to it. Nanny and the rest of us need to know we did everything we possibly could to help Gail, no matter what happens in the end. That's why I want you to take the case." She looked away uncomfortably.

"I am taking the case," I assured her. "So I can sleep at night, too. But you've got to help me find a place to start. What's this about a crackpot caller?"

She pushed her Pepsi bottle away and fiddled with her cigarette pack. "It's a sad case," she finally said.

"I know that already," I assured her.

"Not Gail's case," she snapped. "The caller's."

"Just tell me what he said and let me decide if it's important," I countered. If she was so dang anxious to help her sister, why the hesitation?

Brenda struggled with her conscience in silence while I counted the empty cigarette packs in her wastebasket. Nine crumpled cellophane-covered boxes on top and more beneath. Good god, I hoped her lungs would hold out long enough for her to make up her mind. Eventually, she reached a decision.

"The call was from the judge at her trial," she said reluctantly.

"Judge Peyton Tillman?" I almost shouted I was so surprised.

"Former Judge Tillman," she reminded me. "He's not on the bench anymore. He's a private citizen now. One with some problems. A lot of problems. I really don't think we have enough time to waste taking him seriously. I think his call was motivated by something other than reality."

"Like what?" I demanded.

"He's not like you or me," she explained. "I don't want to presume as to what your character is like, but I have a feeling that you do what you have to do to get the job done, and then you move on. Am I right?"

I shrugged. Sad to say, she was right.

"Peyton isn't like that. He can't let the case go. Gail is the only person he ever helped send to death row and he's never forgiven himself. After he returned to private life, he began calling me late at night and saying that a miscarriage of justice had occurred. Evidence didn't match up." She was silent. "At first I believed him, but when he failed to give me details, I realized that maybe he was drunk or his conscience just couldn't take it."

"Or maybe he's telling the truth?" I suggested.

She shook her head. "He's gone off the deep end. He's calling because he wants me to say that I forgive him." She looked up at me, her sharp eyes sad. "And, to tell you the truth, I can't."

"What does he say when you ask for details?" I persisted. Maybe I was grasping at straws, but since no one was offering me a line, I had nothing else to grab onto.

"Crazy stuff. Like how he's not done gathering proof yet and that he can't tell me anyway because I'm part of the 'system.' He's become paranoid. He sounds like one of those conspiracy freaks."

"I can't blame him," I said. "He got a raw deal during the last election."

Brenda shrugged. "That's the way it works. Judges are supposed to be bi-partisan and they don't run on a party ticket, but you better believe it's party money that gets them there. The Democrats were running scared long before he lost that election. He came under heavy-duty pressure during Gail's trial to leave the door open for the death penalty. In return, the Democrats were supposed to support him all the way in the next election."

"But they didn't," I said. "They left him out to dry."

She nodded. "He traded away my sister's life and got nothing in return. So it's no wonder that he started drinking pretty bad after the trial, and when he got those two DUIs, everybody ran for the hills. That's politics."

"That's people," I said.

We were both quiet for a moment.

"I know what you probably think of me," she finally said. "You think I should be doing more to help my sister. I have been helping, you must understand, as much as I can, when I can keep it private and unconnected to this job. But if it looks like I'm abusing my power as a prosecutor, I could lose everything. Our family has lost enough as it is. The rest of us have to go on, including me."

"I do understand," I said, resigned to finding—or not finding—a new lead on my own. I rose and shook her hand. Her grip was firm and confident, the shake of an athlete. "You're a runner?" I asked.

She smiled and nodded. "The only two-pack-a-day runner in the state. I'm trying to quit."

"Running or smoking?" I asked.

"Smoking." She gave a rueful smile. "I don't think I can ever afford to stop running."

I walked back to my office, thinking about Gail's sister and what a long way she had come from the farmlands of North Carolina. I admired her intelligence and respected her drive, but at the same time, it reminded me of how many years of my own I had wasted by making bad choices and foolish friends. I could easily have been Brenda. And I could just as easily have been Gail. Instead, I found myself somewhere in between.

CHAPTER FOUR

One man's crackpot is another man's salvation. Which is why—despite Brenda's skepticism—I headed for Peyton Tillman's law offices that afternoon after stopping to refresh myself with a plate of chopped-pork barbecue and hush puppies first. His office was located in an old Victorian house along a stretch of Hillsborough Street that had somehow escaped renovation. It was the first in a row of four dilapidated buildings. One end of the wide front porch sagged forlornly toward a scruffy lawn, and the upstairs floors were obviously deserted. It appeared that Peyton Tillman, Esq. and a massage therapist who also offered acupuncture and hypnotherapy were the house's only remaining occupants. Either Peyton Tillman had fallen on hard times or he was in the process of dropping out of the establishment that had screwed him.

I liked Peyton Tillman the moment I saw him. He had a sleepy hound-dog face: all wrinkled with heavy jowls, a disappointed mouth, long nose and sad brown eyes. The emotion sat on top of his skin, as if he had lost the mask the rest of us wear. He was in his early fifties but still had a full head of brown hair that curled just above the frayed collar of a worn white-cotton shirt. The shirt was custom-fit and displayed his initials embroidered in deep blue on the breast pocket. He wore no jacket, and his tie was slung carelessly over one shoulder like an aviator's scarf.

He had an intense look of concentration on his face that did not change even when he charged into the outer room of his office at the sound of my entrance and crashed into a trash can at the side of his secretary's desk. The commotion made little difference to his employee: her soft snores continued to fill the outer room with a gentle rhythm as her boss careened past. No wonder she was snoozing. She was at least eighty-five years old and dressed in a rose-colored faux Chanel suit trimmed in white piping from the 1950s. Her silver hair was permed in tight curls against her skull, and a pair of rhinestone glasses hung from a pink cord around her neck. An upper plate dangled loosely beneath her pink lips and I watched, fascinated, as the false teeth wobbled with each prim breath.

"Oops," my host said, righting the wastebasket and shoveling a stack of discarded paper back inside it. Was this the same man rumored to be such a Romeo with the coeds? He seemed more like the type to get his tie caught in his pants zipper. His voice dropped to a whisper. "Who are you? Are you sure you have the right office?"

No, I wasn't sure. But not in the way he meant it. "I'm a private investigator looking into Gail Honeycutt's murder conviction," I whispered back. "I have to talk to you. I'm not leaving until I do." I tried to look determined, as if I might attach myself and a ball and chain to his sleeping secretary if he refused.

He looked me over intently, and I must have passed his initial muster. "Let's talk back in my office so we don't wake Miss Rollins," he said in a hushed voice. "She had a bad night. Her husband is very sick."

I tiptoed past his sleeping sentinel into a shabby-looking room, wondering what her official job title might be and how I could get hired as one. Director of Employee Stress Reduction? Head Goof-off? I'd be good at either.

His office was a lot like the exterior of the house. Once elegant; now shabby. Echoes of the building's former glory were evident only in the faded flocked wallpaper and crumbling fireplace.

"Have a seat," Tillman said, removing a stack of brown folders from an ancient wingback chair. He blew the dust off the cushion and wiped the back with a handkerchief before he would let me sit down. "I don't get a lot of visitors," he explained. "I do most of my work out of the office. Many of my clients are elderly and have difficulty getting around."

A lawyer who made house calls? I wondered if he did windows, too.

"Oh," I murmured politely, settling into a mound of decaying velvet that smelled of mildew and old wine. "You've gone back into private practice?"

"That's right." He sat behind a massive oak desk, parking his feet on one edge of it and sending a stack of folders tumbling to the floor. "I primarily practice family and real estate law these days. Trusts and estates. Medicaid planning. Mostly to help out my elderly neighbors. I'm semi-retired, I guess you could say. I work just enough to keep me busy."

He straightened his tie as if suddenly remembering he was currently engaged in business, then glanced at his watch. "I apologize, but I do have an appointment in half an hour, so I can't give you much time. How can I help?"

He didn't seem like a fruitcake to me. Maybe a little addled, but who among us isn't? "As you know, Gail is scheduled to be put to death in a month," I said.

He didn't answer. Only the small throbbing of a vein in his forehead gave away his distress.

"I thought maybe you could help me," I explained quickly when he remained silent. "I've been hired by the family as a last-ditch effort to try and clear her. But I can't seem to find a shovel."

He stared at me even more intently. I had the uncomfortable feeling that I was being sized up for a cooking pot. "Brenda Polk told you about my calls, didn't she?" he said abruptly. "She thinks I'm nuts and told you about it. But you want to make sure I've been certified before you write me off. Is that it?"

I blinked. I had not been prepared for a frontal assault. I did the only thing I could do under the circumstances. I lied. "Not exactly," I began.

"I don't believe you," he interrupted quickly. "Tell me the truth or you're out of here."

"Okay," I admitted, taking a deep breath. "Brenda Polk thinks you're nuts and I want to make sure you've been certified before I write you off."

He nodded in satisfaction. "In that case, we're done. I don't have time for crap like that these days."

"Who does have the time for Gail Honeycutt?" I asked, thinking of my hurried appointment with the D. A. earlier that morning. "It seems that everyone is running out of time on this case. Including me. But no one is running out faster than Gail." I glared at him, irritated. "Well, in one month, Gail's going to be dead and then the rest of us will have all the time in the world."

His feet fell abruptly from the desk. He leaned forward in his swivel chair. "I stand corrected," he apologized as he scrutinized my face and somewhat unorthodox attire. I prefer to wear sheath dresses circa 1964, when I can find them, and that morning I had paired my favorite purple number with some lime-green sandals. Listen, I'd been in a hurry and how many of us own a pair of purple shoes that we would wear in public?

I waited while he checked me out, determined not to crumple under the pressure. He wasn't being rude, I decided. He had simply discarded the veneer of elaborate manners that disguises the curiosity of well-bred southerners. Either that, or he also had no time for such niceties these days.

"I can tell a lot about a person just by looking at them," he finally said, leaning back in his chair with a sigh. "That's one thing I learned on the bench."

A short silence followed this pronouncement. I considered commiserating with him on the loss of his judgeship but discarded the notion as obvious pandering. I didn't think he was the type who responded well to butt licking.

"Judge Tillman, if you have any information on the Honeycutt case," I tried instead, "I am begging you to share it with me. Please. I agreed to take the case because I'm a sucker for the underdog. Or maybe I'm just a sucker. I knew that the clock would be ticking the entire time, but let me tell you, it's harder than I imagined hearing that clock tick away the hours. I don't have a single lead and I have got to start somewhere."

Another long moment of silence dragged by before he spoke. "I might know something that could help," he finally said. He stared out the window. "It wouldn't do you much good without collaboration."

"Maybe you could tell me what it is," I suggested. "And I could find the collaboration for you? I am, after all, a trained investigator." Okay, I was fibbing about the "trained" part, but I still hoped to slip it by the human lie detector sitting before me.

"It's not that easy." Tillman stared intently at me again, and I saw a spark of some long-forgotten passion flare in his eyes. Here was a man trying to convince himself that an intangible like justice didn't matter. I knew the look only too well. I saw it in my mirror every time I fell in and out of love. If you can't hold it, you can't break it. Bullshit. That attitude never worked. He knew it, too.

"Do you think she's innocent?" I asked. "Can we start there?"

"Yes, she's innocent. Probably." He looked down at the clutter in front of him, not seeing the folders or the papers waiting to be signed. "I've saved many a guilty man from lethal injection," he added. "And the one time I gave in, I ended up sending an innocent woman to her death. There's a lesson in that for me, I suppose."

"Who did you give in to?" I asked. "Does this have anything to do with the evidence you have on Gail's case?"

"Not in the way you think." He had a deep voice that was softened by a rich southern accent honed to a purr by expensive prep schools and college. The dissipated drawl, I called it. "I gave in to political pressure, not blackmail. I did think she was guilty at the time, but not any longer."

"Can't you tell me more than that?" I asked, frustrated. "Just point me in the right direction. Gail's grandmother is the one that hired me and there's something about that old lady. I just can't let her down."

"I remember the grandmother well," he said unexpectedly. "She always sat in the second row at the far right of the bench. Never missed a day of the trial." He nodded thoughtfully, sized me up once more and seemed to reach a decision. "It's complicated," he began. "The work I have put into the case, privately you understand, has led me in an unexpected direction.

This direction is a complex one, and I cannot make my accusations idly. In fact, you would do well to keep my involvement completely confidential. As I am sure you understand, my credibility is severely impaired around here."

"Only with some people," I protested.

"Nonetheless, anything I say is likely to be taken less than seriously." He held up a hand when I started to disagree. "Please, I am well aware of where I stand in the public eye. People think I'm a fool, a drunk and a philanderer. I am none of these things. What I really am is another matter."

"I want to help you," I interrupted firmly. If he got started on self-analysis, I'd be there until the end of the month and Gail would be a goner.

"I believe you do." He stared at me again. "You're an outsider and, in this particular case, that's good. But if I let you in on what I know, you must promise that you will listen to me when it comes to what is needed in terms of collaboration. And you must take steps to protect yourself because you will be in danger. Is that understood?"

Jesus, I thought. Who was he talking about? The governor? Naw, couldn't be. North Carolina's current governor wasn't independent enough to be involved. Rumor had it that he couldn't shake the piss off his pecker without permission from his wife.

"I can listen," I promised.

"Good. Be at my house at ten o'clock tonight. Here's my card. My home address is on the back. I'm meeting a friend earlier in the evening, but I can see you at ten. Bring your bathing suit."

"Pardon me?" I said.

"Bring your bathing suit. I have an old injury and I spend an hour each evening in my hot tub, undergoing hydrotherapy. If we want to talk, the hot tub is as good a place as any. We won't be overheard."

"The hot tub?" He was losing me. Or, perhaps, he had lost it entirely.

"Ten o'clock," he repeated. "The hot tub is on a deck in my backyard." He opened a briefcase and swept a stack of papers inside. "Don't worry, I'm not crazy. I'm just careful. Our conversation can't be bugged if we're in the hot tub. You'll understand more by tonight. But for now you must excuse me. I have an appointment a few blocks away and I can't be late. My client is very excitable and a recent widow. It's not good for her to become upset." He slipped on a tan jacket and straightened his cuffs carefully until they peeped from beneath his sleeves. "Forgive me for being so mysterious. It's necessary under the circumstances."

With that, he walked out of his office, leaving me surrounded by mountains of papers and presumably confidential files. My imagination exploded. I considered searching every scrap for some clue to his new evidence. Maybe I should check his side drawers for half-emptied bottles of bourbon while I was at it, just to get a clue as to his reliability.

Unfortunately, the slumbering Mrs. Rollins had awakened and arrived to put the kibosh on my rummaging plans. She caught me, quite literally, with my hand in the cookie jar.

"I baked those especially for Peyton," she informed me icily. "Did he invite you to partake?"

I shook my head guiltily and shut the side desk drawer where I had discovered a Tupperware container of chocolate-chip cookies.

"I thought not." She glared at me, and I could feel my face start to flush. There's something about a stern old lady that strikes terror into my heart. I felt as though my soul was being X-rayed.

"Peyton is such a lovely boy," she said grimly, standing in the doorway like a ghost of school teachers past. Which, as it turns out, she was.

"I taught him in the fourth grade, you know," she informed me. "Political science. They called it current events back then. He was the best and the brightest. It's such a shame."

Her voice was remarkably steady for an old woman. I suspected her right hook might be as well. I nodded, not wanting to inflame her further for fear she would pull out a yardstick and start rapping my knuckles with it. She took my nod as encouragement to continue.

"It was the war, I believe," she said. "That's what changed my Peyton. It planted some seed of instability, some guilt, that he lived while others died." She shook her head and the rhinestone corners of her eyeglasses glittered in the light like the eyes of a cobra. My feet seemed unable to move until I was dismissed. I stood, mute, being lectured on, of all things, the Vietnam War.

"What an odd war that was," she mused as she inched closer to me. "It seemed so unreal. So very far away." Her quavery sigh filled the room as she began to fuss over her former pupil's desk, ineffectually stacking papers and aligning pens. She did not actually order me out of the office, but she managed—by her rigid posture—to let me know quite clearly that she was not leaving the room until I led the way.

I could have kicked her little-old-lady butt, but I could never have withstood the lecture that would have followed. So I gave in. "He seems like a nice man," I said, rising to go. We circled each other cautiously, like a pair of elderly samurai anxious to preserve our honor without ever actually drawing swords.

"Yes," she hissed. "He's a wonderful man. His only fault is that he makes up his mind about people too quickly." She stared pointedly at me. "He trusts people too easily. Sometimes people he shouldn't."

"I'm not one of those," I assured her. "We're on the same side."

The look she gave me made my back straighten automatically and called forth some ambiguous apology from my gut. I felt a need to confess, but to what? I could cop to having beaten up some boys in the playground, but that had been decades ago. It wouldn't satisfy her. She was out for first blood.

"I hope you're right, young lady," she said, her eyes boring into mine. "Peyton Tillman is very important to a great many old people in this neighborhood who would be lost and confused without him. And he is like a son to me. No one else would hire me." Her voice softened and, for the first time, she seemed her age. I let out an involuntary breath.

"Look at me," she demanded. "I'm ancient and I do him little good. But he insists on paying me to sit in his outer office and sleep. It's the difference between going with and going without when it comes to food and medicine for me and my husband, you understand." She made no apology; her genteel dignity was innate.

"I understand," I said quickly. I was no stranger to poverty and scraping by.

"I would not like to see him hurt again," she finished up firmly. "The people of this state are the poorer for losing him. He is a good man. We all make mistakes. His were minor. They cost us all dearly."

"I won't let him get hurt again," I promised. Geeze, Tillman must have turned in one hell of a term paper on current events to merit such loyalty.

"So long as we understand each other." The thin smile that stretched across her light pink lips made me glad I'd never had her for a teacher. "Good day, Miss Jones," she said in a soft voice as her eyes narrowed to slits.

So, the sleeping giant knew my name. And my rank and serial number as well, no doubt. I left, reminding myself—no matter what else I did—to keep on Mrs. Rollins's good side.

After that encounter, I felt it necessary to fortify myself with a few beers at the Player's Retreat, then flirted awhile with the counterman at the 42nd Street Oyster Bar guided by the theory that a man in such close proximity to oysters might turn out to be a pearl in the sack. After a quick trip home to change, I was back to work.

It was just past ten when I turned off Oberlin Road onto the quiet, oak-lined streets of Cameron Park, one of Raleigh's oldest residential areas. It had been built on the outskirts of town at the turn of the century, but now found itself smack in the middle of the action. It was bordered on one side by Hillsborough Street, which led straight downtown to the Capitol Building statue honoring the Confederate dead. Although the neighborhood had changed over the past decade, it was still home to many elderly people whose families had lived there for generations. Their houses were dark, shut down for the night, doors bolted tightly against the creeping threat of crime. The sidewalks were empty. North Carolina State University was only a few blocks away, but a rabid block association kept parking and zoning restrictions so strict that few students ever stumbled drunkenly through the neighborhood to arouse the geriatric dogs that lived there.

Peyton Tillman lived on a small side street that wound around one corner of a narrow central park. The house was a two-story whitewashed stone structure nestled on a ridge halfway down a heavily wooded hill. Oaks and pines sheltered the dwelling from traffic on the road above it and discouraged all but the most determined of visitors. Either he had inherited a pile of dough or the Tillmans had lived there for years—houses like this went for nearly half a million in Cameron Park these days. No wonder the professors and little old ladies were pulling up stakes and selling out to the medical crowd.

I negotiated the slippery stone steps gingerly, grateful that I had worn my high-top tennis shoes. The night smelled wet and green. I could hear frogs peeping in the creek at the bottom of the park, their singing a high-pitched dirge against a gentle backdrop of gurgling water. The frogs, at least, had decided that spring had arrived.

So much for conserving energy: nearly every room in Peyton Tillman's house blazed with light. I felt as if I had stumbled onto the Holy Grail in the darkness. Two stories of wide windows cast illuminating patches over the descent that continued behind the house into the depths of the park. I rang the doorbell and waited. I rang it again and waited some more. Still no response. Which of these brightly lit rooms was he nodding off in? I peeped in a few downstairs windows with the practiced sneakiness of a small-town PI and quickly grasped that Peyton Tillman was, hands down, an even worse housekeeper than *moi*. Papers were strewn about on tables and floors. Cabinet doors sagged open, drawers to end tables tilted toward the floor and books were stacked in piles all around the area rugs. Well, how do you like that? His *casa* was *mi casa*. But I saw no Peyton. I shuddered to imagine his bathroom and bedroom. This was a bachelor pad supreme.

I slipped on some ivy-covered stone near the corner dining room and the thought of tumbling into a distant creek reminded me: the hot tub. He was already soaking his weary bones and war-torn body in the hot tub. Where had he said it was located? It could only be in the backyard; both sides were too steep for anything but the most determined of creeping plants and a narrow stone walkway. I followed the path around one side of the house and discovered a large wooden deck built on pilings that angled out over the steep hillside. Unlike the rest of the house, it was shrouded in darkness. The hot tub was sunk near the far edge of the deck and I could barely make out Peyton Tillman lying in it, his head tilted back as he gazed at the stars through a canopy of bare branches.

"Sorry I'm late," I called out. "I stopped off for liposuction so I could fit in my bathing suit."

Okay, it was a bad joke. But ignoring it was in even worse taste.

"Peyton?" I asked in the silence. "It's Casey Jones. We had an appointment."

When he didn't reply, I grew apprehensive. I'd heard stories of people drinking themselves to sleep in a hot tub and waking up in the hospital looking like giant prunes. "Peyton!" I called out more loudly. His name echoed over the hills of the park, silencing the frogs. The sudden stillness made me even more uneasy. The only sound was the gurgling of water in the hot tub. I fought an urge to flee back to the well-lit house, and I glanced around the patio perimeter to see if I was being watched. I was suddenly sorry I hadn't brought old Mrs. Rollins with me for protection.

"Peyton—it may be time for the rinse cycle." Still no answer. I took a deep breath, climbed the steps to the deck and plunged into the darkness. The deck floor was damp around the hot tub, as if someone had been careless and sloshed about. Just as I reached Peyton, I slipped on a wet spot near the base of the tub and went down hard, landing on a mound of towels carelessly heaped on the floor. My upper body sprawled across the deck and I banged one elbow on the tub edge. The pain rang all the way down my arm and I rubbed it furiously before I noticed that something sticky and sweet-smelling was coating my skin. It seeped from my bruised elbow into a dark shadow. I panicked and reached for the tub's edge, hoping to hoist myself upright. Instead, I touched something soft and equally sticky. I dropped back down, this time landing in a puddle of dark liquid. I half-squeaked and half-screamed my repulsion. What the hell was dangling over the tub? I've grabbed some unknown parts in the dark before, but there was no way I was touching that one. I crawled away from the puddle on my knees and pulled myself up by the deck railing. All limbs unfolded normally; I was battered but unbroken.

I could not say the same for Peyton Tillman. Even in the darkness, I was close enough to finally see that something was very wrong. He was leaning against the far edge of the tub, his neck tilted back at what I now saw was an unnatural angle. One arm floated on top of the water, held aloft by the buoyancy of the bubbles. The other arm hung carelessly over the lip of the hot tub—this was what I had touched in the dark. I peered at the lit digital dial of the tub, searching for a light control. The timer showed less than seven minutes remaining on the jet cycle. The light dial had three choices. I went for all the illumination I could get. A blue filter capped much of the brightness, but I saw enough of the foaming light purple water and enough of Peyton Tillman's still face to know that he had been leaking blood into the tub for a long time. Carefully, I stepped around the pool of blood that had collected on the deck floor at the base of his fingertips. It was too late to preserve the evidence. I had already smeared most of it across the deck.

I detoured around the towels anyway and felt his neck carefully for the artery. He was dead. I ran my fingertips lightly over his face and shoulders. Despite the heat of the water, the upper part of his body that protruded from the tub had surface-cooled in the night air. That meant that his blood had stopped circulating some time ago. I bent down in the dim glow from the hot tub's lights and examined his wrists. Three long slits had been gouged vertically, beginning at the base of each palm, leading up toward the inner elbow. Each cut was deep and more than three inches long. This was no half-assed attempt at suicide. The warm water had bled him dry quickly from the one floating arm, tainting the water its seeming purple. The arm that hung over the edge of the tub had drained more slowly, I suspected, but the blood loss from either arm would have been enough to do the job alone.

Why in the hell had he chosen to do it? Why invite me over and then kill himself? Did he feel such a personal responsibility for Gail's life that he felt a need to offer his own in penance?

I sat down on a wooden bench that edged the patio railing to consider my options. Just then, the breeze shifted and the sweet smell of pooled blood insinuated itself into my nostrils, reminding me that I had Peyton Tillman's blood soaking my left side. The thought instantly triggered a wave of nausea. Without warning, I vomited up oysters and beer with a generous side of pretzels. There was nothing to do but lean forward and let fly, hoping to god I didn't puke right in the pool of evidence. My tennis shoes would never recover, I knew, and I wasn't too sure about my ego either. I was covering myself with something, but it sure as hell wasn't glory. It took a good five minutes for the attack to pass and for me to collect my thoughts. I knew I had to call the police and I knew it would not be pretty when I did. Bill Butler would have a coronary, but probably not until after he had arrested me for disturbing the scene of the crime in a rather spectacular fashion.

The delay in calling the police gave me time to realize that I had one chance and one chance only to try and decipher what Peyton Tillman may have had to say to me that afternoon. It was stupid, I knew, but it had to be done. I'd look through his house before I called in his death. No one could have saved him at that point, I rationalized, he'd been dead for a half hour or more. Another half hour would make little difference. The trouble was, I had no gloves and I could not afford to leave a single fingerprint behind. If anyone ran the prints, they'd get an instant hit, and my felony record would be revealed in all its glory for Bill Butler and the rest of the Raleigh Police Department to see. I'd have to find a way to search without leaving any trace behind.

The hot tub reached the end of its cycle, and an ominous silence descended on the deck. The water stilled and tiny trickles of deep red satin spread from his wrist into the blue water like varicose veins. The silence made me want to see his face. It was turned away from the light and his features were difficult to distinguish in the shadows. I wasn't sure what I was looking for: a sign of peace, perhaps, of resolution, of answered questions or resignation? What I found was nothing. All expression had been bled from his face. The essence of whoever Peyton Tillman was drained away forever.

I left him and began searching as quickly as I could, entering through the half-opened sliding back door into the kitchen. The only gloves I could find were two large oven mitts in the shape of an alligator and a cow. I felt like a demented children's TV show host waving those babies around, but they were better than nothing. Especially when I reached the living room and realized that I was in for even more trouble than I had thought. Someone had been there before me. Peyton Tillman was no slob. His house was messy because it had been searched by someone in a hurry, the contents returned in haste. Piles of magazines slid to the floor with a nudge of my foot. Contents of drawers had been replaced upside down. Closet shelves had been swept of their holdings, the surfaces filled again with armloads of whatever the searcher could grab from the pile on the closet floor. Books had been opened, shaken and tossed carelessly back on shelves upside down and sideways. Given the circumstances, I would not find anything in the house during my own search, I knew. I walked through the upstairs rooms anyway, my oven puppet mitts casting bizarre shadows on the stairway walls. Nothing. A ransacked bedroom, empty guest rooms and a hallway cluttered with debris pulled from cabinets and linen shelves, then left on the floor. The searcher had grown even more careless when he'd reached the second story or, perhaps, had been in more of a hurry. Had he or she known that I was coming? How long ago had they left?

And had they helped Peyton Tillman along in his death? It hit me then that I was, at best, a colossal idiot. Peyton Tillman had no more slit his wrists than I was Madonna. I had found no note, no words of remorse or apology. I returned to the kitchen, packed the alligator and cow mitts back into their drawer and wiped the knob off carefully. I found the outside lights to the patio located on a switch behind the refrigerator and flipped them on with my clean elbow. Bright lights flooded the grotesque patio scene, making the dead judge look like a character from a play, a Roman senator playing out his final act.

With more illumination, I had better luck examining the body. The cuts on his arms were not only deep, they were also methodical and evenly spaced. How could a man bleeding profusely from one wrist have the time and strength to scar himself so precisely on his remaining arm? I examined his neck. No signs of ligature, no scrapes or cuts. I ran my fingers lightly through his hair, knowing Bill Butler would have killed me if he could have seen me. The back of the skull curved smoothly except for a knot toward the base of the neck. I could not look closer without moving the body, and even I knew I'd gone far enough.

Task finished, I crept back to the kitchen and picked up the phone. I used a paper napkin as a shield, though I doubted the killer had called out for pizza. Bill answered on the third ring.

"It's Casey," I told him. "I'm at Peyton Tillman's house. Someone's killed him. He's in his hot tub. I slipped in the blood because it was dark, and I might have puked a little bit. Otherwise, I haven't touched a thing."

To his credit, not a breath of disbelief tainted the silence that followed. "Don't move," he said. "I'll get the address and call the CCBI. Just sit down and wait. And, Casey, don't say a word to anyone until I get there. Okay?"

I don't know if it was the unexpected kindness in his voice, the fact that I liked Peyton Tillman or plain old PMS. Whatever the reason, when I returned to the deck I sat down and cried while I waited. The adrenaline was wearing off and the enormity of what had happened was beginning to sink in.

A good man had died. And a woman would die soon if I could not find out what secrets had died with him. It seemed an impossible burden, and I was sorry I had accepted it. Maybe Peyton Tillman would be alive if I had said no.

What the hell. There was no one to see me. I went ahead and let myself get it all out before anyone else arrived. The truth is, I believe in crying when there's good cause. But I do confess that when I cry, I like to cry alone.

CHAPTER FIVE

The CCBI is the City-County Bureau of Investigation, a special joint task force that looks into all homicides, or, in the case of big deal citizens like Peyton Tillman, suspicious deaths. The fact that they were on their way proved that Peyton had been a judge; it didn't prove they believed he had been killed.

Cops around Raleigh have better sense than to tear down the quiet streets of Cameron Park with sirens blaring at eleven o'clock at night. Instead, at least ten cars arrived silently en masse behind a cruiser with flashing lights. They pulled over to the curb surrounding the park in a weird coordinated maneuver that made me think of secret government organizations and people disappearing from the face of the earth. I shivered and realized I was still wearing no more than my bathing suit and a pair of sweats. I rubbed my arms, not caring that I was smearing Tillman's blood even more, and leaned out over the railing of the deck watching the official figures approach, their shadows descending down the hill—to give me a hard time. I couldn't pick out Bill Butler in the crowd. Too bad. I needed a friend. Even one I couldn't seem to get along with.

A beefy uniformed guy arrived first, huffing and puffing from the effort. He was very pink under the glare of the patio light and his light-blond hair was buzzed against his scalp in a crop of stubby bristles. He looked like one of the three little pigs, only in uniform. He was still huffing and puffing as he stared at the pool of smeared blood and the nearby vomit. Then he glanced at the dead judge and gave me the once-over. I figured he was deciding whether to have a heart attack or comment on the mess. "You the one called it in?" he finally asked.

No, I wanted to say, I'm just a friendly neighbor who took this rare opportunity to sneak over and wallow in Peyton Tillman's hot tub—and blood—without permission. Instead, I nodded silently and he ignored me in favor of pulling out a flashlight. He proceeded to inch his way around the far side of the house, casting a small spotlight on the damp stones, as if they might tell him something.

The others arrived within the minute. They were thinner and a lot more serious-looking than the first guy had been. Most of them ignored me. Two headed my way: Bill Butler and a brunette I didn't know. But I disliked her on principle since she was very tall and thin. Worse, her hair had been twisted into a casually elegant knot, the kind of style that would have made my own over-processed strands stick out like some bloodless victim of Nosferatu's.

"Casey, this is Anne Morrow," Bill said. "She's in charge of the investigation. Tell her everything you told me on the phone and answer any questions she might have."

"Aren't you going to handcuff me and read me my rights?" I asked hopefully.

"In your dreams," he replied. "I have to get back to work." Before I could think of a retort—or thank him—he was gone. It was a bad sign.

"Everyone's a comedian," I grumbled, aware that the slender detective was staring at me with a carefully neutral expression on her face.

She took a seat beside me on the bench while a team of forensic specialists went to work on the patio, hot tub and judge. "It's nice to meet you," she said unexpectedly. "It's so seldom that one meets a witness who admits to smearing the blood across the crime scene and puking on the remaining evidence. Most of the time, they don't wait around for us to arrive."

"Very funny," I mumbled. "The two of you are a regular Abbott and Costello routine."

"Actually, Bill Butler and I are not a team at all. In any sense of the word. Does that make you feel any better?"

"Am I that obvious?" I asked, pleased despite myself. They were no more than a pair of pals. The green flame in my heart subsided.

She shrugged. "It's more what I hear about the two of you than what I just saw. I wouldn't exactly call this a romantic setting."

"Not tonight, anyway," I agreed.

"You're lucky you know Bill," she said abruptly. "It's going to make a very, very big difference in the way you're treated. It's none of my business, but I'd say you owe him one. Now, start from the beginning and tell me everything you know."

I started from the beginning and told her everything I knew. For real. I knew the CCBI would never let me get within a mile of the investigation and I wanted whomever had killed Peyton Tillman caught. I told Detective Morrow just that.

"So you're convinced he didn't kill himself?" she asked.

"Come on, what do you think?" I waved an arm toward the corpse, which was being photographed by a pale man who looked more cadaverous than his subject. "I haven't seen cuts so precise since I aced eleventh-grade shop class. And I think he may have a bump on the back of his head."

"You think?" she asked icily.

"I have good eyes," I confessed. "I didn't touch a hair on his head."

"I wouldn't imagine you would," she replied. "A cool-headed professional like you. I'm sure you were far too busy throwing up." But then she smiled, and I decided that Anne Morrow was all right, even if she did weigh about twenty pounds less than me and have a good five inches more in height.

"When did you join the force?" I asked after she had probed for more details on what I knew about Peyton Tillman.

"About six months ago. But I've been on the job for over eleven years. I put in most of my time up in Asheville. I'm from there and I joined the local state bureau right after college."

"College?"

"B.A. in criminal justice from John Jay in New York City. MBA from Indiana. Went home to marry the boy next door.

Divorced his ass, ditched the SBI and came here. First female detective in the history of this department."

"An admirably succinct biography," I offered.

"What's your story?" she asked back.

"Poor white trash—but smart white trash—makes good. Leaves behind the Florida panhandle and heads north. I had an ass that I divorced as well. Found out that I start to shiver whenever I venture above the North Carolina state line. I guess I stayed here because I had nowhere else to go."

"That's as good a reason as any," the detective said.

We were interrupted by a man who looked like Marcus Welby after a three-week bender. He even held a black medical bag. He looked like he needed toothpicks to prop open his eyes, but maybe staring death in the face all day does that to you. "You can move him now if you want," he told Detective Morrow.

"What can you tell me right now?" she asked.

"Not much." He glanced at me.

"You can talk in front of her," Morrow said. I was pleased, and did my best to resemble a responsible law enforcement colleague who just happened to be dressed in a bathing suit and covered with blood and puke.

"This hot tub business plays hell with my assumptions," he explained. "I'm going to have to take the internal temperatures of organs before I can be sure. Timing on this one is going to be difficult."

"But if you had to guess...?" She had obviously asked the same question many times before.

"Based on my scientific observation that he does not yet resemble a California raisin, I'd say that he's been dead for at least an hour and a half, but no more than three. I can't say with my usual certainty because blood flow was continued after death by conditions in the tub. He does have a bump on the back of his skull that I need to examine more closely. It may tell me more."

"Understood," she said, and the man was gone. Damn. Detective Morrow would have made a great queen. She was calm, in charge and to the point.

"So, do you think it was suicide?" I asked when she was done with her questions.

She snapped her notebook shut. "I don't know what I think right now. But I'm going to have to ask you to take off your clothes."

"What?" I stared at her.

"I need to bag your clothes. Seeing as how you did a belly flop in the most important part of the crime scene. DNA evidence is big these days. I suspect you have it dripping off you."

"You keep saying, 'crime scene.' You don't think it was suicide. You know it's connected, don't you?" I replied.

"Connected?" she asked.

"To my investigation into Gail Honeycutt."

She held up a well-manicured hand, but I didn't hold her good grooming against her. "Stop right there, Casey. I have no idea what this is connected to and I'm not about to start guessing this early. I'd say that I'll let you know, but you and I both know that I won't. To be very honest with you, you've used up all of your goodwill and more here tonight. All I can tell you is that a lot of people might have wanted Tillman dead. It's an occupational hazard of being a judge. Put away a bad guy. Bad guy gets paroled. Bad guy comes looking for you. Your investigation is very low on the list of possibilities. But I will consider it, I assure you. If you want my opinion, Tillman was seeing you because he was suffering from a bad attack of conscience. Period." She waved over a detective who had been hovering on the edges of our conversation. "Can you get the boys to bring some large bags over?" she asked him. "I need her clothes."

"What? I'm supposed to strip down right here?" I protested. Okay, so I had stripped for a lot of cops in the past. But it had always been voluntarily—and in the privacy of my own home.

"You can do it here or at the station," she said calmly.

Funny what you can squeeze into when you have no other option. "I have a change of clothes in the car," I said glumly, fairly certain the trunk held an oil-stained work shirt and torn gym shorts several sizes too small. I'd freeze my ass off changing, but that was good. It gave me a shot at fitting into the shorts.

"Go with her," Anne Morrow told the other detective.

"I think you can trust me not to bolt," I said sarcastically.

"I was more concerned about your safety," she replied calmly before she nodded good-bye and headed toward the body.

Damn. I hadn't considered that aspect myself. If someone had conked Peyton Tillman over the head, slit his wrists and left him to bleed to death because of me, who was to say that I wasn't next?

I am often paranoid. But never without good reason. After I changed in the darkness and handed over my bloody clothes, I decide the smartest thing I could do under the circumstances was to nip over to the office and pick up my gun. I keep my Astra locked in the bottom drawer of my desk. The bullets are stored in the top drawer, right next to my supply of Tampax. Just knowing they're there is an incentive to keep my PMS under control.

It was after midnight, and not even the whores on Hargett Street looked interested in staying awake. Downtown was dead in the chilly March night. A cup of hot coffee and a half dozen warm Krispy Kreme doughnuts would have hit the spot right about then. I needed something to replace all the starch I'd left on Peyton Tillman's deck. But I was only a few blocks from the office, so I decided to pick up my gun before I headed for Person Street. Besides, approaching Bobby D. with a full box of Krispy Kremes is a dangerous maneuver. You're likely to lose a hand.

Our office is located on McDowell Street, a few blocks from the convention center and within spitting distance of the Raleigh Police Department. Usually, the neon sign is blinking twenty-four hours a day, and the blinds are left open for anyone passing by to take a peek. But that night the sign had been switched off and the blinds were closed. It gave me a bad feeling. I parked out front and approached the door cautiously. Was Bobby sick? The door was locked—another oddity. As I slid the key in the lock and turned the handle, I heard a strange thumping from inside the office. It did little to add to my confidence. It was dark and I fumbled for the light switch.

Bobby was bound hand and foot to a straight-back chair teetering under his weight. A white cloth blindfold wound around his head and had knocked his toupee askew so that it sprouted from one side like a weed clinging to the side of a cliff. He was gagged with another cloth, and his face was a dangerous red beneath the strip of white. He's not a gentle perspirer on the coolest of days, and, even at a distance, I could see that he had soaked his leisure-suit shirt through. The thumping I heard came from his attempts to stand up in the chair—something he has enough trouble with when he isn't bound hand and foot.

"Whoa, Bobby. It's Casey—take it easy." What should have been a funny sight wasn't. Bobby really did look about one minute away from a heart attack. I broke three fingernails untying the gag and blindfold. A small price to pay for the rare stream of thanks that issued from his freed lips.

"Jesus Christ, Casey—you saved my life. Anything you want, it's yours. Just name it. You can take the whole fee on the Taylor case. What else do you need? God, I would have died if you hadn't come along. I was seconds away from death. I tell you, I looked my future in the eye and saw nothing but black. Zippo. Nada. The Grim Reaper was knocking on my door."

Another second of this and he'd start begging me to drop him off at church.

But Bobby was still Bobby. Soon his grateful ranting was replaced by a torrent of invective aimed at his attacker. "I'm going to kill whoever did this to me. That lousy creep. What a coward. Sneaking up on someone like that. I had a date, you know. Took me weeks to get her to agree. She'll never believe me. I'll rip him from limb to limb. Only I never saw whoever it was. He must have been huge. Incredibly strong. Thank god you weren't here. You would have been killed. I tried to fight him off, but he overpowered me."

I lifted his toupee and felt the back of his head. A small knot was forming at the base of his skull. Nice work. I'd seen it before. On Peyton Tillman.

"You got sapped from behind, Bobby," I told him. "You couldn't have fought back."

He slumped back down in the chair and waited quietly while I freed his hands and legs. "It's true," he finally said in an ashamed voice. "I never heard the guy, never saw him. All of a sudden, the lights just went out. Figuratively speaking. When I came to, there I was, all trussed up like a Thanksgiving turkey. Jesus, do you know what it's like to not be able to breathe? I felt helpless."

"No one could have done anything under those circumstances," I assured him. "I promise not to tell a soul. Did he take anything?" And what, I wondered, was he looking for?

"Hell if I know. Take a look at this mess."

It was true. Our office would never qualify for the cover of Good Housekeeping on the best of days, but it didn't usually look like a twister had just passed through. That night it did. File cabinets were turned over. Bobby's paperwork was scattered across the rug. His trash can full of beer had been emptied onto the floor. Manila folders covered the carpet. I followed the mess down the hall and discovered that my own small office had been equally destroyed. All the drawers of my desk had been jimmied open, the contents emptied onto the floor. That son of a bitch.

I dropped to my hands and knees and searched. My revolver was gone. I pawed through what was left of my top drawer. So was my fake permit and copy of the registration. Damn it. It had taken a long time to get that gun and clean papers. Now I was back to square one. My file cabinet had also been trashed, but that gave me less concern. I only keep old files in the cabinet. I carry the current files with me wherever I go. Which reminded me of something. I bolted out the front door and checked the Valiant. It gleamed undisturbed beneath a streetlight. But when I went back inside, I was in for a nasty surprise: Bobby lay on the floor like a small mountain of flesh rising from a paperwork plain. And he wasn't moving.

I knelt beside him and felt for a pulse. None. Oh, god. No CPR class could have prepared me for such an emergency. I would need every ounce of my considerable weight to reach his heart through all that flesh. And if the phones had been disconnected, we were screwed. I grabbed the receiver and found a dial tone. Taking a deep breath, I called 911 even as I searched for the tip of Bobby's breastbone. I probably sounded like an hysterical female, but who cared? At that moment, that's exactly what I was. At least help was on the way.

Meanwhile, I found the proper spot, took a deep breath and began to pump. Or, rather, began to jump. I knelt beside him on the balls of my feet, pressing with all my strength, hopping up and down like a crazed troll as I forced my entire weight down on Bobby's chest. It worked. His body began to jump slightly in rhythm with mine. That meant I was getting through. I paused after twelve repetitions and steeled myself for what came next.

I had never touched Bobby's lips in my life and had fervently hoped I might go to my grave without doing so. But these were dire circumstances. I tilted his head back and zeroed in on my mark, closed my eyes and began mouth-to- mouth. "Pretend you're smooching Marlon Brando," I thought and locked lips. It wasn't so bad, I told myself. After all, I was the one who had been puking earlier—not him. Besides, while Bobby D. could be a disgusting pig, he was my disgusting pig.

God bless quiet weekday nights: the ambulance was there within five minutes. I could hear the sirens screaming down the street. The sound drove me to new heights of pumping frenzy. By the time the paramedics burst through the door, I probably looked like I was trampolining.

"We've got him," one of them said, grabbing my shoulders and pulling me away. I tumbled across the rug and lay still, gasping for breath. Talk about your calorie burners.

"Paddles," I heard one of the men say. I rolled out of the way as another man rushed past with a portable cardiac unit. This part I would skip. I turned away and held my breath until I heard a voice say, "He's breathing. Let's go."

I was nearly trampled in the rush, but at the very last minute, a pair of hands pulled me to my feet and helped me toward the door.

"Where are you taking him?" I asked. "I'll meet you there."

"Wake Med." The doors slammed and they were gone.

I could have ridden in the ambulance if I had been quick enough, but I had no desire to leave my car with my files in it behind. In fact, given the current state of my office, I was hiding those files, and pronto. I locked up the office—calling the cops to report my gun stolen was out of the question since I wasn't supposed to have one in the first place—climbed inside the Valiant and headed for Krispy Kreme.

Once safe in the anonymity of their parking lot, I transferred my current case files to a small depression in the trunk beneath the spare tire and covered them with an oil-encrusted pillowcase I used as a cleaning cloth. Then I refueled on coffee and doughnuts and headed for Wake Med.

They wouldn't let me see him. My makeshift attire and bloody arm didn't help. I looked like an escapee from a softball game for the criminally insane. In the polite way of southerners, the emergency-room receptionist let me know I was wasting my time and ought to come back tomorrow. Bobby was hooked up to monitors and booked for a bed in the cardiac-tracking unit. "He'll be all right," she promised me, her drawl making the words sound even more soothing. "You'd be amazed at what they can do these days. If he's breathing, they'll keep him alive. Just you wait and see. He'll be back to normal by next week."

I wanted to request a few improvements while they were at it, perhaps some liposuction and a personality transplant or two. But I was too relieved to joke about him and left, exhausted, to head home.

Just on the other side of Raleigh, I realized that I was one of only two cars on Wade Avenue. The other car followed at a distance, but matched my speed consistently. Paranoia set in. Visions of being run off the road by Peyton Tillman's murderer started playing out in my mind. I spent so much time looking in the mirror, it was a miracle that I didn't crash into one of Raleigh's famous oaks.

When the other car turned off on the Beltline, I was so relieved I pushed the pedal to the metal and zoomed down 1-40 as fast as my souped-up Valiant could take me. I made a beeline for MacLaine's where my friend Jack held court and occasionally actually worked during one of his shifts as a bartender. There was no way I was going home tonight. If my apartment had been tossed like my office and Peyton Tillman's house, I didn't want to know about it. I was too tired to face it. Let him rob me. I owned little of value and my case files were snug in my trunk. The only thing confidential in my apartment required batteries and was stored in a bedside table. If my home had been trashed, I'd deal with it in the morning. What I was most worried about was my safety, which meant bunking elsewhere.

Thanks to a flagrant disregard of the law, I made it to the bar before it closed. The entire place was dark and nearly deserted. Just a few drunks lurching toward love in the back room. Jack was wiping down the bar and looking bored. The cook sat at the far end of the counter, nursing a beer and a shot.

"Casey baby, dangerous lady." Jack stopped and looked a little closer. "Christ, you look like you've been through a blender. The blood smeared on your arm is very fetching. And that outfit. Well..." He paused. "I'm left speechless."

"Thanks. Occupational hazard." I told him about my night. He had a different idea about who the office burglar might be.

"I hope it wasn't Tony," he said.

"Who the hell is Tony?" I asked.

"Remember that bartender you caught double dipping last weekend?"

"It seems like a hundred years ago, but, yeah, I remember his dishonest ass."

"He got fired and he found out who you are. He's real pissed."

"How did he find out who I was?" I asked.

Jack shrugged. "I gotta tell you, Casey, you're not exactly low key. A lot of people know who you are and what you do. You ought to start wearing a disguise when you work as a spotter."

"It would be tough to disguise these babies," I said, poking my chest out.

"True. A connoisseur like me would always be able to tell."

I didn't have the energy to sustain the joke. Being stalked by a crazed ex-bartender was not exactly what I needed at the moment. "How seriously pissed is he?" I asked.

"Hard to say, but I think he's a little nutty. And word is, he owns a gun."

"Oh, great. That makes one of us."

"Where's yours?"

"Gone with the wind."

"I don't like the sound of this," Jack said. "I don't usually pull this paternal crap on you, but I think you better spend the night at my place. If you can take the mess."

"I have a shovel in the car," I offered.

"How about handcuffs?" he said hopefully.

"I have those, too. But what I don't have is the energy."

He nodded agreement. "No problem. We'll just snore the night away together."

"I don't snore," I said indignantly.

He raised his eyebrows. "Oh?"

"I don't snore, do I?" I asked, less assured.

"I'll let you know in the morning."

If either one of us snored that night, neither one of us was in a position to remember. We both fell asleep within seconds of hitting the pillows.

CHAPTER SIX

Jack lived in one of those anonymous brick apartment complexes that had infiltrated the Triangle over the past decade to attract young professionals struggling along on their first salaries after college. There were days I envied his access to the swimming pool—but never his neighbors. Both they and their apartments tended to look alike. In fact, when I woke the next morning, I couldn't even remember if I was in a motel room or someone's home. A glance at the floor told me I was at Jack's: his unique laundry system calls for him to drop his clothes in a big pile wherever he happens to take them off, which is usually next to his bed. I'd probably find half of my own long-lost wardrobe in the mess, but I was too achy to mount a search.

"I can't move," I mumbled. "My left side hurts like a son of a bitch from where I fell on Tillman's deck."

Jack stirred sympathetically and promptly fell back asleep. An elbow near his kidneys did the trick.

"Ouch, Casey. Geeze! Whatever happened to 'good morning, darling'?" He opened his eyes and glared, a bear reluctant to leave hibernation.

"I said I can't move. That spill last night was a nasty one. I'm so stiff I can't think of anything else."

"What a coincidence. So am I." He took my hand and wrapped it around the evidence.

"Forget about it, Romeo. I have work to do. Last night I was scared. This morning I'm pissed. Pissed and sore."

"What you need is a long soak in a hot tub."

I thought of Peyton Tillman's body draining to a pale luster in his. "I don't think so," I said. "Not for another ten years, at least."

"Okay," Jack agreed. "A brief massage. But only because you had such a lousy night."

I lay on my stomach and Jack expertly worked the kinks from my muscles while I groaned in contentment. As my body relaxed, my mind began to sharpen. I was sad, but mostly I was determined to find Peyton's killer. And what I didn't need was an angry ex-bartender on my heels.

"You really think that guy is going to stalk me?" I asked Jack. "Can't he just find a new boss to rip off and leave me alone?"

"That was a good job he got bounced from," Jack explained. "Lots and lots of money. Lots and lots of women."

I felt better after hearing that. I had just saved the women of the Research Triangle an awful lot of infections.

"Can you help me out with something?" I asked him, thinking over my options on the Gail Honeycutt case.

"I live to serve," he lied.

"I keep hearing that there are rumors about Roy Taylor having been dirty, but I never hear them from anyone who actually believes it. It's weird. Can you ask around and find out if there was anything going on?" Jack knew a lot of people in the Triangle, including the ones who never even thought about getting out of bed until midafternoon. "It would have been a while ago," I added. "And maybe it had something to do with drug arrests. That's what he was working on when he died."

"I'll ask," he agreed. "Anything else I can do for you while you're giving marching orders?"

"I'm gonna need a new gun," I said, thinking out loud. "Know where I can get one?"

Jack put both thumbs at the base of my spine and began to work them up and down the column. It was better than sex, if you took into account the fact that I was allowed to simply lay there. "Can't help you with that one," he said after thinking things over. "I'm a lover, not a fighter."

"Yeah?" Thanks to the back rub, my spirit was now willing, though my flesh was weak. "It's time to prove it."

By the time I got home, most of Durham was hard at work behind their desks or in the corridors of the many schools and medical facilities anchoring the city's economy. I entered my building almost cheerfully, gathering my strength for what I had to do that morning. If my apartment was trashed, so be it. The contrast wouldn't be all that great.

One look around told me that my sanctuary was safe. The place looked like hell, but the usual hell. Either the burglar had found what he was looking for in my office or he didn't know where I lived—yet.

My phone machine was blinking and I thought guiltily of Bobby D. I really needed to drop by and see how he was doing. I called for an update and found he was recovering well. Then I played the phone messages and waited for a tongue-lashing from Bill Butler. It never came. Silence may be golden, but it's not when you really care about someone, act like an ass in front of him, can't seem to be able to get beyond it and wish that he would realize it and let it slide. No such luck with Mr. Butler. But at least some of the waiting messages were encouraging. Nanny Honeycutt had called to ask if Peyton Tillman's death had anything to do with the investigation—which meant that the news had made it into the morning papers—and added that she'd arranged for a set of the court transcripts of Gail's trial to be delivered to my office. An efficient woman. The last message was from a voice I didn't recognize. It was a woman with a reedy hillbilly accent that turned "can't" into "cain't." She had to have been from the North Carolina mountains, probably near the Tennessee border.

"I don't know if you remember me," she said, stretching every word into two syllables or more. "But I got your number off the card you gave me down here at WCC last Sunday. You can't call me back on account of I'm in prison, but I guess you know that." She gave an embarrassed wheeze that I took for a laugh. "I don't know if I can help you, but if you come see me, I can try. I do know something peculiar that went on but I can't say no more about it right now on account of people are listening. I'm gonna put you on my visitor's list. Gail's my friend and I guess I ought to help her since she's being so stubborn she won't help herself. My name is Susan Porter, but my friends call me Dolly. But tell the guard you want to see Susan or they mightn't not let you in. And don't worry, I'm not in for anything bad. You didn't look like the type who gets scared, but I just thought I'd throw that part in just in case it gets you here quicker." With that, she hung up.

The woman had rattled off her speech as if afraid she might be discounted by the listener before she'd had her say.

I certainly wasn't going to discount her. I couldn't afford to. I had nothing else to go on. No way they'd let me near the Tillman investigation. If there was a connection to Roy Taylor's death, I'd have to establish any link through Gail.

With that in mind, I headed for Raleigh. There was one task I could not put off any longer. It would be hard, but I had to do it.

I inched along East Park Drive, looking for the right house number. It turned out to be a small house behind a larger one, so I missed it initially and had to double back. Old Mrs. Rollins didn't answer the bell at first; I knew someone had to be home, so I persisted. When she finally came to the door, she was still in her bathrobe and her face was puffy from crying. She looked even older than she was, and frail enough to blow away in a stiff wind. Gone was the dignified guardian of the day before. A grieving old lady had taken her place.

"It's you," she said, her fist clutching a crumpled ball of wet tissues.

"I'm so sorry, Mrs. Rollins. Really I am." There was little else I could say.

"It wasn't you that killed him," she answered, making it clear that she didn't think Tillman had committed suicide any more than I did. "But I want to know who did kill my Peyton. I'll give you all the money I have to find his killer. My husband and I, we don't have much, but it's yours if you can do that for me."

"No need for that," I assured her. "I promise you, I'll find out who did it."

"See that you do, young lady." Her face grew older as her anger dissipated. I was afraid of what might take its place.

"Is there anything that you could tell me that might help?" I asked.

She thought about it, the tissue dangling from her bony fingers. An antiseptic smell wafted out the front door; something sickly and sweet lived in their dark little house. I heard someone coughing several rooms away and the blare of a television set turned up loud.

"No," she finally said. "But I'm too upset to think clearly. In a few hours, I am going to sit down and think of everything he did and everything he said in these past few months." The grim line of her mouth told me that she meant every word. "I am going to call everyone he knew and ask them the same thing. If I find out anything, I'll let you know." She paused and looked me up and down. "I hope I am not misjudging your character, Miss Jones."

I straightened involuntarily. "I'll try my best."

"Do that." The coughing sounds grew more alarming, and she shut the door softly in my face, with only a nod for goodbye. The hunch of her shoulders as she turned away told me that the murder last night had taken the life out of more people than just Peyton Tillman.

It was close to one o'clock and time to face the mess in the office. I hoped that none of Bobby's slimy clients would be waiting outside the door, wondering what had happened to him. But the only person even remotely nearby was Ruby, the meter maid. We waved at each other from opposite ends of the sidewalk, and then I took a deep breath, unlocked the door and went in. It was still a mess—and weirdly empty without Bobby D.'s bulk.

My first instinct was to simply throw everything into a box and heave it into the large Dumpster out back. But Bobby was a purveyor of information extraordinaire and I couldn't just chuck his files. They were his pension fund, so to speak. On the other hand, I wasn't about to put them back in order. I compromised by jamming them back into the file cabinets. Needless to say, I kept the blinds closed while I performed even these minor housekeeping chores. I had a reputation to protect, after all. The office still looked as if it qualified for federal disaster aid when I was done, but it would have to do for now.

I put my own office back in passable order quickly, shoving the outdated files into stacks and leaving them for a rainy day's worth of organizing. I reassembled my desk and carefully returned the contents to the proper drawers. The thief had left behind a box of bullets. Fat lot of good they did me now. Maybe I could lob them at the next creep who attacked me. If I got lucky, I'd nick his eye.

When I was done, I faced the fact that I was putting off going to the hospital to see Bobby. I hate hospitals almost as much as I hate prisons—and for the exact same reasons. You can't walk in and out of your own free will, and there's always someone in a uniform telling you what to do. But Bobby was Bobby, and I loved the fat turd. I steeled myself, collected his messages off his machine and dawdled during the short drive down New Bern Avenue to Wake Med.

I should have known better. A mere massive heart attack had not put a dent in Bobby's ego. He was lying in bed like a South Seas island king, lolling among a cluster of nurse's aids, ogling the female flesh around him and cheerfully enduring the maze of tubes that led to his arms and chest. His stomach was barely concealed by the hospital gown, and the sheets were fetchingly arranged around his knees.

"Please, Bobby," I said, pulling the covers up to his midriff. "Enough people are sick around here as it is."

"Har, har," he laughed—a sound that most closely resembled the fighting call of the bull seal. "You're so funny, you're going to give me a heart attack."

"Don't joke about that," a small Filipina aid warned him, a frown crossing her pretty face. She finished sponging his arm with an antiseptic pad while simultaneously sidestepping his groping hand. Getting near Bobby was like dancing with an octopus. One misstep and you'd never get untangled. Expertly, she reattached an IV drip then checked the dials on a nearby monitoring machine. Two other aids were fussing around a cart filled with cups of medication.

"Just give me all the morphine you can find," Bobby instructed them. They tittered nervously—and moved the cart farther away from his bed. I knew the conventional hospital reasoning well: if you're well enough to joke about narcotics, you're well enough to go without them.

"Who sent the flowers?" I asked, eyeing an arrangement of carnations on the windowsill. "It looks like you just won the Kentucky Derby."

"The babe I had the date with last night," Bobby confided. "I guess she forgives me."

Or was grateful he didn't have his heart attack later on in the evening while she was on the bottom, I thought to myself.

"A nurse called her for me," Bobby said. "Must have laid it on thick. She just can't live without Big Daddy. None of them can." He har-harred again and all but one of the aids hurried their chores, anxious to be done with their honor intact. I can't say that I blamed them.

"This was some bad shit going down," I said, sitting on one edge of the bed. I wasn't worried about him groping me. He knew he'd get a belt across the kisser if he tried.

"Yeah. I've been meaning to ask you what the hell it was all about anyway." He coughed and the Filipina aid looked momentarily alarmed, but when we both saw that the cardiac monitoring beat remained steady, she relaxed.

"You're going to be fine," she told Bobby, patting his tummy as if rubbing a Buddha for good luck. "You've made an amazing recovery. I think you're going to be good as new."

"Thanks, babe. But if I need a little mouth-to-mouth?"

"She can give it to you," the woman replied quickly, nodding at me as she fled from the room.

"I already did," I announced to Bobby as the remaining aids left us to our privacy.

"Yeah? My one chance, and I missed it." He was quiet for a minute. "Guess you saved my life."

"Guess I did."

"Course, you put it in danger in the first place." He looked smug.

"I beg your pardon?" I was incredulous.

"I don't think it was any of my clients breaking in," he said. "The worst cases I get are nasty divorces, and I'm not even working on one of those right now."

"Yeah, I know," I conceded. "I think it's connected to Gail Honeycutt somehow."

"What are we going to do?" Bobby asked. For someone who is supposed to be my boss, he asks me that question a lot.

"Get to the bottom of it quick?" I suggested. "At least I'm going to try. You're going to stay here and get well."

He looked disappointed. "The food here sucks. No flavor. No salt. No seasonings. No butter. No hot sauce. No fun."

"God," I sympathized. "That's terrible. It's probably nothing but a bunch of vitamins and minerals and proteins and other icky stuff that's good for you."

"They won't even let me have a phone," he complained. "They want me to rest." He thumped his chest. "I'm fine. It was just a small lapse, is all."

"Small?" I patted his hand. "I was doing back flips on your stomach for five minutes until the paramedics arrived."

"I know, I know. I owe you one. Just don't go getting sentimental on me."

"No chance of that," I assured him. "But what can I do to help?"

"There's a little black book in my top desk drawer. Or it was there."

"I know," I said. "I put it back there this morning."

"Can you go through it and call up every one of the female persuasion and let them know where I am? Only don't call if there's a cross by her name, that means she's history. And if there's a star by her name, don't leave a message on her answering machine because that means she's married. I want to know who my true friends are."

"Done," I assured him. "What else?"

"Get this thing solved quickly, would you? I want to get back to work soon, and I'm not in the mood to wrestle with another maniac."

His comment reminded me that I needed to question him again about the previous night. I brought him through the events of the night before one more time, just to make sure he'd told me all he could. This time the assailant was nearly seven feet tall with massive hands that threatened to squeeze the life out of him. Plus, he'd had incredible biceps, hairy forearms and a menacing growl for a voice.

"I've got it," I said. "You were attacked by Bigfoot."

"Wait till he comes after you," Bobby said. "See how much you like it."

"Look," I said. "I need a favor. Do you know anyone in the Durham Police Department who might have worked with Roy Taylor before he was killed? I'd like to talk to someone there confidentially. See if I can find out where these rumors about him being dirty started."

Bobby thought for a moment, then shook his head. "It's been a while since I dipped my toe over there in Durham. I don't think I'll be able to help. Better go ask that Butler guy if he can help. You know who I mean, the one who gives you such a hard time. The one you like so much."

"Bill Butler," I said glumly. "Is that how you view our relationship?"

"Hell, no," he declared. "But I'm not about to give you my opinion on that one. I want to die a natural death. But not for a couple years yet."

"At last we can agree on something," I said, rising to go.

"Did I tell you the food here was terrible?" he asked as I was halfway out the door.

"Forget it, Bobby," I warned him. "I'm not bringing you any junk food." I blew him a kiss and fled before he asked for a real one.

Bobby'd had the heart attack, not me. Which meant I could stuff my face with impunity. I got a couple of chicken biscuits and a quart of iced tea from Hardee's. The tea was so sweet it made my teeth ache. Two cups of that stuff and not even Claus von Bulow could pull you out of the diabetic shock.

I parked outside the Raleigh Police Department and munched on my lunch, debating the pros and cons of going inside.

What the hell, was I a woman or a mouse? Plus, I looked a sight better than I had last night. And maybe I'd run into Detective Anne Morrow and could weasel some info out of her about Peyton Tillman's death.

The desk sergeant let me know that Bill Butler was indeed on duty, then phoned upstairs to see if I was on the A list. Despite my atrocious behavior, I was. I rode up in the elevator contemplating my own stubborn immaturity.

"Make it quick, Casey," Bill said, pulling a chair up to his desk. "There was another rape out near Peace College last night. Do you know what it's like when a serial rapist starts hanging around a girls' college? I've had calls from every trustee and damn near every parent between New Bern and Asheville. Never mind that the guy is raping homeless women down by the railroad tracks. Everyone's afraid the purity of their daughters might be defiled."

"Want me to act as decoy and kick his ass?"

He eyed me. "No thanks. I'd prefer to bring him in alive."

"I came to apologize," I said. "I've been a complete asshole and I don't know why." Actually, I did know why. But calling Bill a complete asshole instead was unlikely to get me what I wanted.

"You want something," he said. "Is that why you're being nice to me?"

I sighed. "Is there no trust between us?" I asked. "Whatever happened to simple human trust?"

"Can it, Casey. We're both divorced. That's what happened to it. When you come sniffing around my desk, apologizing, I start to get nervous. Forgive me if I'm blunt and just say that I prefer you as a ball buster. The southern belle act isn't going to cut a lot of ice with me."

"That's a relief," I said. "My eyelashes were getting tired from all that batting." I leaned forward and fixed him with my best smile. "But I really am sorry about being such a jerk. Are you?"

"Am I sorry for being such a jerk?" he asked. "Is that supposed to be a friendly remark or something?"

"Something," I said.

He tried to hide his smile but failed. "Okay," he conceded. "We're both jerks. Now what is it that you want?"

"I want to talk to someone on the Durham police force who knew Roy Taylor," I said.

"Ah, Casey." He was disgusted. "I told you to leave that case alone. You already stepped in it deep last night. I'm not saying it's connected. I'm just saying it's bad karma."

"I can't leave it alone, Bill," I explained. "I know I'm not going to be allowed near the Tillman investigation. But what if it is connected? What if I helped it along in some way? I can't just walk away. And what if Gail Honeycutt didn't do it? You can't undo putting someone to death."

"I got a bad feeling about this," he warned me. "A very bad feeling indeed."

"So you won't help me?" I asked with a sigh.

"I'll think about it," he said. "I do know some people over there. And one of them worked with Taylor pretty closely. But that doesn't mean he'll talk to you. A guy's not going to be too friendly to someone who's helping the killer of his dead pal, know what I mean?"

"Just ask," I said. "Pretty please?"

"I'll see what I can do." He fiddled with some papers on his desk. "Going to Tillman's funeral?" he finally said.

"I hadn't thought about it," I admitted. But I had. I had thought about walking into the funeral home and seeing all those old people from Peyton's neighborhood there to mourn his death. I wasn't anxious to see his old secretary again. I could almost feel Mrs. Rollins's eyes on me, asking me why I hadn't protected him better.

"It's Friday, if you're interested. Two o'clock. Church of the Good Shepherd."

"Is this a date?" I asked. "How romantic."

"Actually, I'm already going with someone, and I don't think it's a good idea if you meet. But, yeah, I'll be there."

Ouch. Who the hell was he going with? The lovely Detective Morrow? Some sweet babe from the administrative pool? Little green threads of jealousy tightened around my heart.

"I mean, anyone can come," he offered helpfully. "It'll be in the papers."

"I might," I said, rising to go while my dignity was still intact.

"You look a lot better than you did last night," he offered, checking out my black T-shirt and black stretch jeans. I'd worn boots because, after last night's events, I wanted to feel as if I could drive home a point or two against an assailant if need be.

"I'll bet I do," I said. "Thanks for putting in a good word with Detective Morrow. She's all right."

"That she is," Bill agreed. "She runs rings around the guys. Really knows her stuff. Not bad looking, either. Doesn't have your unique sense of style, of course." He grinned, and I could feel that smile way south of my border.

"She's not bad at all," I said. When he was being sweet like that, it was tough to resist mooning over him. Bill Butler had my number all right. I took one last look before I left. He had a great face, with wrinkles you could trace with your fingers. It was a face that had been lived in, and it made the young faces I was accustomed to waking up with in the morning seem bland and uninteresting. "Go home and get some sleep," I ordered him. "You worked straight through the night, didn't you?"

He nodded. "I've got to protect the flower of southern womanhood."

"Careful," I told him. "Your northern cynicism is showing."

He flashed me a smile, despite himself.

"See you," I added, lingering in the doorway. Our eyes met and then I left, happy yet vaguely irritated at the way he could make me go soft with a single grin.

I returned to the office to pick up Bobby D.'s little black book, then spent a solid hour dialing all the ladies in his life to let them know that he had suffered a mild heart attack. Keeping his code straight was a pain in the butt, but I think I managed to leave most of the marriages at stake still intact.

By the time I finished, it was too late to swing by the women's prison to visit Gail's friend. Instead, I picked up the cardboard box full of trial transcripts sent over by Nanny Honeycutt and told myself I could read them all in a night. Evelyn Wood had nothing on me.

The Durham Bulls were playing their season opener against the Wilmington Blue Rocks, and I was sorely tempted to take the night off and go. Last year, I'd spent two weeks with a severe crush on the hunky home umpire, until I realized that he was wearing his protective padding beneath his blue shirt and that was why he was built so impressively. Dreams dashed, I had turned my attention to the game and actually gotten into it. The thought of spending a chilly March night beneath the stadium lights munching on hot dogs, drinking beer and examining the tushes of twenty-something baseball players appealed to me. Unfortunately, duty called. It would have to be a night curled up in my salvaged armchair, paging through the transcript of Gail's original trial.

Not that it wasn't fascinating stuff. However, I was barely a third of the way through by the time I fell asleep.

The next morning, I stopped by the office, which had not been magically cleaned in my absence, and spent a few minutes idly combing through the replaced contents of Bobby's desk for items of interest. It wasn't often I got the chance. Other than a zillion fast-food coupons, I didn't find much. The absence of condoms alarmed me, but then he probably bought them in bulk and used the cartons as side tables for his king-size water bed.

When I finished my snooping, I had to face the fact that it was time to return to the Women's Correctional Center. I wouldn't be able to talk to Gail again without advance notice, but her friend Susan Porter was a different story.

I locked up and was almost to my car when Ruby, the meter maid, stopped me to talk. Ruby was barely five feet tall, and her skin was so black it glowed with a blue sheen during the hot summer days. I'd seen her subdue men three times her weight and talk down even bigger brothers. Ruby didn't screw around.

"What's the story on Bobby?" she asked in her soft voice. "His car's been parked at the corner for a couple of days now and the office is dark."

I told her what had happened. Ruby let me slide on parking quarters most of the time. That made her a woman worthy of my trust.

She whistled. "No kidding? He got attacked? That's rough. I've been attacked a few times myself, as you can imagine. But I was always able to see my attacker. You tell Bobby not to worry about his car. I'll keep an eye on it for him."

"Thanks," I said. "Know anyone interested in getting the office back in order for us? I can't face it. I'm on a big case."

She thought for a moment. "My sister Keisha might be interested. She has a pretty good office job over at RD Construction, but she needs some extra money right now on account of her kid needs some kind of special glasses."

"If she'll get that damn office back in order, the glasses are on me," I promised. "I don't care what it costs." Nanny Honeycutt would never know what a good cause she was contributing toward.

"Done," Ruby said and we shook hands on the deal. "I'll call her and let you know when she's available."

On the drive to the prison, I was so busy watching the sun trying to peek out from behind a mass of gray March clouds, that I almost ran into the side of Kentucky Fried Chicken at a tricky intersection off New Bern. My brain was starting to mildew from all the cool, damp air. Spring sunshine was a badly needed remedy.

I'd never seen the guard at the front gate of the prison before. He was a stocky Hispanic man with a jolly face. When my name checked out on the approved visitors' list for one Susan Porter, he waved me through. "Dolly's usually in back of the cafeteria this time of day," he told me. "She's a smoker."

Who wasn't a smoker when they were stuck in prison? I'd gone through enough packs during my eighteen months to give an entire third-world country lung cancer. It was one reason why I never even touched a cigarette these days.

I followed the tidy brick walkway to the general population area. My heart was pounding far less than it had been on my previous visit. Maybe time really does heal all wounds. Or maybe bigger ones just come along to replace them.

Many of the prisoners were eating lunch. I passed by the cafeteria and could hear the clink of silverware and the hum of voices. Women's prisons are noisy, much noisier than men's. All the inmates had to do all day was talk—and talk they did: at each other, with each other, to the guards and to themselves. And people wonder why I don't like to sit around and make conversation these days. You try spending eighteen months listening to nonstop chatter and see if that doesn't transform you into a voluntary deaf-mute.

I found Dolly sitting on a concrete bench beside a huge black woman with a large pink scar running down her cheek from her ear to her chin. Both women wore white aprons over their prison garb and had jammed their hair into fine mesh nets. They were smoking cigarettes and talking to each other in low tones. As I drew near, the black woman rose to go, slapping a high five with Dolly as she headed for the kitchen door.

"Dolly?" I confirmed. She seemed even skinnier and more haggard than before. I sat on the bench beside her. It was still warm from the large woman's body.

"That's me. You're the lady detective." She blew out a cloud of cigarette smoke and examined me from head to toe, taking her time. Her voice was even reedier than on the telephone, its Appalachian twang unmistakable. She had at least three teeth missing in the front of her mouth and tried to cover the remaining teeth with her lips when she talked, making it even harder to understand what she was saying.

"The guard called you Dolly," I told her. "He even knew where to find you."

"That's Herman for you," she said with a thin laugh that turned into a cough. She was crouched over nervously, like a cowering dog. I had no idea how to get her to relax.

"Sounds like the guards are pretty friendly here," I said. "That's good."

"How do you know Gail?" I asked when she remained silent.

"The kitchen," she explained. "For a while, they let Gail work in the kitchen, until her first appeal was turned down. Then they moved her into isolation."

"To protect her?" I asked.

The girl looked up at me. "What from? You don't have to worry about being hurt in here, lessen you can't mind your own business or you done something terrible and brag about it. Like boiling your babies in hot water."

"Ouch," I said. "Someone did that?"

Dolly looked surprised. "'Course not. I was just using an example."

"Isn't shooting your husband considered pretty terrible?" I asked.

She shrugged and took a drag on her cigarette. "Depends on the husband." She laughed, and I waited while it turned to a cough and she recovered. "Not me, though, I never killed nobody."

"Why are you in here?" I asked.

"Jury says I shot a man working at a 7-Eleven up at Black Mountain," she said. "He lost his spleen. But I didn't shoot him."

"Mistaken identity?" I asked dryly.

"No mistake so far as I was concerned." She looked up at the gray clouds. "It was my brother done it. We look a lot alike. I was driving the car. I didn't know he was going to rob the place. He told me he was going in for an RC Cola."

"The jury believed him over you?" I asked, mystified.

She shrugged. "Him and my mama. She said he was at home with her when it happened and that I was always getting into trouble."

I was horrified. Mommy dearest, indeed. "Your own mother sold you out?" I asked.

95

Dolly shrugged again. "She needed my brother around the house and he's the firstborn. She just did what she had to do."

I understood why the guard had called her an even bigger loser than Gail.

"How long you in for?" I asked.

She considered the question. "Hard to tell with armed robbery. Parole boards don't like women who get involved in shit like that. They think I'm Bonnie without the Clyde. Full term, I got me four more years. Maybe I can get out in two."

"I'm sorry," I said.

"I'm not," she admitted. She ground out the cigarette and rolled her shoulders, then turned her face up to the sky as if she were speaking to someone a lot higher up than me. "I like it here. It sure as hell beats where I was. I'm in no hurry to get out."

"Why did you call me?" I asked her.

"I thought maybe I could help Gail. Me and her got to be pretty good friends," she explained. "She don't make fun of me like some other people I could mention. I slip her notes with her dinner, and she leaves me notes under the dirty dishes when we pick up the trays. So after you gave me your card, I asked around to see if anyone had ever heard of you."

"Had anyone heard of me?" I asked.

Dolly nodded. "Sure. You kept that girl in Zebulon from going to prison, and there's another girl in here says you helped her get a reduced sentence by proving she didn't know she was smuggling drugs in her boyfriend's backpack."

"I wondered where Sally ended up," I said. "She doing okay?"

"Yup. Got her two girlfriends and a good job in the beauty parlor so she can shop for more. I don't think she'll be smuggling drugs for no boyfriends after she gets out."

I laughed in spite of myself. "Why won't Gail let anyone help her?" I asked.

The girl scuffed the sidewalk with the tips of her high-tops. They were screaming orange. I admired her taste in footwear and told her so.

"Thanks. They're cheap. I like yours, too." She stared down at the bright red high-tops I'd changed into. Boots are too flashy for prison since they don't let the girls wear them in there. "I bet no one gives you a hard time."

"No one who lives to tell the tale," I said and was inordinately pleased when I got a laugh from her that was cleaner than the ones before.

"About Gail?" I prompted her.

"Yeah. Gail." She fiddled with the strings on her apron. "I ain't no genius, you understand? I'm not trying to pretend I know things other people don't."

"But?" I said on cue.

"But I know enough to know that Gail didn't kill her husband. She wouldn't have had a gun in that house. She was afraid of them."

"Okay," I said. "So why does she act so guilty?"

"Because she feels guilty," Dolly explained. "Like my mama made me feel so guilty I took the rap for my brother. Gail thinks that if she hadn't of had so much to drink that night, she might have been able to keep her husband from being killed. It don't matter to her who pulled the trigger. What matters is that she didn't stop them."

Well, there you had it. An uneducated hillbilly girl had gotten closer to the real truth about Gail Honeycutt than a decade's worth of Ph.D.'s.

"She talked to you about her feelings?" I asked.

"Sure she did," Dolly explained. "She don't know I'm talking to you right now, though. She'd be mad."

"Why?"

Dolly looked at me like I was the stupidest damn thing she'd ever run across. "'Cause she wants to be punished," she explained slowly. "She thinks she deserves to die. But I don't. That's why I'm talking to you."

"Who does Gail think did it?" I asked.

"She don't know," Dolly explained. "But I can tell you something peculiar that happened over the past year."

"What?" I asked casually, not wanting to scare her by showing how much it might mean to have even a scrap of information to go on.

Dolly lit another cigarette and offered me a hit. I declined. If I ever want nicotine again, I'll start licking ashtrays. Tastes the same to me. She stared at the burning tip as she spoke. "When I got arrested, the officers weren't none too nice to me. They threw me up against a wall even when I told them I'd go to the station with no fuss. They handcuffed me behind my back and it hurt. They shoved my head down into the car seat. No one in a uniform was nice during the whole trial. It weren't until I got here that people started treating me right. And I damn sure never had a visit from none of the officers who tracked me to Mama's house."

"What's that got to do with Gail?" I asked.

"They visited Gail," she explained. "Gail don't talk about who they were, but I saw them come see her last Christmas, one by one. Three of them in all."

"Three of what?" I asked. "Police officers?"

Dolly nodded. "They weren't in uniform or nothing, but I know a cop when I see one. It's their hair, you know, and those shirts they wear and the boots and the way they walk."

I knew only too well what she meant. In fact, my extensive knowledge of typical policeman attire went even deeper than shirts and boots. "Maybe they were private investigators?" I suggested. "Trying to help Gail?"

"Ain't nobody tried to help Gail until you," Dolly pointed out. "These guys were cops. Besides, Anna who makes the sugar cakes recognized one. She says he's from Durham. Why would a cop from Durham come to see the person who killed another cop from Durham?"

Why indeed? "You got me there," I said.

"Well, find out why," Dolly ordered me. She looked at her watch. It was a cheap Timex with a battered wristband. "My break's over. That's all I had to tell you. I just think it's funny is all. Those policemen hated Gail. They weren't coming here to say they forgave her." Suddenly Dolly leaned forward and spit on the grass. "They ain't gonna forgive or forget."

"Can you ask Gail who they were?" I asked. "And give me a call?"

She shrugged. "I can try. I did ask once before and she wouldn't say a word. But maybe I can sneak it out of her. It's hard now that we don't get to sit and talk. All we got is notes, and sometimes we get to talk through the back window of her building when no one's looking."

"Do what you can, please?" I asked. "In the meantime, I'll try to find out on my own."

"Sure," she promised, extending her hand for a good-bye shake. It was as limp and brittle as a broken bird's.

"It was nice to meet you, Dolly," I told her. "There's no flies on you."

Her guard dropped and a smile escaped. She forgot to hide her teeth, and I was treated to a pirate-like, almost dashing grin. Then it disappeared. "Can you help her?" she asked me, her twang vibrating with worry. "They're gonna kill her. And once you're dead, you're dead."

"I'm going to try," I promised. I watched her slip back inside the low brick building. When she opened the door, a wave of familiar noise billowed out into the quiet courtyard: the clanking of pots, steel on steel, steam hissing, voices shouting above the din. Institutional music. Dolly's life. One that was better than the life she'd had before.

I signed out under the watchful eye of Herman, the front-gate guard.

"How's Dolly doing?" he wanted to know.

"She's doing all right," I said. "She said nice things about you."

"Dolly's a good girl," Herman explained. "She just had a piece of bad luck. And she always seems to say the wrong things to the parole board. It's almost like she doesn't want to get out early. I guess you could say she's one of life's losers."

I nodded and hurried to my car, thinking about that. Everyone thought Dolly was one of life's losers, but I'll tell you what—she was happy where she was, even if she was in a prison. Most of all, she was going out of her way to help someone worse off than herself. So how big of a loser could she be?

CHAPTER SEVEN

Spring arrived the day of Peyton Tillman's funeral. I awoke bleary-eyed to find green shoots peeping up through the new grass in my backyard, and every songbird within three miles busting a gut in relief. I felt like singing myself. I opened the windows and breathed in the richness of warm air tinged with the tang of tobacco from the Liggett & Myers plant on Main Street. Two squirrels were chasing each other up the trunk of my oak tree, and a cat sat on top of the red-cedar fence washing itself meticulously. All I needed was Bambi bouncing across the backyard and I'd be in a goddamned Disney movie.

I selected a black dress with a neckline that wouldn't horrify the elderly mourners sure to be out in force at Tillman's funeral. My leopard-skin pillbox hat, fishnet hose and a pair of slut pumps completed the ensemble. Maybe I've seen *Witness For The Prosecution* one too many times, but I don't feel a black dress is complete without black heels.

The Church of Good Shepherd was on Hillsborough Street, just a few blocks from the police station and barely half a block from the Capitol building. Its graceful spire rose high above the smaller buildings surrounding it. The front sidewalk was cluttered with men in dark suits and women in dark dresses. I was the only leopard-skin pillbox-wearer among the bunch, and most of the female mourners had opted for support hose over fishnets.

I was early, but the front five pews on either side of the center aisle were already occupied by row after row of senior citizens. It was as if, by tacit agreement, Peyton Tillman's neighbors and his parents had decided to block out his less enduring supporters. I didn't blame them. Politicians, business leaders, civic activists and former friends who had deserted

Tillman in droves when he was alive now crammed the church to pay homage. Fat lot of good it did Peyton now. I took a seat at the far edge of the sixth row, squeezing in beside a large black woman in a floral dress whose hair had turned a peppery white from age.

I searched the front row for Peyton's parents. An impossibly old couple was seated near the altar on the right side, next to a tall blond who sat sniffling into a white handkerchief. Both the old man and woman were shrunken with age, and the father had a metal walker parked in the aisle by his side. They stared straight ahead, stony-faced, at the closed coffin holding the remains of their only child. No one, I thought to myself, should ever have to go through what those two old people are feeling right now.

The blond at their side interested me. She was at least forty-five, much older than any of Peyton's typical girlfriends, if you wanted to believe the rumors. She had elegant features—very English-looking—and upswept hair veiled in black mesh. Her makeup was minimal and no Tammy Faye Baker rivulets of mascara marred the dignified grief of her face. She wasn't a sister; Peyton had no siblings. A girlfriend, perhaps, or a colleague.

"That's his fiancée," the black woman next to me whispered, cooling herself with a paper fan she had brought for the occasion. A portrait of Martin Luther King was imprinted on its surface, and his image flickered past my face with every sweep of her hand.

"He was engaged?" I whispered back.

She nodded. "For almost six months now. Very nice lady. An interior decorator, I believe."

"How come no one knew about it?" I muttered, aware that others around us were trying to eavesdrop. The lady in front of me actually reached up to her hearing aid and adjusted the volume.

My seatmate eyed me cautiously. "I hope you and him..." Her voice trailed off.

I shook my head quickly. "No, of course not. I just didn't know he was engaged."

"He liked to keep his private life private," the woman explained. "I guess you can understand why." She lifted her brows and rolled her large brown eyes toward the rows of public figures behind us.

"Yes, I can understand why," I agreed. "How do you know him?"

"I raised him," she confided to me in a proud voice. "His parents wanted me to sit in the front row with them, but I prefer to keep a low profile." With that, she gave a big whoosh of her fan—sending a whiff of lilac my way—and stared straight ahead at the coffin, her mouth trembling slightly from the strain of sudden memories. I knew she was probably hurting more than almost anyone else in the church. I patted her hand. She gave me a curious look before staring back at Peyton Tillman's coffin.

Above me, the stained-glass windows of Good Shepherd blazed in the spring sunshine, sending tongues of red, blue and gold cascading over the marble altar. I had a funny feeling that the figures of heavenly angels etched in the windows were staring at me, but then I realized that the sensation came from closer to home. I glanced over the rows of elderly mourners and discovered old Mrs. Rollins, Peyton Tillman's elderly secretary, looking my way. I stared back and she nodded. I returned the gesture. She'd let me know what she wanted when the time came.

Just as the priest entered through the altar, there was a commotion at the back of the church. The heavy wooden door wobbled a few times before swinging open. Like an extra from a Monty Python movie who had taken a wrong turn, a man with one leg hopped in apologetically, his crutches planted wide and his tie slung haphazardly over one shoulder. He glanced up at the eyes pinning him in their focus, then hurried to the very back row. It was then that I noticed that the last few pews were occupied by an astonishing variety of men in their late forties and fifties. Most had that uncomfortable look men get when they've been forced to scrub for an unfamiliar function, like a bunch of bachelor uncles hiding behind the food table at a wedding reception. I spotted long hair and beards; short hair and rigid jaws; polyester suits; jeans gussied up with tweed jackets. Every now and then, there was a bomber jacket or a well-tailored suit. Heavy work boots all lined up in a row, fidgeting in unison and creating the constant scuffling of creatures forced to sit still against their nature. I definitely wanted to meet that group once the funeral was over.

The day had turned even warmer. As the service dragged on, my eyelids began to droop. I thought I smelled honeysuckle creeping in under the raised window to my right. I'd have killed for a hammock. I heard a faint hiss of steam and suppressed a groan. The radiator was kicking to life, oblivious to the unexpected heat. I was about to disgrace myself by falling asleep and hitting my head on the pew in front of me when my seatmate elbowed me back to consciousness.

"Who's that man staring at you?" she whispered. "He's giving me the heebie-jeebies."

I followed her gaze. She was glancing one row behind us toward the middle of a pew on the opposite side of the church. Bill Butler sat stiffly at attention among a group of off-duty officers. Detective Anne Morrow sat several people further down the row, looking elegant in a black pantsuit. Bill was oblivious to my presence. The man sitting next to him was not. I stared back into his very green eyes, their vibrant color apparent even at a distance. He was an incredibly good-looking man: tall, trim with wide shoulders, thick black hair that feathered back without looking fussy and well-proportioned features perfectly sculpted above a wide mouth. He looked away quickly, but not before a jolt of electricity crackled through the air between us.

"I don't know who he is," I whispered to my seatmate, though I knew he had to be a cop.

She shook her head. "Looks like trouble to me. Do yourself a favor and marry an ugly man. I've done it twice. They know how to treat a woman right."

After that, I had no problem staying awake. Through the remainder of the service, I wondered who the man might be. I whispered a hurried good-bye to my seatmate once the last hymn was over. I was almost at the door when I caught the back of one of my black heels on the crutches of the one-legged man that were in the aisle. I tripped, groped to regain my balance, snagged the other heel on the edge of the aisle runner and landed with a plop in Captain Ahab's lap. I'd never make it as a ballet dancer. Fortunately, the rest of the congregation was too busy collecting their belongings to pay any attention to my Keystone Kops routine.

"Sorry," I muttered, struggling to hoist myself off his lap.

"Anytime, lady. Nice hat." I looked down into a pair of cheerful blue eyes above a ragged white beard. "Sorry about the crutches," he added. "I'm having a new leg made but it's not fitting right yet so I'd just as soon go without."

"Casey Jones," I told him, introducing myself. "Can you move over?" He elbowed his seatmate and obliged. I slipped into the back pew next to the motley crew of assorted men. "Who are you guys anyway? How do you know Peyton?"

"Nam," the man told me. "You're looking at the Triangle Chapter of the Vietnam Veterans Association."

"That's right," I said. "Peyton served two tours, didn't he?"

"More than any of us had the balls to do," the man added, then looked ashamed at his choice of language within such hallowed halls.

I stared down the row. "A lot of you turned out."

"Peyton was a good guy," the man explained. "He used to come to all the meetings. Never made a big deal out of it. Gave us a lot of money, too. He had more than the rest of us. Didn't milk it for the publicity either."

"No," I agreed. "He kept it pretty quiet. I wonder why?"

The man thought about it. "Didn't want to remember but couldn't forget?" he suggested. The man next to him nodded his agreement.

I saw the crowd surging down the aisle: middle-aged politicians being pushed from behind by impatient senior citizens who, I suspected, were taking full opportunity of the chance to poke and prod at the fat cats before them. I didn't blame them. I wouldn't mind taking a cane to a couple of them myself.

"I think I'll get out of the way," I muttered, leaping up only to crash into the handsome man with the green eyes.

"Ouch," he said, rubbing his calf and staring down the front of my dress.

"Should have known it would be you," a voice interrupted. Bill Butler glared over the man's shoulder, annoyed. "You're holding up traffic, Casey."

"Excuse me," I spat back and flounced from the church, which wasn't easy, given that I had to careen around a dozen shuffling old mourners to do so. I waited on the front steps with my retort, wondering what bug was up his ass.

Bill didn't give me a chance to ask. "Detective Morrow wants to ask you a few questions," he warned me.

"Is that why you invited me?" I asked, affronted by his cold demeanor. I knew we were in the middle of a personal cold war, but I didn't think things had deteriorated to Arctic temperatures yet.

"Of course not." He stared down at my legs and tried to smile. "I was hoping for a glimpse of your fishnets. Only you would wear them to a funeral."

The man next to him laughed. I shot him a glare. The look didn't faze him.

"Care to introduce us?" I demanded of Bill, uncomfortably aware that the stranger's green eyes were boring into me.

Bill sighed, making it clear that the man was the very person he had not wanted me to meet. "Casey, this is Steven Hill. He's with the Durham force."

I opened my mouth but Bill wouldn't let me get the words out.

"Forget it," he said. "The answer is 'no.' And here comes Morrow."

Detective Morrow, trim and tall in her tailored suit, was heading for me. She slid her sunglasses down over her face before I could read it. Smart lady.

"Casey," she said quietly. "Got a minute?"

"Sure," I muttered, following her to one side of the wide stone steps. Hordes of ancient mourners shuffled past us, their faces vaguely disapproving.

"That was thoroughly depressing," I said. "All those old people."

"Agreed," Detective Morrow replied. "We found some odd marks when we were fingerprinting the house. Know anything about them?"

I stared down at my feet, finding the open toes of my high heels suddenly fascinating. The way my tootsies were squished toward the middle of the triangular opening made my feet look like pig hooves.

Detective Morrow did not find my shoes quite as interesting. "Casey?" she repeated in a much firmer voice. "Know anything about those odd marks?"

"Weird like how?" I asked faintly.

"Clearly the house was searched," the detective said. "Maybe Tillman was looking for something he lost, but I find that unlikely. His prints were all over, as would be expected. Ditto his girlfriend's."

"Fiancée's," I corrected her.

"There were also plenty of blank prints. Latex gloves. And then there were these weird smudges everywhere. Maybe you could help?"

"Weird smudges?" I said slowly. "Weird like someone was wearing mittens or something when they searched the house?"

"Mittens," she said slowly. "In March?"

"Oven mittens," I suggested with a shrug. "It's just a thought."

A small sigh escaped from her lips.

"Not looking much like suicide, is it?" I asked.

She ignored me. "Senator Hawthorne!" she called out, dumping me to hurry to the side of a distinguished man with silver hair. Geeze, but I was feeling as low on the food chain as intestinal bacteria. Maybe I ought to go back to throwing myself on the laps of one-legged war veterans.

"Miss Jones," a cultivated voice called out. Across the stairs, old Mrs. Rollins was dodging other mourners and heading my way with her teacher's mouth set in a grim line. Her hair was swept up beneath a narrow-brimmed hat, and she was dressed in a dark-brown suit from another era. Her glasses glittered in the sun.

The old Mrs. Rollins was back in full force. "Come with me, Miss Jones," she ordered firmly. "There's someone you should meet."

It was impossible to do anything but meekly obey her. I followed her toward a waiting limousine. She opened the door and ordered me inside. "Get in," she snapped, "before some newshound sticks his camera in her face." She glared at a reporter hovering behind me, and the guy took a giant step back as if she was about to turn him into stone.

I slid inside quickly and found myself nose to nose with Peyton Tillman's fiancée. We blinked at each other and stared.

"Casey Jones," I said, extending my hand for a shake. "I'm terribly sorry for your loss." It was a classic southern expression of condolence. Even white trash like me learned the words early.

Her grip was understandably uninspired. "Sylvia Bennett," she said in a tired voice. "Peyton said he was meeting you the night he died."

I nodded. The poor woman looked drained of life. She was the color of over-cooked fettuccine and half as lively.

"I was hoping you could tell me what some of his last words might have been," she said.

I stared. "The police didn't tell you?" I asked.

She stirred uncomfortably, and a whiff of perfume floated toward me. "Tell me what?" she asked in an even smaller voice.

"I'm the one who found him," I explained. "He was dead when I got there."

She closed her eyes and I waited while she composed herself. "He would never have killed himself," she said flatly.

"I know," I agreed.

She was silent for a moment. "We were going to be married this June."

"I'm terribly sorry," I said again, meaning it.

She stared out the tinted window. "I have something for you," she whispered. "Mrs. Rollins says it's the only way."

"For me?" I asked, startled.

"I thought he was being paranoid," she began. Her voice faltered and tears streamed down her cheeks. I waited while she retrieved a handkerchief tucked in one sleeve and cried quietly into it for a moment. "He started keeping these files at my house about a month ago. I want you to have them. Mrs. Rollins says you're the only one we can trust, that I should give them to you."

"Files on what?" I asked, perplexed.

She shook her head. "I don't know. And I don't want to know. They're numbered instead of labeled. It might be some kind of code. But if they had anything to do with Peyton dying, I want them out of my house by tonight."

"I'll come by later," I promised. "Right after the graveside service."

She nodded dully. "Fine. I'm not going anywhere." She gave me her address, than lapsed back into silence. I took it as a sign that our conversation was over. I was going to tell her again how sorry I was, but I don't think she remembered I was still there.

When I climbed back out into the spring sunshine, the crowd had thinned. Mrs. Rollins was waiting for me at the curb, shading her eyes against the glare. "Thank you," I told her. "I won't let you down."

"Better not, young lady," she warned.

I have been to enough graveside ceremonies—two, in particular—to last me a lifetime. I skipped Peyton Tillman's. I wasn't the only one. The funeral procession that passed me as I stood on the sidewalk had shrunk considerably. It was heavy on land boats driven by silver-haired gents and battered wrecks manned by Vietnam vets. Nary a limo except for the lead one. The fat cats had headed back to work. Just as well, I thought, let him be buried by those who had loved him the most.

Peyton Tillman had left me files. Maybe not intentionally, but I was going to get them. I should, of course, immediately turn them over to Detective Morrow. And I would—after I read them through. In the meantime, I would finish reading the court transcripts while I waited for Peyton's fiancée to return home.

Ruby was busy ticketing a long black car with a low-numbered plate when I pulled up in front of my office. She gets a special kick out of nabbing politicos. It's her way of striking a blow for the freedom of the common man.

"Casey," she said, waving a greeting. "Got me a big fish this time. Look at that—a single-digit plate."

I patted her on the back. "You go, girl," I encouraged her.

"My sister Keisha is all ready to help you out," she said. "But it has to be on her lunch hour and weekends on account of her day care is stretched pretty thin."

"That's fine," I said. "But after what happened to Bobby, tell her to be careful if she's here alone late at night."

"What's she supposed to do?" Ruby asked.

"Shove papers back in whatever file she thinks is best. And keep her mouth shut about what she finds."

Ruby nodded. "You got the right woman. That girl don't talk about no one's business, not even her own."

I retrieved a spare key for Ruby to give to her sister, then returned to the office with my stash of files from the trunk. I had a couple of other cases pending behind Gail Honeycutt's, but all of them were incredibly boring and could wait: a farmer over by Fuquay wanted to know who kept joyriding his tractor at night; a woman in North Raleigh had gotten tired of her husband and wanted to divorce his ass—she was hoping I'd give her a good excuse in the form of some glossy eight by tens; and a neighborhood association in Cary had been whipped into a frenzy by rumors of a pet-napping ring heading its way. Did I care to stake out the subdivision's precious pooches and keep them from ending up being hooked to gizmos in laboratories from here to Atlanta? Normally, I did care. But not this month. Everyone else would still be around at the end of March. But not Gail. Not unless I moved faster than I had been.

I reviewed my notes and made a list of everything that bothered me about the night Roy Taylor was killed. It was a short list. One thing bothered me the most: there had been a potential witness in the house that night. Gail's child. Where was the child now?

A call to Nanny Honeycutt snagged me the information I needed: Brittany Honeycutt was living with one of Gail's cousins near Garner. She had been too young either to remember or to articulate any of the details about that night. Gail had not wanted her to testify. A court-appointed psychologist had agreed it would be too damaging, given how little the girl would have contributed.

Okay, a voice inside my head insisted, but now she's at least eight years older. What could it hurt? Nanny Honeycutt tussled with me a little over my plan—that family sure was protective about the little girl—but in the end she agreed to call the cousin and get her permission. I could see the child tomorrow, on Saturday, since she was not in school. I thanked her and hung up.

I called to check on Bobby D. and the nurse told me he was fine, it was the rest of the hospital that was in pain. It seems Bobby snored loud enough to shake the rafters on the new addition they were building next door. They had his nostrils pried as wide open as the Grand Canyon, but when he was napping, the beds of the other patients rattled as if an earthquake had hit. I thanked her for her colorful update and hung up. The phone rang immediately.

Bill Butler. Now that was a surprise.

"Why aren't you at the graveside service?" he asked.

"Why aren't you?" I said back.

"I asked first."

I sighed. Now we had deteriorated to the level of five year olds fighting over a Twinkie. "I hate graveside services. Don't ask."

"Okay," he agreed. "I'm back on the job. Lots of pressure. Attempted rape last night. The victim escaped with broken teeth. But half of Raleigh's in a panic."

"It wasn't me," I said. "I swear I'm innocent."

"I doubt that sincerely. But for this one, you're off the hook. You don't fit the description." He paused. I was getting mighty curious as to why he had called.

"Why did you call me if you thought I'd be at the service?" I finally asked when the silence stretched to an embarrassing length.

"I just wanted to know how the case was going," he said. "And I had a few minutes free."

"It's going just fine," I told him. "Except I'm being followed by some homicidal maniac."

"What makes you say that?" he asked quickly.

I wasn't about to tell him about the break-in or explain about my illegal gun or why I had failed to call the police. "I think someone's been following me whenever I drive somewhere," I said instead.

"That's easy to mistake when you're nervous," he said, sounding relieved.

"I'm not imagining it," I insisted.

"Maybe not," he conceded. It wasn't good enough for me. I was hoping my silence would intimidate him. It didn't. He gathered back some of the old Bill Butler strength. "Hey, how about a late dinner tonight?" he suggested. "We can talk and try to hammer out some sort of a working relationship here. Get back on track. I'm sorry about how I acted at the funeral. I was a little upset. Seems you might be right about Roy Taylor having been a dirty cop. I got a source over in Durham says it was true. It pisses me off when I'm wrong."

Now that was interesting. "Sounds good to me," I agreed. "Let's meet."

"Great," he said. "I'll call you or you call me about eleven. How's that sound?"

Before I had the wherewithal to realize that he had assumed I'd be free on a Friday night, Bill had hung up. Oh well, I never was good at that particular brand of game playing anyway.

But why had he really called? I'd bet my new black-lace bra that he wanted something from me other than dinner or sex. But what?

It was time to face facts. I had nothing to go on. I needed those files Peyton had left behind real bad. I decided to get to

Sylvia's house early and shanghai her as soon as she arrived. I packed my current case files back into the trunk's tire well and headed for Sylvia's. But it took me a good thirty minutes just to reach her home in a very expensive subdivision of North Raleigh. An inordinate number of oldsters crawling along at five miles an hour seemed to be clogging the roads. When I finally arrived at the address she'd given me, it looked like a huge party was in progress. Land boat after land boat hogged the curb, and a steady stream of elderly visitors flowed into the house.

I should have realized that southerners weren't going to forego an opportunity to eat. This was the post-funeral wake. Inside there'd be platters of turkey and ham biscuits, tea sandwiches, miniature quiches, pound cake out the wazoo, punch and god knows what other goodies. Before the day was out, someone would die of cholesterol overload, and the cycle would begin anew. What a dilemma for an antisocial paranoid like me. Should I brave the mourners for a plateful of munchies? On the plus side, this crowd was old and slow. I'd have an easy time hogging the pickin's. On the minus side, I'd be obligated to listen to a gazillion childhood stories about Peyton, and I'd end up more depressed than the first runner-up in a beauty contest. I decided to hunker down and wait for the crowd to thin. Then I'd go in.

An hour later, the crowd was still thick—and getting thicker on my share of the feast. My eyelids grew heavy in the warm incubator of the car and I dozed off. I woke when a rapping on the car window interrupted my dreams.

A young black woman wearing a rent-a-maid apron was standing politely in the street, waiting for me to get my ass in gear.

"Yes?" I asked, rolling down the window.

"Miss Bennett wants to know if you'd like a plate of food to eat while you're on stakeout, or if you'd prefer to remain undisturbed."

Well, damn. I guess the grieving fiancée was a lot more on the ball than I gave her credit for. "I'd like a boatload of food," I told the woman. "Heavy on the starches and meat. And maybe a ton of pound cake."

"Ice tea?" she asked politely. "Looks like you could use some caffeine to me."

I nodded my head in drowsy agreement. "And please tell Miss Bennett I send her my thanks."

"Would the gentleman like anything?" the girl asked, her eyes sliding further down the street.

"The gentleman?" I asked, turning around so I could get a better look.

"The man in the red car. Miss Bennett said he was probably with you. He's right there..." She pointed to a bend in the crowded road. "He was right there," she amended herself. "I guess he's gone."

"Just bring me his share," I suggested. "When he shows up again, I'll give it to him."

"Be right back with your boatload," she promised, though her sweet voice never wavered. She was a stealth smart-ass, it seemed.

She was as good as her word, but by the time she appeared with the food, I still hadn't figured out who the hell the man in the red car could be. An image of a crazed ex-bartender flickered through my mind. But how tacky to stalk me at someone's wake, for chrissakes. I wished Jack hadn't mentioned the fact that the fellow had a gun. I'd have given up the entire portion of chopped-pork barbecue heaped before me for the clean feel of my Astra in my hand.

Since my options were few, I got my revenge by eating the mysterious stranger's food right after I polished off mine. Two plates of food and two glasses of iced tea later, I felt like a hog the night before first frost and had to piss like a race-horse. Fortunately, the wake showed signs of slowing down. Mourners had started to filter out the front door and totter toward their cars. As their cars pulled away, one by one, they crept forward at a whopping three miles an hour. It could take days just to clear the street. Finally, everyone was gone except for two catering vans parked in the concrete driveway. It was time to go inside.

"I'm sorry but Miss Bennett is sleeping," the same maid told me after I emerged from my desperate dash to the bathroom. "She just got to sleep a few minutes ago."

I didn't have the heart to wake her. I'd waited a good three hours. I'd just have to wait a little bit longer. Maybe I'd take the opportunity for a little more shut-eye myself.

If I could have afforded a maid, I'd have snapped up Sylvia Bennett's in a heartbeat. "Would you care to relax in the den?" she asked. "Miss Bennett seemed anxious to see you. I'm sure she wouldn't mind."

I sank into an immaculate white couch and was soon breast-deep in pillows. I removed my high heels and groaned in ecstasy. My doggies were barking up a storm. Without asking, the maid brought me a beer—god bless her well- trained heart—and I spent a few hours sipping imported brew and channel surfing old movies on a fifty-two-inch color television. I felt like an upper-crust coach potato. So this was how the other half lived.

It was dark and the evening news was long over by the time Sylvia Bennett reappeared. She was wearing a green velour sweat suit and her eyes were bleary with sleep and dried tears. She shuffled into the den and slumped down on the couch next to me, staring at what was on the television screen: *An Affair To Remember*. I switched it off.

"You okay?" I asked.

She stared at my beer. "That looks good."

"I'm sure your maid would bring you one. Personally, I think she should be nominated for the Nobel Peace Prize."

The comment almost earned a smile. "She is a good person," Sylvia agreed. "One of Peyton's cases from when he was a judge. He put her on probation when she was seventeen and ordered her into drug rehab and a remedial high-school diploma program instead of jail," she explained. "When she came out, she needed a job and a place to live so she could stay away from her old 'friends.' I needed someone to help me with this house."

"It is a big house for one person," I said.

She shrugged. "My grandmother died six years ago and left me more money than I know what to do with. But I hate this house. It makes me even more lonely than I already am. I was planning to sell it and move in with Peyton."

We were both quiet then, our silence interrupted only when the maid entered the room with another cold beer for me on a tray. She had brought a cup of hot tea for Sylvia.

Sylvia didn't argue. She sipped and watched the maid move quietly from the room. "Have you noticed that the only person taking care of me right now was a complete stranger a year ago?" she asked. "And that I have to pay for the privilege?"

"She seems pretty devoted to you," I said. "Who cares how long you've known her?"

Sylvia stared at her hands. They were immaculately manicured, unlike my own chipped mess. I had to fight the urge to hide them behind my back.

"Is there anything I can do for you?" I asked politely, though I was itching to grab the files and run.

"Yes. You can get those files out of my house. They're in the study." She rose slowly, as if she were decades older than she was, and I followed her down a long hall to the far side of the house. She talked as she led the way. "The police don't know much," she said. "They don't seem to think it's suicide. They wanted to know what I thought of you. I told them I'd never met you in my life." She smiled at me grimly. "Too bad we had to meet under these circumstances, huh?" She was parodying the comment she must have heard a hundred times earlier that day.

"What else did the police say?" I asked. "If you feel comfortable telling me."

"They wanted to know if Peyton had received any threats recently. If he'd seemed unusually bothered. If his finances were healthy. That sort of thing."

"What did you tell them?" We reached the door of a locked room, and I waited while she unearthed a key from the base of a nearby wall shelf.

"I told them that no one had threatened Peyton to my knowledge, that he was upset about the Taylor execution next month and that he had more money than he knew what to do with."

She threw open the door and we entered a perfect replica of a nineteenth-century study, complete with Oriental rug, expensive mahogany furniture and original Currier & Ives on the walls. "You're a decorator?" I asked.

She shrugged. "Not going to change the world much, is it?" She walked over to an antique rolltop desk and fumbled for the upper catch. "I'm not giving the files to the police," she said. "They don't even know I have them."

"Why not?" I asked as she searched through the slots of the desk.

"When I figured out that Peyton was having some problems," she explained, "I suggested he go to the police. He said he couldn't. That they were part of the problem."

"Part of the problem?" I repeated. "He said 'they.' As in plural? Was he talking about the Roy Taylor case?"

She frowned, then opened the side drawers and continued to search. "I don't know what he was talking about," she finally answered. "I just know it was more than one folder. There were about nine or ten in all, labeled with numbers that were maybe ten digits or more long. There might have been dashes, too. I can't remember. I asked Peyton what they were all about, but he said it was nothing. Just some old questions that needed asking about a matter that might help Gail Honeycutt. He said it all happened before he ever met me. He said something like, 'I can't believe it was right there in front of my eyes and I didn't put it together.' He wouldn't tell me more than that. He said it was safer if I didn't know."

Suddenly, her shoulders sagged. She pulled out the straight-back chair that matched the desk and slumped down in it, putting her head down on the green-felt blotter. In a moment I heard her sobs. This was it. The woman had lost her shit. "They're not here," she said between sniffles. "And you know what? I can't deal with any of this." She began to cry harder.

I did what any sensible, caring person would have done under the circumstances: I left to find the maid.

She was wiping down a counter in the kitchen. "She's in trouble," I said and the girl immediately understood. "Did the doctor give her anything?"

She nodded and retrieved a prescription pill bottle from a hiding spot behind a six-pack of cola stored on top of the refrigerator. "I keep them hidden," she explained. "I'm sure you can understand why."

"She's in the study," I said. I followed the maid as she came to her employer's rescue, watching discreetly from across the room as she coaxed Sylvia into swallowing two pills. She wet a washcloth and wiped Sylvia's face tenderly. I felt like a nosy child peeking through the keyhole of her parents' bedroom.

"I don't want to go back to bed," Sylvia whimpered as her maid took her hand and led her from the room.

"Don't have to," the maid promised in a soothing voice, leading her back into the quiet comfort of the den. She helped Sylvia lie down on the overstuffed sofa, then arranged huge pillows around her head and on both sides of her body. She drew a throw blanket up under Sylvia's chin, then dimmed the lights. "Don't sleep," she told her. "Just lie there and rest. I'll take care of Miss Jones."

By the time we reached the kitchen, I figured poor Sylvia was back in dreamland.

"Good thing you're here," I observed.

She shrugged. "I'm no stranger to lousy breaks. We'll help each other."

"Was the study kept locked during the wake?" I asked, once we were well out of earshot.

She nodded. "Something missing?" she asked.

"Something important," I told her. "Papers. Some file folders. Stuff like that."

She considered the problem. "Someone could have come in through the window. Or found the key on the shelf. It's not a great hiding place."

"Anyone peculiar at the wake?" I asked.

"They were all peculiar," she answered.

117

"Were you here the whole time the funeral service was going on?"

"Sure." She nodded. "Never leave a house empty during a funeral. That's the time when someone is most likely to break in. I ought to know."

"And you didn't notice anyone strange hanging around? Or hear any unusual sounds?"

She shook her head, pulled out a kitchen chair, sat down and began to sip what was left of a beer she had been drinking. "Are we going to call the police?" she asked.

"No."

"I've got a record," she said, after a pause.

"I know. Sylvia told me. I'm not accusing you at all."

She was silent for a moment. "I wish I could help you," she said. "Especially if it would help out Miss Bennett. But anyone who knew what they were doing could have taken those papers at just about any time today and I would have no way of knowing." She glanced at me. "The man in the red car?" she suggested.

She was smart. I was surprised she'd ever been caught. Ten to one, her boyfriend had made the mistake. "What did he look like?" I asked, dropping any pretense that I knew who he was.

She shrugged. "White with sunglasses and dark hair. Had all his hair. That's all I saw."

"Not much."

"Not much," she agreed.

I stared out the window above the kitchen sink. Clouds had rolled in with the night. It was very dark outside. "Know anyone who could come stay here?" I asked. "Keep an eye out for you and Sylvia?"

My voice gave me away. The maid paused with the beer bottle lifted halfway to her lips. She locked her eyes on mine. "Someone big?" she asked.

I nodded. "Preferably a member of the Worldwide Wrestling Federation."

She thought for a moment. "I know someone."

"Good. Tell him to bring his brother along, too."

She nodded grimly, and I turned to go. There was nothing left for me here. "Take good care of her," I said.

"You know I will," she promised, unlocking the back door with a key she kept in her front apron pocket. At least she was careful. Sylvia would be okay until reinforcements arrived.

It was late enough on a Friday night for dinner traffic to have cleared, but the bars had not yet let out for the evening. I was the only car for long stretches of Creedmore Road, a winding artery that connects part of North Raleigh with the rest of town. The surrounding neighborhoods were set back from the road behind protective rows of heavy pine forest. Intermittent strip shopping centers provided the only signs of civilization.

Within minutes, the quieting effect of Sylvia Bennett's grief wore off and I started getting pissed about the theft of the files. Not even the thought of a late dinner with Bill Butler could cheer me. If someone had bothered to steal them from under the noses of dozens of potential witnesses, those files were important indeed. I was damned if I would let some creep stop me from discovering their significance, even if he was talented at breaking and entering.

I drove toward my office, puzzling out the possibilities raised by Sylvia's sketchy description of the files: longer sequences of figures, maybe with dashes in between. Prison numbers, perhaps? Or some sort of code to represent the names of people who knew more than they were telling about Roy Taylor's police activities? What I needed was a secret decoder ring—or maybe just a more straightforward approach. It was possible that Peyton Tillman had simply been engaging in old-fashioned legal research, digging up old court cases and hoping to uncover a judicial basis for overturning Gail's death sentence.

No, none of those theories fit with the little he had told me. He said he had "proof," and that he was looking for more. Plus, Sylvia said that he believed the police were part of the problem.

As quickly as the answer came to me, it was gone—jolted out of my consciousness by a sudden bump from behind that rudely pushed my car forward, sending me momentarily out of control. I looked in the rearview mirror, and, without warning, where there had been darkness, the high beams of a pick-up truck glared, threatening to blind me. The blazing lights drew closer, right on my tail, predator seeking its prey with terrifying concentration. The truck sped up and knocked my rear bumper once more, nudging me to the left of the road toward a muddy shoulder. I swore and gripped the steering wheel tightly, accelerating for the extra control it gave me.

The Valiant took off, and I inched away from the truck just as I rounded a bend and headed up a hill. No good. The truck had more power than my souped-up Plymouth could handle. It caught up with me halfway up the hill and jammed my rear once again. This time, the Valiant fishtailed and I felt the tires slipping. I turned with the skid, momentarily regained control and swerved toward the center of the road.

The truck's engine roared and it closed the gap between us, ramming the rear side panel of my Valiant and sending me spinning closer to the far side of the road. If another car appeared heading the other way at the top of the curve, I would be facing a head-on collision.

Adrenaline surged through my body, directing feet and hands without conscious thought. I steered wildly, first left and then right, desperately seeking a purchase on the smooth road. Just as I thought I was safe, a sharp crack split the air, and I felt something whiz by my right cheek. The front windshield exploded in a spider web pattern, and I realized that the driver behind me had opened fire. I ducked low as another crack exploded within the close confines of the car. It was too much. Without front sight, I was doomed.

The truck engine roared in my ears as the driver poured on the power and rammed me full force from the side. Time slowed and my car spun slowly in circles, centrifugal force clutching at my gut. I thought inanely of the spider ride at the state fair. I was conscious of two full spins, and then my head whipped to one side, hitting the side window.

After that, another cracking sound and darkness.

CHAPTER EIGHT

I woke the next morning in a hospital room with Bobby D. leering over me. Talk about your nightmares. I thought for a moment I was in restraints. Then I realized that he was simply leaning on the top sheet.

"You look like shit," he said cheerfully. "Want a mirror?"

"What are you doing loose?" I replied. "Siphoning out blood supplies? Aren't you supposed to be at death's doorstep?"

"Me?" He settled back in his wheelchair and popped a few wheelies to prove his friskiness. He was wearing a hospital gown, or at least trying to. It covered maybe ten percent of his bulk, and his legs poked out from beneath the green cotton like giant pink tree trunks with hair. "The nurses don't care where I go," he boasted, "so long as I report for my medication."

I bet they didn't care where he went. In fact, I bet they were itching to tell him where he could go.

"This case sucks," I told Bobby, feeling a crusty bump on my upper lip with my tongue. It hurt to talk. "I'm starting to feel like the Roadrunner. There's always someone after me."

"This time they got you," he said, wheeling closer for a better look. "You have a couple of stitches in your upper lip and two black eyes. The left one is just a little mouse, but the right one's gonna be a real shiner. Want me to take a look at the rest of your body?"

"No thanks. I gave at the office." I pulled the sheet up under my chin and felt a sharp ache in one arm. "Someone ran me off the road. On purpose. Hand me my chart, will ya?"

Bobby expertly wheeled to the foot of the bed and tossed a clipboard my way. If they'd known I was awake, the nurses would never have left it within snooping distance. I read the report eagerly. What could possibly be as interesting as one's own injuries? After translating all the goobledy-gook, I figured out that nothing major had been broken, pierced or replaced. But they wanted to keep me forty-eight hours for observation, even in these cost-sensitive times.

"They're not keeping me forty-eight hours," I said. "No way in hell."

"They're worried about head injuries," Bobby explained with the irritatingly superior air of someone who presumes to be an expert on medical affairs. "I tried to tell them that your head was too hard to crack, but they wouldn't listen."

"I've got to get out of here."

"Good idea," Bobby agreed. "The food here is terrible. No salt, no seasonings, no taste, no—"

"Will you stop already about the hospital food? Jesus, don't you ever think about anything else?"

"The nurses," he admitted honestly.

"Dream on." But the mention of Bobby's libido reminded me. My dinner date with Bill Butler had been blown. Remembering that tidbit brought back other memories. The minutes leading up to the wreck were fuzzy, but the information Sylvia had given me on the stolen files returned in a rush. And with it, the conclusion I had reached. "Don't you have a contact in the court system?" I asked Bobby. "A court reporter or something?"

"Babe, this is Wake County. I got me a contact on every corner. In this case, she's small and soft and fluffy. Like a kitten." He meowed enthusiastically, then broke into an extraordinarily horny sampling of *What's New Pussycat?*

"I get the idea," I interrupted loudly. Geeze, Tom Jones singing it had been bad enough, but Bobby D. was worse. He sounded like Burl Ives on acid.

He took the hint. "Tell Bobby what you need and it's yours," he promised.

I explained about the sequence of numbers on Peyton Tillman's stolen file folders. "Sounds like court cases," he said when I was done.

"I thought so, too. But I don't know where to begin."

"That's where Big Daddy can help." He wheeled his huge bulk around the curtain that shielded my bed from the rest of the room, then pulled it back with a flourish. There, a scant ten yards to my right, another human being in pain was revealed. At least I think it was a human being. It might have been an exhibit for the Museum of History. Whatever the creature was, it was bound from head to foot in a bodysuit of bandages. One leg was cradled in an aerial sling, and both arms were set at right angles in plaster casts. Only small openings for the eyes and nose, plus a slit for the mouth, gave evidence that the thing could breathe.

"My god, I'm rooming with Christopher Lee in *The Mummy*," I said. "Get his autograph."

An angry movement beneath my roommate's sheets proved that she was alive and could hear—and had no sense of humor.

"She fell off a scaffolding," Bobby explained. "I don't think she likes the food here, either." He wheeled over to the side of her bed and commandeered her telephone. When an angry howl issued from beneath the bandages, he stared at her in reproach. "You're not going to be using it," he admonished her. "And this is official business."

Poor woman. First she broke every bone in her body, and now Bobby was busting her balls.

I listened in admiration as he dialed a number—from memory, no less—and oozed charm all over the receiver. He knew all the right questions to ask and exactly what I wanted. It took him less than a minute to get to the point. When he hung up, he was beaming in self-satisfaction.

"You're amazing," I told him and meant it. Without Bobby D. and his fingers in every slice of the system, this take-no-prisoners and make-no-friends girl would have been lost long ago.

He preened and patted his belly. "I asked her to pull every case involving Peyton Tillman when he was a judge and to cross-check for Roy Taylor's name or any other Durham police officer."

"Are we likely to find that in Wake County?" I asked anxiously.

Bobby nodded. He knew the score. "Yep. Unless the officer was involved solely as a witness, it would have to be in Wake County. If a case involves a police officer as a defendant or victim, it gets transferred from Durham County to Wake to avoid conflicts of interest."

I tried not to look impressed. It's easy to forget that, beneath Bobby's bad toupee, there lurks a pretty damned-good brain. "When can she have the information ready?" I asked.

"She's going in tomorrow morning while the coast is clear. Expenses are on you, right? She's gonna have to miss church. It's a disappointment."

No doubt. With Bobby in her life, she probably had an awful lot of repenting to do. But I nodded eagerly. Expenses were no problem. Nanny Honeycutt could easily afford to pay a few hundred and to bankroll an intimate candlelit dinner for the two of them when this was all over, even if one of the diners was Bobby D.

"Thanks, babe," Bobby told the outraged mummy as he cradled her phone. He patted her bed-bound foot for emphasis, and a groan escaped through the mouth slit. "She's trying to say, 'You're welcome,'" he translated confidently.

"I don't think so," I told him, eyeing her angry foot movements. "I sure hope those restraints hold."

Bobby let out a giant yawn, looking as satisfied and sleepy as a lion after a wildebeest feast. "I'm gonna go catch me some shut-eye," he declared. "All this detecting has left me exhausted."

"Thanks for the help," I told him. "Come back soon. We'll do lunch."

I shouldn't have reminded him of food. He was off, wheeling out the door and complaining about the hospital meals yet again.

I ignored my roommate's angry hisses, and shut my eyes to think. There was no way in hell I was going to waste two days lying here next to Queen Tut while someone drove around Raleigh running innocent people off the road and gloating about Gail's upcoming execution. Nor was I anxious to lie in wait for the Raleigh Police Department to show up to question me. I gave it a good twenty minutes, and then I crept from my bed, disconnecting the IV drip after checking to make sure I wasn't wasting a good supply of painkillers. It was only an antibiotic, and I was willing to take that chance. The front of my dress was caked with dried blood, but at least all my clothes were present and accounted for in the bottom of my closet. I gathered them in a bundle and tiptoed from the room.

The hospital was filled with visitors of all ages since it was a weekend. No one gave a crap about the woman with two black eyes whose arse hung out the back of her hospital gown. I rode the elevator down two floors to Bobby's wing. I could hear his snores as soon as I turned the corner. God, but I pitied his hall mates. I slipped into his room unnoticed and crept to the narrow closet that held his personal belongings. His key ring was in one pocket of his pants. It had enough keys on it to make the janitor of an apartment complex proud. I could identify his car and house keys, but what the hell did the rest of them open? Lord, I did not want to know. I stole the key ring, along with a pack of breath mints. He never missed a beat of sleep.

I changed in his bathroom. Looking in the mirror was a mistake. I looked like Rocky Raccoon on a very bad day. My right eye was a blotched mess of purple, blue and black bruises that overlapped like running watercolors. The left eye had a mouse the size of a football-chalk smudge beneath it, and there was an attractive streak of red running through the cornea. My lips were swollen, and there were rings of caked blood around each nostril. Very attractive, for a crust.

I cleaned up as best I could, then prayed that my industrial-strength foundation would come through once I reached home. By the time I left Bobby's room, he was still asleep, and, although I barely resembled a human, at least I was wearing human clothes instead of a gown that had a window for a back door.

I had a few close encounters with hospital personnel in the corridors on the way down to civilization and even had to hide briefly in the elevator behind a family of hearty eaters when a doctor I recognized got on at one floor. But no one stopped me, and I was able to stash myself behind a large potted palm in the waiting room while I muttered impatiently for a good half hour until the cab I had called arrived at the visitors' entrance. Soon enough I was on my way to new wheels and more legwork.

Back in the office, I sat in the silence of what had been our happy, noisy home away from home and waited for the office phone messages to rewind. Someone would pay for disrupting our lives, I decided. This case had turned personal a long time ago.

There were two messages for me. The first was from Bill Butler, left just past midnight the night before, according to the time stamp. He didn't sound happy.

"I thought we were supposed to have dinner tonight," he said. "It's not like you to play these stupid games, and I don't appreciate it." He hung up without saying good-bye.

It was too bad he had his jockstrap in a wringer about it, but I had bigger things to worry about. The next message was from Dolly Porter, Gail's prison chum. She talked nervously, her hillbilly twang trampling all over itself in her haste. "I can't talk long," she said. "I got in trouble for smoking after lights out and I ain't supposed to be on the phone at all. I talked to Gail through the window last night. The men who visited her were police officers who worked with her husband. One was named George Washington something, he was easy to remember, and the other two were Pete and Steve. Gail's confused about their last names and she was talking funny. I think she's really doped up. She don't sound too good. Please help her. Please." She hung up, leaving nothing but a flat dial tone.

It was better than nothing. Now I had a few names to go on. I remembered a George Washington Carter from the court transcripts. He had testified about Roy Taylor's final hours. The other names were less familiar. But if a Pete or a Steve popped up in any Peyton Tillman court case, maybe I'd have a lead. In the meantime, I needed a change of clothes and, hopefully, a change of face. Not to mention a little painkiller for my wrenched shoulder and sore kneecaps. I was scheduled to interview Gail's little girl that afternoon, and I didn't want to scare the kid any more than I had to.

Bobby D.'s 1978 Olds Cutlass was big by necessity—I don't think he could fit in any other car—and its huge body made me feel as if I were maneuvering the Titanic through the streets of Durham. This was a car for cruising the moonlit streets of Tijuana. It was not a car I'd care to have anyone I knew see me occupy. Which was why I was driving so fast.

Despite its size, that car could rock: Bobby had chosen the deluxe five-speed manual transmission model with a 350- cubic-inch engine and a four-barrel carburetor. I made it home quickly, showered and changed in record time, slapped on enough pancake makeup to make Lon Chaney jealous, then high-tailed it back to Garner for my afternoon appointment with Brittany Taylor.

The child was everything I had never been: a country princess, slim and pretty, with strawberry blond hair falling in curls to her shoulders. She was wearing a matching denim skirt and rhinestone-studded vest with real leather cowboy boots and playing in the front yard of the small farm she called home when I pulled up in Bobby's car. I saw movement in one window and a curtain flickered, but no one else appeared to greet me.

She watched me with a wary expression as I approached. I had a feeling she could see right through the layers of Ben Nye theatrical foundation to the bruises and scratches underneath. "You're the lady Nanny Honeycutt told me about," she said. She was peeking into a large cardboard box. Tiny mews floated across the yard in the spring breeze, and I inched closer for a better look. A mother cat sprawled lazily on her side, while eight kittens nursed noisily at her nipples. They sounded like a washing machine. "Don't touch them," the girl warned me. "They're only a few days old."

I kept a respectful distance from the furry little critters as requested, though I longed to cuddle one or two. Even a hard-boiled cynic like me finds it impossible to resist a bright-eyed kitten on a spring day.

Brittany seemed extremely innocent for her age. Most eleven-year-old girls around these parts—even in rural Garner—were far more sophisticated. They cruised the local shopping mall, wore blue eye shadow and picked up Fort Bragg servicemen in cyberspace. Damn few were cuddling fuzzy kittens while wearing a matching cowgirl outfit. Brittany was too clean as well, I thought, not a hair out of place, not a dab of mud on her outfit, not a blemish on her pretty heart-shaped face. Her hands and fingernails were immaculate, and she lived on a farm? I wasn't sure if that was a good sign or a bad sign. I preferred a genuinely sullen pre-teen over a Stepford kid any day.

"Did Nanny Honeycutt tell you why I was coming here today?" I asked.

"You want to ask me about the night my mom shot my dad," she said rather matter-of-factly.

"That's right. I guess you've talked to a lot of people about it over the years."

"Just doctors," she explained. "And a judge one time. He was nice. I liked him. He had a sad face. He said he was sorry about what had happened to my dad. He promised he wouldn't make me talk in front of a roomful of strangers. He even let me use his copy machine for fun."

I felt a pang when I realized she meant Peyton Tillman. I didn't tell her he was dead. "I know that judge," I said. "He's a very nice man. I'll probably ask you a lot of the same questions he did. Is that okay?"

She sighed, as if I were boring her. "I guess so," she said. "Are you a judge?"

"No, I'm a private detective," I said. "I'm trying to help your mom."

"My mom's in prison," the child explained calmly. "People don't think I know about it. I pretend like I don't know because it upsets them. And I don't want the kids at school to know."

"That's right," I said. "Your mother is in prison."

"Have you seen her?" she asked.

"I visited her last week."

"Why can't I go to see her?" the child asked. "I would be good."

"Your mother is afraid that seeing her will upset you," I explained. "She says that prison is no place for a little girl."

Brittany considered this in silence, then shook her head. "I don't care," she said. "I still want to see my mother."

"Okay," I said. "I can understand that. I'll talk to her next time I see her."

She relaxed at my promise. "What did you want to ask me?" she said.

"Do you remember that night?" I asked. "I mean from personal experience, not from what other people said?"

She shrugged. "I guess I remember some things. I was only three."

"What do you remember most?" I asked, searching her face for clues.

"The noise," she said promptly, but her voice faltered as if a hidden fear had crept unexpectedly into the sunny afternoon. "I woke up because there was a big boom and I was afraid to get out of bed. I sat up and waited. I kept thinking my mom or dad would come in. Then I heard two more booms right after that."

She had heard the gunshots. One or two to wake her, two more right after she'd sat up in bed. "What happened then?" I prompted her.

Her unnatural composure began to crumble. Her lower lip trembled. "I waited a long time, and no one came," she said. "Then there were two more big booms. I hid my head under the pillow and I wet the bed. It got cold, but I was afraid to move. I was crying for a long time and then the lights in my room came on. Some men in white wanted to know if I was okay. Policemen were there, too. They carried me out a back door and I could hear my mom crying inside the house, and no one would tell me why."

I sat quietly for a moment, thinking of what she had said. It wasn't an experience anyone was likely to forget. "When you were lying in bed," I asked slowly, "and you had the pillows over your head, did you hear anything else besides more booms? Anyone talking? Footsteps? Or even a car?"

She shook her head solemnly. "Just the roaring and lots of light."

"A roaring?" I asked. "Like a lion roars or like a train roars?"

"Like in that movie about the aliens," she explained. "When the spaceship gets near and there are lots of bright lights and the air gets full of roars."

"Did you tell the doctors that?" I asked.

She nodded, her eyes growing wider. "They asked me if I heard the roaring inside of my head or outside of my head."

"What did you tell them?" God, but shrinks could be goofy.

"Nothing." She shrugged. "The question didn't make any sense."

"Can you tell me anything else?" I asked.

"I wish I could remember more," she said. "But I was really little and really scared. I'm not that little or scared anymore."

"You seem very brave to me," I told her. I smiled at her and she smiled back, a slow upward turning of her mouth.

"Maybe you could hypnotize me?" she suggested. "Like they do on TV?"

"Maybe I should," I agreed. But I left it at that. She remembered as much as she could bear to remember. I wouldn't try to force more on her.

She walked me out to my car, her face a blank mask I could not read. "You'll ask my mom if I can come visit?" she said when we reached the car.

"I'll see what I can do," I answered. "But that's all I can promise. I don't want you to get your hopes up, okay?"

She nodded. I climbed inside the Cutlass and drove back to Durham, wondering if I had gained anything useful from the interview. Too bad I had even minimal ethics. A good hypnotist might be able to help the child remember more. That was when I almost steered the Cutlass into a tobacco barn in my excitement. Out of the mouths of babes indeed. Forget hypnotizing the daughter. It was her mother's memory that could use jogging the most. So why not try it?

I wasn't sure if it would help, and, certainly, it smacked of desperation. But I did know that I had to do something to move things along more quickly. And that I needed some new leads if I hoped to get anywhere.

Besides, I knew where I could find someone who might be willing to give my plan a try.

CHAPTER NINE

By the time I returned to Raleigh, gray clouds had rolled in to darken the afternoon. The old Victorian house that served as Peyton Tillman's office looked even more unkempt in the early dusk. Lights gleamed in the office across the hall from Peyton's, illuminating the shared space just enough to spotlight a funeral wreath that someone had left on the door. Bouquets of flowers had been placed on the stone steps leading up to the house. I wondered if anyone would do the same for me when I died. I doubted it. My clients typically wanted to forget they had ever known me. But that was okay, I wanted to forget most of them in return.

According to the sign, the office opposite Peyton's offered its patients massage therapy, acupuncture and hypnotherapy. Presumably not all at the same time—though I'm sure that someone somewhere would have paid for that privilege. New Age philosophies had followed the influx of northern settlers to Raleigh, along with bagel shops and sixty-dollar hockey tickets. I remained a skeptic, but then I don't trust medical doctors, either. I knocked on the door anyway.

It took a few minutes for someone to answer, and, when I got a good look at his sleepy expression, I suspected I'd caught him napping. He was very tall and dressed in a torn lavender T-shirt. A pair of jeans drooped around his bony hips. No shoes. Long brown hair scraggled to below his collarbone, and his pointed chin could have used a beard, except that then he would have looked just like Jesus—and have had to endure everyone telling him so.

"Yes?" he said pleasantly. "Can I help you?" He looked me over. "I'm not sure I'll be able to help with injuries like that." His voice was a warm baritone.

"I'm not here for treatment," I explained. "I'm a private detective looking into Peyton Tillman's death."

He motioned me inside. "His dying is about the worst thing that's happened since I moved here from Seattle. Why are you investigating? You don't think he killed himself?"

"No," I said. "I don't."

He gestured toward a lumpy red couch and I sat down gratefully, aware of every sore ligament in my body. The hospital painkillers had worn off and I was fresh out of the illegal kind. A faintly smoky smell permeated the air and I sniffed, trying to place the aroma.

"Sage sticks," he explained. "American Indians use them to clear a space of evil spirits. I'm trying to cleanse the house of the sorrow that Peyton's death has brought. I could feel it in the air this morning when I came to work." He wiggled his hands through the air like one of those goofy modern dancers. "Premature death robs the universe of energy. Violent death tears at its fabric."

"So you don't think it was suicide either?" I asked wryly.

"I know it wasn't," he answered, folding his frame into a bright-yellow beanbag chair. "I told the cops the same thing when they asked me about his state of mind. They were here, you know. The cops. A patrol car arrived the night he died. I think to guard the office. They stayed all night and the next morning tons of cops were here going through his papers. His old secretary Mrs. Rollins showed up to glare. She gave them an earful about catching his killer. She's not buying suicide, either."

I had to give Detective Morrow credit for sending a car over so promptly to seal the office. A lot of detectives would have missed that. I needed to treat that woman with respect—or she'd fry my butt.

"You live here, too?" I asked, glancing around the cluttered room.

He looked embarrassed. "Right now I do. My girlfriend and I broke up and she got the apartment. I haven't found a new place yet."

"Oh. Sorry." Lord, but love made people stupid. Everyone knows that the first rule of thumb when living together is: make sure it's your name on the lease.

"How well did you know Peyton Tillman?" I asked.

"He was a regular patient of mine," the therapist explained. "I swapped him for legal work. I think he was really just doing me a favor. We talked a lot during our sessions. He'd been relatively happy lately. His life was in balance. He enjoyed his work and loved the woman he was going to marry." He pulled one long leg back against his chest, stretching the muscles while he spoke. "That's why I told the police: no way Peyton killed himself."

"What were you treating him for?" I asked.

"Peyton came to me for acupuncture, mainly. He had back problems." The man paused, as if hesitant to break the confidence of a dead man. "If you'd ever seen his back, you'd know why. It looked like a road map of welts and scars. I don't know exactly what happened to him in the war, but I do know that he was frequently in pain. And that he seemed to think my treatments helped."

"You can help with pain?" I asked, acutely aware that my entire body felt as if I'd been pureed in a blender.

"Certain kinds," he explained. "Peyton's pain was nerve-related. Yours might be another matter."

He unfolded himself from the chair and ran his fingers over my bruised face, then carefully touched my arm and calf muscles. "Tell me where it hurts," he commanded. After a few seconds of being assured that it ached like a son of a bitch everywhere, he stopped. "We may as well give acupuncture a try," he said. "You can't hurt any more than you already do."

"Okay." I was game. "But that's not really why I'm here. The sign on your door says you also do hypnotherapy."

"That's right. I trained in Portland. Some people think it's helpful when they want to stop smoking or lose weight. It works," he said, reading the skepticism on my face.

"Can you hypnotize someone on tranquilizers?" I asked. "And bring back repressed memories?"

"Depends on the person," he explained. "Sometimes tranquilizers make them more susceptible. Sometimes less." He stared at me. "Does this have anything to do with Peyton's death?"

"Maybe." I explained what I wanted and he listened intently, occasionally asking questions about Gail and the night Roy Taylor had been killed.

"It could be detrimental to the subject," he said when I was done. "In general, people only remember what they can bear to remember. In her case, being incarcerated and heavily sedated, I'm wary that her defenses are down. I'm not trained to deal with any trauma that might arise. I'd only agree to do it if you let me make the call as to when we should stop."

I thought about it. How many other hypnotherapists could I dredge up in Raleigh on a Saturday night? None, if you didn't count the audiences being put to sleep over at Theater in the Park.

"Deal," I said. "I want to go tomorrow when the prison is crowded with Sunday visitors and lots of families. You're going to be Gail's cousin."

"You think?" he said, raising an eyebrow. That was when I noticed he had a row of five small gold hoops running up and down his right ear. Those I could tolerate. I had a part-time naval ring myself. It's the eyebrow hoops that get to me. I always feel an irresistible urge to rip those little suckers right off.

"She has a trillion cousins," I explained. "Gail will probably believe you're a cousin herself."

"Peyton was a good guy," the therapist said after a moment of silent consideration. "I know he regretted that he had been the judge on that case. For a while there, I even thought that maybe his pain had something to do with his guilt."

"So you'll do it?" I asked. "If I can set it up?"

He shrugged again. "Why not?"

"Thanks," I told him. "I think Peyton would have approved."

I called Nanny Honeycutt and set up the next day's visit. She was skeptical, but I was persuasive. She even promised to do her best to get Gail to skip that morning's medication. I didn't want her melting to the visiting-room floor in the middle of our session.

"What's your name?" my new friend asked me after I was done.

"Casey Jones. What's yours?"

"Robert." His face brightened. "Hey, Casey?" he suggested. "How about some ginseng tea and a session with the old needles? It gets pretty quiet around here on a Saturday afternoon. No charge for the service."

Twenty minutes later, my ears, lower back, butt and calf muscles were studded with thin needles. I felt like a blissed-out porcupine. The world seemed to hum around me. God bless Robert, I thought drowsily, as I drifted off to Lala Land. Around me, the smell of sage wafted through the air. If this kept up, I might even consider wearing tie-dyed shirts. But never patchouli.

When I woke, it was dark and Robert was curled up in the beanbag chair, reading a book and sipping a cup of tea with the kind of maddening calm I can never seem to attain.

"What happened?" I asked groggily. "Where was I?"

"I'd say about two or three planes out of your body," he said with a satisfied smile. "How are you feeling?"

I flexed a few muscles and was amazed. "Damn," I said. "You're good."

"Think you can drive home?" he asked as he carefully removed the needles, twirling them between his fingers before plucking them from my skin with a delicate tug.

"If not, I'll just fly," I decided.

"So long as you come back for me tomorrow," he said. "I was meditating about things while you slept. I think the universe is giving me a way to help offset the evil of Peyton's death. I think it's asking me to be an instrument of karmic justice."

An instrument of karmic justice? And all these years I thought I had just been kicking ass. But I was willing to look at it in a different way if that's what the heavens wanted. Casey Jones, karmic avenger. It had a nice ring to it.

I drove home to Durham, sore, but at peace. Tomorrow was indeed another day. That night, I was in bed by nine. It had been a long time since I'd spent a Saturday night alone. At least a week, I'd say. But I slept contentedly through the wee, wee hours with a single purpose—to heal my body for what lay ahead.

The next morning, I tried calling Bobby D. at the hospital to find out if his court reporter contact had made any headway. No one answered. He was no doubt having a personal chat with the kitchen staff. Disappointed, I hung up the telephone. It rang almost immediately.

"What the hell happened to you on Friday night?" a female voice demanded.

"Who the hell is this?" I replied.

"Anne Morrow. I assume you remember me?"

Of course I remembered her. Long and lean and cool and lovely. The girl from Ipanema goes stalking.

"How are you?" I asked in my most civilized tone.

"Tired. How else?" There was a silence. "There are those of us on the Raleigh Police Force," she said, "who think that you know more than you're telling about Peyton Tillman and his final splashdown. I am not among them."

"You're not?" I asked faintly, my heart beating faster. I cannot afford trouble with the police since I have no official detective's license. Technically, many of the things I do could be construed as against the law if a judge wanted to get picky about it.

"No. I think you're shooting straight. But I want to know what happened to you on Friday night. I got a call from a sergeant who was poking around down at the impound lot. Your car was towed there yesterday. He recognized your name from the Tillman case. He says your car is sitting there with at least three bullet holes in it. Care to explain?"

"I pissed off some crazy bartender a couple of weekends ago," I explained. "Caught him stealing. He lost his job and blames me. I heard he was a gun nut. I think he was the one who ran me off the road."

"You're a very popular woman," she observed.

"Yeah. Among all the wrong people."

"Theoretically speaking," Detective Morrow mused out loud, "if any of this had to do with the Peyton Tillman case, you'd let me know, right?"

"Right," I lied.

Two hours later, I picked up Robert, the New Age hypnotist. He was wearing a dress shirt and tie above faded blue jeans. The hoop earrings were gone from his lobe. I thought his attempt at respectability was sweet.

He shrugged when I told him so. "I've never been in a women's prison," he said. "So I wasn't sure what you're supposed to wear."

I laughed. "Since you're a guy, I'd say as little as possible."

Robert stared at me intently as I drove.

"What?" I asked.

He stared even more weirdly. "Nothing," he said.

"Liar."

He stared at me again.

"Will you cut that out?" I asked. I'm not opposed to being ogled, understand, it's just that I'm accustomed to people ogling my body. This guy was staring somewhere to the right of my head and it made me wonder if I'd sprouted horns.

"I can't help it," he explained. "I'm reading your aura—the atmosphere around you. It's changing to the most extraordinary colors."

"Reading my aura?" I asked skeptically.

"Sure. You have colors around you all the time," he explained. "Angry people have dark colors. Peaceful people have lighter colors. Sometimes it changes, depending on your mood. Like right now. I can tell you're not attracted to me."

"Oh yeah?" I asked. "That could give a whole new dimension to the detecting game. Where exactly is the spot you look at to find out if I'm attracted to you or not?" I was imagining a hot-pink glow around my cooter, a little road sign of attraction for the initiated.

"All over. It follows the outline of your body. Actually, being able to read auras can be a real bummer at parties. Sometimes there's not a single woman there who is attracted to me."

"Maybe you should look at auras less," I suggested. "Try looking at their asses like a normal guy."

He laughed. And he was much, much cuter when he laughed.

The conversation held us until we approached the parking lot of the prison. The familiar constriction of my heart and lungs returned, my palms felt sweaty, my breath came in shallow gusts.

"You really don't like it here, do you?" Robert asked. "You're sort of strobing a sickly green right now."

"I feel a sickly green right now," I told him. We marched up to the main desk where Herman, the friendly guard, was on duty. He barely gave me a second glance. I must have looked a normal pink to him.

"Don't stay too long. She's got a lot of visitors scheduled for today," he observed. "They're waiving the usual rules. Guess they figure they'd better hurry." He realized the tactlessness of his remark. "Sorry," he apologized to Robert. "I see you're family. Lots of family checking in."

"Not much time left," I agreed. I gave him a smile. "It's okay, Herman. You're one of the good guys."

Robert was smarter than I gave him credit for. He wasted no time once the guards brought Gail into the visiting room. "Cousin!" he said, giving my bewildered client a hug for the benefit of the guard while simultaneously pushing his chair with a foot so that his back would be to the guard windows once he sat down.

Gail stared at him suspiciously as she sat. She looked tired and disheveled, which made two of us. I was willing to bet she'd skipped the morning medication, as requested. "This is nuts," she said.

I interrupted to head off dissent. "I saw your daughter yesterday," I said.

She stiffened and looked at me warily. "Did you tell her what was going on?" I could hear her temper lurking beneath the coldness of her voice.

I shook my head. "She already knew," I told her. "Or, at least, she knows you're in prison. She doesn't know you're on death row."

Gail relaxed. "Why did you tell me that you went to see her?" she demanded.

"Because if you don't want to go through with this for yourself, do it for her," I urged. "At this point you have nothing to lose."

She sat back and stared at me for a moment. I held her gaze. She'd done more time behind bars than I'd ever had to do, but my ass was still just as bad as hers. She finally dropped her eyes and looked at Robert. "Is this the guy who's going to do it?"

"Yup. Robert, meet Gail. Gail, meet Robert."

"You don't look like a hypnotist," she said in a challenging voice.

"You don't look like a murderer," he returned. It surprised her into laughing, and the ice was broken. My aura warmed a little toward Robert right about then.

"Have you ever been hypnotized before?" he asked Gail.

"Hell no," she said, indignant.

"It won't be like you expect," he explained. "You'll still be aware of where you are. You'll still have a feeling of being here in this room. But you're going to see things at a different level. Like you're underwater or something. And you'll be very relaxed."

"That's cool," Gail said. "It sounds like Valium."

"Big difference," Robert pointed out. "I'm going to be removing barriers to some feelings that you may have," he warned her. "Not blocking them. You're going to experience many emotions. You may feel overwhelmed. Please understand that your mind protects you. I'll be protecting you, too. If I think you're in any danger of psychological damage, I'll stop the session. So don't worry."

"Hey, buddy," Gail replied, "they want to kill me in two weeks. A little psychological damage isn't going to make much difference."

Poor Robert looked a bit taken aback at that, but I was even more surprised. If I didn't know better, I'd say that Gail was flirting with him.

Oblivious, Robert went about his business. "I'm going to use repetitive motion to put you under," he explained. "Just follow my index finger."

I understood then why his back, not Gail's, was to the guard. He began to move the index finger on his right hand back and forth slowly as he urged Gail—in a soothing voice—to relax and let her muscles go limp. His rich baritone had a hypnotizing effect. I felt myself growing drowsy, but pulled myself back to full consciousness just in time. How would it look if the guards busted in and found two females slumped over, eyes wide and one guilty-looking Robert?

Besides, I was in charge of the questions.

"How do you feel?" Robert asked Gail, his voice deep and gentle.

"This is wild," she murmured back. Her voice was lower than usual, and the pacing was disjointed, as if the words had to hit her own eardrums and bounce off before the rest of us could hear. She was sitting erect, but her shoulders slumped and her hands fell open, slack on the tabletop. Her eyes were dreamy, and her mouth parted slightly as she stared at Robert's moving finger. "My legs feel very... silly," she said and giggled. I exchanged a glance with Robert. Gail giggling was not what I had in mind. He nodded.

Quickly, I wrote down the first series of questions for him to ask.

"I'm going to bring you back to the night your husband died," Robert said. Gail stiffened. "To early evening," he quickly explained. "Long before your husband was shot."

Gail said nothing.

"Do you remember being at the bar that night?" Robert asked, checking my notes. "You're at the Lone Wolf bar. Tell me what you see."

She stared at the tabletop, seeing another place and time. "People are looking at me because I'm sitting alone. I've been waiting a long time for Roy to show up and I know I'm drunk, but there's nothing else to do." She frowned. "My mother's at home with Brittany and she's going to be mad if I show up late. She'll be able to tell I'm drunk. Roy said he would give me a ride home. I don't have any other way—" She stopped. "There he is. With the guys. Oh, damn. Roy's shirt is dirty." She sounded baffled. "I ironed it this morning and it was perfect. He spilled ketchup on the front pocket."

"Who else is there with Roy?" Robert asked as I took notes.

Her eyes searched an invisible bar. "George is there. He's always there when Roy is. And that guy Pete. He works with them. Haven't seen him in a while. And some guys I don't know. Roy doesn't like to be alone with me anymore." Her face grew sad. "I've gotten so fat. I know Roy hates it. God, I finished another drink. Roy knows I'm drunk. He's mad at me. I can tell by the way he looks at me I disgust him. But I want another drink."

"Does the waitress bring you another drink?" Robert asked. Gail nodded.

I scribbled another question. Robert looked perplexed, then understood. "Who else is drinking?" he asked.

"Everyone else," she said. "That's all we do. We sit and drink. They just drink slower than me."

"Let's go forward an hour or so. What are you talking about right now?" Robert asked. "Is Roy talking to his friends?"

She nodded dreamily. "Roy's talking to George about the fishing cabin," she said. "Pete's not there. He's at the bar getting another drink. He never orders from the waitress. He's too cheap to leave a tip. I don't like Pete much. I wish Roy wouldn't have him around." She paused. "Roy wants to go up to the cabin with George in the morning. He says it's important. It will be safe up there."

"What will be safe?" Robert interrupted, reading my scrawled note.

Gail shrugged. "Don't know. Besides, Roy can't go to the cabin. We have a family reunion. I promised Brittany we'd all go together. I tell Roy that. But now he's mad. He's going to yell."

She was silent for a moment. "People are looking. We're being too loud. But I don't care. It's not fair. Roy promised Brittany. He knows I'm right. I can tell by his face."

"What does Roy do now?" Robert asked her. "Does he say he's mad at you?"

Gail looked vaguely surprised, the memory still perplexing her. "He ignores me." Her look changed to hurt. "He's talking to George again now. Whispering about something. He doesn't want me or Pete to hear. I'm not part of his life anymore." She paused. "But I can hear a little bit. George is afraid."

"Afraid?" Robert asked. "Of what?"

"I don't know," Gail said. "I can't hear. The bar is too noisy. George looks afraid." She was quiet, listening intently to words said long ago. "George said something about trouble. Oh, no, they can tell I'm trying to listen." She shifted in her chair. "Where is that stupid waitress? I want another drink."

After more coaxing failed to produce anything useful, Robert read my notes and switched direction. "I'm going to bring you forward to a little later," he said, following my instructions. "You're still at the bar. But it's not a happy time anymore. You and Roy are fighting again." Gail's face contorted, first with anger, then with pain. Emotions flickered across her face as if she were watching a movie the rest of us could not see.

"What are you fighting about?" Robert asked. "It's okay to tell me. You're just remembering. No one can hurt you."

"Someone sent me over a drink," she said. "Roy is mad about it even though we're getting a divorce. The waitress said that a guy at the bar sent it. I stood up to see who it was but the waitress said he had gone. She said he was really cute. It serves Roy right, he's ignored me all night. But it makes me sad that the waitress doesn't realize Roy and I are together. She'd never have brought it over if she thought we were married. I know we're not really together anymore but still..." Her voice grew sad. "I wish we could work it out."

"Roy is angry about the drink?"

Gail nodded. "He wants me to send it back. That's stupid. The guy is gone. I'm going to drink it down before Roy can do anything." Gail was quiet for moment, then giggled. "It's gone. Roy can't do anything about it. He's angry. He's shouting at me. I'm yelling back. I tell him that Mama is home with Brittany. She's going to be really mad. We ought to leave, but Roy won't go. He's still talking to George. All they do is whisper. Pete is leaving. He says he's in trouble with his wife. What about me? I'm in trouble with my mother. I tell Roy that and he gets very angry." Suddenly, her dreamy voice changed to one of anger and she began cursing the tabletop like a drunken sailor. I looked up, alarmed, at the guard window. No one seemed to notice. For a few moments, Gail continued to argue with the tabletop. None of it was helpful. I motioned for Robert to bring her along.

"Gail," he said sharply. She fell silent. "Let's go even farther forward in the evening. To when it was time for you to go home."

"Roy thinks he's going to drive." She laughed, and the sound was ugly. "No way. He's had more than me. He just won't admit it. He's trying to grab the keys." She lifted a hand in the air. "No way he can have them." A frown crossed her face and her lower lip stuck out in a pout. "No fair. George grabbed the keys and gave them to Roy. They're all against me. They always are. I'm not his partners. I'm just the wife. And not even that anymore. What do I count?" Her face grew dark.

"What is it?" Robert asked anxiously. "What's happening?"

"My legs feel funny," Gail explained. "Rubbery. My mouth is dry. I need another drink but Roy wants to go home." Her voice faltered. "It's hard to walk. Maybe I counted wrong..." Her voice trailed off. We waited, but she was silent.

"Gail?" Robert asked. "Where are you now?" She did not reply.

I scribbled on the pad. "Gail," Robert said in a firm voice. "It's a little later. You're home now. Are you at home right now? Do you remember?"

"Mama is really angry at me. She's yelling. Where is she going?" Her face crumpled, and for a moment, I was afraid Gail was going to start crying. Instead, anger took over. "She about broke the door on the way out. I'm calling her in the morning to tell her so. I hear her car in the driveway. She's driving too fast. She'll still be mad at me tomorrow. I can't deal with it. My stomach hurts. I think I might be sick." Her voice trailed off and she sat in silence, staring at Robert.

"Gail?" Robert asked. "What are you doing right now?"

She did not answer.

"Gail, pretend there's a big black theater curtain in front of the scene," Robert said. "I'm going to count to three and when I get to three, I'm going to raise that curtain. When I do that, I want you to tell me what you see."

Gail nodded, and Robert counted slowly to three. But when he was done, Gail simply continued to stare at the tabletop. "Gail?" Robert asked more softly. "What do you see?"

She did not reply.

Robert turned to me. "That's it for that night," he said firmly. "She won't go back. I can't push her. It may be she was too out of it to know what happened."

I sighed and showed him the next series of questions. I wanted to learn more about the prison visits from the Durham police officers.

"Gail," Robert said, his voice sharp again. She sat up straight. "We're leaving that night behind. I want to take you forward a long time now. Past the trial, past coming to jail."

"I'm in jail," she said in a flat voice.

"Yes," Robert agreed. "You're in jail. And you've had some visitors. Police officers. Do you remember? It was around Christmastime."

"You mean George?" she asked. "He came to see me. I was surprised. I thought he hated me. I thought he was sure I killed Roy."

"When did he come to see you?" Robert asked.

"Right after New Year's," Gail said. "But George wasn't mad. He was sad. He said he would help me. But he was just talking. After that, I never heard from him again." She was silent for a moment. "There's nothing anyone can do."

"What's George's last name?" Robert asked.

"The same as a president," Gail explained dreamily. "George Washington. And then something else. I can't..." Her voice trailed off and she looked perplexed.

Robert read my notes. "Is it Carter?" he asked. "George Washington Carter?"

She nodded. "Yes. That's George."

"Did someone named Pete come to visit you?" Robert asked. "What was his last name?"

Gail shook her head. "Don't know. Don't want to know. Roy never liked him much. I never knew his last name. Just Pete."

"When did he come?" Robert asked. "What did he want?"

Gail's voice hardened. "He came after George. I don't know what he wanted."

"You're back at that day now," Robert said. "What is he asking?"

"He wants to know if George came to see me. He's asking me about Roy now, about what Roy said the night he died. Why does he want to know that? He was there. What does it matter now?" She was quiet, as if listening to someone else. "He's trying to be nice, but I'm not sure if..." She sat up straighter. "Why is he being so nice? I don't even know him. I'm going to sit here until he leaves."

She sat perfectly still as the clock on the wall ticked away seconds.

"Is he gone?" Robert asked.

"He's gone," Gail said.

"What about Steve?" Robert asked, peering down at my notes. "Did someone named Steve come to visit you?"

Gail stiffened. "Yes," she whispered. "A few days after Pete. He says he's sorry about what happened to Roy. He says they worked together and had been good friends. I think he's a liar. Roy never mentioned him to me." Her voice grew sad. "He says he forgives me. He acts like he thinks I killed Roy. But he says he forgives me anyway. I don't want his forgiveness. There's nothing to forgive." Another silence passed and when Gail spoke again, she sounded incredulous. "He's trying to flirt with me." Her voice grew angry. "I'm going to die, and he tries to flirt with me? I tell him to leave. That I don't want his forgiveness." Gail was quiet, watching and listening. "He won't leave. He wants to talk to me about something," she explained.

I scribbled a note on the pad. "What does he want to talk to you about?" Robert asked.

"He says he wants to buy the fishing cabin from me." Gail sounded perplexed. "The fishing cabin? What difference does that make? What do I care about the cabin? It's not mine anyway. It never was. It belongs to Roy's stepfather. Roy lied to me about it. He said his parents bought it for us as a wedding present, but that wasn't true. I found out at the trial that his parents were only paying the mortgage until we could take over. We never had enough money to do that. But I'm not telling him. It's none of his business." Her voice trembled with rage. "This jerk is trying to get me to sell him the cabin cheap. I think that's why he came to see me. I can't believe it. He didn't care about Roy. He just wants a bargain. I tell him to go away again. But then he wants to know if George and Pete have come to visit and what they said. I won't talk to him anymore. Not for a minute. I make him leave. I call the guard and make him leave."

Gail's face had grown red and Robert was looking uncomfortable. I quickly pointed to my last question before they both bailed on me.

"What was his last name?" Roy asked. "Who is Steve?"

"I don't know and I don't want to know," Gail said angrily. "I think he was working for the prosecutors. He wasn't Roy's friend. He was lying. Why did I talk to him at all? I'm so stupid. I'm always so stupid about things like that."

Her voice swelled with anger and Robert looked alarmed. I shrugged. There was nothing more I could learn anyway.

When he brought Gail out of her trance, she looked at us apprehensively. "Let's do it," she said.

"We already did," Robert told her.

She stared at him, face doubtful. "We did?" she asked.

He nodded. "Take your time. What do you remember?"

She thought back. "I guess I remember talking to you," she said. "I remember being mad. I remember being here but at the same time it felt like I wasn't here." She looked at me. "Did you get anything that might help?"

"Maybe," I told her. "I'm going to try."

I could have added that she shouldn't get her hopes up, but I didn't need to. Gail was not the kind of person who indulged in hope.

"Listen," I told her, trying once more to keep my promise to her little girl. "Your daughter wants to see you. I think she's old enough to handle it. Can't you give her that choice?"

"No," Gail said, crossing her arms. "I haven't been much of a mother to her, but I know one thing: little girls shouldn't see their mothers on death row. So don't bring her here." She glared at me. "And don't you ever let anyone else bring her here without my permission. I'll come back and haunt you after I die if you do."

"Whoa," I said quickly as we rose to go. "I have no intention of bringing her here without your permission. Get a message to me if you think of anything else." We headed for the door. I was ready to get out of there. The whole thing had been creepy. And god almighty—come back to haunt me after she dies? Honeycutt women are scary enough alive.

"That was weird," Gail said to no one in particular as we were leaving. "Kind of like too many tranquilizers."

By the time I dropped Robert off and returned home to Durham, I was ready for some good news. I didn't get it.

There was a message from Bobby D.'s court reporter contact to call her back at home that evening. When I reached her, she sounded glum.

"I didn't find anything," she admitted. "Bobby's going to be disappointed. I hate to let Big Daddy down."

Bobby would be disappointed? What about me? "Are you sure?" I asked. "Did you check all of Tillman's cases?"

"I checked all of the Wake cases in the last fifteen years," she said. "Not just Tillman's. I ran a search for any cases involving Durham police officers and, except for Roy Taylor, there's not much there."

"I was so sure it was something," I said, disappointed.

"Have you tried searching the Durham County files?" the woman suggested helpfully.

"But Tillman was a Wake County judge," I said.

"It's policy to rotate judges to the next county every few years for at least six months," she explained. "That way no one gets too cozy or sure of what cases he's going to get."

"You're kidding?" I said. "Tillman presided over cases in Durham County?"

"Absolutely," she said. "Maybe your answer is there."

Maybe indeed. And now I had more than a vague bunch of Durham police officers to go with. If I could get into the Durham County court computer system, I'd run a search for any Tillman cases involving Durham officers named George Washington Carter, Pete or Steve. Better yet, first I'd search the department's roster for possible last names. I knew someone who could help.

Despite my aching body—or maybe because of it—I needed a drink. I called Jack at home, but no one picked up. I took a chance and drove out to MacLaine's. It was empty and a bored-looking Jack was on duty.

"I thought it was your night off," I said.

"Nothing else to do," Jack explained. "And Timmy wanted off."

"Did you hear anything yet on that thing I asked you about?" I whispered.

Jack dropped his voice to an exaggerated whisper. "You mean any drug or corruption scandals involving Roy Taylor or any other Durham police officer? Not a word."

"Sorry," I said in a normal voice. "I'm a little paranoid right now. For good reason."

He peered at my face, seeing what I had tried to conceal with makeup. "No wonder. What the hell happened to you?"

I told him the story of my car chase while he bought me a drink.

"This is not good news, Casey. You're taking a beating on this case."

"I know," I admitted. "Now I'm looking over my shoulder every time I go anywhere. You think it's that crazy ex-bartender?"

"Could be Tony." He thought about it. "Want me to ask around?"

"Please. And I have one more favor."

"Name it." He spread his arms across the bar, a hopeful leer on his face.

"Down boy," I told him. "I hurt too much to sneeze, much less do the horizontal hokey-pokey."

"No sweat," he said. "I just like leering at you. You're one of the few women who can appreciate it."

I took it as a compliment. "Do you know the bartender out at the Lone Wolf?" I asked. "It's a cop bar off 1-85 near the Starlite Drive-in."

"Sure," Jack said. "He owns the place. Used to be a cop himself, but he liked to be on the other side of the bar a little too much for purposes of public safety. He got out and bought the bar about ten years ago. Usually works it himself, has a little help on busy nights and weekends. You need to talk to him?"

I nodded. "Yeah. Can you set it up?"

"Sure. We've had a couple drinks after hours a few times. You know, that 'bartenders hang out after work to bond' kind of thing."

"Thanks." I sipped my drink. "God, my body aches. I feel like I just flunked out of the rodeo."

"I could close up early and take you home for a foot massage."

I considered the offer. "The bottoms of my feet may be the only parts of my body that don't ache."

"Okay, then," Jack said. "It's decided. I'll get you slightly drunk, then you can crawl in bed and lie back. I'll oil and caress your tootsies."

"You're a saint," I told him. "I mean it."

"Hey," he said, "That's what friends are for."

CHAPTER TEN

When I need to burrow inside the bowels of the Durham Police Department, I head—where else?—to the men's room on the third floor to wait for my pal Marcus Dupree to show up. It's never a very long wait. Marcus has a thing for men's rooms. Several things, in fact. For one, his effeminate mannerisms make Liberace seem butch. The bathroom may be the only place in downtown Durham where he can be himself without fear of encountering raised eyebrows. Second, Marcus is a male typist surrounded by underpaid women and humorless policemen. That makes him a stranger in a very strange land. I think he feels safest alone in a stall with four wooden walls around him. Finally, Marcus is a chain-smoker—he prefers Virginia Slims—and not even North Carolina allows smoking inside public offices these days. Rather than lurking outside the front door where he'd suffer verbal abuse from the lowlifes being dragged in for questioning, Marcus prefers to sneak his smokes in the privacy of the urinal.

Of course, it's not so private when I'm around.

"Lord give me strength, Miss Casey," Marcus scolded me. "Do you have to sneak up behind a person like that? You like to give me a heart attack."

"Don't worry. If I don't, those will." I nodded toward his cigarette.

He fanned the air guiltily, his long fingers caressing the smoke. "Now you know I cannot survive a minute with those people out there unless I have my nicotine. Girl, they make me so nervous. If it's not all those perpetrators staring at me and licking their lips, it's the new recruits making the same old jokes or those heifers in the typing pool jealously eyeing my wardrobe.

It's not my fault I'm slimmer and prettier. What we need around here is a weight-control program. Those floors are going to give out soon if they don't encourage a little lunchtime restraint."

"Now, Marcus," I told him. "We can't all have your metabolism."

"That's so." His face brightened. "There is only one me."

Truer words were never spoken. Marcus was an original. He came from one of those southern families—and there were many—that didn't blink an eye when one of their own emerged from the womb as a flamer. He'd grown up sitting with the women at family functions, cooking pound cake with the best of them, ironing lace doilies, bleaching curtains, learning the art of southern hostessing and generally being left alone to be whoever the hell he wanted to be.

Rather than going to church each Sunday and praying for his homosexual soul, Marcus had a mama and a whole passel of sisters who attended services solely to thank the Lord for sending them a wonderful provider. And well they should have prayed: Marcus was the oldest of ten children and the man in the house. He'd already sent two little sisters and a brother to the University of North Carolina, then bankrolled two more siblings through technical school. He was only a typist, but he was going to make damn sure that the rest of the Dupree family tree took root in richer soil. I hoped Marcus was treasured by someone. I know I would have snapped him up in a heartbeat, if not for the fact that we definitely played on opposite teams.

Marcus was peering at my face. "Girl, get out of whatever you're in. No man is worth it," he counseled me. "Be strong. Walk out that door. Play some Gloria Gaynor. She'll give you the strength you need."

"This is not the work of a boyfriend," I assured him. "You ought to know me better than that. This is the work of an enemy. An unknown one as yet."

He touched a bruise with gentle fingers. "He sure got his licks in."

"You'd make a good nurse," I told him. "Why don't you go back to school?"

"Money, honey child. Dinero. And I don't mean Robert. Maybe when Humphrey, that's Mama's youngest, graduates from college."

"You're a good man, Marcus," I told him.

"What do you want from me today, Miss Casey?" he asked, glancing toward the door. "You better hurry. Sergeant Bennett has got himself a case of the trots and he's going to be back in here moaning and groaning soon. I must say, it does spoil the ambiance."

"You remember the Roy Taylor case?" I asked. "About eight years ago?"

"Sure," he said. "It was *Frankie and Johnny* revisited. He was her man, but he done her wrong. So she plugged him."

"Maybe," I said. "But I don't think the wife did shoot him, and if I don't find out something new real quick, the state is going to administer a lethal injection to her in about two weeks."

Marcus was silent as he considered the situation. "You're a cynical woman, Miss Casey," he finally said, "and if you don't think she did it, then I hate to say it, but—they may have the wrong person sitting up there on death row."

"That's right," I said. "And it's a hard mistake to correct once the deed is done. That's why I need you to rummage around in the department files and get me some information and names. A man named George Washington Carter testified at the trial. I think he was a partner of Taylor's. See what you can find on him. Also, I need to know who else used to work closely with Taylor and in what capacity, especially if they're named Pete or Steve. I'm sorry, but I don't have any last names. And anyone else you can come up with. Plus, I need their current home addresses."

Marcus made a face of delicate horror. "That's easy to do," he said. "But if I get caught, it's hard to explain."

"I know," I admitted. "I'll give you five hundred dollars. More if you need it. My client can afford it. That's a lot of schooling for one of those little brothers of yours."

"It sure is," he agreed enthusiastically. "And since when has Marcus Dupree ever blinked an eyelash in the face of danger?"

"And what eyelashes they are," I added, patting his smooth cheeks. "I'd kill for those long, lovely lashes."

"You want something else," he guessed at once. "You're being too nice."

"I'm sort of an obvious person, aren't I?" I asked, disappointed.

He nodded. "But that's cool, Miss Casey. It's your style. So get out there and work it."

I worked it. "I need a password to get into the Durham County court database. I need to search for cases involving some specific people over the past ten years or so."

"Meaning those people I'm going to uncover for you?" he asked.

I nodded. "You catch on quicker than body crabs, my dear Marcus. Did I mention that I needed your information by this afternoon?"

"No, but I figured it was something like that, what with the price being paid and all." He smiled. "Rush jobs are my specialty. I'll go cruising through the files during my lunchtime. No one pays any attention to me anyway. It's not like they're going to be asking me to join them down at Elmo's Diner. I'm lucky if they wave a sandwich my way. I'll call you at one o'clock with what I find and give you the court password then. I have to make a few calls for that. And I might need more money."

"No problem. I'll be at my office." I gave him a business card and he palmed it carefully, tucking it into the back pocket of his immaculately pressed pants. "Just let me know what you need for petty cash," I added.

"Miss Casey," he protested, checking his Jheri curls in the mirror and adjusting a subtle wave that dipped toward one nicely shaped eyebrow. "There is nothing petty about me. You ought to know that by now."

While I waited for Marcus to call back, I spent a couple of hours back in the office cruising through old *News & Observer* files on my trusty Mac. I didn't find out anything involving Durham County court cases presided over by Peyton Tillman.

But that was to be expected. I'd be more likely to get a hit if I could poke around the *Durham Herald* files. Unfortunately, they'd had the bad taste to upgrade their security system when they retooled their computer network last fall. I didn't have a password into it just yet. I was thinking of canceling my subscription in retaliation.

Marcus called right on time with the last names I needed, giving me a little bit more to go on.

"Got a pencil?" he asked in a hushed voice. "There's something fishy down here in Denmark, and it's not the Ladies Auxiliary."

"Oh, yeah? What gives?"

"I remembered George Washington Carter once I got a peek at his file photo. Tall, fine-looking brother with a chiseled triangular nose that looks like an Aztec god's. The color of ebony, and skin that don't need no Elizabeth Arden to shine. He used to work the Durham Bulls games as a security officer for extra cash, and I hardly knew where to put my eyes. On him or the next batter up."

"What do you mean he used to work the games?" I asked.

"He's AWOL," Marcus explained. "Missing in action. Listed as inactive, but I poked around. He disappeared about two months ago, and no one has seen him since. Left behind a pregnant wife. They're trying to keep it quiet because it looks bad for the department. I remember hearing rumors about some cop turning gay and leaving his family behind for the wilds of San Francisco or something like that. I think it must be him everyone is talking about."

"Bullshit," I said. "You'd have known if he was gay, nosy as you are."

"That's true." Marcus agreed. "And with a face like his, it's likely I'd have been first in line."

"Give me his last known address."

Marcus rattled off an address near Northgate Mall. "There's more," he told me. "A fellow named Pete Bunn worked with Taylor. Chunky old white man. I didn't know him. Had mean eyes in his photo, like an old warthog. Retired last month."

"Retired?" I asked. "How old was he?"

"I knew you would ask me that question," Marcus said, pleased. "So I detected around. He was fifty-eight."

"Older than a lot of guys retiring from the force," I observed.

"That's true," Marcus said knowingly. "But in this guy's case, the timing was odd."

"Odd enough to make you think he might have been forced to retire?" I asked. "Was there anything in his file to indicate he was dirty?"

"No," Marcus said. "His file looks clean. But whose doesn't? I just think it was kind of sudden. If he'd stayed a few months longer until June, he'd have hit another year of service and his pension would have gone up. So I smelled trouble in River City."

"Good work. Now who the hell is Steve?"

"Well," Marcus said slowly. "There's plenty of Steve's and Steven's in the department. You know these southern white women. They have no creativity when it comes to naming their children. But the one you want is Steven Hill, I'm pretty sure of it."

"Go on," I told him, thinking that the name sounded familiar.

"The reason I am saying it's him," Marcus explained, "is that their personnel records show that all three of these men worked with Roy Taylor back in the good old days. It gets a little complicated. Are you with me on this?"

"Like a tick on a yard dog," I assured him.

"All three men worked with Roy Taylor as beat cops patrolling Durham's southwest district. It's a pretty rough district. I myself would never walk there late at night without a pack of Rottweilers at my side. When things started getting really bad on account of that crack cocaine, the department formed a special crime unit to try and stamp out drugs all over Durham. You can imagine how successful that was." He gave a disapproving sniff. None of Marcus's many siblings had even dreamed of doing drugs and their big brother was the reason why. He was a gentle human being, but he'd have kicked their asses from here to Tallahassee if they had so much as thought about inhaling.

"And these men were all on that special drug unit?" I guessed.

"You got it. Along with Roy Taylor. But they didn't have much time together before Roy was killed. Less than a year."

"What happened to them after Roy died?" I asked.

"The remaining three stayed together for a while, but your George Washington fellow asked for a transfer back to a patrol beat. It's not often someone asks to be demoted, understand."

"Maybe he was a hands-on guy?" I suggested.

"He can put his hands on me any old time," Marcus agreed.

"But first we have to find him."

"A boy can dream, can't he? Anyway, the two remaining unit officers, Bunn and Hill, were assigned to one of the new crime area target teams when they started organizing the department differently in the nineties. CAT teams, they call them. Don't you just love that? I suggested they wear black cat suits to go along with the theme, but no one ever got back to me on the idea."

"Probably too expensive," I consoled him.

"Their CAT team focused on some of your choicer Durham neighborhoods, roaming around as needed. They were working heavy drug areas until about four years ago, when Bunn transferred into white collar and Hill came to headquarters, where he's been moving up pretty fast for a white man. He's a captain now, working in professional standards. They think it sounds better than internal affairs, but it's the same thing. Good place to be right now. Plenty of opportunity for work."

This was an understatement. A series of public-relations disasters had plagued the Durham Police Department over the past ten years, all of them unrelated, yet seemingly never-ending. Good cops grew more and more demoralized by the day, as the actions of their less honest brothers in blue exposed them to public ridicule. The stories seemed endless: a drunk off-duty sergeant nabbed for shooting at a little old lady civilian who accidentally bumped him at a stoplight; an on-duty 911 operator selling drugs over the department phone lines; beat cops taking the "beat" part a little too seriously and bringing in suspects that were more blue than black by the time they arrived for questioning; a string of ranking officers resigning due to sexual harassment, taking illegal honorariums, having conflicts of interest and just about everything short of running a prostitution ring out of headquarters. I figure that if they could have come up with a way to accept credit cards, someone would have jumped on that angle, too. Durham's new city manager had recently brought in a no-nonsense police chief who seemed serious about cleaning up the department. He'd have to be more stubborn than a mule at mealtime to succeed.

"To tell you the truth," Marcus added, interrupting my thoughts, "I'm surprised the Hill guy is already a captain. Him being white and all. And not a college boy, either. 'Course, he looks like one of those college boys what with his expensive haircut and all."

Steven Hill. The name was familiar, yet it would not come to me. The wreck had really knocked the stuffing out of my memory. Maybe I should have stayed for that forty-eight hours of observation after all.

"You're a genius," I told Marcus. "What about their home addresses?"

Pete Bunn had retired to a farm in Chatham County. Steven Hill lived in a new subdivision off 15-501, one of those model communities where all the houses look so much alike that you have to double-check the address each time you pull into your own driveway. The neighborhood was closer to Chapel Hill than Durham, and that made it more expensive. Ratting on your fellow officers paid well.

"I don't want to push my luck," I admitted to Marcus. "But about that password I need to get into the Durham County court files?"

"Since when has Marcus ever let you down?" he demanded. He read out several telephone numbers and a string of access codes. "It's going to cost you an extra two hundred dollars. I'm sorry. My source got a little greedy. But she wants a convertible for the summer real bad. I told her we'd pay for the optional tinted windows, but that was all."

"You did good," I told him. I promised to drop by his house with the cash soon, then rang off and got to work. I wasn't worried about being caught hacking. Many of the bigger law firms in the Research Triangle paid out the wazoo for direct access to the new computerized court-records system. I'd be just one more law clerk poking around in cyberspace. I even recognized one of the phone numbers that Marcus had given me. He was routing me through the largest law firm in Durham as a precaution before I tapped into the court system itself. If anyone cared about my presence online, they'd just figure the fat-cat partners were earning their $300 an hour, per usual. I liked the irony of the situation since that particular law firm had once stiffed me on a perfectly reasonable bill for a job well done. Maybe I'd download some kiddie porn onto their office network when I was done, then alert the FBI to move in, just for fun.

It took the entire afternoon to locate the case files I wanted, but I found them. Peyton Tillman had indeed rotated through the Durham County court system during his tenure on the bench. He'd heard a few embezzlement cases, one kidnapping and a politically touchy sexual assault by the head of a medical unit at Duke Hospital, but drug cases made up most of his docket. What can I say? Durham was more than the City of Medicine.

I found my link to Roy Taylor and his unit buddies when I poked into Judge Tillman's drug-case transcripts further. Curiously, they occurred after Roy had died and involved his former partners as witnesses or arresting officers. Most of the cases had never gone all the way through to trial, and many involved only the preliminary motions. These cases had most often been plea-bargained down to lesser charges. In many instances, it seemed to me that the defendants had gotten a real deal. How anyone caught with a kilo of cocaine and processing paraphernalia can walk away with a misdemeanor charge of simple possession is beyond me. With standards like that, you'd have to be a Columbian drug lord in order to actually do time. I wanted to know why.

I then searched for cases involving any judge and Roy Taylor's partners. There was plenty to find. If I hadn't personally faced a cocaine-possession charge in my youth—and been forced to learn the nuances of federal and state charges it entailed—I might have missed the subtleties of what the transcripts were telling me. But I never forgot a hard lesson once I'd learned it, and, by the end of the afternoon, I thought I had the answer: someone was dirty. Evidence had disappeared, witnesses recanted and memories grew foggy on the stand. Whatever the cause, prosecutors had found themselves with evaporating cases and been forced to accept plea bargains that let the bad guys off the hook. Had all four of the team been dirty, I wondered. Most cases had occurred after Roy's death. So if Roy was dirty, he wasn't the only one. Were all of the other three officers dirty? Or only some of them? Did the entire Durham Police Department stink worse than a cow pond in summer?

No wonder Judge Tillman had said he needed more proof before he could go public. So did I.

I thought of calling Bill Butler for help. That was when I remembered where I had heard the name Steven Hill before: at Peyton Tillman's funeral. He'd been the handsome green-eyed stranger with the clothing-optional stare. No wonder Bill had tried to keep us apart. And how lovely for Bill to have concealed Hill's real status. It was definitely time to give him a call with my special thanks.

At first the administrative officer who answered the phone refused to put me through. But when I promised to rip her neck off and breathe fire down her throat if she didn't do what I asked, she had an unexpected change of heart. Sometimes, people just need an incentive.

"Nice, Casey," Bill said. "First you blow me off and then you threaten some poor girl two years out of school."

"Save it," I said. "Number one, I was in the hospital on Friday night, having been put there by the person you insist I'm imagining is following me around town. Thanks for the cards and flowers, by the way. It was so nice to return home to find your supportive phone call."

There was silence. "I didn't know," he said.

"Anne Morrow knew," I pointed out.

There was another silence. "Detective Morrow is playing her cards on the Tillman case close to her chest," he said. "If there was no reason to tell me, she wouldn't have."

"But you did know that Steven Hill had been one of Roy Taylor's partners, didn't you?" I asked. "And you kept that information from me even after I begged you to find me someone who had known him so we could talk?"

"Tillman's funeral wasn't the time or place for you to go interrogating Taylor's old partners," Bill said. "The world does not revolve around you and your cases, though I know that comes as a shock. Steven Hill and Tillman served together in Vietnam. He was there to show respect, not answer questions."

"What is really going on here?" I demanded. "Are you and Hill butt buddies or something?" Okay, it was rude, but I'd left my better judgment behind on that dark road when I got banged around by an anonymous truck. Besides, he could have showed some concern for my poor, battered body. A little sympathy would do, if outright concern was too much of an emotional gamble for his delicate male ego.

"Everything is about sex with you, isn't it?" Bill shot back. "Your mind is in the gutter."

"At least I have a mind," I retorted. "And use it on occasion. Excuse me if I offended you. But tell me this: why are you protecting Steven Hill from having to answer a few simple questions from me?"

The silence that followed this remark made me nervous, I admit. When Bill finally spoke, his tone told me that our friendship would never be the same. "Because Roy Taylor was a dirty cop," he said. "And I'd like to spare his family from knowing it. Okay? They already lost a son. Soon, they'll have to take the rap from all the bleeding-heart liberals for Gail Honeycutt being put to death. I think that's enough for one family to go through. Don't you?"

"Who says Roy Taylor was a dirty cop? Steven Hill?"

"Who else would know the truth?" Bill countered. "That's his job."

What an idiot. Cops will stick together until one of them draws a gun on the other, and even then they'll think twice before returning fire. And they say women are overly loyal. At least we can recognize two faces on one body when we see it.

"Did it ever occur to you that maybe Hill is the dirty one?" I asked. "And please don't tell me that you're good friends and you'd know it if he was."

"We're not particularly good friends," Bill said stiffly. "I met him at a conference. But if he's a dirty cop, I'll eat my badge. He's helping to lead some initiative to reduce corruption, for chrissakes. He's as far from the street and temptation as you can get. Plus, the guy has been decorated more times than the windows at Macy's."

Oh, those colorful ex-New Yorkers.

"Bill, use your head," I pleaded. "When did Hill call you up to renew your casual acquaintance? It was after I took the case, wasn't it? He's using you to get information on me."

"That's ridiculous," Bill said. "He didn't even know that I knew you until Tillman's funeral."

"Everyone knows that you know me," I informed him. "And most people think you're—" I stopped. I didn't want to open that particular door for fear it would be slammed shut in my face. "Never mind," I said. "But people are well aware that we know each other. Take my word for it."

"I think you're giving yourself too much credit," he said. "Steven Hill never even heard of you until I introduced you to him."

"Bullshit," I said. "And I want to talk to him. Immediately. If you stand in my way, I'll start talking a lot louder, only I'll be talking to all the wrong people. I'll go right over your head and right over his head. It won't look good for you, I promise you."

He didn't waste any more time arguing. "I'll ask him," he said. "You're a hard woman, Casey."

"Hey," I told him. "Sometimes a hard woman is good to find."

Arguing with Bill Butler was thirsty work. I needed a drink. A real one. The kind that doesn't require a paper umbrella. I called Jack at work to see if he was interested in some company.

"It's quiet as hell," he told me. "You're welcome to hang out. But I've got news you might want to follow up on. The owner of that cop bar is expecting you. His name is Johnny. He says he'll tell you what little he knows. Plus I heard something about the Durham cops, but it happened a few years ago."

"Like what?" I asked.

"The usual when you're talking about drugs. Busts where money and product disappeared. Dealers saying they had a lot more cash on them when they were arrested than was ever reported. Evidence disappearing and finding its way back onto the street. That kind of thing."

"Any names keep popping up?" I asked.

"Nope. It was all pretty vague, but the guys I know seem to think the rumors were true. They say it's stopped, probably because of heat from internal affairs. With all that publicity, they can't afford to screw around anymore."

I believed him. Jack's sources are impeccable. The guys that Jack knows are the drug dealers who never get arrested, the ones who sell socially acceptable drugs to white people instead of crack at the street level. I didn't know their names and I didn't want to. But I believed Jack when he said he believed them.

"Thanks," I said. "And if you'll forgive me, I'll take that drink at the Lone Wolf instead."

"No problem," he said. "Just watch that Johnny. He waters the good stuff."

He didn't water mine. The owner of the Lone Wolf served me a Tanqueray over ice that was stiff enough to put starch in a dead man's drawers. He was less eager to serve up information. I sipped my drink and waited while he refreshed a few old regulars who were methodically drinking themselves into a stupor at the other end of the bar. Johnny was a giant of a man, well over six feet tall, with a rectangular head and massive limbs. All he needed was a few studs sticking out of his neck, and he'd be ready for Halloween. He must have been terrifying as a street cop. He was still pretty scary as a bartender.

"Okay," he finally said once he ran out of other customers and was forced to acknowledge my presence again. "I told Jack I'd help out if I could, so give me the lowdown and I'll see what I can do." His voice was deep and rumbling, like a storm rolling in on the horizon.

"You remember the night Roy Taylor was killed?" I asked.

"Who doesn't? Tourists came in here for months afterward. Pain in the ass. It's not like he was the first person to get killed after drinking here. Cops, guns and alcohol. What do you expect?"

I didn't ask for details. If the Lone Wolf hadn't been a cop bar in the first place, it would have been shut down a long time ago.

"What can you tell me about that night?" I asked.

He sucked idly on a toothpick, treating me to a glimpse of massive yellow teeth. I'd seen more attractive smile on mules.

"Not much," he said. "Roy was drunker than shit and his old lady was even worse. It was crowded, and she was a royal pain in the butt when it came to getting her fat ass out the door. Roy had to drag her and she knocked two regulars off their stools at one end of the bar, then fell over a table near the front, breaking a couple of beer bottles and some glasses. Roy said he'd settle up later, but never got the chance. I just let it slide."

How magnanimous of him. Sparing Roy Taylor's estate a whopping $15 bill for damages. "That's it?" I asked.

He shrugged again. "They were drunk. They fought. They left. End of story. Told the police the same thing."

"Someone bought Gail Taylor a drink that night. Any idea who?"

"You're joking, right?" he asked, the toothpick bobbing up and down. "How the hell should I know? It was a lot more crowded than now."

Considering that I was the only customer besides the dusty retirees at the far end of the bar, this was easy to believe.

"What about George Washington Carter?" I asked.

"What about him? He invented peanut butter. Big effing deal. The stuff gives me gas."

"Carter," I enunciated slowly. "Not Carver." With social skills like his, he should be working with people in comas. "He's a Durham police officer who disappeared a couple of months ago. He was here with Roy Taylor the night he died. You know him?"

He looked sullen and eyed the regulars for distraction. But they were too busy watching wrestling on the tube to order another drink.

"Did you know him?" I prompted.

"Yeah, I knew him," he finally said. "One of those black guys who thinks he's white. Hung out here all the time with Roy."

Translation: while the problem may have been that George Carter was the world's lousiest tipper, it was more likely that Lurch here was not happy that a man of color had been drinking at his bar, even one who was a Durham police officer and good friends with his paler brethren.

"Any idea why he disappeared?" I asked.

Lurch shrugged. "Heard he was eating tube steak out San Francisco way."

Charming. "That's hard to believe," I said. "He had a pregnant wife."

Lurch shrugged again. "So his wife slept with someone. Doesn't mean it was him."

Geeze, I was starting to hate the guy and he hadn't even watered down my drink. "When's the last time you saw George Carter?" I asked.

"Night before he disappeared," he admitted. "Came in with a guy named Pete Bunn. A real jerk. They had a couple of pops, then took off."

"This bar is sort of a dead end for cops, isn't it?" I asked. "Your customers have a habit of meeting untimely ends or disappearing."

"Look lady, I don't know exactly what that crack meant, but I think I've answered enough of your questions for one night, okay?"

I agreed. I gave him my card and elicited a meaningless promise to give me a call if any regulars could contribute more.

I left needing a drink just as badly as I had when I arrived.

CHAPTER ELEVEN

The next day, I had a choice: while I waited for Bill to come through with an appointment with Steven Hill, I could either question George Washington Carter's abandoned wife or I could track down Pete Bunn. I let the weather decide for me. It was warm and sunny, and I was in need of vitamin D. My poor country bones were weary of concrete. I needed a trip to Chatham County.

By ten o'clock in the morning, I had left the new subdivisions of outer Chapel Hill behind. Pine forest surrounded Highway 15-501 on both sides, broken only by stretches of farmland growing green beneath the warm spring sun. Pete Bunn, the retired Durham police officer who had worked with Roy Taylor, lived close to Pittsboro, a small country town that had recently been adopted by hordes of potters, artists and sculptors, much to the dismay of the locals. Bunn's land was marked only by a mailbox with a post-office box number and, predictably, I missed the turnoff. I doubled back, using the driveway of the horse farm next door as a turnaround. No one stirred when Bobby D.'s big car lurched toward the stables.

Returning to 15-501, I turned right, then followed the long driveway, as it wound over hills and around sharp curves, to Pete Bunn's farm. Obviously, he valued his privacy. I wasn't sure what I would say to him when I arrived at his doorstep, but I was acutely aware of three things: one, he had been among the last people that I knew of to see both Roy Taylor and George Carter alive; two, I lacked firepower, thanks to the office ransacker; and three, I wasn't in the mood to add a bullet hole to the list of my current injuries. I reminded myself to ask Bobby D. if I could borrow one of his many firearms, and continued up the dusty lane.

Just as I reached the crest of a hill and spotted a white farmhouse nestled in a hollow below me, I noticed a small dust storm making its way toward me: another vehicle on its way out toward the main road. I automatically slowed down. It wasn't a very wide road, and we'd have to pass each other eventually. But the vehicle in front of me picked up speed, churning dust until I could barely make out that it was a truck. It roared past in a whoosh of engine and dirt, blinding me and forcing me to veer over onto the grass. I caught a glimpse of taillights through the dust before the truck reached the top of the hill and disappeared from sight.

Any normal person would have considered the situation and retreated. Not me. I made my way toward the farmhouse, pulled the big-ass Cutlass to a stop in the front yard beside a white Chevy Impala. I pounded on the front door for a good three minutes without success. Okay, I thought, if that had been Pete Bunn in the truck, he was mighty late for an important appointment. At any rate, there was no one home and that left me free to snoop.

But what would I do if he returned to find me poking around his property? Trespassing was a surefire way to get my cellulite studded with lead, and I wasn't anxious to have a backside that resembled a Little Debbie raisin cake. I had a better idea. I made my way back to the main road without seeing anyone, and returned to the horse farm. A hand-painted sign proclaimed it to be the LAZY K RANCH. That was an understatement. Not a dragonfly stirred in the spring heat. I followed the sounds of whinnying to a paddock behind a long barn, where I discovered a plump woman with gray hair combing a colt. She agreed to rent me an overweight nag, which looked as though it was about two months away from the glue factory, provided I could demonstrate that I knew the difference between a trot and a canter. I was pretty sure my horse had asthma, but agreed to swap twenty dollars for a few hours of freelance exploring.

"She's old, but sneaky," the owner explained, slapping on a saddle and tightening the straps. "You've got to be firm with her or she'll try tricks like this." She kicked the mare in the stomach, causing its belly to deflate with a hearty whoosh that emanated from both ends of the nag. The saddle slipped to one side, where it dangled a mere inches from a sudden urine stream. "See what I mean? That's why we call her Miss Bitch, even though her real name is Beauty."

I decided that Miss B. and I would get along just fine. We had a lot in common, including a nickname.

I took Miss B. through her paces under the disapproving eye of her owner and was finally cleared for takeoff. It felt good to be back in the saddle again. Men always wonder why women love riding horses so much. I'd tell, but it's a state secret. As I rode off toward a nearby hill where Pete Bunn's farmland abutted the pasture, I remembered a story I'd heard from a Chatham County deputy a few months ago. It seems that one night last spring, four migrant workers had been caught on a barn's security video having their way with a mare from a Chatham County farm. Three of the men had left town and headed south toward the border, suffering from acute embarrassment. The remaining miscreant had served six months in jail, no doubt being paid back by incarcerated horse lovers. I wondered if the Lazy K Ranch and Miss B. had been in on the action.

"*Mi quapita,*" I whispered to Miss B. She didn't blink an eyelash. Definitely not the same horse.

Pete Bunn's farm was separated from the Lazy K by a chicken-wire fence that sagged to the ground along much of its perimeter. This was fortunate. I don't think Miss B. could have jumped a rabbit hole, much less a fence. We picked our way over the wire and, when she spotted a nice clump of new grass ahead, Miss B. impressed me by picking up steam. Soon we were deep onto Pete Bunn's land, and I had the passable excuse of having gotten lost should he discover me on his property. I would simply claim to be sorry and make like heigh-ho, Silver back to the Lazy K.

I wasn't sure what I was looking for, so I started with the farmhouse. It was still deserted. I tied Miss B. to the porch railing, then searched for a way inside. No such luck. The doors and windows were locked securely. I did not want to force my way inside, at least not if it meant breaking a window or leaving other telltale clues of my visit. I contented myself with peering into the darkness of the interior. It was a tidy if uninspired home, heavy on brown-checked upholstery, cheap pine furniture, television sets and vinyl-covered kitchen chairs. The usual decor for an old bachelor cop. When I returned to the porch, I found that Miss B. had christened the front steps with her own unique housewarming gift, no small feat considering she'd had to back up to do it.

"You're one talented lady," I told her, remounting for more exploration. I didn't bother to clean it up. What the hell was Pete Bunn going to do? Call in a forensic team to run tests on horse poop?

It wasn't a working farm, just a small farmhouse next to a modest barn used primarily for storing tools. The rest of the property consisted of empty paddocks and lots of green pastures. There wasn't an ounce of livestock to be found—unless you counted the butterflies swarming over the untended fields and the mounted deer head I'd seen through one of the farmhouse windows. Maybe Pete Bunn hadn't owned the place long enough to get his god's little acre going yet.

After surveying the empty fields, I meandered through the surrounding pine forest and discovered a clearing about a quarter of a mile from the house. It was linked to the main dirt road by a lane hardly wide enough for the combined size of Miss B.'s rump and mine. The clearing included an impromptu dumping site about twenty feet across, the kind found on farms everywhere. Rather than cope with the hassle of EPA regulations or local restrictions, lots of landowners chose to dump dead livestock, brush, barn muck, used oil and other assorted junk in an isolated spot away from the watershed. We'd had our own dumping ground when I was a kid, and I helped Grandpa sprinkle powdered lime over the carcass of a newly departed animal many times.

Of course, Pete Bunn had no livestock, and the farm wasn't a working operation. So what the hell did he need a dumping ground for?

I dismounted and snooped around the junk pile, lifting up old mattress springs, rotting wooden crates and piles of branches without discovering much. I found nothing more exciting than a partially burned black-and-green checked lumberjack shirt stuck to a set of old mattress springs and an ancient army boot with the sole rotted out. The shirt intrigued me, but then I discovered a whole mound of discarded clothing—including women's clothing from the 1930s—and thought it likely that Pete Bunn had been cleaning out his attic. More searching revealed a couple of old farm tools, a smashed-up baby safety seat, some cracked flower pots and a small mountain of rotting pecans. Nothing to write home about, though I bemoaned the loss of so many potential pecan pies. Ah well, at least I'd enjoyed a nice afternoon with a nonhuman beast. There were worse ways to pass the time. I hoped Pete Bunn was as innocuous as his farm was and decided to return later for a person-to-person chat.

By the time I headed back to Durham, it was late afternoon, and I felt rested and ready to tackle an interview with the missing George Carter's wife. His neighborhood was easy to find.

Durham is an odd town when it comes to urban renewal. Beautifully restored historic homes stand side by side with ramshackle mill houses owned by absentee slumlords. Even the best neighborhoods are never more than a few blocks from the worst. Yet it seemed to work, having the good alongside the bad like that. Durham was a town that didn't try to hide its problems. It was one reason I liked calling it home.

George Washington Carter lived in a solid middle-class neighborhood just off of Duke Street, about half a mile before the 1-85 interchange. It was a five-block-square area of brick ranch homes perched on neat rectangles of well-tended lawns. In other words, the kind of neighborhood where people grilled out in the backyard on Sunday afternoon and watched you with wary eyes when you strolled by their yards, especially if they'd never seen you before. It was not the kind of neighborhood you walked away from without warning. Where in the world had George Carter gone?

An old black Toyota was parked in the driveway of his house, so someone was home. I was in luck. His wife answered the door before my finger touched the bell.

"Thank god you're here. I'm running late." She thrust a plump brown baby into my arms and rushed past, reaching the driveway about the same time the little tyke began to yowl. "His name is George Jr.," she called back to me. "Jiggle him and he'll stop. I just fed him and changed his diaper. I expressed some milk for later. The bottles are on the second shelf of the refrigerator. I'm working in the emergency room of Durham Regional tonight. Call if you have problems. I'll sign your time sheet when I get home."

I looked down at the baby. He stared back blankly, his dark almond eyes trying in vain to focus on my face. I'm not an expert on children, but this little sucker couldn't have been more than a few months old. His head wobbled on his neck as though it was attached with a ball bearing. "I'm not the baby-sitter," I shouted after her before she could zoom away.

She dashed back and snatched away her pride and joy before I could kidnap him. The kid stopped crying the second he felt his mother's touch. I tried not to be insulted.

"Who the hell are you?" she demanded, blocking the front door with her thin frame. For someone who had just had a baby, she was downright emaciated. Her dark skin could not disguise the even darker circles under her eyes, and her head seemed almost shrunken beneath the mountain of beaded braids piled on top. Her nurse's uniform hung off her limply, as if worry was eating her away from the inside and the baby was working on her from the outside.

I figured I had ten minutes tops before the real baby-sitter showed up. I'd have to make it quick. I pulled out my identification—which was not and never had been strictly legit, but could fool most people outside of law enforcement—and gave her a brief rundown on why I was there. She heard only the part she wanted to hear.

"You're trying to find George?" she asked, opening the door wide and gesturing for me to come inside. All suspicion vanished as her face lit up with hope.

I hated myself for causing her voice to rise with optimism. If George didn't want to be found, it was unlikely that I would ever be able to find him. I'd been down that empty road before. "Sort of," I explained. "It's all part of my broader investigation into Roy Taylor's death."

"He was good friends with Roy," she explained. "It took a lot out of him when Roy died." With that, she was off and running. The words rushed out of her in a torrent. Either she was desperate for help in finding her husband or she was a single mother on overdrive.

"We'd been dating about a year when Roy was murdered," she added. "Before that, he and George were as tight as can be. They really had a connection. Do you think George's disappearance had anything to do with Roy's death? That happened such a long time ago."

Before I could stop her, she marched into a small living room that was miles cleaner than my own, plopped George Jr. on the couch, then pulled out two fat photo albums from beneath the coffee table. She opened one and showed me several pages of photos featuring her husband and Roy Taylor. They were drinking beer, grilling burgers, holding up long strings of fish and goofing for the camera—a pictorial of male bonding in action. "That's at Roy's fishing cabin," she explained. "They went up there all the time. It was on some smaller lake a few miles from Lake Gaston. I don't know exactly where. It was strictly no women allowed. We hadn't been together long enough then for me to tell him to cut out that shit." She complained happily, clinging to the normalcy of bitching about her husband, pretending that he hadn't disappeared more than two months ago.

"I was happy he was friends with Roy," she continued. "It was hard for George back then, finding friends on the job. At the time, he was the only African-American patrolling their beat. They hired a lot more later on. Roy was the only one he could talk to about the job. They really got along. It tore him up when Roy was murdered. He didn't even hear about it until I told him the next afternoon. He'd driven up to the cabin in the morning, before the murder hit the papers. I broke the news to him when he called me later that afternoon—"

"George went up to the cabin alone?" I interrupted. "Before he knew Roy was dead?"

She nodded. "He promised Roy he'd do some repair work on the icebox up there. George was handy about things like that. I don't know what to do now when something gives out. I don't have a clue."

Neither do the rest of us, I thought to myself.

"He was so upset when I told him about Roy," she said. "Later on, he told me that he'd just sat there, staring off the end of the dock, wondering why Gail had done it. Wondering if he could have stopped it from happening. He'd followed them home that night, you know, to make sure they arrived safely. But he left right away because Gail's mother was waiting for them, angry they'd been so late returning from the bar. He didn't want to interfere. He kept thinking that if only he had stayed a little while, things might have been different. He was never the same after that. I sometimes wonder if Roy's death was what made George..." Her voice trailed off into silence.

"Made George what?" I prompted.

She was staring at the photos of her missing husband and I wasn't even sure she heard me.

"You have to help me," she finally said after a long moment of silence. Her baby had gone to sleep on the cushion beside her, oblivious to his mother's sorrow. "The police don't really care that George has disappeared. They think he was dirty, I know they do. They kept asking me stuff like, did he drink? Did he do drugs? Did he gamble? They didn't believe me when I told them no way."

Her voice faltered before she continued. "It was true that he started drinking more after Roy died," she admitted, "but it was never a problem. And he pretty much quit entirely once I got pregnant and couldn't join in. I tried to tell the police that but they wouldn't believe me. Then some guy named Steven Hill came over and said that he used to work with George. He said he would help find George, but I didn't know then that he worked for Professional Standards. He didn't want to find George, not really, he just wanted to find evidence that George was dirty."

"Was he dirty?" I asked. "I'm sorry, but I need to know."

She took it calmly. "Look around you. Does it look like George was taking payoffs? He used to work security at Durham Bulls games and high school basketball games just to earn a few extra dollars. And he was home with me the rest of the time. He didn't have the energy to be dirty. And he sure didn't have the money."

She had a point. George Carter had not been living in the lap of luxury. "Maybe he was gambling or on drugs or in debt?" I suggested.

This time she glared. "George went to church, worked three jobs, mowed our lawn every weekend and spent most of his free time massaging my back once I got pregnant. Does that sound like a drug fiend or gambling man to you?"

Actually, it sounded like a brother from another planet. But I didn't offer my opinion. I tried another tact. "Had anything unusual happened to upset him before he disappeared? Strange phone calls? Visitors you didn't know?"

She nodded. "The cops asked me the same thing. I told that Steven Hill guy about the judge visiting, but that was all. He said they already knew about it and had looked into it. He told me I better keep it to myself." Her voice dropped. "He acted like maybe the judge was dirty. That maybe he and George had been doing something wrong together. I didn't believe it for a minute."

"What was the judge's name?" I asked.

"I forget," she said. "He came to see George just after Christmas. George told me later that it was a sad story. That the judge had been drinking a lot and he'd been voted out of office and just wanted to talk to George about things. He told me not to worry. The visit had been about nothing. But he was really quiet for a few days after that, and I remember that he disappeared for an afternoon the next Tuesday when he was supposed to have the day off. He said he'd been called back into work, but, later on, I wondered."

That would have been the day George Carter visited Gail on death row, I thought. "You know that judge is dead, right?" I asked. "He was killed last week."

She froze. "You don't think George had anything to..." She could not finish the sentence.

I shook my head. "I don't know what to think," I confessed. "Are you sure George didn't get any unusual phone calls before he disappeared. Maybe from other officers, people he worked with?"

She shook her head. "If he did get any calls, it wasn't when I was home."

"Tell me exactly what the police did when you reported George missing?" I asked. I wanted to know exactly who had been involved in the search and how.

She stroked her son's thick hair idly while she composed her thoughts. "I called them around dusk the day that George disappeared. He'd left that morning to buy the baby a car seat. They won't let you take the baby home from the hospital unless you have one, and I was due at any time. After that, he was going to go cut some firewood. A guy he knew from work had volunteered to let him clear away some fallen trees from Hurricane Fran. We'd just gotten the chimney repaired and cleaned. We were going to use our fireplace for the first time that night. George said he'd be back by early afternoon, but he wasn't. I was nine months pregnant and freaking out. I called everywhere. I even called that damn cop bar and he wasn't there. The bartender said he'd been there the night before with Pete Bunn. I wasn't too happy when I heard his name. Pete had worked with George a long time ago and there had been some trouble later on. I didn't want to talk to him, but I was desperate. I finally called him around six o 'clock. He was on the job, and I asked him if he'd seen George. He hadn't."

"Pete Bunn?" I asked. "He was on the same drug unit as your husband a couple of years back, right? Before George went back on patrol?"

She nodded. "But George never liked him much and didn't stay in touch after he left the unit."

"What was the trouble about?"

She looked disgusted. "Testifying at the trial for Roy's murder. Pete had been there with Roy and George the night before, at the bar, but he refused to admit it and begged George not to tell anyone. He didn't want to take the stand. He said his wife would kill him if she knew he'd been out drinking. George hated people who lied. He thought Pete should have taken the stand and explained what a good cop Roy was."

"If George didn't like Pete, why do you think they had drinks together the night before your husband disappeared?"

"I don't know," she admitted. "I was surprised to hear he'd been seen with Pete. All George told me that night was that a friend needed to talk to him about something and he was going to be late coming home from work. People called George a lot when they were having trouble. He was a good listener. Everyone loved him." Her voice faltered as she realized she was speaking in the past tense. She paused, regaining her composure. The silence that followed was broken when the baby decided to drop a load in his diapers, a task that involved some spectacular sound effects. It sounded like an elephant stepping on a carton of water balloons and bubble wrap. I had an urge to run for high ground but, without missing a beat, Carter's wife just plucked a fresh diaper from a stack on the back of the couch and efficiently changed the child as she continued.

"When George got home that last night," she said, "he was really quiet. I was already asleep, being pregnant and all, but I woke up when he got in bed, and I could tell he was just lying there awake. He wouldn't say what was wrong, but I know something was." She was silent for a moment, remembering. "I told the cops about Pete and they followed up, but said it was nothing. They said George and Pete had a few drinks then left the bar separately. That Pete had worked the late shift after that, filling in for some guy getting married the next day."

"So Pete Bunn didn't know where your husband was when you called him the Saturday he disappeared?" I confirmed.

She shook her head. "No one knew where he had gone. I called everyone I could think of. I know you're supposed to wait twenty-four hours, but I was so worried. It was a nightmare. I was so upset I started having contractions, and that freaked me out even worse. I finally phoned George's sergeant and he sent some guys over right away. Steven Hill joined them about an hour later and promised he'd do everything he could. They sent out a bulletin describing George's car. No one had seen him. He was just... gone." She stared down at the photo album in her lap, running her thin fingers over the images of her missing husband. "I stopped having contractions. My mother came over. We waited and waited. A week went by. Then two. George Jr. was born. I went back to work. I had to." She looked up. "That's about it."

"Why are the police so sure he left voluntarily?" I asked. The baby was starting to squirm, and I was afraid he'd begin bawling, bringing our interview to an end.

"George called me," she said in a voice so low I had to lean forward to hear her correctly.

"He called you?" I asked, surprised.

She nodded. "The police put a tap on our phone, in case he had been kidnapped or something. At least that's what Steven Hill said. I think now he was hoping to catch someone calling George about a payoff or something illegal."

"And George was taped trying to phone you?"

"That's what they said," she murmured softly. "He called late one night. You could hear heavy traffic in the background. His voice was muffled. He sounded far away." Her voice broke. Now it was a tossup as to who would start crying first, her or her son.

"What exactly did he say?" I asked gently.

"Something like, 'I can't do this anymore. I'm sorry but it's better if I just go.' And then the connection was cut off."

"That's it?" I asked.

She nodded.

"Not much to go on," I said.

She wiped a tear from her eye. "I think they had other evidence," she admitted in a faint voice. "Steven Hill didn't say exactly what. He told me he would keep it quiet. I didn't know whether to believe him or not, but he said if I just hung in there, he'd try to find George and bring him back. Or, at the very least, there was a chance that I could draw part of his pension if nothing was ever proved about possible wrongdoing."

"But you still don't believe that your husband was doing anything wrong?"

She shook his head. "I know George, and he was a good cop and a good man. I mean, he is a good man."

Funny, those were the exact same words many people had used to describe Roy Taylor. But if a good man is so hard to find, why do they always seem to end up dead, maimed or missing?

"What was he wearing the day he disappeared?" I asked. "And was there anything else missing from the house? Clothing or a suitcase?"

"Nothing was missing but the clothes he had on his back," she said. The baby began to cry and she rubbed his tummy gently while she reached for the second photo album with her free hand and turned to the last page. "You can see for yourself what he was wearing. We took photos of my belly that morning because it was so huge. I used up the last few shots on the roll taking pictures of George dressed as a lumberjack. We joked that he was the only black man in the history of Durham County to ever wear a flannel shirt."

My heart jumped at her words. Have you ever had your life changed just by hearing a single phrase or with a single glance? It happened to me that day. I stared down at the last known photos of George Carter and I knew at once that he was dead. There he stood, posed on the front steps of his home, holding a chainsaw over his shoulder like a rifle, a goofy smile on his face. He was just as my pal Marcus Dupree had described him. He was tall and graceful, his face seemingly etched from stone, his aquiline features a deep brown, the triangular nose prominent between chiseled cheekbones. But it was his shirt that made me certain he was dead. George Carter was wearing a green-and-black checked flannel shirt and I had seen the pattern before—in Pete Bunn's farm dumping pile. Yes, George Carter was probably dead.

"Why are you staring at him that way?" his wife asked anxiously.

I looked up into her tear-filled eyes. "Nothing," I lied. "I just recognized him from some Durham Bulls games. I always wondered who he was. He's a striking looking man." And an innocent one, too, I thought to myself. If he was dead as I feared, chances were good he wasn't my killer.

"Yes, he is striking," Carter's wife agreed softly, running her fingers over his image. "And such a good man, too."

I couldn't take it anymore. Innocence is an intolerable sight to an old cynic like me, yet I could not bear to be the one to topple her world. I murmured my thanks and left as soon as I could, making meaningless promises on my way out the door. I left her sitting there, late for work with no baby-sitter in sight, still staring at the photo album.

I'd planned to go visit Roy Taylor's fishing cabin that night— an awful lot of people had seemed interested in it, and I thought an exclusive search party was in order. But the information about George Carter was too important to ignore. I had to talk to Pete Bunn immediately. He knew something about Carter's disappearance or I'd eat that green-and-black shirt.

Knowing that Carter was dead and probably parked on Pete Bunn's farm, I wasn't about to revisit him without a gun. And if my gun was gone, the only option was to beg Bobby D. for one of his. After all, I'd already commandeered his car. What was a pistol or two between friends?

This meant either a trip to the hospital to ask Bobby's permission or a clandestine visit to his apartment. Efficiency won out. I already had his entire ring of keys and it would be at least a week before they let him out of the hospital. With any luck, I'd have his gun back in place by the time he was sprung. I stared at

Bobby's keys. God knows what closet doors I could open with those—or what skeletons might fall out.

It was a short drive to West Raleigh where Bobby D. maintained a love pad on the ground floor of a large Victorian house near N.C. State University. Like Bobby, the place was large: large rooms, large kitchen, large closets, large television screen, large velvet portrait of Elvis—in his porcine Vegas days, of course—hanging on the bedroom wall above a king-size bed. The apartment was as immaculate as always. Bobby had a whole squadron of middle-aged girlfriends only too happy to scrub his love nest clean. I've never understood why so many women clean up after men to prove their love, while men get away with proving their love by letting the women clean.

I checked the refrigerator and had a good laugh over the Weight Watchers entrees, since I knew he ate them four at a time. Then I selected a couple of French bread pizzas to nuke for an early supper as I searched for his gun cache. I knew he had a collection somewhere; he always bragged when he added one to his stash. I found it in a gray metal box hidden in the closet. He owned enough firepower to arm a small street gang.

I selected seven handguns and laid them out on the kitchen table, trying to decide on one. The first two were Lorcins— garbage guns designed for disposable death. They were cheap enough to fire and toss away, but just as likely to blow up in your hand. What was Bobby doing with them anyway? I shuddered and put them aside. The rest were more reliable.

He had a Colt .45, Ruger .357, a SIG Sauer semiautomatic and a 9mm H&K. I considered the Colt .45 seriously because it was a revolver and I was reluctant to go waving an unknown semi around. In the end, I chose a Smith & Wesson .44 magnum with a barrel long enough to dry clothes on. That sucker was more than ten-and-a-half-inches long. Overkill, perhaps, but a nice weight. Clutching the solid grip, I felt like Jesse James. Most important, I had handled one before. I returned the other guns to their hiding place and left an IOU for the .44, just in case. I didn't want Bobby D. to go off half-cocked, so to speak, if he discovered it missing.

I felt ready to face the mysterious Pete Bunn. Just the same, it wouldn't hurt to let someone know where I was going, just in case I ended up next to the vanished George Carter. But who could I call? There weren't a whole lot of people who would care if I were missing. I had no idea where Jack was this time of day, and I was not anxious to explain my current situation to Bobby D. since there was little he could do and he had his hands full groping nurses and complaining about the hospital food. I'd have to swallow my pride and give Bill Butler a call.

I sat at the kitchen table eating French bread pizza while I dialed. Bill was at his desk and none too pleased to hear my muffled voice. "Sorry," I said. "We have a bad connection. There seems to be pizza on the line."

"That gets old after a while," he warned me.

"Sort of like I do?" I suggested.

"Sort of like I feel," he countered. "I have news for you. I was just about to give you a call."

"Yeah?"

"Hill will talk to you, but it has to be tonight. He's got something big kicking in tomorrow and won't have any extra time for weeks. He's not happy about taking time out for this crap, but he'll do it as a favor to me."

I was silent. Out of surprise. I had not expected Steven Hill to agree.

"Did you hear me?" Bill repeated.

"It has to be a public place," I told him. I wasn't liking what I was hearing about Hill. And I don't like acting any stupider than I am.

"Oh, for god's sakes," Bill said, exasperated. "If it makes you feel better."

"It does. Tell him to meet me at the Lone Wolf at nine o'clock tonight. He'll know where it is. I'll hear what he has to say."

"I'm sure he'll be thrilled."

I had to hand it to Bill—as a transplanted northerner, no one could touch him when it came to the sarcasm department.

I drove back to Durham, revising my strategy and feeling secure knowing that the Smith & Wesson was wedged in the glove compartment. I'd see what Steven Hill had to say to me tonight and talk to Pete Bunn in the morning.

Better yet, I thought, as I passed by a pickup truck loaded with a pack of baying beagles, I wouldn't talk to Pete Bunn at all. At least not yet. I'd revisit his deserted farm tomorrow instead, only this time with some help. I had an old friend named Slim Jim Jones who would be just the person to call.

The Starlite is the only drive-in movie theater left in this part of the state. People from counties around flock there to watch first-run movies and stuff their faces with popcorn, dill pickles and twenty-five cent hard-boiled eggs. If you're more into drive-by than drive-in, the owner also runs a gun shop out of the concession stand.

I drove past the flickering screen wistfully. I loved parking in the front row, not budging my big southern butt from my big Detroit car, lying half-comatose in the privacy of my automobile, overeating on junk food, popping open a beer and muttering comments at the actors. It made me feel so very American. Unfortunately, I could not stop to linger. I had miles to go before I could sleep.

The owner of the Lone Wolf looked as if his mother-in-law had just walked in holding hands with his mistress. He was definitely not pleased.

"Johnny," I lied, "how nice to see you again." What I really wanted to do was pistol-whip him with my new ten-inch barrel, then throw him in the Dumpster out back with the rest of the garbage.

"Save it," he growled, scowling at a table where Steven Hill sat waiting for me. "I suppose you're responsible for bringing that jerk into my bar?"

"That jerk?" I widened my eyes innocently. "Is he not a fellow brother in blue?"

"He's a professional snitch, and half the guys who come in here spend their time on the job avoiding the likes of him. Kindly get him out of here before my business takes a nosedive."

I glanced around the main room. A dozen or so overweight men and women sat drinking themselves into oblivion. It looked like a convention of Weebles, except that they not only wobbled, they also looked like they might fall down at any moment. "Seems like you're doing all right to me," I said. "Better than last night." A bored-looking waitress yawned in one corner. "Look at that," I added. "There's even an alert staff member standing at the ready to handle the every whim of this overflow crowd."

He walked away without asking if I wanted a drink. Whatever happened to good old-fashioned southern hospitality?

"We meet again." Steven Hill rose from the table as I approached and flashed me a smile guaranteed to melt all panties within a ten-mile radius. Fortunately, I wasn't wearing any.

"Seems to me that we never really met properly in the first place," I corrected him. I shook his hand just to let him know that I was no wimp in the muscle department, then took a seat. He was drinking Red Dog beer. I am immune to all trends and ordered Bud Lite. The bored waitress took my order, gave Hill a not-so-subtle look and slouched away to do my bidding.

It was odd. Steven Hill was every bit as handsome as he had been at Peyton Tillman's funeral. His eyes were as green, his dark hair thick and feathered, his body still as muscled beneath an immaculate golf shirt and pressed pants. But, up close, the man excited me about as much as a pile of dirty laundry.

He was too perfect, I decided. Like a man hiding in a Halloween costume. Who knew who really lived behind that mask?

"You're staring at me," he said, sounding pleased. Women probably stared at him a lot.

"You look about twenty years younger than Peyton Tillman," I said. "How is it that you were old enough to serve in Vietnam?"

"Oh, I'm old enough. I just have good bone structure. My mother was part Cherokee."

The old part-Cherokee trick, eh? Half the people in this state assuaged their white consciences by claiming to be part-Cherokee. "You were friends with Peyton Tillman, weren't you?" I asked.

He looked away. "I knew him. We weren't friends. Why are you asking about him?" When I didn't answer, he continued. "My only tour coincided with his last one. He's five years older than me. Was, I mean. It's too bad what happened to him."

"Yeah," I agreed. "Too bad. When was the last time you saw him alive?"

He put his beer bottle down on the tabletop. When he smiled at me, I knew just how Little Red Riding Hood felt. "I thought you were looking into Roy Taylor's death. Why all the questions about Tillman?"

I shrugged. "Just curious."

"So am I. About a lot of things. You're an interesting woman."

He flashed me his megawatt smile again and all I could think was: here I sit covered with bruises from an accident, and he hasn't said a word? Instead, he's trying to come on to me? My makeup can't be that good.

"Really," he insisted when I didn't answer. "When all this is over, I'd love to get to know you."

When all what was over? "Hmm," I said vaguely.

When I ignored his come-on, Hill aimed his smile at the approaching waitress and had more luck. She tried to put my beer in my lap she was so busy licking her lips back. "Nice-looking," Hill confided when she sashayed away. "But I prefer an intelligent woman. You intrigue me. Tell me about your work."

I gritted my teeth. He was laboring under the misapprehension that women were either beautiful or intelligent. In my world, they could be both.

"I heard you went to see Gail Honeycutt on death row," I said. Time to nip his stirring of the loins in the bud, so to speak, and head him off before the pass.

His eyes slid away as he searched the room out of habit. I knew his type. He never looked at the woman he was with because he was too busy checking out whether the grass was greener in someone else's pasture.

"I'm not the only one of Roy's old partners who went to see her," he said. "No crime in that."

"How did you know other officers visited her?" I asked.

He shrugged. "I heard. In fact, I think that's where I got the idea."

He was a closed-mouth bastard. He'd talk all night and not say a word if I wasn't careful. I plowed on. "I hear you work in Professional Standards these days."

He frowned. "It's not popular, but it has to be done. I'm not going to apologize for being an honest cop. The future of the department is on the line."

"I also heard you helped Missing Persons look for George Carter when he disappeared."

He stared at me. "You're finding out a lot in a short period of time."

I shrugged. "It's my job."

"Then you'll understand that it was my job to look for Carter." He took a swig of beer. "Missing Persons called me in because they knew I'd worked with him and thought I might know where he'd gone. What they didn't know was that George was on my division's hit list. Suspected of being in on a couple of bad-news deals. I tried to keep it from his wife. She doesn't need to hear that right now, but it's pretty obvious that he left before we could move in on him."

"Because of his last phone call," I said.

"The phone call and a lot more I can't tell you about."

"Confidential department matters?" I whispered loudly. My sarcasm was wasted. He just nodded.

"That's right." he said. "And I'd like to keep it that way. It gives his wife a chance to collect on his pension one day."

"Is that entirely honest of you?" I asked innocently. "If the man was dirty, does he deserve a pension?"

He gave me a sharp glance. "I said I was honest, not heartless. Look, I don't see what this has to do with Roy's death. Roy died eight years ago. And it's pretty obvious that Gail did the honors.

George took off a couple of months ago. It's a stretch to think the two events are related."

"True," I said, pleased I was finally getting under his skin. Was that sweat I saw forming on his perfect brow? Casey Jones, interrogator supreme. "Let's get back to Roy," I suggested. "How close were you?"

He shrugged. "We got along fine," he said. "We worked together. We weren't best friends or anything. No offense to Roy, but my wife at the time couldn't stand his wife. Thought she was trashy. I guess she was right. Offing your husband is pretty trashy, wouldn't you say?"

Depends on the husband, I thought to myself. "You didn't hang out with Roy doing the guy thing?" I asked. "Go fishing up at his cabin?"

His eyes flickered. He was one suspicious dude. "I'm not a big fisherman. Not enough action for me. Where was his cabin anyway? I know he and George were always up there. Wasn't it Lake Gaston or somewhere nearby?"

"Beats me," I lied. Why should I give him any information? He wasn't giving me any. "Why didn't you testify about what a great guy he was during Gail's trial?" I asked. "Like George did?"

He tapped his fingers against the beer bottle. "That's easy. It was a high-profile case and everyone wanted a piece of the publicity. George testified because he'd seen him last. But when it came to being a character witness, I had to stand in line behind the brass. They never got down to us peons."

"You're not such a peon anymore," I pointed out.

"Hey, I earned my promotions, okay?"

Geeze, he was verging on surly. Maybe I should have flirted back after all.

"Why did you agree to see me?" I asked, hoping to bring us back to calmer ground.

He looked at me over the neck of his beer bottle, hesitating before he spoke. "I'm one hundred percent sure that Gail killed Roy," he explained. "But I figure it can't hurt if the rest of the world is one hundred percent sure, too. Besides, the more you know, the more you'll see that it was nothing more than another useless domestic murder caused by too much alcohol and not enough love."

"That's pretty poetic," I observed.

He ignored me. "I've been a cop for almost twenty years. I know why and how people murder other people. There's nothing all that mysterious about it."

"Then why the wall of blue?" I asked.

Hill leaned forward, his face earnest. "Casey, I know you're a professional and take your cases seriously, but this is one job where you could end up hurting a lot more people than you're going to help. Roy Taylor was my friend, but the truth is that he was a dirty cop and I'd like to keep that from his family. It's the decent thing to do. Can you understand that?"

"What about his wife?" I asked. "She's paying with her life."

"What about her?" he said. "She killed him. She has to pay the price."

"Sorry, I'm not convinced," I told him. "And I have no proof that he was dirty, except other people's opinions. Do you have proof?"

He looked annoyed. "Leave it alone, Casey. Believe me, my department has enough proof to bury Roy Taylor."

"He's already buried," I pointed out.

He glared. "Look, I worked with the guy at one time. I knew what was going on. I'm not going to say more than that. Now Roy is dead. What's the point in bringing it up? You're only going to hurt people."

"Do you keep in touch with Pete Bunn?" I said, hoping to throw him off-balance.

He remained unshaken. "I talk to him every now and then, just like I keep in touch with a lot of my old partners. We're not friends."

"Did you know he had retired early?"

"Yeah, I knew." He signaled the waitress for another beer.

"Why did he retire early?"

He paused. "Pete had a drinking problem," he finally said. "A bad one. When his wife divorced him, it got worse. They put him on white collar because it kept him off the front line. But he took a swing at a lieutenant colonel after a liquid lunch one day. He was gone a week later. He's lucky he kept any pension at all."

"Do you know where he is now?"

"What do you mean?" he asked. "Is he gone?"

I shrugged. I wanted to know how much Hill kept up with his old partners and decided to lie. "That's what I'm asking you. He doesn't seem to live in Durham, and I can't find him. Do you know where he's gone?"

"Who knows where Pete went. Maybe the shore. He liked to fish and drink. That was about it. Maybe he moved to Myrtle Beach or something. Who knows. And come to think of it, who cares?"

I cared. And I also knew. What I couldn't tell was if Steven Hill knew that Pete Bunn was living on a farm in Chatham County.

"I read through the transcripts of all court cases involving the drug unit you used to serve on," I told him.

"All of them?" he asked, so thrown he actually ignored the opportunity to smile at the fawning waitress again.

"I read fast. And there are a couple of odd things about those cases."

"Odd like how?" He sounded confused.

"Odd like it seemed to me that the charges got dismissed or reduced an awful lot of the time."

He tapped his fresh beer up and down on the tabletop, staring at the initials some drunk had carved into the cheap wood.

"Well?" I prompted.

He looked up. "I'm only telling you this because those cases are years old by now. I'm not breaking any confidentiality considerations."

"Of course you're not," I agreed.

"We were building up our network," he explained. "Putting in place informants, trying to build jackets on the bigger suppliers. Those cases involved street dealers. We let them go so they could become informers."

"That's a lot of informers. What'd they do? Run around informing on other informers?"

"Are you trying to be funny?" he asked suspiciously.

"No, just trying," I assured him.

"Look, the system stinks," he said. "But that's the way it works. We had to let them walk. If you check the record, I think you'll find that the guys who came up behind us made a lot of collars thanks to our work."

"I'm sure I will," I agreed. I was buying his story about as much as I believed the pre-discount prices at outlets.

"Ask Pete Bunn," he said confidently. "I'm sure he'll tell you the same thing."

"I bet he will," I said cheerfully. I swear I didn't mean to be snotty. But Steven Hill sure took it that way.

He pushed his chair back from the table and rose up to his full six-feet-plus height. "I gotta go," he said abruptly. "I'd say I've been helpful enough. Good luck with your investigation." He walked out the door—leaving me with the tab—only pausing long enough to accept a slip of paper from the waitress. I don't think it was a shopping list, at least not in the traditional sense of the term.

I put a ten on the table and followed him to the front door, watching as he climbed into a late-model Porsche that was painted a candy-apple red. It was exactly the kind of car that a wanker like him would drive. He peeled out of the driveway in a burst of gravel, and disappeared down Club Boulevard.

"You must be a real charmer," Johnny called out from behind the bar. "He couldn't get away fast enough."

"Really," the waitress agreed. She gave me a triumphant smile. "If I had a man like that," she said, "I wouldn't let him get away so easily. Good-looking and with a Porsche, too. Yum, yum, did he make my motor hum."

"Just cross your legs, honey," I advised her. "It'll pass."

I knew she'd be even more insulted when she saw the tip I'd left.

I got up early the next day to call my friend Slim Jim Jones. He had been awake for hours, milking the cows, slopping the hogs and plowing a plot near the house for a truck garden. Slim Jim lived on one of the last real working farms in Wake County, where he worked hard at being a devoted son to his crusty old mama. He had to get up mighty early in the day to protect the livestock from her trigger-happy, shotgun-toting habits. Mama Jones was suffering from failing eyesight and had been known to blow away a cow or two under the delusion that they were linebackers from the N.C. State football team gone bad and out to rob and rape her. They ate a lot of hamburger out on the Jones farm. You just had to chew carefully.

"Slim Jim Jones," I said enthusiastically into the phone. "How is my favorite long, cool drink of water this morning?"

"Cut the crap, Casey," he replied in a nasal voice that had never lost its mountain twang. "That sweet stuff don't work with me. What do you want?"

Poor Slim Jim. He really could not make up his mind whether he liked me or not. He'd been grappling with the issue for going on ten years now. Secretly, I think he adored me. Why else would I annoy him so much? Besides, he always came to my rescue when I asked, even if he did grumble at first. A few months ago, he'd even helped me track down the killer of a fat-cat real-estate developer, even though neither one of us had been all that sorry to see him dead.

"You still doing that search and rescue stuff for the Red Cross?" I asked casually. You had to sneak up on Slim Jim, or you'd spook him and he'd refuse right off the bat.

"Sure. Me and the boys found an old lady who'd wandered away from her rest home just last month. It was pretty cold, too. She'd have died if Tuck hadn't found her under some leaves."

"The boys" were Nip and Tuck, two of the smelliest bloodhound mixes ever sniffed by the human nose. They'd been named by Slim Jim's mama, who was a Damon Runyon fan and never read anything more current. Those dogs had special oil glands that produced a funky odor akin to fermented toe jam. You could tell they were coming from twenty miles downwind.

But they were good trackers and Slim Jim handled them well. He talked tough, but I knew for a fact that he kept two electric blankets out in the barn for those mutts and would have let them into his bed if he hadn't been afraid they'd be mistaken for women and blown away by nearsighted Mama Jones.

"Can you help me out on a job?" I asked. "I'll pay you two hundred dollars."

Slim Jim whistled. "Can't do nothing illegal for you, Casey."

"This is legal," I assured him. Hey, my fingers were crossed, okay? "When have I ever steered you wrong?"

"Ain't got enough hours in the day to get into that," he said in a rare burst of humor. Two hundred dollars vastly improved his naturally sour disposition. "Where and when?"

I told him where and negotiated the when. He would meet me out in Chatham County by two o'clock, but had to be back home by six at the latest to finish the evening farm chores. That left me two to three hours to search Pete Bunn's farm. It seemed plenty long enough.

I got there early, confirmed that the farm was still deserted, then hooked up with Slim Jim at the country store down the road. He was chewing tobacco with the store's owner and showing off Nip and Tuck. Like a lot of southerners with the mountains in their blood, Slim Jim was of Scottish descent. It showed in his craggy features. But he was also tall and lanky, with a long turkey neck and a peculiar way of cocking his round head sideways that made him look even more like a bird. At the moment, he was staring at Nip and Tuck like a proud papa.

Some unidentified breed had shaken Nip and Tuck's family tree somewhere down the line and they lacked the size and height of pure bloodhounds. Instead, they looked like mutant basset hounds wearing black-and-tan pajamas that were several sizes too big.

"Can they can track?" the store owner was asking dubiously. "They seem awfully low to the ground."

"Better than any two hounds I've ever had." Slim Jim spit a wad of tobacco on the ground a few inches from my feet as I approached. It was his way of saying hello. I joined them in admiring Nip and Tuck.

"What kind of job are you up to today?" the owner asked. I shot Slim Jim a warning glance and answered for him.

"Just a practice run out by the Haw River," I lied. "We're trying to convince the sheriff to use Nip and Tuck for lost-hiker searches, so he wants to see them do their stuff." Nip and Tuck began to howl, as if sensing my lie. I gritted my teeth and scratched behind their floppy ears to calm them, knowing I'd have to practically boil my hand to remove their stench when I was done.

"This some sort of secret mission?" Slim Jim asked as I climbed in the front seat of his truck and directed him down 15-501.

"You might say that," I said.

"But nothing illegal?" he asked me again.

"Of course not." I tried to sound offended but was completely stumped for a cover story. I ended up having to tell him the truth.

Slim Jim surprised me. "So you think maybe this fellow's body is buried somewhere on the farm?" he asked calmly when I was done. "And that the fellow who owns the farm did it?"

"That's right. Think Nip and Tuck can find the body?"

He nodded. "If it's there. But I can't guarantee it. Hell, we get a good enough whiff of that shirt and I might be able to track him down myself." He gave me a grin that framed two missing teeth. I smiled back. Slim Jim so rarely made a joke that it was best to encourage him when he did.

We parked the truck in a clearing near where the Haw River crossed 15-501. Anyone driving by would figure we were fishing. Nip and Tuck had fallen asleep in the truck bed and we had to drag them out by their scruffs before they would wake up.

"They're just conserving their strength," Slim Jim claimed as they flopped down in the sun and began to snore. I hoped he was right.

The day had turned hot, a rare flash of summer in early spring. I was sorry I'd worn a purple sweat suit as protection against poison ivy. By the time we reached Pete Bunn's land, I was sweating like a sow in a sauna. Meanwhile, Slim Jim hadn't broken a sweat. Love those country boys. A little hot sun doesn't go to their heads.

The heat didn't seem to bother Nip or Tuck either. They snuffled along at Slim Jim's feet, eating insects while they waited for a command from their master. He had both on a long twin tether, but the dogs seemed in no hurry to wander away. In fact, Slim Jim had to drag them forward most of the time. I was getting more dubious of their skills by the moment.

"When do we start?" I asked.

"Soon as we get there," he drawled.

I stopped and got my bearings. We were on the edge of the pine woods overlooking the hollow that cradled the farmhouse. I wanted to confirm that no one had returned home. I crept to the edge of the woods and saw nothing but rolling hills and an empty front yard. "Coast is clear," I announced. "Follow me."

We made our way down the narrow dirt lane to the dumping-ground clearing. Flies buzzed over the mound of junk, and an unseen creature scurried across some leaves on the far side of the pile. It took me a few minutes to locate the green-and-black checked shirt but I finally found it where I had stuffed it into an empty plastic milk crate. Slim Jim examined it carefully.

"You're lucky, Casey," he said.

"Why's that?"

"This here is blood. It'll give Nip and Tuck something to go on. Otherwise, it's been out in the rain and sun for a long time." He held out the shirt and I examined some rust stains near one torn edge. I'd missed them before, but Slim Jim was right: they could be blood.

"Any more of his clothes in there?" Slim Jim asked, peering at the junk pile.

I shrugged. "Lots of clothes in there, but it's hard to tell what else might have been his. It looks like the guy dumped a whole thrift shop here."

"Okay then," Slim Jim decided. "We'll go on what we got." He cradled the shirt around Nip's face and then around Tuck's while he whispered instructions in their ears.

"What are you telling them?" I demanded.

He gave me the evil eye. "My training methods are secret," he informed me, letting fly with a wad of tobacco juice that splatted to the ground near my feet.

I rolled my eyes and wiped the sweat off my forehead. I keep my hair pretty short, but at the moment, in the afternoon heat, it felt like I had a RuPaul wig weighing me down. I should have worn a baseball hat to shade me from the sun.

The dogs had grown still and sat side by side on the edge of the clearing, staring at Slim Jim. Their haunches quivered with contained excitement. Slim Jim unleashed both hounds, and, holding the shirt like it was a checkered flag at the Daytona 500, he waved it toward the ground and commanded, "Seek! Seek!"

Those smelly low-slung hounds leaped into action with an enthusiasm I reserve solely for Krispy Kreme doughnuts. They dashed out of the clearing and began running in ever- widening circles, their tails wagging furiously and their ears dragging on the ground like miniature dust mops.

"The ears help trap the scent close to the nose," Slim Jim explained as we waited for Nip and Tuck to pick up a trail. "They can smell nine hundred times better than we can."

"They smell all right," I agreed.

Suddenly, Nip gave a sharp bark and took off toward the main road. Either he was taking the easy way downhill or he'd found a trail.

"Is this working?" I asked between gasps as we followed both dogs toward the farmhouse.

"Can't tell yet," Slim Jim explained, not even winded. "They're dogs. They like to take their time."

They didn't like to take their time nearly enough for me. For what looked like nothing but a bunch of dog fat and loose skin, those two suckers could move. They dashed around the house, into the barn and out again, along the perimeter of a backyard lawn and then into some bushes leading to the pastures. We had no choice but to tag along, with Slim Jim exhorting them to "seek" and "seek" until I was ready to stuff the shirt down his throat.

Thirty minutes later, I had sweated away at least three pounds and was ready to throw in the towel. Just as I was about to admit it, a remarkable change came over Tuck. He froze and flopped to the ground, his nose resting on his front paws. His tail curled up in a plume, the tip pointing over his head like a one-way sign. He began to make an eerie whistling sound.

"He's found a trail," Slim Jim whispered. I felt a prickling rise on the back of my neck. It was one thing to go looking for a body out of desperation. It was another to find one.

Nip joined his brother and lay quietly at the head of the scent trail, with the same posture and the same obedient stillness.

"Ready?" Slim Jim asked. "When I let them go, they're going to really go."

"Ready," I promised.

"Find it," Slim Jim commanded his dogs and they leapt forward, baying in unison. Their howls echoed over the hills like a primordial warning, primitive sounds of triumph meant to terrify as they closed in on their quarry. We jogged to keep pace, following Nip and Tuck over a rolling hill, part of the broken-down fence and into the pine woods again.

"They're taking us back to the clearing where we started," I said, disappointed. "We're going in circles."

"Trust them," Slim Jim told me, his lean frame darting forward. "Nip and Tuck know what they're doing."

The dogs picked up their pace, squat legs pedaling furiously. They arrived at the clearing a minute before we did. We found them laying obediently at attention, their noses pointed toward the far end of the junk pile.

"It's the shirt," I said. "They've probably found the rest of the shirt."

"It's not the dang shirt," Slim Jim answered crossly, annoyed at my lack of faith. "They're trained for flesh, okay? Help me look around."

He took the lead and began moving old junk to one side, eroding part of the pile away. Together, we dragged the set of old box springs, the smashed baby seat, broken flower pots and a small mountain of yard debris to one side.

"This section of the pile seems mighty dense to me," Slim Jim said. "Why would someone want to go piling all the big stuff in the far corner like that?"

Why indeed? I was starting to believe those two bloodhound impostors knew their stuff. It took us almost twenty minutes to uncover the far corner of the pile. Nip and Tuck inched forward with each object we removed, until their noses quivered on the edge of the cleared area.

"It's here," Slim Jim said confidently. "You were right, Casey. The boys are never wrong. There's something here."

Slim Jim was right. Nip and Tuck were right. I was right. It was only George Carter who wasn't all right. Because there, beneath the far end of the dumping ground, was an area of earth that had been disturbed and packed back into place. We scraped away a base layer of leaves and discovered the faint outline of an uneven rectangle big enough for George Carter's body.

Slim Jim imitated his dogs and got down on all fours, sniffing the ground. "How long did you say this fellow has been missing?" he asked me.

"A couple of months," I told him. "Maybe two and a half."

"Then we'd better hurry," Slim Jim decided. He picked through the junk pile and selected a couple of broken farm tools with sharp enough points to serve as makeshift shovels. Together, we worked one corner of the rectangle, carefully probing beneath the earth's surface and removing chunks of loose dirt by hand. We worked for half an hour, the mound of earth beside us growing, as did the dogs' whining.

"You sure?" I asked for about the fifteenth time.

"I'm sure," Slim Jim answered grimly. "I feel something."

He scraped away another layer of dirt. We were concentrating on an area two feet square and had reached three feet in depth. Nip and Tuck were practically turning inside out with excitement. Even I could smell the change in the air.

"Almost got it," Slim Jim announced. His face shifted and he blinked rapidly, withdrawing his hand from the hole. "Look for yourself," he told me, moving away from the grave toward fresh air.

"You okay?" I asked. "You look kind of green."

"Sure." He spat a wad of tobacco juice on the ground. "Just not enough lunch. Smell's not what I expected." He edged away and gulped for breath.

I crawled forward on my knees to where Slim Jim had been digging, and scraped away a thin layer of dirt. The outline of an arm emerged, or what was left of one. It curved inward toward the remnants of a hand that had detached from the body. Deterioration of the flesh was advanced, but cool weather had helped preserve the underlayer, and you could still tell that the victim had been a black man. I didn't need to see any more.

"It's him," I said, almost incredulously. "We actually found him." I looked down at Nip and Tuck. "You two are getting the thickest T-bone steaks you ever saw when all this is done."

I should never have mentioned food. Poor Slim Jim—he was game for the hunt, but green for the quarry. He dashed to the far side of the clearing, heaving the remains of his lunch into the brush. It was nice to have someone else throwing up for a change.

Nip and Tuck gave us a hard time when we tried to leave the site. Like Ghandi supporters, they went limp and refused to budge. We practically had to carry them from the scene. Slim Jim was baffled. I was pissed. Lugging seventy pounds of dog fat around is thirsty work. But soon Nip and Tuck were fast asleep in the truck bed, having earned their rest.

Slim Jim and I sat in the truck back at the country store, sipping Pepsis and eating banana moon pies. Trust me, it's an old country remedy for nausea. "What do we do now?" he asked.

"I don't know. I need to think," I admitted.

"Durnnit, Casey," Slim Jim complained. "You act like you didn't expect to find nothing. Don't you have a plan?"

Strictly speaking, no. But I was trying to come up with one fast.

"I think it's a good bet that Pete Bunn killed him, don't you?" I thought out loud. "I mean, with the body being found on his land and all."

Slim Jim shrugged. "Pretty stupid place to dump a body, if you ask me. I'd have put it on someone else's land."

"Yeah, but he could keep on eye on it there," I said.

Slim Jim glanced at his watch. He had more important matters on his mind. "Listen," he said. "I got to be back by six or Mama will have my hide."

And mine with it, I thought. "I could go to the governor," I suggested, still working out a plan. "Lay out this new evidence and try to get him to postpone Gail's execution while they look into this bad-cop angle."

"Which governor?" Slim Jim asked. "Our governor? Cuz that dog ain't gonna hunt with him, if you know what I mean. He's not postponing no execution this year. He's not real keen on letting killers go, if you hadn't noticed."

Slim Jim acted like he was from the sticks, but he was no fool. He was right about the governor. He would only cave in under extreme pressure, and there was still no direct evidence to link the deaths of Peyton Tillman and George Carter to Roy Taylor's murder. What was needed was a little spin control—and enough public pressure to force the governor to make his decision out in the open where he could be judged by the good citizens of the state.

"I've got an idea," I said. "But it will have to wait until morning. It will be too dark soon. That means I have to guard the body tonight."

Slim Jim whistled. "You're going to sit up awake in those woods all night?" he asked. "Listening to every sound and waiting for that Pete Bunn fellow to show up? Casey, you're a country girl, but you've been living in the city a long time now. I can't see you doing it, to be honest with you."

"I don't have a choice. If anyone is on to us and tries to move the body, we'd have nothing. Gail would be dead before we could find another connection."

"Don't have a connection now," Slim Jim pointed out with the practicality of a farmer.

"No," I admitted. "But I have enough to stop the scheduled execution date while they look to see if there is one. I just need to make some phone calls." I hesitated before I climbed out of the truck, not wanting to come right out and ask the favor. It was a big one after all. Slim Jim stared at me, waiting out my silence.

"Ah, all right," he finally said, reading my unspoken request. "I'll keep you company tonight. But I got to wait until Mama gets to sleep." He snorted to clear his sinuses, then began to chew his tobacco again. No wonder he never had a girlfriend. You'd have to wear a bib just to kiss him good night.

It was nearly eleven o'clock by the time I met Slim Jim back at the country store. I'd made my phone calls, though it took a while to track down the right reporter and even longer to locate a television-news announcer that the reporter thought could be trusted.

"All set?" Slim Jim asked. He held a small canister of chewing tobacco. Talk about camping light.

"Didn't you bring anything else?" I asked.

He stared at me blankly. "We're just spending one night out there, right?"

I nodded.

"Then what else do I need?" he asked and started the engine.

"We probably should have brought your mama and her shotgun," I said, somewhat embarrassed that I was toting a sleeping bag, my knapsack with a flashlight and the .44 magnum inside it and enough fried chicken from Hardee's to feed a starving Confederate battalion.

"I did bring one of her shotguns," he drawled. I could sense his grin in the dark. "Never know when it might come in handy."

He shot a rabbit with it. Then he skinned it and ate it for a midnight supper after building a hidden fire between a ring of boulders left behind eons ago when the Haw River had changed direction. It was about the most exciting thing that happened during the first half of the night. We took turns snoozing on the sleeping bag and keeping watch over the clearing. There wasn't a rustle that we could attribute to human movement, just a night full of owl chatter, deer footsteps, possum squeaks and an attempted raid on the fried chicken by a horde of hungry raccoons. I was on duty for that skirmish. We lost a few drumsticks, but I managed to save the rest. Raccoons can be tough, but I'm even tougher when it comes to protecting my biscuits and white meat.

I walked back to the main road every hour on the hour, but Pete Bunn's farmhouse remained dark and deserted. I was starting to get a bad feeling about the man. Somehow he'd been warned away. And once he saw his farm all over the evening news, we'd probably never see him again.

It was close to three o'clock in the morning when I heard a truck engine. It began as a far-off drone and grew louder as the vehicle made its way down the long driveway. Slim Jim was snoring softly beside the dying fire, and I left him in peace. I crept down the trail to the main farm road, the .44 firmly gripped in my hand. Clouds blocked the moonlight, shrouding the farm in darkness, but I could see the taillights of a truck glow red and then blink off at the base of the hill. Someone had pulled up in the front yard of the house. The engine cut out and the silence was abrupt. I could hear my heart beating in my chest and the pine needles crackling beneath my feet. I couldn't get any closer without giving up cover.

The sound of glass breaking traveled up the long drive. If it was Pete Bunn returning home, he'd forgotten his keys and was climbing in a window. But I had my money on someone else. Someone who had fewer scruples than I did when it came to breaking and entering.

I was about to chance being spotted on the road for the opportunity to get closer when a hand gripped my elbow. I jumped a good two feet in the air, swallowed a scream between clenched teeth and almost peed in my pants.

"It's me," Slim Jim whispered. "Don't you even think about going down that road."

"Damnit, Slim," I hissed. "You scared the crap out of me."

"Hush up," he commanded in a barely audible voice. "The sound'll float right down into that hollow."

"I need to see who it is," I muttered.

"No, you don't," he said. "I can't let you go down there. Sorry."

Geeze, he had a grip like a Sears Craftsman vise. I wasn't going anywhere until he decided to let go. I shut up and waited.

About thirty minutes later, we heard the truck engine rev to life. Slim Jim pulled me back into the woods, and we watched as the headlights bounced up the hill toward us. "Don't move," he warned me.

The lights swept over our heads in an arc as the driver reached the pinnacle of the hill and slowed for the curve. I thought my heart would burst from my chest. Slim Jim's hand tightened on my arm until the vehicle regained speed and disappeared down the hill toward the highway.

"I thought he was going to stop," I said, gasping for breath and rubbing my elbow.

"He was searching for something," Slim Jim decided. "He broke in through a window and was searching the house." He sounded pleased, as if he was enjoying a new game and having a mighty fine time.

"How do you know it's a 'he'?" I asked crossly. I wasn't sure I liked Slim Jim invading my turf.

"I got good night sight and he was driving a black Ford F-150 with reinforced rear wheels," Slim Jim answered with annoying confidence. "How many women do you know who drive one of those?"

Good point. I started down the road toward the house and was tackled from behind. Slim Jim was turning out to be a wee bit overprotective.

"Get off me," I hissed. "I almost blew my foot off. I'm carrying a .44 magnum, you idiot. Let go of me. I want to see what he wanted in the house."

"If he found what he was looking for, it's gone." Slim Jim explained. "If he didn't, you're not going to find it, either. I can't take the chance he might come back. Every hunter knows you don't go charging through the brush after some varmint unless you know what that varmint is."

I hated it, but Slim Jim was right.

"I'd kill to brush my teeth," I told Slim Jim early the next morning as I rinsed my mouth with leftover iced tea and spit it out on the campfire embers. It sizzled and sent a pleasing wisp of steam up into the brisk morning air. Dawn would break in a matter of minutes; the dark was nothing more than a shadow hovering in the pine trees at this point.

"Waste of time," Slim Jim offered. He was polishing off the remains of his midnight supper. "Sure you don't want some rabbit?"

I shook my head. I was a country bayou girl, but I'd grown up eating gator and leaving the bunnies alone so they could terrorize vacationing presidents.

"I feel great," I announced. "You'd think my back would hurt and I'd be cold, but I feel great. I must be getting over my injuries."

"Clean air," Slim Jim offered. "Night out is good for the soul."

I checked my watch. "Reporters are waiting. I gotta go make my calls."

"And I gotta go."

There had never been any question that Slim Jim would disappear once the reporters and cameras arrived. He kept such a low profile that I often wondered what the hell he was really up to. Sometimes he disappeared for nights on end and old Mama Jones wasn't talking. I never asked. I'd learned to mind my own business unless I was paid not to.

We erased all evidence of our night spent guarding George Carter's body, then headed back toward the truck. The man at the country store eyed us curiously when we entered the place.

We were an odd couple indeed to be spending evenings together in the wilds. "Where's the dogs?" he asked.

"Hell, they're home sleeping," I explained. "Too damn early for them." That confused him into minding his own business. He even let me use his phone, though he did linger near the junk food rack, dusting off cellophane wrappers while he eavesdropped. Slim Jim waved good-bye through the window as I dialed. He looked relieved that his duty was done.

I called the N&O reporter I had alerted the night before. I chose her because she had written the series on Gail's little girl and displayed more sensitivity than most when it came to covering the trial. As arranged, she was ready and standing by with a news crew from Channel 5. They had invaded the all-night Bluebird Diner outside of Pittsboro and eaten heartily while waiting for my phone call.

"I wasn't sure you'd really call," she said. "I'd have had a lot of pissed-off people on my hands."

"I'm a woman of my word," I assured her. "Just remember our deal."

"Don't worry," she promised. "I will."

I gave her directions to Pete Bunn's farm. She promised to be there in fifteen minutes. I waited for the full fifteen just to be safe, then made my second call.

"Chatham County Sheriff's Department," a voice muttered into the phone.

"I'd like to report a dead body," I said calmly.

The country-store owner was so surprised he forgot to dust the Devil Dogs.

CHAPTER TWELVE

The Chatham County sheriff was wasting his time trying to interrogate the N&O reporter and the Channel 5 news crew.

"How the hell did you get here before us?" he demanded. Not a person spoke. "Don't give me that first-amendment crap," the sheriff warned, but still no one answered. I didn't blame them. I was saying as little as possible myself.

He was a tall man with huge shoulders and a big belly that overflowed above his belt. And his tan sheriff's uniform was so starched it could have stood at attention without him. His hat was pushed back, revealing a basketball-shaped scalp, completely devoid of hair. Worst of all, he had tiny dark eyes that gleamed beneath a prominent forehead. I was glad I lived in Durham County.

He trained his small eyes on me. "What the hell were you doing here?" he asked impatiently. "Tell me again how you discovered the body."

Overhead, the cloud cover had thickened. The threat of rain had been hovering over us all morning and the gray day mirrored my suddenly ominous mood. My plan was not going as well as expected. I'd never met the Chatham County sheriff and he had turned out to be a whole lot smarter than I had hoped. He looked downright scornful as I repeated my lame story about coming out to the farm early the evening before in order to question Pete Bunn in connection with a missing-persons case I was pursuing. I said I had grown suspicious when no one was home. "I decided to walk around the property," I explained. "When I got to this junk pile, I was poking around and found a man's shirt with what looked like blood on it, and when I moved some stuff around to investigate, I noticed the shallow grave. It was getting late and I was afraid to stay. So I came back early this morning and found the body."

"Had to move an awful lot of junk around to find that grave," he said in a dry voice. It sounded like the warm-up hiss of a rattlesnake.

We were interrupted by the arrival of an out-of-breath deputy. He had huffed and puffed his way up the hill from the house to deliver his news.

"The house has been broken into and searched," he reported. "It's trashed. Everything is upside down, dumped on the floor. No blood, though."

The sheriff stared at me and waited.

"Don't look at me," I protested. "I didn't go near the place."

He turned his back and spoke to another one of his deputies. "Anything yet? You're trained in that crap. What or who is it?" he demanded.

The crew of deputies had worked hard and uncovered the entire body in little more than an hour. What was left of George Carter now stared up at the treetops, oblivious to the activity swarming around him.

"Black male, about six feet five," the deputy reported. "Gunshot wound to the chest. Probably an exit wound. I'd say he was shot in the back. He's wearing jeans and part of a shirt. No identification. Body's been in the ground awhile. A couple months, at least, would be my guess. "

"This the Pete Bunn fellow you've been trying to question?" the sheriff asked.

I shook my head. "Pete Bunn is white."

The sheriff looked disgusted. "Then who the hell is this?"

The news crew had begun to roll film in order to capture the unearthed body and I was careful to step out of the way. Slim Jim Jones wasn't the only one who preferred to keep a low profile.

"Where do you think you're going?" the sheriff demanded. He crooked a finger the size of a link sausage and beckoned me to come closer. I inched a foot toward him and stopped.

"Any idea who this might be?" he asked in a dangerously calm voice.

I coughed modestly. "I have an idea," I said.

"Please enlighten me," the sheriff commanded between clenched teeth.

"There's a Durham police officer who disappeared about two months ago who fits the description of the body. His name is George Washington Carter. He used to work with Pete Bunn. It might be him." As I spoke, I noticed a deputy slip quietly from the clearing and head toward one of the patrol cars pulled up in the driveway. Word would be out soon.

"Why do you think he's here?" the sheriff asked, sounding as if every syllable he spoke to me caused him great personal pain.

"I don't really know," I lied.

Her timing could not have been worse: as if on cue, the newscaster from Channel 5 planted herself next to the clearing and began to report in a loud camera voice that dripped with professional concern. "Sources close to the investigation have identified the body as that of a Durham police officer missing since January," she confidently announced. "The name is being withheld until the family can be notified. In another surprise twist, some investigators are claiming that his death is related to the sensational Roy Taylor murder of eight years ago and may also be linked to the recent suicide of former Superior Court Judge Peyton Tillman. While this connection is still being confirmed, some local law-enforcement officials have expressed private concern about the upcoming execution of Gail Honeycutt for Roy Taylor's death. Speaking on the condition of anonymity, one insider told this reporter that new evidence linked to the body you see behind me could clear Gail Honeycutt and lead to new indictments in the Roy Taylor murder."

Not bad, I thought. Now all I had to do was come up with the evidence.

The sheriff was staring at the newscaster with tightly drawn lips and a thunderous expression.

"At least someone knows what's going on," I ventured.

His answering glare could have curdled milk still in a cow.

By noon, the clearing had turned into a law-enforcement circus. A squadron of state troopers had arrived to restore order and give the locals a helping hand. The State Bureau of Investigation had also joined the crew once word got out that the victim was probably law-enforcement. The SBI officers were conspicuous by their sex (male), their attire (three-piece suits) and their technology (earpieces, cords, walkie-talkies, beepers). Those guys had more gizmos going than Circuit City on a Saturday morning.

The Channel 5 crew had departed so that their scoop could lead off the afternoon news, but other television stations had arrived. It had been a slow news month so far, highlighted by a wild dog terrifying rabies-fearing mothers in Cary and a loose tiger cub thought to be roaming Durham. The intrepid dog remained at large, eluding all attempts at capture and achieving the status of a canine Che Guevara. Meanwhile, the tiger cub had turned out to be an obese tabby cat. Every reporter in the Triangle was dying for a real news story and they were there to get one. Unfortunately, no one knew what was going on beyond the information I had fed to my selected reporters. The others were desperate for details, but none of the officers was talking. There was nothing to do but eavesdrop on the argument raging in one corner of the clearing.

The sheriff stood at the center of a tightly knit huddle of law-enforcement officers. Behind them, the combined forensic team snapped photographs and bagged evidence. The officers were arguing jurisdiction, I was pretty sure, and I had my money on the sheriff to win. He looked like he could whip the fur off a grizzly and would, if he ever got a chance. He was definitely king of the hill.

Until a new contingent arrived, that is. Like a gang of gentlemen thieves in a bad Western, a line of four men dressed in suits appeared at the head of the trail through the woods, their figures silhouetted by a rare burst of sunshine. They advanced in unison, badge wallets flipped open to display shiny metal. The city of Durham was weighing in with a high-level team of investigators—they hadn't sent the junior varsity. Another line of suited detectives stood behind the first, and I spotted Steven Hill in the center of it all. His eyes locked on mine from across the clearing. I was the first to blink.

He wasn't quite human, I thought, not with emerald-green eyes like that. If I'd had a wooden stake with me, I'd have held it at the ready, because I could smell that he was after blood. Specifically, mine. His look told me that.

My only chance for escape was that Chatham County would win the jurisdiction argument. But that hope evaporated when I saw two grim-looking men dressed in black suits and sporting short haircuts bring up the rear of the Durham squad. Immediately, most of the SBI agents scurried over to them and began to argue in low tones. Local FBI field agents.

Okay, I thought. Keep calm. Keep very calm. So Steven Hill had the FBI backing him. They were unlikely to shoot me on the spot.

The sheriff wasn't waiting around to lose the pissing contest. As soon as he saw the new arrivals, he stepped away from the crowd and began to wave at someone at the far side of the clearing. Everyone was so busy arguing that few people noticed at first when a small earthmover appeared with a Chatham County deputy at the wheel. The driver began to carefully scoop up the remains of the junk pile in the vehicle's jagged-edged front loader. I hid a smile. If the sheriff wasn't going to be allowed to play his way, he was going home—and he was taking the whole sandbox with him.

"Move it out," he told the driver. "Bobby's pulled up a truck at the end of the lane. Put it in the bed and come back for another load. We'll go through everything down at the ball park where we can spread it all out."

"What the hell do you think you're doing?" an SBI repre-sentative demanded, sticking his astonished face into the sheriff's.

The sheriff pushed him aside like an annoying vine. "Forensics team is done with the site work," he said calmly. "And there's too much of a chance that evidence will be lost or destroyed if we leave it here. Look at all these damn people. I'm securing the evidence. We'll go over it in a private location. Get your men out of the way."

"You can't do that," three SBI men all yelled at the same time, stepping in front of the sheriff to block his way.

Their shouts were drowned out by the bellows of a cameraman who had been filming the earthmover as it loaded. "Holy shit!" he shouted. "Holy shit! Holy shit!"

A male reporter stared at him, mystified. "What the hell is it, Barry?" he asked. "Are we rolling or not?"

Definitely not. The cameraman's equipment dangled to one side, unnoticed, as he started toward the small bulldozer. He pointed with an unsteady arm. "Look," he said. "Look in the front of the loader."

The driver had already made his turn and was heading out the trail but the shouts of the crowd stopped him. He looked back over his shoulder, beseeching the sheriff for instructions.

The sheriff, looking increasingly uneasy, glanced at the cameraman, hesitated, then waved the driver to return. The vehicle pivoted back toward the clearing with the bright-yellow loading claw held high in the air.

"It's in there!" the cameraman shouted, pointing to the claw. Regaining his composure, he raised the camera and once again began to film.

The sheriff waved his hands down, directing the driver, and slowly the claw began to descend. It tipped forward as it did so and debris spilled over the lip, all the branches and junk tumbling out into a pile.

"It's there," the cameraman insisted. "I saw something. Look—there it is!" The dead body of a stocky white male tumbled from the loader and flopped unceremoniously atop the junk pile. Its head pointed downward, and one arm was extended in an arc, as if he were flamenco dancing.

A silence descended on the clearing. In the distance, a pack of hounds bayed at some unknown animal, their bugling sounding like the keening of some weird funeral song.

An officer inched closer. "It looks like he's been shot in the head several times. Small caliber," he said.

"Jesus Christ," someone else said. "Who is it?"

"I know," a cold voice announced. "It's Pete Bunn. He owns this farm."

Everyone stared at the speaker in surprise. When I joined in, I found that Steven Hill was staring back at only one person—me. And I knew I was in real trouble then.

I sat on a log, guarded by two troopers, while half of the state's law-enforcement officers searched the junk pile under the direction of a very determined Steven Hill.

"What are we looking for?" a deputy asked as he hoisted up a broken jug and peered inside it.

"A weapon," Steven Hill said calmly. "And, if I'm not mistaken, here it is." He used a branch to poke beneath a mound of molding leaves unearthed during the search. He hooked the trigger of a small handgun with the stick and held the gun up to the crowd. The weapon gleamed pewter in the afternoon sunlight. My heart flip-flopped when I saw it. I knew that gun well. An Astra Constable. And it had once been mine.

I went in for questioning voluntarily. Very voluntarily. If they arrested me and processed my fingerprints, my life as I knew it would be over. They'd quickly discover I had a felony record in Florida and that my N.C. investigator's license was a fake. Not only would I lose my job and most of my friends, I was pretty sure they could also come up with enough legal violations to put me back behind bars. My only hope was to keep it friendly.

Too bad that wasn't what Steven Hill had in mind.

They put me in a small room painted such a blinding white that it gave me a headache just looking at the ceiling. I stared out the window at the deepening twilight and wondered who had been dispatched to break the bad news to George Carter's widow. I was glad it hadn't been me. Would George Jr. cry when his mother began to sob? Or would he gurgle unknowingly?

Voices brought me back to the room. Everything I said was being immortalized by tape recorders and a video camera. It was a regular party. Hill sat at the head of the table, flanked on each side by two other Durham investigators. All, I suspected, were from the Professional Standards Division or the Detective Bureau's Homicide Squad. One of the FBI agents sat in a chair against a wall, looking bored. The other agent had disappeared. That made it six to one. I wasn't even counting the Chatham County sheriff who, through sheer stubbornness, still clung to the case by the skin of his false teeth. He sat next to me at a far end of the table, staring at me as if I were a perplexing specimen that defied classification. I was doing my damnedest to treat him with respect. At this point, I considered him my only friend in the room—which tells you how very desperate I was. But at least he was outside of Steven Hill's sphere of influence.

"Were you aware that Pete Bunn was the subject of an ongoing investigation by the Professional Standards Division?" some sourpuss with glasses asked me.

"No, of course not," I said. "How could I know that? When I met with Mr. Hill, he wasn't talking."

Mr. Hill? Ack. But now was not the time to be anything but a well-behaved, demure lady investigator. I'd have batted my damn eyelashes at that point if I'd thought it would do me any good.

"Any idea who illegally accessed the department's data files?" Hill asked in a neutral voice. Uh, oh. That meant Hill knew I'd been snooping around in his personnel records. This could get personal real quick.

"How could I know that?" I answered again. "I don't work for the Durham P.D." No way was I giving up my pal Marcus Dupree. They could break out the bamboo shoots and start sticking them under my chipped fingernails. I wasn't talking.

"You've got to admit that it seems a little odd that you would find Carter's body so easily, after professionals have searched for him for months." This was offered by another officer. And it made me mad. I forgot to be demure.

"First of all," I said. "I am a professional. Second, I haven't run across a shred of evidence that anyone ever actually bothered to look for Carter. It seems to me everyone just assumed he'd taken off on his own. If you had bothered to look, you would have found him. All I did was go out to question the last person outside of his family known to have seen him—and that was Pete Bunn. That's standard investigative procedure. Maybe finding the bloodstained shirt was lucky. Or maybe I was just more thorough."

"Would it surprise you to learn that we did go out to the Bunn farm shortly after Carter's disappearance and that we questioned him thoroughly?" a beefy Durham cop asked. "He was as baffled as the rest of us that Carter had disappeared."

I looked at Steven Hill innocently, but I hoped the Chatham County sheriff got the message. "It wouldn't surprise me to learn that at all," I answered. "I bet I can even guess which one of you went to see him."

Only one person in the room got my true meaning and it was the wrong one. Steven Hill's glance flickered over me like a lizard's tongue, and, instead of being a warning, it was something far worse: it was a cold and confident dare that let me know it was useless however hard I worked. He had laid the groundwork far too well. I was no one to these men, while he was one of their leaders.

I was going to lose either way. If Steven Hill was an honest cop, he thought I was dirty, and that meant I was going down. If he was a dirty cop, he had placed himself in the perfect job to cover his tracks, and that meant I was going down, too. There was no way I was going to extricate myself without help. But I didn't know where to turn. I couldn't just sit there and continue to tap-dance around Hill's loaded questions. He was gunning for me, and, if I hadn't gotten the message yet, Hill's next question made it very clear.

"Do you own a gun?" he asked.

"What's that supposed to mean?" I asked.

"It's very simple. Do you own a gun or not?"

"Of course I own a gun," I answered, evading the issue. "I'm a private investigator. Why are you asking? I can't possibly have shot George Carter. I hadn't even heard of the man two months ago. As for Pete Bunn, are you trying to say that I'm stupid enough to kill him then lead the cops to the exact spot where I've hidden the body and the weapon?"

The men shifted uncomfortably, but Hill had a point he wanted to make and my answers weren't going to stop him.

"You might well do exactly that," he said. "Did you figure the sheriff here would be so grateful for having you lead him to Carter's body that he wouldn't bother to look through the rest of the junk pile? Was this some sort of game you were playing?"

"Are you serious?" I demanded. "Am I a suspect here? Or are you just being a complete asshole?" Okay, I know I said I was going to tone it down, but come on—the guy was out to hang me.

But Hill's remark had provoked the wrong person.

"What exactly is it you're trying to say?" the sheriff asked, turning to Hill. "That my reputation for stupidity tempts criminals into being even more stupid than I am?" He ignored the disapproving stares of the other men with the calm of a man who has selectively enforced local law for years and been reelected a zillion times by his neighbors as a result. He had true job security: every person in Chatham County owed him a favor. If the city cops wanted to be morons, his attitude said, that was fine by him. But he didn't want to waste any more time than he had to. "What would be this little lady's motive?"

I forgave him the "little lady" the moment he said it. He was saving me the trouble of asking myself.

"Money," Hill said. "Gail Honeycutt's family would pay a lot to have her off death row. Killing Carter and Bunn makes it look like Roy Taylor may have been mixed up in something illegal. It would be enough for a stay of execution. It might even be enough for a pardon."

"Oh, so now you think the governor is stupid, too?" the sheriff asked. The others scowled, annoyed that the sheriff was failing to toe the line.

"All I'm saying," Hill said, "is that we're verifying if the weapon we found is the one that killed Pete Bunn. We're running the serial number on the gun right now. If it comes back registered to Casey, then she's in trouble. A lot of trouble. She'd be a whole lot better off if she just let us know the truth right now."

Something in his voice gave him away. He was too confident. That was when I knew for certain that Steven Hill was the one. He had killed Pete Bunn and Peyton Tillman. And probably George Carter. And maybe even Roy Taylor, too. Because only the person who had stolen my gun and registration would be so confident it was traceable back to me. He was going to let me take the fall—which meant he had planted more evidence along the line to implicate me. I had to find it before anyone else did.

My one hope was that my gun registration was fake. As someone who had served more than a year in jail, I was not allowed to legally own firearms in North Carolina. The trace would come back showing that my gun had been purchased by one Pearl Woods of Mecklenburg County. Further investigation would reveal that Pearl had been dead for forty years. I know, because I'd paid a lot of money for a gun with a clean pedigree.

I wondered what Hill would do when the trace came back. He couldn't pull out the fake registration papers without making it clear that he had been the one to steal them from my office. If I could get someone in power to believe my story, Hill's reaction to the gun trace might confirm that I was telling the truth.

"I want to make a phone call," I announced.

Hill looked pleased, like he had me on the run. The others were annoyed. I was screwing up their schedule. Fortunately, the sheriff came through again.

"I need to make some calls myself," he said. "Since she's here voluntarily, why don't we take a break?" Just to prove he could, the sheriff rose, hitched up his belly so it cleared his belt and strode from the room. It was a nifty move. I didn't have his belly, at least not yet, but I could stride with the best of them.

The FBI agent stopped me at the door and glanced at Steven Hill.

"It's okay," Hill said, waving a dismissive hand. "Let her make her call."

You arrogant son of a bitch, I thought, pressing my lips together to keep from speaking out loud. I'm going to stuff your

Armani tie up your ass by the time I'm done. I pushed past the agent and was petty enough to step on his foot on my way out the door. I hoped my size-nine clompers hurt.

I rode down the elevator to the lobby's main bank of phones wondering who the hell I could call. Every favor extended, every favor ever owed ran through my head as I scrambled for someone to come to my aid. When this whole mess was over, I really needed to spend a little more time winning friends and influencing people. Loners ended up, well, alone. Like I was right now.

I weighed my options. Since I hadn't been arrested yet, introducing a lawyer into the situation was unlikely to do anything but raise the very issue I wanted to avoid. Bobby D. could get me out of any jam, but he was laid up at Wake Med, snoring and belching his way into the Patient Hall of Fame. Bill Butler had made it clear that he was on Hill's side. I could call Jack, but what could he do? He was a bartender. Get the cops so drunk they let me go? There was Slim Jim, but I was frankly afraid of what he might do. Slim Jim's anti-government sentiments had been simmering for years. I had visions of a horde of mountain men descending on Durham police headquarters, faces shrouded with bandannas as they dynamited a hole in one of the supporting walls and whisked me away to perpetual exile somewhere along the Blue Ridge.

In the end, I called the only person I could call: Detective Anne Morrow of the Raleigh Police Department. As I dialed the number, I sent up a small prayer. This case was making me downright religious. She had been investigating Peyton Tillman's death for at least ten days by now. Maybe she had found something to make her suspect that it could be related to Roy Taylor's. If so, she might at least listen to what I had to say.

She was off-duty and out of the office. I must have sounded as desperate as I felt because the officer covering her phone offered to beep her for me. I gave him the pay phone number and waited, eyes closed, rehearsing what I would say. I'd confess to everything but my felony record. It was ancient history anyway. Other than that, it would be the whole truth and nothing but the whole truth.

The phone rang four minutes and thirty-three seconds later. I snatched up the receiver on the first ring. "It's me," I said quickly. "Casey Jones. I'm in trouble."

"I'll say," she answered. "You just interrupted a hot date."

I'd forgotten that normal people might be out on dates or hanging out with their families. Casey Jones, social outcast

"Sorry," I said. "But this is really, really serious. My ass is in a sling."

"Go on," she said. "I'm listening."

God bless her and her unborn children, too. I raced to explain before she could cut me off. I told her about everything: Judge Tillman's fiancée and the missing court case files, George Carter's death just after Tillman had visited him at Christmas, the partners' visits to see Gail on death row, the bodies found on Pete Bunn's Chatham County farm and, finally, all about Steven Hill, my stolen gun and my fake registration. I did not tell her why it was fake. She did not ask. After three murders and charges of corruption and conspiracy, illegal possession of a firearm was not that big a deal.

When I was done, Morrow remained silent. "Are you there?" I asked.

"I'm here," she said. In the background, I could hear the clink of silverware and the hum of conversation: normal people leading normal lives in a restaurant that seemed a galaxy or two away. "I'm thinking," she added.

"You believe me?" I asked.

"I believe that you think you've found the answer," she said. "Now I'm just trying to put it all together and decide what I think. Those are some pretty heavy-duty accusations you're making against a decorated cop."

"So you know Hill," I said, my hope evaporating. He had her fooled, too.

"No, but I've heard of him. He keeps a high profile."

"You have to help me," I pleaded. "No one else will believe me."

"You got that right," she agreed. There was a silence. "You know you left your case files in your car the night you were ran off the road," she said. "The sergeant down at the impound brought them to me. I read through them. You're pretty thorough. Some of your counter theories about who killed Roy Taylor were pretty good. They should have been looked into."

I knew I had forgotten something that night: my files. "It was just theory back then," I said. "Now I have more proof."

"Yes, and part of it may be a bullet I found in your cooler. Ballistics called this afternoon. It was a .45 caliber ACP."

"The same as killed Roy Taylor," I said with relief. "The same issued to Durham police officers."

"Don't get too excited," she warned me. "Half the people in law-enforcement use them. And half the people outside of law-enforcement, for that matter."

"Please, Detective Morrow—I know you don't know me well, but you've got to help me out here. Steven Hill has everyone fooled."

A tap on my shoulder sent me jumping a good foot in the air. The Chatham County sheriff stood behind me, his arms folded. He looked like he had been listening for a long time "Give me the phone," he ordered, holding out a huge, work-worn hand.

I handed it over, too scared to protest.

"This is Stanley T. Johnson, Chatham County sheriff Who's this?" he barked into the receiver. His tiny eyes narrowed as he listened, and huge furrows appeared in his rounded forehead. "Yeah," he answered. "I heard it all. I'm not sure how much of it I believe, but I can tell you this— something hinky is going on, and I don't like it. This Hill fellow is smoother than the belly of a well-fed pup and mighty lucky when it comes to finding evidence. He found that gun quicker than a pig rooting truffles. Maybe you ought to give this little lady the benefit of the doubt." He passed the phone back to me and glanced at his watch.

"Thanks." It was all I could manage to say.

He tried to glare, but his beady eyes no longer seemed mean. "When this is all over, you owe me one, little lady," he said.

"Deal."

He nodded and marched out the front door like he couldn't wait to get back to Chatham County, where the living was easy and the criminals were high. He was leaving this mess to the city cops.

Forty-five minutes of uncomfortable questioning later, the door to the conference room opened. A small, portly black man entered the room. He was losing his hair on the top of his head, and what little remained on the sides had turned gray. A pair of gold-rimmed glasses framed his myopic round eyes, and, as he entered, he blinked in the room's sudden glare. He was dressed in a golf shirt and pair of khaki slacks, and the front of his shirt was stained with what looked like a blob of barbecue sauce. In short, he was about as unassuming a person as I had ever seen. Yet all five of the Durham police officers present, including Steven Hill, rose to their feet. Even the FBI agent stopped looking bored.

Detective Anne Morrow followed the little man into the room. She was wearing a short black dress that ended a good six inches above the knees, and she looked incredible in it. Ignoring the assembled men, she spoke directly to me. "Casey, do you know Chief Robinette? He just took over the Durham Police Department a few months ago. I know him from Indiana State. He was a guest lecturer on computer crime one semester."

The chief took off his glasses and wiped them clean on one corner of his golf shirt, blinking at me like a baby owl as he did so. "It was actually a course on the use of money transfers and foreign bank accounts in laundering cash," he corrected her in a deep baritone. "Anne was one of my worst students. I bored her, I'm afraid." He gave her a fond smile, then turned to the waiting officers. "If you boys don't mind," he said, "I'd like to speak to Miss Jones here in private for a few minutes. Why don't you take a dinner break?"

Steven Hill opened his mouth as though he wanted to say something, but his burly coworker grabbed him by the arm and pulled him from the room before he could speak. The silence was complete as the room emptied of everyone but me, Chief Robinette and Detective Morrow.

Chief Robinette switched off the tape recorders and video camera, then took a seat at my elbow. "Okay, Miss Jones," he commanded. "Tell me exactly what you told Anne."

I did. He listened carefully and, when I was done, asked me several questions, mostly about the probable dates of Roy Taylor's service on the force and when he had been partners with Carter, Bunn and Hill. He wanted to know if I had ever been personally involved with Steven Hill and apologized when I took offense. He also questioned me closely about the body of court cases involving Taylor's former drug unit recognizing, as I did, that this was the common link.

"I have the transcripts," I volunteered. "I downloaded them into my system. They're in Raleigh. I could print them out in an hour. It would be faster than searching all the records again."

The chief exchanged glances with Detective Morrow.

"I can take a look at them," she volunteered. "I know drug law pretty well from my stint in Asheville. I could summarize for you. It would give you a good idea of what you're dealing with."

The chief nodded, then stopped and frowned. "On the other hand, Anne, I'd like you to accompany me to visit George Carter's family. I feel that I should inform his wife personally, and, with no offense to you, I may need a woman's touch. After that, I'd like you to be present when I inform certain individuals in the city government of these unfolding events."

Was he for real? He was personally going to notify George Carter's widow of his death? Suddenly, I felt as if I—and the Durham Police Department—were in very good hands.

"No problem," Detective Morrow said. She spoke to me and I took her words as they were intended: as an order. "I'm going to be tied up for a couple of hours here. We can save time if you'll get the transcripts, then meet me back here." She stopped and reconsidered. "No, don't meet me here. You live in Durham, right?"

I nodded.

"Do you feel comfortable meeting me at your home?"

I nodded again.

"Okay, good," she said, checking her watch. "I'll meet you at your house in three hours. I need your address." She slid a pad of paper across the table and I wrote my address below the scribbles of one of the Durham investigators. He had been drawing a hangman's scaffold and noose.

"And Casey?" Detective Morrow added as she folded the piece of paper and stowed it away in her evening bag. "You know not to open your door for anyone else but me, right?"

"Right," I agreed emphatically.

CHAPTER THIRTEEN

I drove back to Raleigh feeling as if the years of following cheating spouses were behind me, as if I had finally cracked a case that really mattered. I wouldn't call Nanny Honeycutt with the good news, not yet. But I'd be able to make the call soon if Chief Robinette and Detective Morrow took me seriously. With resources like theirs, I was convinced that before long, they would come up with evidence that directly linked Steven Hill to Roy Taylor's death. And even if they couldn't get him right away, the fact that Hill might be involved coupled with pressure from the public, might force the governor to at least issue Gail a stay while the matter was investigated further.

These thoughts kept me occupied as I idled in what was supposed to be the fast lane of I-40, but had instead been reduced to a parking lot due to an accident on the other side of the median. I glanced in the rearview mirror: more than a mile of cars and trucks stretched behind me, and the line in front seemed just as long. A couple of impatient jerks, inevitably driving pickup trucks, were trying to sneak ahead using the shoulder, but most people waited patiently for the mess to be cleared. Never mind that the accident wasn't even on our side of the road. Southerners don't just rubberneck at accident sites, they pull out the popcorn, sit there and gawk. I crawled forward and waited my turn. It was a bad one: a four-car accident plus a tractor-trailer that had jackknifed across all three westbound lanes trying to avoid the wreckage. I knew it would be hours before the road to Durham was fully clear. I'd have to find another route back home after I picked up the transcripts.

The office looked lonely without Bobby D.'s familiar silhouette hogging the front window. Unexpectedly, I missed him. It seemed so empty, like the whale pool while Baby Shamu was napping. I also felt guilty I hadn't been to the hospital in days. Who was he complaining to about the food? And, more to the point, had he discovered yet that I'd stolen his keys?

I let myself inside, collected the mail, threw away everything but a check from a now rich ex-wife, then sat to work printing out the transcripts of the court cases. It took only a few minutes to route the documents to the laser writer, but there were so many pages that the actual printing would take nearly an hour. I spent a few minutes cleaning my office, then put my feet up on the desk and closed my eyes. My back ached from spending the night on the damp ground, and I longed to change into something a little more attractive than the stained sweat suit I was wearing. Unfortunately, the only outfit at my office was a pale-green shantung-silk dress from the fifties that I'd bought at the Bargain Box for two dollars. It needed heels to set it off, and I was not about to subject myself to such torture tonight.

I had almost dozed off when I heard a series of faint clicks at the front door, as if someone had turned the knob to see if it was locked. My senses were still on hyper-alert—I could have heard a mouse sneeze in China at that point. The lights in the front room were off, and my hole-in-the-wall office was so far in the back, that the only indication that I was here would be a faint gleam from the hallway. Slowly, I eased into a sitting position, holding my breath as my chair creaked in protest. I fumbled in the bottom of my knapsack for the magnum. The barrel rested against my thigh heavily as I pressed my back to the wall and inched down the hallway. I lifted the gun against my chest, then shrank back against the doorjamb and peered into the main room. I could see the outline of a figure fumbling with the doorknob on the other side of the Venetian blinds that covered the glass door. There was a loud click, and the door began to ease open. Then two things happened simultaneously. I stepped into the main room and shouted "Freeze," like I was some leftover Charlie's Angel, and the lights in the office blazed on so brightly that they blinded me.

"Don't shoot," a female voice squeaked in panic.

My vision cleared. A slender black woman dressed in a T-shirt and jeans held her hands high in the air, her eyes wide with terror.

"Who are you?" I demanded.

"Ruby's sister Keisha. You hired me to clean the office after the break-in. I'm just finishing up the filing. My mother said she could baby-sit, and I thought I'd try to get it done by Monday." She spoke faster than Speedy Gonzalez, as if trying to talk down the gun in my hand.

She did look a lot like her sister Ruby, my favorite meter maid. I lowered the gun and let out a long breath. "Sorry. You don't know what I've been through this week."

She peered at my grimy sweat suit and bruised face. "Don't think I want to know," she said. She glanced at Bobby's file cabinets. "Okay if I get to work?"

"Sure," I told her. "Just make sure the front door is locked."

She double-checked the door, gave me another sideways glance, then got to work reorganizing files without wasting time on any more talk. I was grateful. Ever since I hit thirty, which was a relatively long time ago, I haven't had the energy for normal conversation. I don't mingle and I don't chitchat.

I checked on the progress of the printing and estimated that it would take another forty-five minutes to complete. I wasn't sure I'd be able to stay awake.

Keisha was on the same wavelength. Five minutes later, she popped her head in the door and unsuccessfully fought off a yawn. "I don't think I can do this without coffee, after all." she said. "I'm going to run over to Krispy Kreme for a cup. You want something?"

Ah, salvation. I ordered six doughnuts—a dozen if they were warm—and a large cup of coffee. I also made a mental note to pay Keisha a hundred bucks in addition to buying her son's special glasses. By golly, the woman had initiative.

I spent the next five minutes entertaining myself with daydreams of Keisha working for me and Bobby D. permanently, running out to keep us fueled with warm doughnuts on command. This daydream soon gave way to more base instincts—the need to gloat. By now, Bill Butler would have seen the Channel 5 newscast, and other stations might have expanded on the story. He'd know that both George Carter and Pete Bunn were dead, and even he would be having second thoughts about what the hell was going on in connection with Roy Taylor's death.

I wouldn't say a word about Steven Hill, I promised myself, but I would casually bring up Carter and Bunn. Just dip Bill's nose in it, so to speak, instead of rubbing his entire face in the fact that I was right.

I tried him at the office first. The female voice that answered his phone was slightly familiar. And whoever she was, she certainly knew who I was. "Is this Casey?" she asked. "Bill's not here. He has a date tonight. A hot one."

I remembered. The woman on the phone was the administrative officer I'd threatened with bodily harm a few days before, when she wouldn't put me through to Bill fast enough. She remembered the incident, too—and she was out for revenge.

"I see you're not doing anything tonight," she continued. "Too bad. Not many single men in this town, huh? Especially when you're middle-aged like you are, I expect. Do you want me to take a message for Bill? He probably won't check in until late tomorrow. He's got the day off and he's cooking dinner tonight for that new girl from Records. Have you seen her? Everyone thinks she looks like Heather Locklear. She can't be more than twenty. She's crazy about Bill, too. He's cooking her dinner at his house. Isn't that romantic? He says he's making his mother's spaghetti sauce. I hear it's pretty good. Have you ever had it?"

"No," I answered grimly. "I haven't." The nerve of some people. She was trying to make me feel lousy and she was doing a good job of it. She must have gone to an all-girls' school. She had perfected the art of being a total bitch without once stooping to sounding like anything but the nicest, most sincere friend. The hell of it was that I knew what she was up to, but she was succeeding anyway. I couldn't tell if I felt bad because Bill had a date with some young babe or because I didn't. Regardless, I felt about as desirable as a pregnant water rat.

The girl sighed dreamily. "Some people have all the luck."

"I'll call back later," I said and hung up. I'd even the score in my own good time. Maybe I'd take an ad out in *Prison Penpals* using her name and begging hot males to contact her pronto.

The Krispy Kreme doughnuts arrived warm and cheered me up, but a casual comment of Keisha's did not. I had just finished my fourth doughnut when she popped her head in the door and asked me a peculiar question.

"This business that's been giving you a hard time this week," she said. "Does it involve a tall white guy with dark hair?"

"Why are you asking?" I said, the doughnut turning to tasteless muck in my mouth.

"There was a guy standing in the doorway across the street when I left for the coffee and he was still there when I got back. I thought he might be a bum or something but the Rescue Mission sandwich truck just cruised past and he didn't budge. I just checked and he's still there, hiding in the doorway."

"You ought to have my job," I told her. And, frankly, at the moment I wished she did. We slipped to the front window, and I lifted up a corner of the blinds.

"Across the street," Keisha told me. "There. See the white doorway?"

I looked just in time to see the back of a man's figure as he slipped from the shadows and disappeared into the darkness of the five-story parking garage across the street. "Damnit, he's gone."

"Do you know him?" Keisha asked.

"Probably," I answered.

Paranoia returned in a rush. I finished dividing the remainder of the printed transcripts, stuffed them into my knapsack and made a beeline for the front door. "Don't stay here alone," I ordered Keisha, mindful of Bobby D.'s conk on the head. "Don't worry about the files tonight. They'll keep. And remind me to give you a raise."

She was still staring at me when I hopped into Bobby D.'s Cutlass and took off from the curb, burning rubber like some testosterone-infested redneck. If my mysterious shadow was parked in the garage and I hurried fast enough, I'd be gone by the time he exited and made the series of turns required to pick up my trail on one-way Saunders Street.

I took a deep breath while I waited at a stoplight and tried to get a grip. Just to be safe, I took the .44 from my knapsack and put it in the glove compartment, where I could get at it easily. A few feet away, students and aging rabble-rousers were whooping it up at Sadlack's on Hillsborough Street, taking advantage of cheap sandwiches and even cheaper beer. Some people had all the fun. When this was over, I'd relax for at least two weeks, I vowed. I'd relax and forget all about being followed by angry bartenders or psychotic cops or... I had to stop right there. My thoughts were getting me nowhere.

The light changed and I eased away from the intersection, peering into the rearview mirror. Traffic was always heavy on this stretch of Hillsborough Street where it bordered the N.C. State University campus. Students in groups laughed as they made their way from pub to pub or popped into one of the restaurants along the crowded blocks. Enlisted men from nearby Fort Bragg joined local high-school kids in cruising the strip, hoping to horn in on the action. The result was total chaos, and it was impossible to tell if I was being followed or not. I spent so much time looking in the rearview mirror, I almost rear-ended a Mazda 626 idling in front of me.

After that, I forced myself to pay attention until I got past the crowds and was nearing the state fairgrounds. I needed to make a fast decision. The trip had already taken longer than expected and I was late to meet Detective Morrow. I didn't want to chance further delays by taking 1-40. Sometimes accidents took three or more hours to clear when the built-up congestion was particularly heavy. Instead, I turned right on Blue Ridge Road and headed for Alexander Drive. If I drove like a maniac, I could cut a good ten minutes off the trip.

The fact that my route would also take me past Bill Butler's apartment had nothing whatsoever to do with the decision. At least that's what I thought. Until I neared the turnoff to his complex and found myself steering the Cutlass into the left-hand lane. Look, it wasn't love or jealousy that drove me to his front door. It was suspicion and fear. The man across the street from my office had been tall with dark hair. That could have been the pissed-off bartender from my pre-stalked days or it could have been Steven Hill, though he was probably answering questions for some minion of Chef Robinette's right now. That left someone else who was tall with dark hair, and the only one I could think of was Bill Butler. Contrary to popular belief, tall dark strangers are hard to come by.

I'm not saying I thought Bill was in on the murders with Steven Hill. Bill was a good cop who walked on the right side of the angels. More to the point, he hadn't even moved to Raleigh until a few years ago, long after Roy Taylor was dead. But Hill sure seem informed about my movements. Maybe Bill had fallen for some line about helping out in Hill's own corruption investigation. Hill could have told him that he was looking into Pete Bunn himself, and that what I found out during my investigation might be important. That would be enough to get Bill to agree to follow me around to see what I uncovered. Men can be dumb that way—and Bill was mad enough at me to be real damned dumb.

All I'd do, I promised myself, was drive by Bill's apartment. If I saw the lights on, I'd know he was home and having his hot date. At least then I'd be able to put the possibility that he was helping Hill out of my mind.

Putting my plan into action was more difficult. Blue Ridge Road was a bitch to navigate at night since residential development had long since outpaced the streetlights. Identical brick and wood apartment complexes lined the road on either side. Their names were so bland that they were impossible to remember: Sherwood Forest, Merrye Hills, Nottingham Commons, Pine Woods. After I waited for several minutes to turn left, as a long string of traffic streamed past, I realized I was headed for the wrong apartment complex. I checked my rearview mirror, then pulled back into the main lane. Almost immediately, a horn honked. I checked the mirror again and saw that the warning had not been for me. I could tell by the brighter headlights that a truck had pulled out of the turn lane a few cars behind me and cut off an oncoming car. I took another look, but could not make out what kind of truck, other than that it was black. It worried me.

I slowed, searching for Bill's apartment, and the truck slowed with me. I was really spooked. If I didn't calm down, I'd end up doing something dumb like running off the road from nervousness. On the other hand, the traffic and darkness made it impossible for me to tell whether the truck was really following me or not. This thought gnawed at me until I cracked. I couldn't take the chance, not when I was so close to convincing Chief Robinette that I might be right. I had to get some help quick to make sure I made it back to Durham in one piece.

Now I had two reasons to go by Bill's.

Desperate times call for desperate measures. If I wanted his help, I'd just have to look like I was asking for it. I located Bill's apartment complex and drove rapidly toward a back building near the tennis courts. He lived in a two-bedroom walk-up that, for a guy, was actually pretty nice. Certainly it was cleaner than my own apartment. For one thing, he seldom hung his bras on the doorknobs. I was relieved to see the lights on. If cooking dinner for some sweet thing was his idea of entertainment, I considered it vastly preferable to discovering that he was the one following me around.

Time, age, sleeping on the ground and car wrecks had taken their toll on my weary bones. I was huffing and puffing by the time I reached his third-floor apartment. I also confess that, despite my preoccupation with getting the transcripts safely to Durham, I was acutely aware that I was still wearing the purple sweat suit that made me look like Moby Grape.

Bill's stare made it obvious that he agreed. "What the hell are you doing here?" he asked, blocking the entrance with that lean physique I used to admire so much before he launched a second career trying to boss me around. He was wearing tight jeans and a black golf shirt. How come he had never looked that good when we were going out?

"I don't have time to go into it," I said. "But I need three aspirin and some help getting back to Durham in one piece. It doesn't have to be you, but maybe you could call someone down at the department and get me an escort?"

"What?" he asked with a quick glance over his shoulder. Something smelled delicious in there and my stomach growled. It had been ages since I'd eaten anything substantial. Woman cannot live on Krispy Kreme alone.

"I've got to get back to Durham tonight and I'm being followed," I explained more slowly. "You have to help me. Don't you watch the news? George Carter and Pete Bunn are dead."

"Who?" he asked, looking back over his shoulder again.

I lost my temper at his apparent stupidity, not to mention his preoccupation. "What? Who? What is this?" I asked. "You talking in one syllable words tonight so that she can understand you?" I nodded behind him as he tried to slam the door in my face. I jammed it with my foot and pleaded, "I'm not kidding around. Bill. I really need your help."

"This is beneath you," he said, trying to mangle my foot in the doorjamb. "How did you find out I had a date? Don't you have anything better to do?"

"I am not here because you have a date," I hissed back. "I'm here because some psychotic maniac is trying to kill me with a truck and I need your help to stay alive."

"Who is it, Billy?" a syrupy voice called out from inside his apartment.

"Billy?" I asked, rolling my eyes. Look, I couldn't help it. Bill Butler was the last person in the world I would call "Billy."

"Mind your own business, Casey," he whispered, throwing his full weight against the door. I pushed back. We were nose to nose, at a stalemate, when his date butted in.

I quit struggling and stared. Heather Locklear, my ass. She had a pancake face to go with her syrupy voice. If you scraped off her makeup and stripped her of her Wonderbra, she would have been lucky to resemble Lassie. And twenty years old? Spare me. Maybe in Gabor years. She was pushing thirty if she was a day.

"Who's this?" she asked, draping an arm over Bill's shoulder and smiling sweetly at me. When it comes to marking territory, women can't piss as easily as men. We tend to cling instead. Which was why she was hanging on him like a lamprey eel who's snagged a ride on a fifty-pound sturgeon.

"I'm his wife," I told her, pushing past them both. I wasn't worried about Bill's reaction. What could he do? Belt me in front of her?

"Your wife?" she asked, her sugary voice cracking.

"She's kidding," Bill said in panic.

"No, I'm not," I assured her. Good god. The living room stopped me cold. He had vacuumed the rug so that the nap all lay in one direction, and there were so many lit candles that I kept looking around for the coffin to go with them. "Expecting a vampire?" I asked.

"Looks like one just got here," his date shot back, grabbing a fluffy pink sweater that had, I swear by all that is tacky, a sequined heart embroidered on it. She shouldered past Bill and flounced down the stairs, her high heels making angry little clicks as she milked her exit for all it was worth.

"Sorry about that," I said, sitting down at the cozy dining-table and pulling a plate full of spaghetti toward me. Naturally, his date had been the type to only pick at her food. She'd barely nibbled at the meatballs. No sense letting good food go to waste.

Bill stared at me from the doorway, speechless.

"This is pretty good," I admitted. "Your mother's recipe?"

"Get out of my apartment," he said grimly. He pointed outside like the proverbial father casting his daughter into the blizzard, little bastard and all.

"Look, Bill, I'm sorry." And truly, read my lips, I was. "But you weren't taking me seriously. I really do need your help. I think someone is following me and I have to get back to Durham. They found the bodies of two cops who used to work with Roy Taylor. They're dead. People are starting to listen to me. I have an appointment I have to keep. I can't afford another incident. If we take Alexander Drive, we can be in Durham in twenty minutes, and you could be back here in an hour. Please."

He slammed the door behind him, stalked to the table and sat down across from me. He looked mean leaning toward me in the candlelight, mean and determined and, let's face it, rather gorgeous. I hate to admit it, but I found it kind of exciting. But now was not the time to let my mind wander.

"Casey," he said in a calm voice that made me more nervous than an angry one might have, "let's just admit it. You're losing your shit on this case. You're in over your head. You're a little confused. You're letting your personal feelings get in the way of your job. And you've been paranoid for over a week now."

"I didn't imagine my car wreck last weekend."

He pulled the plate of spaghetti away from me, then snatched away the bread sticks, too. "You said it was probably that bartender you had fired, and I don't think he'd be dumb enough to stick around for an encore."

"You don't know that," I said. "There is a truck following me. I saw it. And I resent the implication that I invented an excuse to butt in on your hot date with Miss Pork Rind of 1936."

He ignored the slur. "This is why I don't like working with women," he told me. "You let your emotions interfere with your judgment." He stopped me when I started to protest. "I'm not saying you aren't truly convinced that someone has been following you. I'm sure your fear is genuine. I'm only saying that it's common to have fears like that after you've been in an accident. I've had the same reaction myself after I've been shot. I keep expecting it to happen again and I look over my shoulder for weeks. But the difference between an amateur and a professional is that a professional acknowledges that what he is feeling is simply a reaction to the earlier incident." He finished up his tidy little speech by munching on a bread stick. "And thanks for ruining my date," he added.

"I don't give a shit about your date," I said. "I care about saving my ass." But an odd feeling was spreading over me like an unstoppable infection. I was starting to doubt myself. The tiniest seeds of self-doubt had been planted and taken root. I suspect it's happened to most women. It can begin when your friend's husband puts his hand on the small of your back. At first, you don't even notice it's happening. You suppress it, unwilling to acknowledge the intrusion into your reality. But then the hand moves a crucial few inches and cannot be ignored. So you tell yourself that you're the one misinterpreting events, that, really, you must have a dirty mind to think that such a nice man would put the moves on you. Finally, when the destination of that creepy, crawling hand becomes inescapable, you leap over the fact that some asshole is trying to use you and instead immediately blame yourself. You begin to ask, "What did I do to lead him on?" and damn if you don't find some excuse to blame yourself.

I don't know when and how women are programmed to react in such a way, I only know we are and that it happened to me. Simply by throwing the words "professional" and "emotion" around, Bill Butler managed to convince me I was a hysterical female who seriously needed to get a grip if I wanted to be considered an equal to men.

"Thanks for your help," I said stiffly, confidence fleeing and something akin to embarrassment taking its place. I grabbed a bread stick. Too bad it wasn't a nightstick. I would have loved to beat him over the head with it.

"Look, don't be sore at me," he had the nerve to say. "I'm not going to hold it against you for ruining my date with a gorgeous woman."

"Please," I said. "She was gorgeous all right—before they invented electricity."

"Come on, Casey," he said, still trying to placate me, "maybe her brain's a little rusty from underuse, but she's not that bad-looking. It's not a big deal, anyway. She's just someone I'm seeing."

"You mean just someone you're sleeping with?" I asked.

He shrugged. "Just trying to keep in practice until you come around."

"Yeah?" I said. "Well, you can keep on practicing until you get it so perfect your pecker falls off, because I am never coming around. I've got you figured out. The way you talk about that woman tells me everything."

"Oh, yeah?" he said. "And what exactly is it that you think you've figured out about me?"

"That you're one of those guys who likes a woman until she sleeps with him, and then you decide you really don't like her after all, because what woman in her right mind would want to sleep with your sorry ass."

"Well, thank you for stopping by, Dr. Ruth," he retorted.

"It's true," I warned him, actually waggling a finger, which is something I seldom do unless I am royally pissed off. "It makes it easier for you to throw women away like yesterday's trash. And that is why you're mad at me. Because I won't go ahead and sleep with you, so that you can go ahead and decide you don't like me. I've spoiled your plans for a three-minute relationship. That is exactly why you have been acting like such a jerk to me."

"That is not why I have been acting like such a jerk to you," he said.

"Aha!" I said triumphantly. "So now you admit you've been a jerk to me."

"I am not," he protested. "And stop saying 'aha!'"

"Aha, aha, aha," I answered maturely. "In fact: ahahahahaha." I ended up laughing like the hysterical female he had envisioned, but sometimes a girl's got to take a stand and just let it fly.

"Fine," he said with an elaborately casual shrug. "Go ahead and laugh at me, if it makes you feel any better."

"Go ahead and send me out there alone so some maniac can follow me, if it makes you feel better," I shot back as I headed for the door.

"Yeah," he replied sarcastically. "I'm really worried about you, Casey. You just can't seem to take care of yourself. All those bodies lying in your wake are one big coincident."

He followed me to the door in an effort to land one more dart on my hide. "If it makes you feel better, I'll watch from the balcony while you walk back to your car," he offered sweetly. "If you're being followed, I can rush to your rescue. I may even leap from the balcony with a single bound."

"You do that," I told him acidly. "Watch for me very carefully. I'm sure it'll make me feel tons better."

I stomped down the steps, angry at myself, angry at him and unsure if I really was a hysterical female or just a plain old moron. When I got to the car, I saw Bill watching me from the balcony. Patronizing jerk. I shot him the bird, and, you know, having him watch did make me feel tons better.

I felt even better when I noticed his date sitting in her car a few spaces down, spying. I rolled down the window as I passed and called out, "He's a great guy. Except for the herpes."

Immature—but worth it.

Traffic had thinned by the time I reached Alexander Drive and broke free of the stoplights on Highway 70. I had checked the rearview mirror carefully for the past three miles but spotted no one on my tail. Annoyed that Bill had been right after all, I took a left and accelerated down the empty road, watching the speedometer climb to a satisfying seventy miles per hour. The official speed limit was half that, but there was no other traffic, and I'd never seen a cop patrolling Alexander Drive in my life. Besides, the road cut straight through the heart of the Research Triangle Park, and it was completely deserted at night. The Park is a 36,000 acre state-sponsored business zone filled with top-secret medical research facilities, software manufacturers, telecommunications companies and other less definable and sometimes downright scary operations. Not even the burglars bothered with the Park at night—security was too tight. Each facility was surrounded by acres of undeveloped woodland with access typically limited to a single entrance road blocked by a manned guard booth. They didn't screw around with rent-a-cops, either; most of the guards looked like moonlighting Green Berets. I passed by several buildings at top speed, their lights soon a blur behind me.

I was three miles into the park when, inches from my tail, four bright headlights blazed on without warning. The high beams cut through the back window and bounced off the rearview mirror into my eyes. A strident horn sounded and the Cutlass was bumped from behind, forcing me to the opposite side of the road. Son of a bitch. The truck was back, and its headlights had been adjusted to glare upward where they could do the most damage. A set of illegal spotlights, often used by deer hunters in defiance of law, were mounted beneath the truck's headlights. Together, they completely blinded me. Between the lights and the roar of its powerful engine, the truck's sudden appearance was like having a UFO appear on my tail unexpectedly—powerful, terrifying and unknown.

I stomped on the gas pedal and downshifted, praying that Bobby's boasts about his engine had not been idle. I could feel the torque kick in and the heavy car pulled away. I leaned forward as if I was riding a horse, urging the Cutlass to go even faster. I took deep breaths, hoping to quell my panic, as I calculated how far I had before we reached the Durham Thruway. There, heavy traffic would make it impossible for my attacker to run me off the road without being seen—and I didn't think he would try in front of witnesses. I still had at least five more miles to go and I was determined to make it. Behind me, in the rearview mirror, the four high beams faded as I put distance between us. But then they began to grow large and bright again as the truck's driver recovered from the surprise of the Oldsmobile's speed and accelerated in response. Damn, the truck was fast. It was making up my advantage quickly. I'd never make it to the thruway in time.

Up ahead, I saw the lights of a building through the trees on my right. It was a research facility for a huge French-based pharmaceutical conglomerate and the only company accessible by Alexander Drive for several more miles. I'd be protected there. But I slowed too late and passed the entrance road before I spotted its turn-off. The well-lit guardhouse was a blur as I sped past. I was trying frantically to come up with another plan.

I made a decision. I slammed on the brakes and the Cutlass fishtailed across two lanes, nearly flipping over on the concrete median that now divided the road. I fought to regain control until the heavy car found its center of weight. I wrestled it to a stop beside the side of the road and cut the lights. With any luck, my pursuer would speed past before he realized what I had done. That would give me time to cut back through the half mile of woods on foot. I could reach the guardhouse and ask the guard to call for help before my attacker figured out what was happening. I knew I'd be safe once I reached light and civilization. Whoever my assailant was, he was anxious to keep his identity a secret.

The truck lights were approaching at a rapid speed. I sat in the darkness of the car, holding my breath, not daring to open the door until the truck zoomed past. I was certain the interior lights would give me away. I rolled across the front seat, grabbed the magnum from the glove compartment and waited as the truck drew closer. It whooshed past at full speed, engine whining from effort.

I opened the door and threw myself onto the shoulder of the road, ready to hit the ground running. Damnit. The driver had spotted the light in his rearview mirror. As I heard the screech of brakes, I ran for the woods without stopping to shut the car door behind me. Jumping over a drainage ditch by the side of the road, I landed badly. Pain shot through my ankle, but I could still run—and run I did. Like hell.

I tore through the trees without heed to any of the lessons my grandfather had once taught me about moving silently through the forest. All I cared about was reaching that guardhouse, and I mentally counted down the distance to go as I ran, ignoring the sharp pain in my ankle.

The ground was slippery with dried pine needles and crisscrossed with gnarly roots that sent me stumbling into trees and bushes every few yards. I careened my way through the dense forest, desperate for a glimmer of light that might lead the way. I stopped, gasping for breath, heard someone else crashing through the brush behind me and took off again at top speed, wheezing for air. There were no pockets in my sweat suit where I could store the gun and the waistband was too loose to grip it securely. I had to hold it to one side as I ran, terrified that if I fell, I'd end up shooting my own head off.

I was moving too fast for safety. I tripped over a fallen log, bounced off a tree, regained my balance, then entered the hell of a forest section where a tornado spawned by Hurricane Fran had upended dozens of trees and sent them crashing to the ground like giant pickup sticks. It was almost impossible to navigate. I ducked between trunks, crawled over debris and frantically scrambled to find my way around thick piles of dried branches. Behind me, the crashing sounds grew louder as my pursuer neared the devastated area.

I banged into a trunk that had fallen crossways across another fallen log and thought I had broken my shin in two. The gun flew from my hand upon impact, and I dropped to my hands and knees, searching the ground with frantic hands until I felt the metal of the butt. I took a deep breath, got back on my feet and forced myself to think. I had to calm myself; there were too many obstacles in the way. Panic would doom me.

I focused on a nearby tree, giving my eyes time to adjust to the darkness. As my pupils dilated, shapes became clear. I could make out a less-cluttered section of the forest ahead, where welcome moonlight cast a pale shadow over still- standing trees and, possibly, a clearing.

I moved over the pine needles more lightly, being careful where I stepped and taking the time to do so quietly. I was too confused by my fall to know at this point which direction led to the research facility and safety. My only option was to keep going and hope that I was right.

My pursuer reached the area of fallen trees behind me. There was a crash and deep curses echoed though the silence of the night forest. I pressed my back against a rough pine trunk and held my breath. "Say something," I willed him. I had to know who he was. Somehow, I believed, it would lessen the terror if I knew who I was up against. I heard scrambling and then more crashing as he attempted to bull his way through the dried brush. A gunshot echoed behind me, and my feet took flight, automatically propelling me away from the sound. Was he stupid enough to shoot blindly into the darkness, hoping to bring me down? Or had he stumbled and fired inadvertently?

I didn't wait to find out. I moved through the forest steadily, finding my stride, moving as quickly as possible away from the crashing sounds behind me.

I stopped as the knowledge hit me. Crashing sounds? There were two people pursuing me, I realized. One farther back than the other. Another gunshot rang out, and I was certain of it then, the echo was weaker. More like a pop. It was a different gun. God, I thought, two maniacs? Shooting off bullets at random?

I jumped over a dead sapling blocking my path and spotted a light through the trees. The guardhouse. It had to be. I dashed forward in relief—and ran chest first into a six-foot metal fence. I bounced off the heavy wire and fell to the ground from the impact, impaling my left hand on a sharp bottom strand that bent up at the base of the fence. My hand began to bleed. Damn it. Who the hell needed a fence in the middle of nowhere? I peered through the thick wire. There was a deep drainage ditch on the other side. The fence had been put up for safety, not privacy. If I followed it back to the road, chances were good it would end when the ditch was no longer a danger.

Behind me, the crashing sounds grew nearer. Another gunshot split the quiet and I winced, trapped against the fence. They were getting closer. Before I could react, another series of gunshots rang out, closer than before. Hot pain flooded my left hip like a nest of fire ants had attacked me. I fell to the ground, cursing. Those lucky bastards. I'd been hit from behind. I grabbed the fence and hauled myself upright. It hurt like hell, but I could still walk. I was slowed down considerably, though, and the crashing sounds just kept coming closer and closer.

I had to change my plan. There was no time to follow the fence. They'd know I had no other choice, and any chance I had at escape would be gone. Running was out, anyway. Hobbling was the best I could manage. It wouldn't take long for them to catch up.

I had no other choice. I'd have to bring them down.

I dropped to my knees behind a large pine tree that had fallen onto a smaller one, creating a prop for my shooting arm. Together, the two trunks shielded most of my body, while the top log allowed me to take steady aim. I gripped the .44 and took my position, sighting down the long barrel, willing my eyes to see through the darkness. Why hadn't I taken one of Bobby's semi-automatics? I'd have to make every shot count.

I was ready when Steven Hill burst through a clump of bushes and stopped just short of the fence. He held a small handgun and cocked his head to one side as he listened for a hint of my presence.

"Over here, asshole," I said loudly.

He turned and I fired twice.

The bullets hit their mark a few inches south of their intended target. I blew off his right kneecap instead of neutering him for life like I'd planned. He dropped to the ground like someone had knocked both legs out from under him. Then he began to scream like a wildcat in heat. I bet every animal within five miles took off running at the sound. Some tough guy. He rolled around on the ground, holding his injured knee and wailing like a baby. His gun lay to one side, forgotten. I scurried to him, ignoring my own wound, grabbed the gun and told him to shut the fuck up or I'd blow his other kneecap off. He didn't argue. I left him thrashing in silent agony as I retook my position and waited for the second pursuer.

Hill had been carrying a Lorcin. There was only one reason for someone like him to carry such a cheap gun—he had intended to kill me and toss it.

"Casey!" someone was calling through the woods. "Casey, are you there?" As the voice grew closer, Hill lost what little composure he had and began to moan again, leading whomever it was right to our spot. "Casey!" the voice shouted, only a few feet away in the darkness. I took aim and waited.

Bill Butler broke into the small clearing, gun in hand.

I couldn't shoot. I hesitated, finger on the trigger, unable to squeeze. For months afterward, I would relive that hesitation again and again. And I would forever send a silent prayer upward that I did not complete the shot. Because Bill ran straight up to Steven Hill and stuck a Glock into his ear.

"Where's Casey?" he demanded. "If you hurt her, you're dead. End of story."

"Hurt her?" Hill croaked, rolling on the ground and holding his knee. "That bitch doesn't need protecting. It's the rest of us who need protecting from her."

Bill ignored him and stood, scanning the clearing. "Casey!" he called out.

"Don't come any closer," I said, stepping out from behind the fallen pines. I wasn't taking any more stupid chances. I held the gun aimed at his waist but my hands were shaking. Badly. I was losing blood. Liquid seeped down my left leg and collected in my sock. I could feel it growing heavy around my sprained ankle. God, what if he had hit an artery?

Bill automatically put both hands in the air. "Jesus, Casey. I'm on your side, remember?"

"Are you?" I asked, more calmly than I felt.

"Yes. I am." His voice rose an octave. "Do you really have to point that thing at me?"

"Yes," I said. "I do."

"Here—take my gun." He held it out, barrel first.

"Toss it."

He stared. "It might go off."

"Then toss it and duck."

Reluctantly, he flipped the Glock across the clearing as if he were playing horseshoes. It fell at my feet with a thud.

"Now, prop him up against that log," I ordered, nodding a Hill. "And sit next to him."

"Why?"

"We're going to play twenty questions," I explained "And you're going first."

"Casey," Bill pleaded. "Come on. This is nuts."

"Shut up and sit down." I said. He slid to the ground next to a whimpering Steven Hill. "Tell him to shut up or I'll blow his other knee off," I added.

"Shut up?" Bill said. "Look what you did to him."

"He's lucky," I explained. "I meant to shoot his dick off."

"Jesus, Casey," Bill croaked, appalled. "What the hell is going on here?"

"You tell me," I answered. "Let's start with what you're doing here."

"I followed you," he said, hands still held high in the air "I was just kidding when I said I'd watch and make sure you weren't being followed. At least, I thought it was a joke. But then I really did see a black truck pull out from behind the clubhouse and follow you out the drive. I realized you'd been right. I hauled ass to my Mustang and followed the truck. I lost it on 70, but I knew you were taking Alexander Drive. I was going over a hundred miles an hour when I saw your car and the truck by the side of the road. You left your car door open and the light was on. I heard the two of you running through the woods. It's not like following you was difficult. You two sounded like moose mating the way you crashed around."

"Shut up," I ordered him. "If I want you to be funny I'll tell you to be funny. Right now I want you to shut up and listen." He shut up.

I believed Bill. Almost. But now it was time for him to believe me. And the only way that was going to happen was if he heard it from Hill himself.

"Move away from Hill," I told him.

"Why?" Bill asked.

"Because I'm going to shoot him if he doesn't answer my questions and my aim might be off again. I might accidently shoot something of yours off instead."

Bill opened his mouth like he wanted to say something but changed his mind and scuttled away from Hill like a crab heading for its sand hole.

"You know what you did," I told Hill. "And I know it, too. But Bill needs enlightening. I want him to hear it right from your mouth."

Hill groaned and rolled toward the edge of the clearing.

"I'm going to ask you some questions," I told him, training my revolver on his left knee. "If I think you're trying to shit us, I'm going to shoot."

"You can't do that," he said, the words muffled by pain.

"Sure I can," I explained. "Watch this." I pointed the gun up and squeezed the trigger. A small branch exploded from a pine tree and dropped to the ground at his feet. Luck. But impressive luck.

Hill groaned and Bill's eyes grew wider. "Just stay put," I warned Bill.

"Stop her," Hill pleaded.

Bill looked at me. I shook my head. None of what Hill said to us in that clearing would ever stand up in court, but that wasn't the point. The point was that I wanted to know that I was right. I wanted Bill Butler to know that I was right. And, lastly, I wanted to hear Steven Hill admit what he had done.

"Better hear what he has to say before you do anything," I told Bill. "I don't think you really know him very well." I turned to Hill. "We'll start with an easy one," I said. "Question number one: who killed George Carter, not giving a shit that his wife was pregnant and he was a good cop?"

He knew as well as I did that he had nothing to lose by telling me. His need to be smarter than us won out over discretion. "Pete Bunn," Hill said quickly. "I swear it was Pete."

"Why?" I asked. "Because you told him to?" He met my question with silence, and I took a step closer, wincing. My left hip was starting to throb, my ankle was aching and a steady trickle of blood had turned my sock into a soggy mess. "Because you told him to?" I persisted.

"Yes," he spit out. "Because I told him to. I promised him a cut of my action if he would."

"What action?" I asked. "You're off the streets now. Who would bother to pay you off?"

I swear there a smug smile just lurking beneath his controlled expression. He was dying to show how clever he had been.

"Isn't it obvious?" he asked.

"Maybe to a scumbag like you," I conceded. "But why don't you fill us Boy Scouts in on the plan?"

He was silent.

"It's the end of the line for you," I assured him. "The only way to save your ass is to start talking. May as well practice your story on us."

"Dirty cops," he explained. "Pretty simple, really. I'd tell them they were under investigation and promise to keep the division off their backs for a percentage of their take. They spoke the same language. No one argued. They just looked at it as a business expense."

"Enterprising," I remarked. "You're sort of the Amway of corruption."

Poor Chief Robinette, I thought. A prostitution ring out of headquarters would have been preferable to this.

Bill was sitting on the ground, staring openmouthed a Steven Hill. "And you ain't even heard nuthin' yet," I thought to myself.

"Why did you have George Carter killed?" I demanded "He'd done nothing wrong. He had a wife and a baby due any day, for god sakes. Why did he have to die?"

I couldn't tell what hurt Hill more. His knee or having to answer my questions. His face was ashen. "Nothing I say can be used in court," he said. "So don't get your hopes up."

"I don't give a crap about court," I assured him. "Or hope. Now talk."

"He finally figured out what had gone down with Roy," Hill said sullenly. "Around Christmastime, Tillman visited him and asked so many questions that George finally figured out what had happened to Roy back in 1989. Stupid do-gooder. Took him eight years to make the connection. He never dreamed anyone but Gail could have done it. When I heard he had visited Gail in jail, I was afraid he'd go to someone in the department next with what he suspected. So I paid Pete to kill him. He was willing. Pete didn't care about George or Roy. He cared about money. Pete had helped me in the past, but the money had dried up when he got transferred to white collar. He wanted more money. He didn't care why I wanted George dead. He just did it."

"Why kill Pete then?" I asked. "He was on your side." I wanted Bill Butler to hear all the details. I wanted him to know that I had been right from the start.

"George shot his mouth off to Pete before he was killed. When Pete put two and two together about Roy, he also threatened to go to the department. But only if I failed to pay him off."

"Pete had helped you in the past by sabotaging drug cases?" I asked.

Hill didn't answer for a moment, then he locked his eyes on mine with an angry glare and nodded. If I didn't know better, I'd say he didn't like me much.

"Say it," I ordered. "Say it out loud so Bill can hear you."

"Yes. Pete and I threw drug cases for money," he spit out. "Lots of money. Roy and George were too goody-goody to help." He looked up at me, pleading. "I'm bleeding to death here," he said.

I ignored him. Not that I thought Bill was stupid, but I wanted to make sure he got the point. "In other words," I said. "Pete decided to blackmail you after he figured out that you had killed Roy Taylor. So you killed Pete. You did it right after I talked to you at the Lone Wolf, didn't you? You didn't want to take the chance that I would spook him. You couldn't let him live long enough to talk to me."

His expression told me I was right. "Go on," I said. "I want to hear you say it. You killed Pete Bunn."

"I killed Pete," he said through tightly drawn lips. "So what? You'll never be able to prove it. I had to kill him. I couldn't afford to have rumors start about me. I needed the job in Professional Standards to cover my tracks."

"And I guess we know that you killed Judge Tillman, too." I said. "You were the old friend he was meeting that night. He was ready to confront you about the compromised drug cases and Roy's murder."

Hill was silent and I didn't press the issue. He had guessed, correctly, that if the D.A. was going to hang him, the Peyton Tillman murder was his best shot. But I wasn't worried. They'd get him for it. Detective Morrow would find enough physical evidence to link Hill to the judge's murder once she focused on him as a specific suspect. No one can kill that cleanly.

"Why did you search their houses?" I asked.

"I was afraid they'd marked their meetings with me down in a calendar or something," he said quickly. "I had to erase any trace of our getting together." I knew he was lying. Smart man. Nothing he was telling me was worth beans without evidence to back it up. But I was smarter. There was evidence somewhere or else he wouldn't have searched for it. I didn't know exactly what the evidence was—but I did have an idea of where it might be.

"You're doing good," I assured Hill, who had resumed his groaning. "Keep it up and I'll toss you a few dozen Percodans." I gritted my teeth, determined not to let my own pain show. But the throbbing had turned into a strobing of fire that was spreading up my left side. I leaned against the trunk of a tree and slid to the ground, unable to stand any longer. God, but my side hurt. Still, the job wasn't done yet. Bill had to hear the rest. He was staring at Hill, mesmerized.

"Who killed Roy Taylor?" I asked Hill. "It wasn't Gail, was it? You bought her a drink that night and sent it over to her table, didn't you? Only it had something in it that didn't show on the standard drug screen. She blacked out, and you killed Roy, making it look like Gail had done it. That's what the wild shots above the doorway were all about. You had to get powder burns on her hands and her fingerprints on the gun. She wasn't even conscious when you did it."

A silence descended on the clearing, broken only by the far-off screech of an owl.

"Who killed Roy Taylor?" I asked again, more forcefully.

Hill stared back, his face pale. He was losing blood fast.

"Let's go," I said to Bill. "We're leaving him here. There's a rabies epidemic in Durham County. With any luck, he'll run across a rabid raccoon or two."

"I did," Hill shouted angrily. "I did. Okay? He was acting like Dudley Do-Right for chrissakes. I'd offered him a piece of the action but instead he was going to turn me in on the drug thing. I had to kill him."

"How in the hell did you think you could get away with it?" I asked. "Didn't you think it would look funny when all of these people connected with Roy Taylor turned up dead?"

"You," he said.

"What?"

"You," Hill repeated. "When you took the case, I figured it was the perfect way to cover my tracks. All I had to do was make it look like you had killed them for the money, as a way to get Gail out of jail."

Bill made an indefinable sound and shook his head.

"It would have worked," Hill insisted. "With that Morrow woman in charge of the Tillman team, it would have worked."

"I'll be sure to tell her you said so," I promised.

There was one more matter to clear up. For me, it was, perhaps, the most important question of all.

"Did you know that Roy and Gail had a daughter?" I asked.

"What?" Hill looked confused.

"At the time you killed Roy Taylor, did you know that he had a step-daughter?" I repeated more loudly. "Did you know when you killed him that there was a three-year-old girl in the next room, cowering under the covers afraid that you would come and kill her next? A little girl who saw the lights of your truck and heard the roar of the engine and thought a monster or maybe a spaceship had visited her house?"

He was silent.

"You didn't know until you read about it in the papers, did you?" I answered for him. I was shaking I was so pissed. I'd been that little girl myself, one who'd heard gunshots and raced to find her parents dead on the ground. I knew what it was going to do to Brittany. "Because if you had known she was there, she would be dead now, wouldn't she? You would have killed her and let Gail go to her grave thinking she had done it. It wouldn't have bothered you a bit." Just thinking about it made me so angry that I struggled to my feet again and took aim at his good knee, planting my legs wide for better balance.

"Don't do it, Casey," Bill yelled, speaking out for the first time. "Don't let him goad you into it. I won't be able to help you if you do."

Hill took Bill's interference as a sign he was on his side. He held up his hands. They were covered in blood from his injured knee. "For god's sake, you've got to get me out of here," he said to Bill. "I'm dying."

"Good," I snapped back, grabbing a low-hanging branch and struggling to stay upright. "Payback's a bitch, isn't it?"

Casey Jones, karmic avenger. But my body was not reacting as it should have. I was growing weaker and it scared me. My head felt funny, like bees were buzzing inside it.

"Are you hit?" Bill asked, finally realizing that I was hurt. He forgot I held the gun and rushed to me. He propped me up against the tree and checked my hip. "You are hit. Oh god, what if it was my gun?"

Even through my pain, I felt relief. Men are amazingly predictable. First, they're overly loyal to their own kind and then, once betrayed, they bring new meaning to the term "silent treatment." Bill Butler did not just act as if Steven Hill had betrayed him and every other cop in the world, he acted as if Hill were invisible. Having heard the truth, Bill was cutting him off completely. I knew then, for sure, that Bill was on my side.

"Put your arm around my neck," he ordered me. It was no time to argue. I complied. He lifted me easily—I was impressed—and started for the fence.

"The guns," I reminded him. He placed me on the ground gently and returned to the pine trees to retrieve the two extra guns. "Good god, Casey, there's enough here for an artillery."

"Bring them," I ordered him. I didn't want Hill taking the easy way out. I wanted him to spend a long, long time in the state's worst prisons, personally getting to know some of the perpetrators he had put behind bars. Preferably, very personally.

Bill removed the clip on his Glock as a sign of faith, then emptied the bullets from the Lorcin and stuffed both guns in a back pocket. This time he groaned when he lifted me. "Christ, how much do you weigh?"

"Muscle weighs more than fat," I reminded him.

"I'm so sorry," he said unexpectedly. "I'm so sorry I didn't believe you. God, I was a complete jerk. You needed my help. You finally came to me for help. And I ignored you completely. I'm an asshole." This confession was accompanied by heavy breathing as he toted me along the fence, searching for an opening.

"I like the new you," I told him. "Confess your unworthiness some more."

"Hey—what about me?" Hill yelled from the darkness behind us. "You can't just leave me here."

"So long," I called back over Bill's shoulder. "Have a nice day."

Bill did not even look back. Like I said, Hill was history.

"There's a spot," Bill said. "Hold on." He plopped me on the ground and I screamed. I know it was rude, but it felt like someone had just stabbed a dozen steak knives into my hip. "Sorry," Bill mumbled. He crawled to the base of the fence where the heavy metal had been pried away from the ground. He used the long barrel of my gun to dig away dirt from the base of the fence on either side of the opening. When he had gouged a trench wide enough to wiggle through, he pulled the wire up, straining against its tension. I was impressed again. He bent the wire enough for us to crawl underneath, saving us who knew how much hiking— or toting—time.

"Are you sure the guardhouse is over there?" I asked.

"Positive," he said. "City boys can track, too, you know." He went first, sliding through the opening on his back before straddling the drainage ditch on the other side. "Stick your legs through," he ordered me.

I was having trouble moving both my legs. I slid the right one through the hole in the fence, then used my hands to maneuver the left one into position.

"Jesus, Casey—that bad?"

I nodded and he began to gently pull me through the opening, lifting the wire with his free hand so that my chest would clear the fence. "No jokes," I warned.

"No jokes," he agreed.

"I have to rest," I admitted. "God almighty, this hurts like a son of a bitch." I probed my hip with my fingertips. The pants were soaked in blood and my hands came away stained with what looked like deep purple in the moonlight.

"Shit, Casey. How badly hit are you?" He cradled me in his arms and carried me over the ditch, then made his way through a few more yards of pine woods. We broke free onto the edge of a well-manicured lawn. The cloudiness of the last few days had disappeared, and, without the canopy of woods above us, the moonlight illuminated the night with a cheery brightness. To my intense relief, I saw the lights of the guardhouse glimmering a football field away.

"Hold still while I check this," Bill ordered. He laid me on the grass and probed my soggy sweat pants.

"Behind," I told him. "I was hit from behind."

"Okay, roll over." He sat cross-legged and laid me over his lap like I was about to get a spanking.

"Don't get carried away," I warned him. "Just because your fondest wish is coming true."

"If you can joke about it, you're going to live," he told me. He peeled down my sweats, then stopped. "Good god," he said.

"What?" I asked, alarmed.

"Who wears black lace underwear on stakeout?"

"What am I supposed to wear, bloomers?"

Either he had a delicate touch or my senses were on overload; I could feel the night wind on my wounded hip like the softest of kisses before I even realized he had bared my butt for inspection. "I don't believe it," he said, whistling.

"What? Did it hit an artery?" I began to squirm.

"Lie still," he ordered. "No, you're fine. But your glutes are amazing. You must work out all the time. This is the flattest butt I've ever seen."

"Pull my pants back up immediately," I ordered him between gritted teeth. "Or you will die."

"I was just paying you a compliment," he said. "Really, they're amazing."

That was when I began to laugh. It was too much for me. I was losing blood, felt light-headed and was relieved to be alive—plus I was finally living my fantasy of being stripped by Bill Butler under the moonlight. Only none of it was happening quite as planned and it struck me as hysterical.

Bill began to laugh, too.

We sat there on the grass, laughing with relief, until the commotion attracted the guards and we could spot two flash lights bobbing our way. "Cover my ass," I ordered Bill, trying to regain my composure.

"No way," he said. "It's the main attraction. You've been shot right in the left buttock. It's a perfect bullet hole. You could put a pencil through it."

That struck us as even funnier. I hadn't laughed that hard since I was a kid and watched my cousin Shelby shoot a possum out of a tree onto his own damn head. Bill and I were downright certifiable by the time the perplexed guards arrived, ready to roust two amorous drunks.

"What the hell?" one of them said.

"I've been shot in the ass," I explained, and Bill and I collapsed into still more laughter when we heard faint "helps!" echoing from the forest.

"I guess he's afraid of the dark," I managed to say between gasps for air.

"There's someone calling for help in the woods," one of the guards said.

"Call the cops," the other one told his partner. "These two are on drugs."

"She's got blood all over her..." The first guard ran out of words as the flashlight played over my skin. "All over her... well, let's go call the cops."

"I am a cop," Bill said, still trying to stifle his laughter. "Call the Raleigh P.D. and tell them where I am." He handed his identification wallet to the guards. "Tell them Bill Butler said to send out the Tillman murder team. I'll fill them in when they arrive."

I stopped laughing. "No," I said as I struggled to tug my pants back on. "Call the Durham Police Department and don't speak to anyone but Chief Robinette. Tell them where we are and that Casey Jones has been shot by a man named Steven Hill. Ask Robinette to send Detective Anne Morrow of the Raleigh P.D. to take charge. He'll know where she is." If anyone got official credit for the collar, it was going to be Anne Morrow.

Bill was staring at me, mouth open, laughter forgotten. "But I'm right here on the scene," he protested. "I came to your rescue."

"Hey, I rescued my own ass," I reminded him. "Bullet hole and all."

CHAPTER FOURTEEN

More than a week after that night in the woods, the governor had yet to issue a stay in the matter of Gail Honeycutt's execution. Gail's sister made numerous phone calls to the governor's personal counsel, and, finally, Chief Robinette and Detective Anne Morrow were called in to see him. Still, no word came.

Throughout this waiting period, a dozen anti-capital punishment protesters kept vigil outside the wrought iron gates of the governor's mansion, standing witness for a woman they did not even know. I wasn't sure what I envied about them the most: their conviction or their detachment.

I don't know how the wait was for Gail, but it was horrible for me. Each morning and every afternoon, I received a phone call from Nanny Honeycutt asking if there had been any word. Each day I had to say "no." Executions had never bothered me before. But it's different when you know the person who's going to die—and when you know she's innocent. The process becomes a relentless march toward cold justice that reduces a person's life to an appointment on someone else's calendar. I didn't like the taste of it at all.

Gail's appeals lawyer wasted no time waiting around for a miracle. When word came through that the Fourth Circuit in Richmond had turned down Gail's second appeal, she immediately filed a final plea with the Supreme Court. This time, new evidence was a crucial part of the argument. I was trying to decide if I was proud or embarrassed to have Clarence Thomas mulling over photos of my bullet-ridden butt when word came from the governor's mansion: the governor had issued a stay. At five o'clock in the afternoon on the Friday of a three-day holiday weekend, the news—that Gail Honeycutt's upcoming execution would be postponed indefinitely pending further investigation—hit the wires.

While reports of the stay were buried in the excitement of vacation and traffic news, the Honeycutts sure got the word. Bobby D.—who'd been released from the hospital twenty-two pounds lighter—was driven crazy by the endless phone calls of thanks.

I went to see Gail the next day. She was not in good shape. The hope was worse for her than the despair had been. She seemed depressed, confused and afraid to hope for more. She was also doped to the gills.

"A stay means he could change his mind," she mumbled, rubbing the knuckles of one hand anxiously. They were red and rapidly turning raw.

"He's not going to change his mind," I assured her. "There's a woman detective in the Raleigh Police Department who's not the type to let it go. She likes the innocent to go free and the guilty to go to jail. She won't let you down."

"What if they don't believe her?" Gail asked, "I notice they haven't let me off death row."

"They will," I promised. "It's just going to take some time. More evidence is being uncovered every day."

"Why did he do it?" she asked. "Why would that man choose to set me up like that? I hardly even knew him. And why would he kill Roy? Roy never hurt anyone. What kind of a person is he?"

"I don't think Steven Hill really is a person," I explained. "He just walks around in a human suit. And I can't tell you why he thought he had the right to take so many lives."

The information Gail had gotten up to then had been wildly distorted on its passage through the family grapevine. She listened carefully as I explained what I thought had happened.

I told Gail that Steven Hill had probably always been a dirty cop, even when he was patrolling a beat. That when he was promoted to the new drug unit, he saw a chance to make a lot more money. He would bury evidence and alter testimony in drug trials in exchange for cash or drugs he could resell. But he needed the cooperation of his unit partners to get away with it. It took a while for the unit's early arrests to wind their way into court. By the time the first wave of trials began, there was a big backlog of cases waiting to be heard. Hill had put off making an offer to the other unit officers, but could not delay any longer. He went to each of the three other men in turn and offered to cut them in on his deals if they would help or at least look the other way. Pete Bunn agreed. Roy Taylor and George Carter were another story. Roy was adamant: he would not do it. George was less certain. He was confused about what to do and looked to Roy for advice. The two men met with Steven Hill and, unknown to Hill, recorded the conversations on tape. Roy was too smart to meet with Hill otherwise.

"I think Roy probably got every conversation he had with Hill down on tape," I explained to Gail. "He knew he'd need proof when he turned Hill in. That's why Roy wanted to go up to the cabin instead of to your family reunion and argued with you about it the night he died. He needed to hide the tapes. Instead, after the fight about the reunion, he gave the tapes to George to hide. George drove up to the cabin the day Roy was killed, not even knowing that he was dead."

"Why didn't George just go to the police with the tapes after Roy died?" Gail asked.

"He didn't know Hill had anything to do with Roy's death," I explained gently. "He thought you had done it. And without Roy to guide him, George lost his nerve about turning Hill in. Instead, he asked to be transferred out of the drug unit and let the issue go."

"Where are the tapes now?" Gail asked. "How can you be sure they exist?"

"I can't," I admitted. "But Hill was looking for something or he wouldn't have torn Tillman's and Bunn's houses apart. Or my office."

"Why didn't he look for them after Roy died?" she asked.

"He didn't know they existed until this past Christmas, when Judge Tillman visited George and started asking questions. George figured out Hill had been the one to kill Roy, not you, and realized the tapes might help prove it. Pete Bunn figured out the same thing and may have learned the tapes existed from George by pretending to be as concerned as he was. But Bunn was more interested in blackmailing Hill then setting you free. In the end, Hill killed them both."

"Why didn't Steve just drive up to the cabin and get the tapes once he found out they existed?" Gail asked.

"He couldn't find the cabin," I explained. "He only knew it was near Lake Gaston. He probably checked the county records after George's death, looking for evidence of a sale made by Roy's estate. Since your stepfather really owned the cabin, there never was property listed in Roy's name, so Hill couldn't find anything. Hill would have known why if either he or Pete Bunn had attended the trial, but he was too busy keeping a safe distance. I don't think Hill knows to this day why he couldn't find the cabin. That's why he came to see you here in prison. He was trying to find out where the cabin was."

"How can all this help me?" Gail asked.

"Maybe Hill doesn't know where the cabin is," I explained. "But the police do. They're searching it now. If the tapes are there, they'll find them."

There was more I could have told her. Like how I didn't know who had actually killed George Carter, but that I did know he had been held at Pete Bunn's farm while Bunn and Hill tried to learn whether George had told anyone what he suspected. Or how they had forced George to call his wife to tell her that he was going up to the cabin, but cut the call off to make it sound as if George was going away for good. Gail didn't need to know more right now. She had enough to absorb for one day. Especially since she was still bombed on pills.

"What if they can't find any evidence that Hill killed Roy?" she asked. "I could be here forever."

"They'll find it," I promised. "With DNA testing, they'll tie him to the murder scenes somehow. Just hang in there and we'll get you out."

She looked unconvinced.

"Gail," I told her. "It's time to start looking ahead. You're going to have a life outside of here again. You need to prepare. It's hard getting out. It's weird and it's scary. I know. But I know you can do it. You have your little girl to think about. You need to start thinking about how to be a mother again."

"No," Gail said flatly.

"What do you mean 'no'?"

"No," she said. "I know what you're leading up to and the answer is 'no.' I don't want you to bring her to see me. Even if I do get out of here, Brittany is staying where she is. I wouldn't know how to be a mother anymore. They've kept me alone in here so long, I've forgotten how to talk to people. And I don't know what to say when people talk to me. I can't even stand to be touched. I'm not fit to raise a child right now."

"How can you say that?" I asked. "She's your daughter."

"Look," she insisted angrily, a spark of life breaking through the drugs that insulated her. "I'm not smart. I'm not lucky. I'm not much of anything, but I am sure that Brittany would be better off staying where she is. It just wasn't meant to be. I'm not changing my mind, so don't try."

"Okay," I said. "I won't. I hope you know what you're doing."

"So do I," she answered.

After that, I left her with a promise to keep her up on any new developments. When I looked back through the window of the tiny visiting room, she looked uncertain and afraid. Uncertain of a life that would be quite different from the one she had come to know, and afraid to hope for too much from it.

On the way out, I passed an elderly couple checking in with Herman, the front-gate guard. The woman was frail and looked older than her husband, as if life had beaten her down more. Her hair was sprayed into a gray bubble; her clothes were plain but well-ironed. The old man stood almost painfully erect in polyester clothes obviously chosen for durability, not style.

"Relationship to the prisoner?" Herman was asking them.

"We're her in-laws," the woman replied in the flat twang of someone raised near the coast. She hesitated on the final word.

Herman raised his eyebrows in surprise. I stopped to watch.

"In-laws?" he asked.

"Yes," the old man repeated firmly. "I assume relatives are allowed to visit?"

"Sure," Herman answered quickly. "But usually you need twenty-four hours clearance," he explained.

"Make an exception," the old man ordered calmly.

"I'll try," Herman agreed, picking up the phone and dialing a superior. As I listened to him explain, I realized that I was looking at the mother and stepfather of Roy Taylor. They were there to see Gail.

"Purpose of the visit?" Herman asked, one hand covering the receiver.

The couple stared at him.

"Purpose of the visit?" Herman repeated more loudly.

The two old people exchanged a glance. The silence stretched long.

"Forgiveness," the old man finally said.

I turned out to be wrong about some of the things I told Gail. For one, they never did get Hill for killing Roy Taylor. They couldn't find enough evidence to bring charges, though they did find enough to convince everyone he had done it. The waitress who had worked at the Lone Wolf back then was fairly certain Hill had been the one to send Gail a drink the night Roy died. He was the best-looking man she'd ever seen, she explained, that was why she had remembered him so well. That and the murder the next day had fixed the whole night in her memory. There was no way to prove that Hill had put something, a drug that wouldn't show up on standard screens, in that drink to cause Gail to black out, but other evidence confirmed his guilt.

A voice analysis of the taped 911 call reporting the shooting produced a match: Hill had been the one to call it in. And a thorough search of the fishing cabin near Lake Gaston had indeed produced audiotapes of several conversations between Steven Hill and Roy Taylor. George Carter had hidden them under the refrigerator by taping a protected bag beneath the cooling coils. But the audiotapes did not contain any direct threats, and the crime scene had long since been renovated. And Hill's confession in the woods would never be allowed into court.

All the prosecutors had was conjecture and the vague recollection of a little girl whose memory had translated the lights and roars of a truck outside her bedroom window into a UFO.

Steven Hill would escape paying for Roy Taylor's death. Instead, they brought him up on the other three murders, including Peyton Tillman's—once his autopsy showed that there was water in his lungs, which proved the judge had been drowned before his wrists were slit.

I called Gail's sister when I heard Hill would not stand trial for Roy Taylor's death. She said going after Hill for the other three murders would have to be enough. Besides, the prosecutors were asking for the death penalty on all three charges and you could only kill someone once. I was disappointed. I had my heart set on gassing, drugging and, possibly, beating Steven Hill to death. Most important, though, if Hill was convicted of any of the charges, Brenda assured me, the governor would hear more evidence in favor of setting Gail free. I hoped to god she was right.

Everyone affected by Steven Hill's crimes was anxious to bring him to trial quickly, especially the Durham Police Department. Every good cop on that force felt betrayed; I heard it said over and over at night in bars, on street corners, in diners after the shift change. Once again, one bad cop had gotten all the headlines while the rest were forgotten. But what could they do?

Plenty, as it later turned out.

Hill's trial was moved far from Wake and Durham counties because of the publicity. Ironically, it was held in Detective Morrow's old hometown, Asheville. She returned in triumph, local girl made good, an avenging angel there to see that justice was done. She deserved every headline she got.

When Steven Hill was brought into the courtroom for the first time, he was confronted by row after row of fully uniformed, off-duty Durham police officers who had traveled many miles to see him pay for his crimes. They sat side by side, jaws set tight, shoulders squared back, staring at Steven Hill. I saw two of the officers who had questioned me that night in the white conference room; I recognized others from previous cases or from their work patrolling Durham's streets. It was a long trial, and the days in the overheated courtroom could seem even longer, but at least a dozen officers showed up every single day, and not one of them ever got up and left until the judge had signaled the end of a session. They rarely reacted to testimony and they never commented to the press. They just stared at Steven Hill with disdainful eyes.

I couldn't have taken their peculiar form of punishment. I would have cracked and been dragged screaming to Dorothea Dix Hospital before the end of the trial.

It got to Hill eventually. He had been remanded without bail, and the nights in jail had to have been rough for a former cop. Payback had begun.

As the days passed, Hill showed up in court looking less and less like a pretty boy, disintegrating before the jury's eyes. He grew puffy from the starchy food, and soon his belly spilled over his suit pants. Wrinkles appeared around his jaw and even the striking green eyes disappeared. It turned out they were the product of contact lenses. He took to wearing heavy black glasses to court instead. His hair turned gray and took on a disheveled look. A hardness settled over his pale skin, making him seem brittle and unpredictable. I wouldn't be fully satisfied until he lost all his hair and his teeth fell out, but I was pleased that the jury got a good look at the man who destroyed three families and killed four men without ever looking back. We all saw the real Steven Hill emerge.

Detective Morrow had headed up the joint investigation into the murders and nothing escaped her notice. Rumor had it that she had ordered the filter in Peyton Tillman's hot tub removed and every hair in it analyzed and compared to Steven Hill's. I don't know if that was true—god help the lab if it was—but I do know that she compiled enough physical evidence to tie Hill to all three recent murder scenes. It was like weaving a spider web of thin strands of proof all linked together to create an inescapable net.

Hill had left a fingerprint on the wooden railing of Tillman's deck, as well as on the handle of the upstairs toilet. Several of his hairs were discovered in Tillman's car. When they had been left there, no one really knew for sure, but the jury was happy to make that call. Tillman's missing files on the tainted court cases were uncovered in Hill's basement, hidden beneath a socket wrench set in a drawer of his tool chest. Most damning of all, traces of skin tissue were detected on Hill's regulation police baton, and tests showed that they matched Peyton Tillman as well as an unidentified third person. It was Bobby D., of course, from the wound inflicted the night Hill broke into our office. Neither Bobby D. nor I volunteered that info.

The evidence for George Carter and Pete Bunn's deaths was even more solid. Hill had grown sloppier with each murder. George Carter's blood was found in Hill's truck, pooled in the grooves of the flat bed beneath the spare tire. The bullets that had killed Pete Bunn matched a gun found among Hill's large collection of weapons. It was a Bren Ten automatic. Very nice, but obscure and expensive. Hill was too cheap to have gotten rid of it. Maybe he should have used that Lorcin he'd reserved for me.

Hill had also left a trail of DNA all through Bunn's house while searching for the tapes the night Slim Jim Jones and I stood listening at the top of the hill: hairs on the back of the sofa where he had stopped to rest, fabric fibers on the sharp hinge of a cabinet door and saliva on the rim of an empty Red Dog beer bottle left on the kitchen table. I suspect that Red Dog had been his tenth or so of the night. Otherwise, he'd never have been so careless. It pleased me to know that having drinks with the man had contributed to his downfall.

Other evidence pointed to George Carter's imprisonment in Bunn's house. Carter's fingerprints were found in the bedroom and his hair fibers in the shower drain. His blood had pooled on the bedroom floor at one time, but had been scrubbed away. A relentless Detective Morrow and her forensics team found the evidence anyway.

When I heard that, I began to believe that maybe Bunn really had been the one to murder George Carter. But Steven Hill was the one who was still alive and he would be the one to pay the price. The jury was North Carolina mountain folk and they bought the Slim Jim Jones argument lock, stock and gun barrel: who in tarnation would be dumb enough to kill someone and dump him on their own farm? Clearly, they decided, it had been Hill, not Bunn, who'd done it.

The hidden tapes played their part. While they had not been enough to bring Hill to trial for killing Roy Taylor, they helped convince the jury that Hill had been the one to shoot George Carter. Only some of the tapes featured Hill's conversations with Carter, but the judge allowed the D.A. to play them in their entirety. Roy Taylor's parents sat in the courtroom that day, alongside of the silent officers, listening as Roy came back to life, hearing their dead son's voice urging Hill to forget the idea, telling him that once he started he would never be able to stop.

"They'll own you," he told Hill. "You'll never be able to go back to being a good cop. Think before you get started."

"You know what your problem is, Taylor?" Hill had replied. "You just don't live in the real world."

I don't know what constitutes the real world these days, but I suspect that Steven Hill was living in it big time by the end of that trial. A parade of drug dealers who'd done business with him followed the audiotapes into evidence and provided comic relief in an otherwise depressing episode. They looked and acted like extras in a bad cop show, but their impact was impressive. Most had eventually landed in jail on other charges and were outraged at not getting their money's worth from their bribes to Hill.

One by one, they took the stand to describe how Hill had offered to destroy evidence for money. By the end of their testimony, Steven Hill looked like the spokesman for the Home Shopping Network from Hell—someone who was willing to auction off justice for whoever could cough up the cash.

There was no point in putting either me or Bill Butler on the stand. I was just as happy. It allowed the issue of my gun and its fake registration to sink in a sea of more important matters. They never traced the gun back to me, anyway, giving Steven Hill something to ponder during his long nights in jail.

After two weeks of relentless hammering away at Hill, the prosecution rested. The defense took less than a week and it was vintage "Some Other Dude Done It." Only Hill and his attorney made the mistake of trying to blame it all on a dead man and the mountain jury didn't want to buy it. If Pete Bunn had been the bad guy all along, who the hell had shot Pete Bunn? I was afraid Hill would try to pin that one on me, but he didn't want me to take the stand for fear of what I could slip in on cross-examination. Instead, his lawyer tried to blame Bunn's murder on unnamed drug dealers. This was a hard sell, given how amiable the dozen drug dealers introduced to the jury thus far had been.

In the end, by the time the judge issued deliberation instructions, even Steven Hill knew he was going down. I figure he spent sixty solid minutes debating the pros and cons of the gas chamber versus lethal injection before he cracked, because one hour after jury deliberations began, Steven Hill cut a deal to avoid the death penalty. He pled guilty to three counts of murder one and took life without the possibility of parole on all three counts—to be served consecutively. He would never be a free man again.

I wondered at his decision. I had flip-flopped on capital punishment again during the trial. If anyone deserved killing, Hill did. But for a cop, what could possibly be worse than a lifetime behind bars, running into people you helped put there? I wished him the worst as they led him away in chains. "Good riddance to bad rubbish," I thought to myself. "Let's see what your fading good looks get you behind bars."

A month after Steven Hill pled guilty to the murders, the governor of North Carolina granted Gail Honeycutt clemency. She would be free before Christmas. Gail's father had a heart attack when he heard the news and died a few hours later. In some ways, I think this released Gail to start a new life every bit as much as the governor's decision did.

The work I'd done had been instrumental in convincing the governor of Gail's innocence, but he would never know it. By rousing consensus, I kept a low profile. Instead, Bill Butler was sent to the governor's mansion to relate what had been said in the forest that night. They took his word for it, and that was good enough for me. All I really cared about was setting Gail free—and rubbing Bill Butler's face in my superior detecting abilities for the next twenty-five years.

Besides, what I lacked in official recognition was more than made up for by the Honeycutt clan. They threw Gail a homecoming party at Nanny Honeycutt's white farmhouse north of Mebane, near the Piedmont foothills. The farm was decorated to the gills for Christmas. Enough lights covered the trees and barn roofs to power the state's electric milking machines for the next century. Even an old Scrooge like me felt a jolt of festive awe when I spotted those lights blazing.

I stopped and stared when I first saw the farmhouse—it looked exactly like the one my grandfather had lived in before he lost his land and savings. I felt as if I were coming home when I walked up the wide wooden steps.

Inside, tables lined a huge dining room, and every surface inch was filled by platters, bowls, baskets and tubs of the Honeycutt specialties: hams baked in milk; deep-fried turkeys; smoked pork loins; fried catfish; barbecue beef ribs; Brunswick stew; and a barnyard of fried chicken. Not to mention green beans, snap peas, squash, canned stewed tomatoes, fried okra, last summer's sweet corn, baked beans, homemade mashed potatoes, coleslaw, Jell-O salad and a token plate of lettuce that went untouched all evening long. Yeast rolls that melted when you bit into them competed with corn bread, hush puppies and homemade biscuits for my starch intake. All of this was washed down by gallons of iced tea or beer and followed by one of a dozen desserts, including cherry, apple, pumpkin and blackberry pies; banana pudding so sweet it made your fillings ache; peanut butter, coconut and caramel cakes; brownies as big as a trivet;

blueberry and peach cobblers; and oatmeal cookies. The peanut butter cake was the best of the lot. I know because I tasted it all.

Nanny Honeycutt had decreed that I should share guest-of-honor status with Gail. A big banner at one end of the room read WELCOME HOME GAIL, and its twin on the other side read THANK YOU CASEY. I posed under it with Gail for at least a dozen photographs. I was the only one of us who could manage a smile.

It was hard to move because the crush of relatives was so great, not to mention I'd eaten far too much for actual physical activity. Instead, I sat in a chair tilted against one wall for most of the night, murmuring meaningless chat to a parade of well-wishers while I watched the festivities. When it comes to family affairs, I'm a much better observer than I am a participant.

Nanny Honeycutt had urged me to bring a date. I thought long and hard before settling on Robert, the versatile acupuncturist who had hypnotized Gail for me. I wasn't interested in him myself, I was just doing my Christian duty as an incurably romantic busybody. I figured with all those female Honeycutts in their tight jeans, at least one of them was bound to glow a nice pink in his direction. Robert was better at mingling than I was. He worked his way through the crowd like a politician. I even overheard him telling one tank of a man that acupuncture could help with the ache in his shoulders and to give him a call. And damn if the good old boy didn't tuck Robert's business card into the front of his bib overalls, as if he planned to do just that.

Eventually, Robert settled down in a chair next to Gail's. Gail had spent most of the evening huddled in a far corner, watching her family with wary eyes. It was too much for her, I knew. Too much noise, too many lights, way too much touching and lots of unaccustomed laughter. I could tell just by looking at her that she felt rusty and not really part of it. It would be a long time before she could relax. A couple of times, I caught her staring at the tubs of iced beer, her eyes looking longingly at the bright metal cans. That was one monkey I hoped she could keep off her back.

Robert felt her isolation, I think, and went out of his way to help her get through the evening. He sat next to her for hours, talking earnestly, his body leaning close and his long face shining with concern. Slowly, Gail unwound. Once, I thought she even smiled.

This was now Gail's life, I thought to myself, as I accepted the thanks of her female relatives and watched the men eat. I wondered how it felt to her to be back in it—and I wondered if they would give her the room to be someone new. A lifetime is a long time to be labeled a loser.

Brittany had arrived early to spend private time with Gail, and she now played with the other children happily, shrieking as they chased each other through the crowd. I saw her go up to Gail once and she received an awkward attempt at straightening her hair bow in return. But neither one of them seemed very interested in taking it further.

Several times after that, I spotted Brittany among the crowd, hugging a large woman I took to be her guardian. The woman was fat and jolly, with massive breasts. She crushed Brittany between them each time they met in the chaos.

After I saw how much the little girl was loved, I changed my mind about Gail's decision to leave Brittany where she was. Maybe Gail wasn't afraid to be a mother, I decided. Maybe she was brave—and smart—enough to let her daughter go. It would be difficult enough for Gail to live with her past; she was sparing her daughter the same burden.

The homecoming party gave me my first look at the Honeycutt men. They were a silent species, more interested in food than in conversation. They jostled each other around the food tables, heaping their plates high while conducting a strange form of communication that consisted chiefly of grunts, single syllable words and an occasional emphatic "Yessiree." Not one of them said a single word to me the entire evening, but an odd thing happened when I was ready to go home. After hugging Nanny in the kitchen and bidding Gail farewell, I collected Robert, unearthed my coat from a bedroom and headed for the door.

The Honeycutt men blocked the way.

They stood silently in a long line that extended the length of the living room. As I made my way past, one by one, they shook my hand. I passed down the line and accepted each work-worn hand with the same solemn silence with which it was offered. By the time I reached the door, I was deeply gratified. It meant a whole hell of a lot more to me than a meeting with the governor.

"That was kind of weird," Robert said as we made our way toward my car. I still hadn't committed to buying a new one of my own and was driving around a 1964 Corvair I'd bought for four hundred dollars in the meantime.

"True," I agreed. "But there's a lot to be said for the strong and silent type. Unfortunately, men that are strong enough for me are seldom silent enough for me, know what I mean?"

Robert ignored me. He'd never dated Bill Butler, what did he care? He was humming as he fastened his seat belt. He was pleased with himself.

"What were you talking about to Gail for so long?" I asked.

"She's going to think about coming to work for me," he explained. "As a sort of receptionist. In return, I'll give her a small salary and free relaxation sessions. I think it will help her start a new life while she waits for her friend Dolly to get out of prison. They're going to share a house when she does. Sort of help each other get used to the real world. It will be good for them both."

I looked at him curiously. "What color was Gail's aura tonight?" I asked.

"The right color," he said with a big smile.

The case of Gail Honeycutt brought me in contact with a wildly different group of people that cut across traditional southern social and class lines. In the months that followed Steven Hill's imprisonment, I found myself following the lives of everyone involved with an unseemly interest. It was fascinating sport.

Mrs. Rollins, Peyton Tillman's ancient secretary, enjoyed a brief flurry of fame when she wrote a letter to the editor of the

News & Observer blaming the local Democratic Party for Tillman's fall from grace and subsequent death.

Her defense of her prized former student was eloquent, if a little confused: Tillman came across as a sort of modem-day Robert E. Lee who could have gone on to build a new vision of southern justice if only those double-dealing, money-hungry cowardly Dems had stood by their man.

She was written up locally and landed an on-air interview with a Raleigh morning radio talk-show host, during which she blasted the hypocrisy of the people in power who had let Peyton Tillman go down in defeat for minor moral transgressions when their own closets were "stuffed full of skeletons." Not since Jeannie C. Riley sang *Harper Valley PTA* had the world heard such a stirring indictment of two-faced behavior. Her fifteen minutes of fame came late in life, but Mrs. Rollins made the most of it when her time arrived.

On a personal note, she also sent me a thank-you card for my work on the case. Her perfect handwriting gave me the shivers.

Ham Mitchell, the puffed-up prosecutor who had originally sent Gail to jail, lasted less than a year in his position and never did get a shot at his dream of state attorney general. He was caught on videotape before a press conference suggesting that North Carolina deal with a recent rash of property crimes by following Iran's example and cutting off the hands of thieves. If only he'd suggested similar treatment for child molesters, he might have gotten off scot-free. As it was, his secretary, Donna, got her front-row view of his public fall from grace. He was replaced as Wake County district attorney by the female capital-crimes specialist who had taught Brenda, Gail's sister, everything she knew. Brenda went on to take her place as the state's specialist in capital punishment, and she occupies that position today. She's working to standardize the jury instruction and sentencing phases of capital trials, in hopes of reaching a fairer application of the law, which is sort of like trying to teach manners to a bunch of chimpanzees. I don't think she'll get very far, but it's nice of her to try.

George Carter's wife got on with her life. She filed a civil suit against Steven Hill for wrongful death and one day, many moons from now, his ill-gotten gains may send George Jr. to college. In the meantime, rumor has it that Chief Robinette stops by her house often to see how she and the little boy are doing. He's not married, but no one in Durham thinks that he'll stay a bachelor for long now. I was pleased with this news. After all, someone's got to get the barbecue stains out of his shirts. He's the chief of police, for god's sake. And he's turned out to be a good one. One of the first things he did was to shut down the Lone Wolf for serving liquor by the drink without food. I figure Johnny, the bar's owner, is impersonating Frankenstein at Halloween parties for chump change these days.

I haven't heard from the Chatham County sheriff yet. I'm sure he's saving up his favor until he needs a really big one. In the meantime, I watch my speed very carefully when I drive through his kingdom. Hell, I don't even neck inside his county line these days.

Sylvia Bennett, Peyton Tillman's fiancée, calls me every now and then to say hello and float an invitation for drinks. I've managed to decline so far. In my opinion, she's one cook who should stay off the sauce. She's doing okay. All her money seems to bore her and she's redecorated her house twice in the past year alone. Her one hope for a meaningful life was taken from her when Peyton Tillman died, and I don't think she has the strength to find another reason to really be someone this time around. But her maid is staying out of jail and helping Sylvia stay out of the mental hospital. That's something, at least.

Slim Jim Jones surprised me and landed in the public eye that fall. A troop of Girl Scouts got lost up on Black Mountain in October, and Nip and Tuck were the first to find them, huddled around a campfire bravely enduring the horrors of eating s'mores without the marshmallows.

To thank them for their actions, the governor awarded medals to Slim Jim and the boys during a widely publicized live press conference. The governor's aids figured that the dogs would be good for his image. Tuck had other ideas.

He lifted his leg on a Louis XIV sideboard during the ceremonies, prompting the governor's wife to kick him in the stomach. Nip lived up to his name by retaliating on her right ankle. The whole debacle was captured on camera by Channel 5 and played over and over during the Thanksgiving weekend when 1.2 million North Carolinians were glued to their couches and television sets, due to the aftereffects of mass gluttony.

By Monday, ten times more protesters than had ever showed up for Gail Honeycutt arrived at the gates of the governor's mansion.

In the end, the governor's wife had to volunteer at a local animal shelter for a solid week just to silence her critics. I hope they made her clean the cages.

Detective Anne Morrow continued to kick butt on McDowell Street. One day, I predict, she's going to run the entire Raleigh Police Department. We meet for lunch every now and then. It's a new experience for me to have a girlfriend. I'm trying to get used to it because I figure it's good for my soul. We talk about girl stuff, like what's the most reliable handgun and if the choke hold should be outlawed or not.

I could learn a lot from Anne Morrow. I ran into her a few months ago when she was out on a date with the great-looking new basketball coach at a local college. I took one look at how happy they seemed and decided that I wanted her life in its entirety, right down to the makeup in her medicine chest. But I suspect she's not willing to hand over any of it. That is one lady who knows what she wants and knows how to go out and get it.

Bill Butler caught his serial rapist. It turned out to be a cook at the Krispy Kreme Doughnuts around the corner from Peace College. I was shocked and appalled that my favorite establishment would be cast in such a nefarious light. I was forced to respond by making numerous trips to the store for boxes of warm doughnuts.

I felt it important that devoted customers show their solidarity for the rest of the hardworking Krispy Kreme employees.

My show of loyalty cost me five extra pounds, but I worked them off lifting my elbow at a new bar that opened up around the corner from my apartment. Cops hang out there, and, one time, late at night, I heard them talking about how I had caught Steven Hill. They had no idea that I was sitting at the end of the bar, listening to their tales. They also apparently had no idea of the real facts of the case. But it made a great bar story and I loved to think that I would live forever in the lore of the Durham P.D. My career at the bar was short-lived, however. Tony, the dishonest bartender I'd help to have fired, showed up there for work one night, and I decided to find another clean, well-lighted place.

I don't know yet if relaxation massage will lead to love between Gail and Robert. But, believe me, stranger couples have happened. Bobby D. and every one of his many girlfriends is proof. I figure if a wedding invitation ever arrives, then I'll know for sure that their auras were compatible.

Bobby D. returned to work with a rejuvenated ticker and never even knew I had borrowed his car. I confessed to the use of his Smith & Wesson, but he was more pissed that I had eaten two of his French bread pizzas.

"I depend on those to take the edge off my hunger," he complained the day that I confessed all. He'd been back in the office for a week and the steady supply of girlfriends bearing welcome home dishes had finally abated. Empty Tupperware containers littered the front office, and I estimated that Bobby had already put back on half of the twenty-two pounds he'd lost.

"A small price to pay for victory," I reminded him. "I'm looking forward to that check from Nanny Honeycutt."

His face lit up. "It'll be a honey, all right." He hummed happily as he contemplated the cartons of French bread pizzas he could buy with his proceeds.

"I hate to dash your dreams," I reminded him, "but you did say I could keep the entire fee as thanks for saving your life."

His face fell. I'm not sure he thought his life was worth it. As always, though, Bobby rallied to look on the good side. "No matter. I'll still profit from the publicity. We're getting more respectable every day."

"Hey," I corrected him. "I'm getting more respectable. You're just getting fatter."

"Someone has to be the brains behind the operation," he said cheerfully as he peered into a plastic pan and dug out the remains of some homemade fudge with a chubby finger.

"You keep eating that stuff and you'll have another heart attack," I warned him.

"That's what I'm hoping for," he confided. "Then you'll have to lock lips with me again." He wiggled his eyebrows at me.

I looked at him for a minute, the memory fresh in my mind, then turned and walked away.

"Where ya going, Babe?" he called after me.

"To brush my teeth," I told him.

Life slowly returned to abnormal. Keisha finished cleaning up the office for us eventually, and she continues to come in every now and then to bring order to our chaos. Bobby pays her very well. He has to—she's seen every one of his confidential files. Her little boy got his special glasses and then some.

Hell, she could buy him the Hubbell telescope with what she's earned by now.

As for me, a funny thing happened on the way to the bank. The day after Steven Hill tried to blow off my butt, I snuck out of my hospital bed and visited the hospital's automatic teller machine in hopes of coaxing enough cash from it to pay for a snack from the lobby machines (Bobby D. turned out to be right: the food there was horrible). When my balance flashed on the screen, I felt like the winner of a slot-machine jackpot in Vegas: I was $20,000 more flush than I had anticipated.

I've never been great about balancing my checkbook, but this seemed a substantial slip-up.

When I was released from the hospital, I traced the funds to a cash deposit made several days before our chase through the woods. I knew at once that Steven Hill had been trying to set me up for the murders by making it look like I'd been paid for killing Tillman, Carter and Bunn as a way to set Gail free. He had used a deposit slip stolen from my office during the break-in and he forged my handwriting pretty damn well.

What a shame his plan had been nipped so early in the bud.

I kept the money.

I didn't even have to think about it.

Hill couldn't complain without admitting his guilt. All I had to do was pay taxes on it and spend the rest. Life can be simple if you let it be. I thought hard about how I should spend it, though. I needed a new car, but Nanny Honeycutt's fee would cover that. I needed a new gun, but even a clean one was unlikely to cost more than five hundred dollars.

I decided that what I really needed was a vacation, one that would take me far from the "real world," as defined by Steven Hill. Of course, I didn't want to go alone. And I hadn't gotten through this case all on my own, as much as I hated to admit it. Past history aside, one man had been there for me when I needed him and he'd been working as hard as I had over the past month. It was time to put my pride aside and recognize that, like it or not, he was an important part of my life.

Which is why I took Jack with me on a three-week cruise through the Caribbean on a private forty-foot sailboat. A man who gives foot massages is worth his weight in ballast.

I didn't forget Bill Butler, though. I sent him a postcard from Nevis that read "The weather is here. Wish you were beautiful. Love, Casey."

Jack and I had a great time. We swam, we fished, we sunned, we sinned and we spent every penny of Steven Hill's ill-gotten gains beneath the bright Caribbean sun. Jack sat back and let someone else make the drinks for a change.

I ate fish baked in banana leaves, with fresh tomatoes and chilies, danced drunkenly on the deck each night to recorded calypso music and swore to lifetime friendships with a crew whose names I could never remember once morning and sobriety came. That's what happens when you can order paper umbrella-topped drinks without feeling like a pain in the butt for the bartender.

A week into the adventure, Jack said he felt like a gigolo. I told him not to worry. I told him that's what friends are for.

When I got back to work, tanned and ready to deal with my backlog of cheating spouse cases once more, Bill Butler tried to make my near-death up to me. In fact, he's still trying. He's said he is sorry a million times and has long since ceased telling me what to do. But I've kept telling him that he's going to have to kiss my .45 caliber ass for the next twenty years in order to atone.

Besides, I had asked the gods for a sign as to our future together and I got one in spades: the medical report came back stating that measurements proved the bullet that had ripped a hole in me came from Bill's gun.

If that isn't proof positive that Bill is, quite literally, a pain in the ass, I don't know what is.

Bill tried to make that one up to me by pulling out his badge and biting into it when I reminded him that he'd promised to eat his badge if Steven Hill was dirty. Unfortunately, he broke a crown chomping down, and I had to drive him to the dentist for emergency repairs. He bitched the entire way.

In a way, I'm glad he screwed up so royally. It allows me to lord it over him for years to come. I expect I'll get tired of my petty revenge eventually, and then we'll probably give our ill-fated non-love affair another try. It's tough to walk away completely. I keep thinking of him carrying me through the woods and the way we laughed ourselves silly over a bullet wound beneath the Carolina moon.

For whatever reason, somewhere, underneath it all, we connect—and I can't say that about myself and very many people. Maybe it's a good connection; maybe it's a bad connection. I don't know. I just know that I miss it when it's not there. So I keep hoping that one day the planets will align just right and we can test the bond between us.

In fact, I might just ask Robert if he also does astrology. I'd like to know when that might be.

For now, Bill and I spend our days happily arguing the finer points of every topic we discuss. It appears that we disagree on everything. For example, Bill says that Steven Hill got what he deserved. That death was too good for him. He thinks Hill's paying the price for what he did every day for the rest of his life.

I'm not so sure. Someone like Steven Hill could end up running the prison and loving it. He's cruel. He's cunning. He's amoral and smart. And he's still alive.

I asked Bill once why Hill was allowed to plead down to life in prison when Gail never had that chance. He told me that he thinks the system works just fine and that, in the end, justice prevails.

Me? I don't agree. Everyone says that justice is blind. But I think that, most of the time, she's just looking the other way.

# # #

ABOUT THE AUTHOR

Katy Munger is the author of fourteen novels, writing under her real name as well as her pseudonyms, Chaz McGee and Gallagher Gray. She was born in Honolulu, Hawaii, raised in North Carolina, lived for a number of years in New York City and now calls North Carolina home. She is a former book reviewer for *The Washington Post*, a co-founder of Thalia Press and an original author of Thalia Press Author's Co-op, which seeks to connect established writers with new e-book audiences. All of her work is also available in e-book format. You can learn more about the author and her work at www.katymunger.com.

WITHDRAWN

CPSIA information can be obtained at www.ICGtesting.com
Printed in the USA
LVOW11s1104210216

476055LV00001B/96/P